#1 BESTSELLER
"A RIVETING, SUSPENSE-FILLED READ!"
—*Los Angeles Times*

"SURPASSES LUDLUM'S EARLIER TRI-UMPHS . . . A BOOK YOU CAN'T PUT DOWN, BY A MASTER PLOTTER." *(King Features Syndicate)* "EXCITEMENT AND SUSPENSE ON EVERY PAGE." *(Milwaukee Journal)* "A SPELLBINDING TALE OF VIOLENCE AND EVIL." *(Cleveland Press)* "A ROLLER-COASTER OF CONFLICT AND CON-SPIRACY . . . EVOKING THE SPECTER OF A MILITARISTIC GERMANY REBORN." *(John Barkham Reviews)* "LUDLUM GETS THE READER HOOKED FOR THE WHOLE CAREENING RIDE." *(Pittsburgh Press)* "A HYPNOTIC STYLE THAT LURES US ON, PAGE AFTER PAGE AFTER PAGE." *(Washington Star)* "THE POUNDING TENSION NEVER FALTERS." *(Cosmopolitan)* "IT GRABS THE READER BY THE THROAT AND NEVER LETS GO." *(Houston Chronicle)* "A COMPELLING, FRIGHTENING, HAIR-RAISING CLIFF-HANGER." *(Chicago Sun Times)*

THE HOLCROFT COVENANT

ROBERT LUDLUM

THE HOLCROFT COVENANT

*A Bantam Book / published by arrangement with
The Robertmary Company*

PRINTING HISTORY

*Richard Marek edition published March 1978
9 printings through August 1978*

Bantam edition / February 1979

2nd printing .... February 1979	5th printing .... March 1979
3rd printing .... February 1979	6th printing .... August 1980
4th printing .... March 1979	7th printing .. December 1980

ISBN 0-553-14775-7

Published simultaneously in the United States and Canada

PRINTED IN THE UNITED STATES OF AMERICA

16 15 14 13 12 11 10 9

For Michael and Laura—
A lovely, talented, wonderful couple.

THE
HOLCROFT
COVENANT

Prologue

The hull of the submarine was lashed to the huge pilings, a behemoth strapped in silhouette, the sweeping lines of its bow arcing into the light of the North Sea dawn.

The base was on the island of Scharhörn, in the Helgoland Bight, several miles from the German mainland and the mouth of the Elbe River. It was a refueling station never detected by Allied Intelligence and, in the cause of security, little known among the strategists of the German High Command itself. The undersea marauders came and went in darkness, emerging and submerging within several hundred feet of the moorings. They were Neptune's assassins, come home to rest or going forth to press their attacks.

On this particular dawn, however, the submarine lashed to the dock was doing neither. For it, the war was over, its assignment intrinsic to the origins of another war.

Two men stood in the well of the conning tower, one in the uniform of a commanding officer of the German Navy, the other a tall civilian in a long dark overcoat—the collar turned up to ward off the North Sea winds—yet hatless, as if to defy the North Sea winter. Both looked down at the long line of passengers who slowly made their way toward the gangplank amidships. As each passenger reached the plank, a name was checked off against a list, and then he or she was led—or carried—aboard a submarine.

A few walked by themselves, but they were the exceptions. They were the oldest, some having reached their twelfth or thirteenth birthdays.

The rest were children. Infants in the arms of stern-faced army nurses, who surrendered their charges to a

I

unit of navy doctors at the plank; preschoolers, and early graders clutching identical traveling kits and one another's hands, peering up at the strange black vessel that was to be their home for weeks to come.

"Incredible," said the officer. "Simply incredible."

"It's the beginning," replied the man in the overcoat, his sharp, angular features rigid. "Word comes from everywhere. From the ports and the mountain passes, from the remaining airfields all over the Reich. They go out by the thousands. To every part of the world. And people are waiting for them. Everywhere."

"An extraordinary accomplishment," said the officer, shaking his head in awe.

"This is only one part of the strategy. The entire operation is extraordinary."

"It's an honor to have you here."

"I wanted to be. This is the last shipment." The tall civilian kept his eyes on the dock below. "The Third Reich is dying. These are its rebirth. These are the *Fourth* Reich. Unencumbered by mediocrity and corruption. These are the *Sonnenkinder*. All over the world."

"The children . . ."

"The Children of the Damned," said the tall man, interrupting. "They are the Children of the Damned, as millions will be. But none will be like these. And these will be everywhere."

1

"Attention! Le train de sept heures à destination de Zurich partira du quai numéro douze."

The tall American in the dark-blue raincoat glanced up at the cavernous dome of the Geneva railway station, trying to locate the hidden speakers. The expression on his sharp, angular face was quizzical; the announcement was in French, a language he spoke but little and understood less. Nevertheless, he was able to distinguish the word *Zurich;* it was his signal. He brushed aside the light-brown hair that fell with irritating regularity over his forehead and started for the north end of the station.

The crowds were heavy. Bodies rushed past the American in all directions, hurrying to the gates to begin their journeys to scores of different destinations. None seemed to pay attention to the harsh announcements that echoed throughout the upper chambers in a continuous metallic monotone. The travelers in Geneva's *Bahnhof* knew where they were going. It was the end of the week; the new mountain snows had fallen and the air outside was crisp and chilling. There were places to go, schedules to keep, and people to see; time wasted was time stolen. Everyone hurried.

The American hurried, too, for he also had a schedule to keep and a person to see. He had learned before the announcement that the train for Zurich would leave from track twelve. According to the plan, he was to walk down the ramp to the platform, count seven cars from the rear, and board at the first entrance. Inside, he was to count again, this time five compartments, and knock twice on the fifth door. If everything was in order, he would be admitted by a director of La Grande Banque de Genève,

3

signifying the culmination of twelve weeks of preparations. Preparations that included purposely obscured cablegrams, transatlantic calls made and received on telephones the Swiss banker had determined were sterile, and a total commitment to secrecy.

He did not know what the director of La Grande Banque de Genève had to say to him, but he thought he knew why the precautions were deemed necessary. The American's name was Noel Holcroft, but Holcroft had not been his name at birth. He was born in Berlin in the summer of 1939, and the name on the hospital registry was "Clausen." His father was Heinrich Clausen, master strategist of the Third Reich, the financial magician who put together the coalition of disparate economic forces that insured the supremacy of Adolf Hitler.

Heinrich Clausen won the country but lost a wife. Althene Clausen was an American; more to the point, she was a headstrong woman with her own standards of ethics and morality. She had deduced that the National Socialists possessed neither; they were a collection of paranoiacs, led by a maniac, and supported by financiers interested solely in profits.

Althene Clausen gave her husband an ultimatum on a warm afternoon in August: Withdraw. Stand against the paranoiacs and the maniac before it was too late. In disbelief, the Nazi listened and laughed and dismissed his wife's ultimatum as the foolish ravings of a new mother. Or perhaps the warped judgment of a woman brought up in a weak, discredited system that would soon march to the step of the New Order. Or be crushed under its boot.

That night the new mother packed herself and the new child and took one of the last planes to London, the first leg on her journey back to New York. A week later the Blitzkrieg was executed against Poland; the Thousand Year Reich had begun its own journey, one that would last some fifteen hundred days from the first sound of gunfire.

Holcroft walked through the gate, down the ramp, and on to the long concrete platform. *Four, five, six, seven. . . .* The seventh car had a small blue circle stenciled beneath the window to the left of the open door. It was the symbol of accommodations superior to those in first class: enlarged compartments properly outfitted for conferences in transit or clandestine meetings of a more personal nature. Privacy was guaranteed; once the train was moving, the doors at either end of the car were manned by armed railway guards.

Holcroft entered and turned left into the corridor. He walked past successive closed doors until he reached the fifth. He knocked twice.

"Herr Holcroft?" The voice behind the wood panel was firm but quiet, and although the two words were meant as a question, the voice was not questioning. It made a statement.

"Herr Manfredi?" said Noel in reply, suddenly aware that an eye was peering at him through the pinpoint viewer in the center of the door. It was an eerie feeling, diminished by the comic effect. He smiled to himself and wondered if Herr Manfredi would look like the sinister Conrad Veidt in one of those 1930s English films.

There were two clicks of a lock, followed by the sound of a sliding bolt. The door swung back and the image of Conrad Veidt vanished. Ernst Manfredi was a short, rotund man in his middle to late sixties. He was completely bald, with a pleasant, gentle face; but the wide blue eyes, magnified beyond the metal-framed glasses, were cold. Very light blue and very cold.

"Come in, Herr Holcroft," said Manfredi, smiling. Then his expression changed abruptly; the smile disappeared. "Do forgive me. I should say *Mister* Holcroft. The *Herr* may be offensive to you. My apologies."

"None necessary," replied Noel, stepping into the well-appointed compartment. There was a table, two chairs, no bed in evidence. The walls were wood-paneled; dark-red velvet curtains covered the windows, muffling the sounds of the figures rushing by outside. On the table was a small lamp with a fringed shade.

"We have about twenty-five minutes before departure," the banker said. "It should be adequate. And don't be concerned—we'll be given ample warning. The train won't start until you've disembarked. You'll not have to travel to Zurich."

"I've never been there."

"I trust that will be changed," said the banker enigmatically, gesturing for Holcroft to sit opposite him at the table.

"I wouldn't count on it." Noel sat down, unbuttoning his raincoat but not removing it.

"I'm sorry, that was presumptuous of me." Manfredi took his seat and leaned back in the chair. "I must apologize once again. I'll need your identification. Your passport, please. And your international driver's license. Also, whatever documents you have on your person that describe physical markings, vaccinations, that sort of thing."

Holcroft felt a rush of anger. The inconvenience to his life aside, he disliked the banker's patronizing attitude. "Why should I? You know who I am. You wouldn't have opened that door if you didn't. You probably have more photographs, more information on me, than the State Department."

"Indulge an old man, sir," said the banker, shrugging in self-deprecation, his charm on display. "It will be made clear to you."

Reluctantly, Noel reached into his jacket pocket and withdrew the leather case that contained his passport, health certificate, international license, and two A.I.A. letters that stated his qualifications as an architect. He handed the case to Manfredi. "It's all there. Help yourself."

With seemingly greater reluctance, the banker opened the case. "I feel as though I'm prying, but I think . . ."

"You should," interrupted Holcroft. "I didn't ask for this meeting. Frankly, it comes at a very inconvenient time. I want to get back to New York as soon as possible."

"Yes. Yes, I understand," said the Swiss quietly, perusing the documents. "Tell me, what was the first architectural commission you undertook outside the United States?"

Noel suppressed his irritation. He had come this far; there was no point in refusing to answer. "Mexico," he replied. "For the Alvarez hotel chain, north of Puerto Vallarta."

"The second?"

"Costa Rica. For the government. A postal complex in 1973."

"What was the gross income of your firm in New York last year? Without adjustments."

"None of your damned business."

"I assure you, we know."

Holcroft shook his head in angry resignation. "A hundred and seventy-three thousand dollars and change."

"Considering office rental, salaries, equipment and expenses, that's not an altogether impressive figure, is it?" asked Manfredi, his eyes still on the papers in his hands.

"It's my own company and the staff is small. I have no partners, no wife, no heavy debts. It could be worse."

"It could be better," said the banker, looking up at Holcroft. "Especially for one so talented."

"It could be better."

"Yes, I thought as much," continued the Swiss, putting the various papers back in the leather case and handing it to Noel. He leaned forward. "Do you know who your father was?"

"I know who my father is. Legally, he's Richard Holcroft, of New York, my mother's husband. He's very much alive."

"And retired," completed Manfredi. "A fellow banker, but hardly a banker in the Swiss tradition."

"He was respected. Is respected."

"For his family's money or for his professional acumen?"

"Both, I'd say. I love him. If you have reservations, keep them to yourself."

"You're very loyal; that's a quality I admire. Holcroft came along when your mother—an incredible woman, incidentally—was most despondent. But we split definitions. Holcroft is once removed. I referred to your natural father."

"Obviously."

"Thirty years ago, Heinrich Clausen made certain arrangements. He traveled frequently between Berlin, Zurich, and Geneva, beyond official scrutiny, of course. A document was prepared that we as"—Manfredi paused and smiled—". . . as biased neutrals could not oppose. Attached to the document is a letter, written by Clausen in April of 1945. It is addressed to you. His son." The banker reached for a thick manila envelope on the table.

"Just a minute," said Noel. "Did those certain arrangements concern money?"

"Yes."

"I'm not interested. Give it to charity. He owed it."

"You may not feel that way when you've heard the amount."

"What is it?"

"Seven hundred and eighty million dollars."

2

Holcroft stared at the banker in disbelief; the blood drained from his head. Outside, the sounds of the huge station were a cacophony of muted chords, barely penetrating the thick walls of the car.

"Don't try to absorb it all at once," said Manfredi, placing the letter to one side. "There are conditions, none of them, incidentally, offensive. At least, none we're aware of."

"Conditions? . . ." Holcroft knew he could hardly be heard; he tried to find his voice. "What conditions?"

"They're spelled out very clearly. These vast sums are to be channeled into a great good for people everywhere. And, of course, there are certain benefits to yourself personally."

"What do you mean there's nothing offensive that you're . . . 'aware of'?"

The banker's magnified eyes blinked behind his glasses; he looked away briefly, his expression troubled. He reached into his brown leather briefcase, which lay at the corner of the table, and pulled out a long, thin envelope with curious markings on the back side; they were a series of four circles and appeared to be four dark coins affixed to the border of the flap.

Manfredi held the envelope across the table, under the light. The dark circles were not coins but waxed seals. All were intact.

"Following the instructions given to us thirty years ago, this envelope—unlike your father's letter here—was not to be opened by directors in Geneva. It is separate from the document we prepared, and to the best of our knowledge, Clausen was never aware of it. His own words to you would tend to confirm that. It was brought to us within hours after the courier delivered your father's letter, which was to be our final communication from Berlin."

"What is it?"

"We don't know. We were told it was written by several men aware of your father's activities. Who believed in his cause with great fervor; who considered him in many ways a true martyr of Germany. We were instructed to give it to you with the seals unbroken. You were to read it before you saw your father's letter." Manfredi turned the envelope over. There was writing on the front side. The words were in German and written by hand. "You are to sign below, so to state that you received it in the proper condition."

Noel took the envelope and read the words he could not understand.

DIESER BRIEF IST MIT UNGEBROCHENEM SIEGEL EMPFANGEN WORDEN. NEUAUFBAU ODER TOD.

"What does it say?"

"That you've examined the seals and are satisfied."

"How can I be sure?"

"Young man, you're talking with a director of La Grande Banque de Genève." The Swiss did not raise his voice but the rebuke was clear. "You have my word. And, in any event, what difference does it make?"

None, reasoned Holcroft, yet the obvious question bothered him. "If I sign the envelope, what do you do with it?"

Manfredi was silent for several moments, as if deciding whether or not to answer. He removed his glasses, took a silk handkerchief from his breast pocket, and cleaned them. Finally he replied. "That is privileged information. . . ."

"So's my signature," interrupted Noel. "Privileged, that is."

"Let me finish," protested the banker, putting back his glasses. "I was about to say it was privileged information that can't possibly be relevant any longer. Not after so many years. The envelope is to be sent to a post-office box in Sesimbra, Portugal. It is south of Lisbon, on the Cape of Espichel."

"Why isn't it relevant?"

Manfredi held up the palms of his hands. "The post-office box no longer exists. The envelope will find its way to a dead-letter office and eventually be returned to us."

"You're sure?"

"I believe it, yes."

Noel reached into his pocket for his pen, turning the envelope over to look once again at the waxed seals. They had not been tampered with; and, thought Holcroft, what difference *did* it make? He placed the envelope in front of him and signed his name.

Manfredi held up his hand. "You understand, whatever is contained in that envelope can have no bearing on our participation in the document prepared by La Grande Banque de Genève. We were not consulted; nor were we apprised of the contents."

"You sound worried. I thought you said it didn't make any difference. It was too long ago."

"Fanatics always worry me, Mr. Holcroft. Time and consequence cannot alter that judgment. It's a banker's caution."

Noel began cracking the wax; it had hardened over the years and took considerable force before it fell away. He tore the flap open, removed the single page, and unfolded it.

The paper was brittle with age; the white had turned to a pale brownish yellow. The writing was in English, the letters printed in an odd block lettering that was Germanic in style. The ink was faded but legible. Holcroft looked at the bottom of the page for a signature. There was none. He started reading.

The message was macabre, born in desperation thirty years ago. It was as though unbalanced men had sat in a darkened room, studying shadows on the wall for signs of the future, studying a man and a life not yet formed.

FROM THIS MOMENT ON THE SON OF HEIN-RICH CLAUSEN IS TO BE TESTED. THERE ARE THOSE WHO MAY LEARN OF THE WORK IN GENEVA AND WHO WILL TRY TO STOP HIM, WHOSE ONLY PURPOSE IN LIFE WILL BE TO KILL HIM, THUS DESTROYING THE DREAM CONCEIVED BY THE GIANT THAT WAS HIS FATHER.

THIS MUST NOT HAPPEN, FOR WE WERE BE-

TRAYED—ALL OF US—AND THE WORLD MUST
KNOW WHAT WE REALLY WERE, NOT WHAT THE
BETRAYERS SHOWED US TO BE, FOR THOSE WERE
THE PORTRAITS OF TRAITORS. NOT US. AND PAR-
TICULARLY NOT HEINRICH CLAUSEN.

WE ARE THE SURVIVORS OF WOLFSSCHANZE. WE
SEEK THE CLEANSING OF OUR NAMES, THE RESTO-
RATION OF THE HONOR THAT WAS STOLEN
FROM US.

THEREFORE THE MEN OF WOLFSSCHANZE WILL
PROTECT THE SON FOR AS LONG AS THE SON
PURSUES THE FATHER'S DREAM AND RETURNS
OUR HONOR TO US. BUT SHOULD THE SON ABAN-
DON THE DREAM, BETRAY THE FATHER, AND
WITHHOLD OUR HONOR, HE WILL HAVE NO LIFE.
HE WILL WITNESS THE ANGUISH OF LOVED
ONES, OF FAMILY, CHILDREN, FRIENDS. NO ONE
WILL BE SPARED.

NONE MUST INTERFERE. GIVE US OUR HON-
OR. IT IS OUR RIGHT AND WE DEMAND IT.

Noel shoved the chair back and stood up. *"What
the hell is this?"*

"I've no idea," replied Manfredi quietly, his voice
calm but his large, cold blue eyes conveying his alarm.
"I told you we were not apprised. . . ."

"Well, *get* apprised!" shouted Holcroft. "Read it!
Who *were* these clowns? Certifiable *lunatics?"*

The banker began reading. Without looking up, he
answered softly. "First cousins to lunatics. Men who'd lost
hope."

"What's *Wolfsschanze?* What does it mean?"

"It was the name of Hitler's staff headquarters in
East Prussia, where the attempt to assassinate him took
place. It was a conspiracy of the generals: Von Stauffenberg, Kluge, Höpner—they were all implicated. All shot.
Rommel took his own life."

Holcroft stared at the paper in Manfredi's hands.
"You mean it was written thirty years ago by people like
that?"

The banker nodded, his eyes narrowed in astonishment. "Yes, but it's not the language one might have expected of them. This is nothing short of a threat; it's un-

reasonable. Those men were not unreasonable. On the other hand, the times *were* unreasonable. Decent men, brave men, were stretched beyond the parameters of sanity. They were living through a hell none of us can picture today."

"Decent men?" asked Noel incredulously.

"Have you any idea what it meant to be a part of the Wolfsschanze conspiracy? A bloodbath followed, thousands massacred everywhere, the vast majority never having heard of Wolfsschanze. It was yet another final solution, an excuse to still all dissent throughout Germany. What began as an act to rid the world of a madman ended in a holocaust all its own. The survivors of Wolfsschanze saw that happen."

"Those survivors," replied Holcroft, "followed that madman for a long time."

"You must understand. And you will. These were desperate men. They were caught in a trap, and for them it was cataclysmic. A world they had helped create was revealed not to be the world they envisioned. Horrors they never dreamed of were uncovered, yet they couldn't avoid their responsibility for them. They were appalled at what they saw but couldn't deny the roles they played."

"The well-intentioned Nazi," said Noel. "I've heard of that elusive breed."

"One would have to go back in history, to the economic disasters, to the Versailles Treaty, the Pact of Locarno, the Bolshevik encroachments—to a dozen different forces—to understand."

"I understand what I just read," Holcroft said. "Your poor misunderstood storm troopers didn't hesitate to threaten someone they couldn't know! 'He will have no life . . . no one spared . . . family, friends, children.' That spells out murder. Don't talk to me about well-intentioned killers."

"They're the words of old, sick, desperate men. They have no meaning now. It was their way of expressing their own anguish, of seeking atonement. They're gone. Leave them in peace. Read your father's letter . . ."

"He's *not* my father!" interrupted Noel.

"Read Heinrich Clausen's letter. Things will be clearer. Read it. We have several items to discuss and there isn't much time."

*   *   *

A man in a brown tweed overcoat and dark Tirolean hat stood by a pillar across from the seventh car. At first glance, there was nothing particularly distinguishing about him, except perhaps his eyebrows. They were thick, a mixture of black and light-gray hair that produced the effect of salt-and-pepper archways in the upper regions of a forgettable face.

At first glance. Yet if one looked closer, one could see the blunted but not unrefined features of a very determined man. In spite of the pockets of wind that blew in gusts through the platform, he did not blink. His concentration on the seventh car was absolute.

The American would come out of that doorway, thought the man by the pillar, a much different person from the American who went in. During the past few minutes his life had been changed in ways few men in this world would ever experience. Yet it was only the beginning; the journey he was about to embark on was beyond anything of which the present-day world could conceive. So it was important to observe his initial reaction. More than important. Vital.

"Attention! Le train de sept heures . . ."

The final announcement came over the speakers. Simultaneously, a train from Lausanne was arriving on the adjacent track. In moments the platform would be jammed with tourists flocking into Geneva for the weekend, the way Midlanders scrambled into Charing Cross for a brief fling in London, thought the man by the pillar.

The train from Lausanne came to a stop. The passenger cars disgorged; the platform was again packed with bodies.

The figure of the tall American was suddenly in the vestibule of car seven. He was blocked at the doorway by a porter carrying someone's luggage. It was an irritating moment that might have provoked an argument under normal circumstances. But the circumstances were not normal for Holcroft. He expressed no annoyance; his face was set, unresponsive to the moment, his eyes aware of the physical confusion but not concerned with it. There was an air of detachment about him; he was in the grips of lingering astonishment. This was emphasized by the way he clutched the thick manila envelope between his arm and his chest, his hand curved around the edge, his fingers pressed into the paper with such force they formed a fist.

It was the cause of his consternation, this document prepared a lifetime ago. It was the miracle *they* had waited for, lived for—the man by the pillar and those who had gone before him. More than thirty years of anticipation. And now it had surfaced at last!

The journey had begun.

Holcroft entered the flow of human traffic toward the ramp that led up to the gate. Although jostled by those around him, he was oblivious of the crowds, his eyes absently directed ahead. At nothing.

Suddenly, the man by the pillar was alarmed. Years of training had taught him to look for the unexpected, the infinitesimal break in a normal pattern. He saw that break now. Two men, their faces unlike any around them, joyless, without curiosity or expectation, filled only with hostile intent.

They were surging through the crowds, one man slightly ahead of the other. Their eyes were on the American; they were after him! The man in front had his right hand in his pocket. The man behind had his left hand concealed across his chest, beneath his unbuttoned overcoat. The hidden hands gripped weapons! The man by the pillar was convinced of that.

He sprang away from the concrete column and crashed his way into the crowd. There were no seconds to be lost. The two men were gaining on Holcroft. They were after the envelope! It was the only possible explanation. And if that were the case, it meant that word of the miracle had leaked out of Geneva! The document inside that envelope was priceless, beyond value. Beside it, the American's life was of such inconsequence that no thought would be expended taking that life. The men closing in on Holcroft would kill him for the envelope *mindlessly*, as if removing a disagreeable insect from a bar of gold. And *that* was mindless! What they did not know was that without the son of Heinrich Clausen the miracle would not happen!

They were within yards of him now! The man with the black-and-white eyebrows lunged forward through the mass of tourists like a possessed animal. He crashed into people and luggage, throwing aside everything and everyone in his path. When he was within feet of the killer whose hand was concealed under his overcoat, he thrust his own hand into his pocket, clutching the gun inside, and screamed directly at the assailant:

"Du suchst Clausens Sohn! Das Genfe Dokument!"

The killer was partially up the ramp, separated from the American by only a few people. He heard the words roared at him by a stranger and spun around, his eyes wide in shock.

The crowd pressed rapidly up the ramp, skirting the two obvious antagonists. Attacker and protector were in their own miniature arena, facing each other. The observer squeezed the trigger of the gun in his pocket, then squeezed it again. The spits could barely be heard as the fabric exploded. Two bullets entered the body of Holcroft's would-be assailant, one in the lower stomach, the other far above, in the neck. The first caused the man to convulse forward; the second snapped his head back, the throat torn open.

Blood burst from the neck with such force that it splattered surrounding faces, and the clothes and suitcases belonging to those faces. It cascaded downward, forming small pools and rivulets on the ramp. Screams of horror filled the walkway.

The observer-protector felt a hand gripping his shoulder, digging into his flesh. He spun; the second attacker was on him, but there was no gun in his hand. Instead, the blade of a hunting knife came toward him.

The man was an amateur, thought the observer, as his reactions—instincts born of years of training—came instantly into play. He stepped sideways quickly—a bullfighter avoiding the horns—and clamped his left hand above his assailant's wrist. He pulled his right hand from his pocket and gripped the fingers wrapped around the knife. He snapped the wrist downward, vising the fingers around the handle, tearing the cartilage of the attacker's hand, forcing the blade inward. He plunged it into the soft flesh of the stomach and ripped the sharp steel diagonally up into the rib cage, severing the arteries of the heart. The man's face contorted; a terrible scream was begun, cut off by death.

The pandemonium had escalated into uncontrollable chaos; the screaming increased. The profusion of blood in the center of the rushing, colliding bodies fueled the hysteria. The observer-protector knew precisely what to do. He threw up his hands in frightened consternation, in sudden, total revulsion at the sight of the blood on his own clothes, and joined the hysterical crowd racing away like a herd of terrified cattle from the concrete killing ground.

He rushed up the ramp past the American whose life he had just saved.

Holcroft heard the screaming. It penetrated the numbing mists he felt engulfed in: clouds of vapor that swirled around him, obscuring his vision, inhibiting all thought.

He tried to turn toward the commotion, but the hysterical crowd prevented him from doing so. He was swept farther up the ramp and pummeled into the three-foot-high cement wall that served as a railing. He gripped the stone and looked back, unable to see clearly what had happened; he did see a man below arch backward, blood erupting from his throat. He saw a second man lunging forward, his mouth stretched in agony, and then Noel could see no more, the onslaught of bodies sweeping him once again up the concrete ramp.

A man rushed by, crashing into his shoulder. Holcroft turned in time to see frightened eyes beneath a pair of thick black-and-white brows.

An act of violence had taken place. An attempted robbery had turned into an assault, into a killing, perhaps. Peaceful Geneva was no more immune to violence than were the wild streets of New York at night, or the impoverished alleyways of Marrakesh.

But Noel could not dwell on such things; he could not be involved. He had other things to think about. The mists of numbness returned. Through them he vaguely understood that his life would never again be the same.

He gripped the envelope in his hand and joined the screaming mass racing up the ramp to the gate.

3

The huge aircraft passed over Cape Breton Island and dipped gently to the left, descending into its new altitude and heading. The route was now southwest, toward Halifax and Boston, then into New York.

Holcroft had spent most of the time in the upstairs lounge, at a single chair in the right rear corner, his black attaché case against the bulkhead. It was easier to concentrate there; no straying eyes of an adjacent passenger could fall on the papers he read and reread, again and again.

He had begun with the letter from Heinrich Clausen, that unknown but all-pervading presence. It was an incredible document in itself. The information contained in it was of such an alarming nature that Manfredi had expressed the collective wish of the Grande Banque's directors that it be destroyed. For it detailed in general terms the sources of the millions banked in Geneva three decades ago. Although the majority of these sources were untouchable in any contemporary legal sense—thieves and murderers stealing the national funds of a government headed by thieves and murderers—other sources were not so immune to modern scrutiny. Throughout the war Germany had plundered. It had raped internally and externally. The dissenters within had been stripped; the conquered without, stolen from unmercifully. Should the memories of these thefts be dredged up, the international courts in The Hague could tie up the funds for years in protracted litigations.

"Destroy the letter," Manfredi had said in Geneva. "It's necessary only that you understand why he did what he did. Not the methods; they are a complication without any conceivable resolution. But there are those who may try to stop you. Other thieves would move in; we're dealing in hundreds of millions."

18

Noel reread the letter for perhaps the twentieth time. Each time he did so, he tried to picture the man who wrote it. His natural father. He had no idea what Heinrich Clausen looked like; his mother had destroyed all photographs, all communications, all references whatsoever to the man she loathed with all her being.

Berlin, 20 April 1945

My Son.

I write this as the armies of the Reich collapse on all fronts. Berlin will soon fall, a city of raging fires and death everywhere. So be it. I shall waste no moments on what was, or what might have been. On concepts betrayed, and the triumph of evil over good through the treachery of morally bankrupt leaders. Recriminations born in hell are too suspect, the authorship too easily attributed to the devil.

Instead, I shall permit my actions to speak for me. In them, you may find some semblance of pride. That is my prayer.

Amends must be made. That is the credo I have come to recognize. As have my two dearest friends and closest associates who are identified in the attached document. Amends for the destruction we have wrought, for betrayals so heinous the world will never forget. Or forgive. It is in the interest of partial forgiveness that we have done what we have done.

Five years ago your mother made a decision I could not comprehend, so blind were my loyalties to the New Order. Two winters ago—in February of 1943—the words she spoke in rage, words I arrogantly dismissed as lies fed her by those who despised the Fatherland, were revealed to be the truth. We who labored in the rarefied circles of finance and policy had been deceived. For two years it was clear that Germany was going down to defeat. We pretended otherwise, but in our hearts we knew it was so. Others knew it, too. And they became careless. The horrors surfaced, the deceptions were clear.

Twenty-five months ago I conceived of a plan and enlisted the support of my dear friends in the *Finanzministerium*. Their support was willingly given. Our objective was to divert extraordinary

sums of money into neutral Switzerland, funds
that could be used one day to give aid and succor
to those thousands upon thousands whose lives
were shattered by unspeakable atrocities committed in Germany's name by animals who knew
nothing of German honor.

We know now about the camps. The names
will haunt history. Belsen, Dachau, Auschwitz.

We have been told of the mass executions,
of the helpless men, women and children lined
up in front of trenches dug by their own hands,
then slaughtered.

We have learned of the ovens—oh, God in
heaven—ovens for human flesh! Of the showers
that sprayed not cleansing water but lethal gas.
Of intolerable, obscene experiments carried out
on conscious human beings by insane prac-
titioners of a medical science unknown to man.
We bleed at the images, and our eyes burst, but
our tears can do nothing. Our minds, however,
are not so helpless. We can plan.

Amends must be made.

We cannot restore life. We cannot bring back
what was so brutally, viciously taken. But we
can seek out all those who survived, and the
children of those both surviving and slaughtered,
and do what we can. They must be sought out
all over the world and shown that we have not
forgotten. We are ashamed and we wish to help.
In any way that we can. It is to this end that we
have done what we have done.

I do not for a moment believe that our
actions can expiate our sins, those crimes we
were unknowingly a part of. Yet we do what we
can—I do what I can—haunted with every
breath by your mother's perceptions. Why, oh
eternal God, did I not listen to that great and
good woman?

To return to the plan.

Using the American dollar as the equivalent
currency of exchange, our goal was ten million
monthly, a figure that might appear excessive,
but not when one considers the capital flow
through the economic maze of the *Finanzministerium* at the height of the war. We exceeded our
goal.

Using the *Finanzministerium*, we appropriated funds from hundreds of sources within the Reich and to a great extent beyond, throughout Germany's ever-expanding borders. Taxes were diverted, enormous expenditures made from the Ministry of Armaments for nonexistent purchases, Wehrmacht payrolls rerouted, and monies sent to occupation territories constantly intercepted, lost. Funds from expropriated estates, and from the great fortunes, factories, and individually held companies, did not find their way into the Reich's economy but, instead, into our accounts. Sales of art objects from scores of museums throughout the conquered lands were converted to our cause. It was a master plan carried out masterfully. Whatever risks we took and terrors we faced—and they were daily occurrences—were inconsequential compared to the meaning of our credo: Amends *must* be made.

Yet no plan can be termed a success unless the objective is secured permanently. A military strategy that captures a port only to lose it to an invasion from the sea a day later is no strategy at all. One must consider all possible assaults, all interferences that could negate the strategy. One must project, as thoroughly as projection allows, the changes mandated by time, and protect the objective thus far attained. In essence, one must *use* time to the strategy's advantage. We have endeavored to do this through the conditions put forth in the attached document.

Would to the Almighty that we could give aid to the victims and their survivors sooner than our projections allow, but to do so would rivet attention to the sums we have appropriated. Then *all* could be lost. A generation must pass for the strategy to succeed. Even then there is risk, but time will have diminished it.

The air-raid sirens keep up their incessant wailing. Speaking of time, there is very little left now. For myself and my two associates, we wait only for confirmation that this letter has reached Zurich through an underground courier. Upon receipt of the news, we have our own pact. Our pact with death, each by his own hand.

Answer my prayer. Help us atone. Amends must be made.

This is our covenant, my son. My only son, whom I have never known but to whom I have brought such sorrow. Abide by it, honor it, for it is an honorable thing I ask you to do.

Your father,
HEINRICH CLAUSEN

Holcroft put the letter facedown on the table and glanced out the window at the blue sky above the clouds. Far in the distance was the exhaust of another aircraft; he followed the streak of vapor until he could see the tiny silver gleam of the fuselage.

He thought about the letter. Again. The writing was maudlin; the words were from another era, melodramatic. It did not weaken the letter; rather, it gave it a certain strength of conviction. Clausen's sincerity was unquestioned; his emotions were genuine.

What was only partially communicated, however, was the brilliance of the plan itself. Brilliant in its simplicity, extraordinary in its use of time and the laws of finance to achieve both execution and protection. For the three men understood that sums of the magnitude they had stolen could not be sunk in a lake or buried in vaults. The hundreds of millions had to exist in the financial marketplace, not subject to discontinued currency or to brokers who would have to convert and sell elusive assets.

Hard money had to be deposited, the responsibility for its security given to one of the world's most revered institutions, La Grande Banque de Genève. Such an institution would not—could not—permit abuses where liquidity was concerned; it was an international economic rock. All the conditions of its contract with its depositors would be observed. Everything was to be legal in the eyes of Swiss law. Covert—as was the custom of the trade—but ironbound with respect to existing legalities, and thus current with the times. The intent of the contract—the document—could not be corrupted; the objectives would be followed to the letter.

To permit corruption or malfeasance was unthinkable. Thirty years . . . *fifty* years . . . in terms of the financial calendar was very little time, indeed.

Noel reached down and opened his attaché case. He slipped the pages of the letter into a compartment and pulled out the document from La Grande Banque de Genève. It was encased in a leather cover, folded in the manner of a last will and testament, which it was—and then some. He leaned back in the chair and unfastened the clasp that allowed the cover to unfold, revealing the first page of the document.

His "covenant," Holcroft reflected.

He skimmed over the words and the paragraphs, now so familiar to him, flipping the pages as he did so, concentrating on the salient points.

The identities of Clausen's two associates in the massive theft were Erich Kessler and Wilhelm von Tiebolt. The names were vital not so much for identifying the two men themselves as for seeking out and contacting the oldest child of each. It was the first condition of the document. Although the designated proprietor of the numbered account was one Noel C. Holcroft, *American,* funds were to be released only upon the signatures of all three oldest children. And then only if each child satisfied the directors of La Grande Banque that he or she accepted the conditions and objectives set forth by the original proprietors with respect to the allocation of the funds.

However, if these offspring did not satisfy the Swiss directors or were judged to be incompetent, their brothers and sisters were to be studied and further judgments made. If all the children were considered incapable of the responsibility, the millions would wait for another generation, when further sealed instructions would be opened by executors and by issue yet unborn. The resolve was devastating: *another* generation.

THE LEGITIMATE SON OF HEINRICH CLAUSEN IS NOW KNOWN AS NOEL HOLCROFT, A CHILD, LIVING WITH HIS MOTHER AND STEPFATHER IN AMERICA. AT THE SPECIFIC DATE CHOSEN BY THE DIRECTORS OF LA GRANDE BANQUE DE GENÈVE —NOT TO BE LESS THAN THIRTY YEARS, NOR MORE THAN THIRTY-FIVE—SAID LEGITIMATE SON OF HEINRICH CLAUSEN IS TO BE CONTACTED AND HIS RESPONSIBILITIES MADE KNOWN TO HIM. HE IS TO REACH HIS COINHERITORS AND ACTIVATE THE ACCOUNT UNDER THE CONDITIONS SET FORTH. HE SHALL BE THE CONDUIT THROUGH

WHICH THE FUNDS ARE TO BE DISPENSED TO
THE VICTIMS OF THE HOLOCAUST, THEIR FAM-
ILIES AND SURVIVING ISSUE. . . .

The three Germans gave their reasons for the selec-
tion of Clausen's son as the conduit. The child had entered
into a family of wealth and consequence . . . an *American*
family, above suspicion. All traces of his mother's first
marriage and flight from Germany had been obscured by
the devoted Richard Holcroft. It was understood that in
the pursuit of this obscurity a death certificate had been
issued in London for an infant male named Clausen, dated
February 17, 1942, and a subsequent birth certificate filed
in New York City for the male child Holcroft. The additional years would further obscure events to the point of
obliteration. The infant male Clausen would someday *become* the man Holcroft, with no visible relationship to his
origins. Yet those origins could not be denied, and, therefore, he was the perfect choice, satisfying both the demands and the objectives of the document.

An international agency was to be established in
Zurich, which would serve as headquarters for the dispersal of the funds, the source of the funds to be held
confidential in perpetuity. Should a spokesman be required, it was to be the American, Holcroft, for the others
could never be mentioned by name. Ever. They were the
children of Nazis, and their exposure would inevitably
raise demands that the account be examined, that its various sources be revealed. And if the account *was* examined,
its sources even hinted at, forgotten confiscations and
appropriations would be remembered. The international
courts would be swamped with litigations.

But if the spokesman was a man without the Nazi
stain, there would be no cause for alarm, no examinations,
no demands for exhumation or litigation. He would act
in concert with the others, each possessing one vote in all
decisions, but he alone would be visible. The children of
Erich Kessler and Wilhelm von Tiebolt were to remain
anonymous.

Noel wondered what the "children" of Kessler and
Von Tiebolt were like. He would find out soon.

The final conditions of the document were no less
startling than anything that preceded them. All the monies
were to be allocated within *six months* of the release

of the account. Such an imposition would demand a total commitment from each of the offspring, and that was precisely what the depositors demanded: total commitment to their cause. Lives would be interrupted, sacrifices required. The commitments had to be paid for. Therefore, at the end of the six-month period and the successful allocation of the funds to the victims of the Holocaust, the Zurich agency was to be disbanded and each descendant was to receive the sum of two million dollars.

Six months. Two million dollars.

Two million.

Noel considered what that meant to him personally and professionally. It was freedom. Manfredi had said in Geneva that he was talented. He *was* talented, but frequently that talent was obscured in the final product. He'd had to accept assignments he would have preferred not to take; had to compromise designs when the architect in him dictated otherwise; had to refuse jobs he wanted very much to do, because financial pressures prohibited time spent on lesser commissions. He was turning into a cynic.

Nothing was permanent; planned obsolescence went hand in hand with depreciation and amortization. No one knew it better than an architect who once had a conscience. Perhaps he would find his conscience again. With freedom. With the two million.

Holcroft was startled by the progression of his thoughts. He had made up his mind, something he had not intended to do until he'd thought things through. Everything. Yet he was reclaiming a misplaced conscience with money he had convinced himself he was capable of rejecting.

What *were* they like, these oldest children of Erich Kessler and Wilhelm von Tiebolt? One was a woman; the other, a man, a scholar. But beyond the differences of sex and profession, they had been a part of something he had never known. They'd been there; they'd seen it. Neither had been too young to remember. Each had lived in that strange, demonic world that was the Third Reich. The American would have so many questions to ask.

Questions to ask? *Questions?*

He had made his decision. He had told Manfredi he would need time—a few days at least—before he could decide.

"Do you really have a choice?" the Swiss banker had asked.

"Very much so," Noel had replied. "I'm not for sale, regardless of conditions. And I'm not frightened by threats made by maniacs thirty years ago."

"Nor should you be. Discuss it with your mother."

"*What?*" Holcroft was stunned. "I thought you said . . ."

"Complete secrecy? Yes, but your mother is the single exception."

"Why? I'd think she'd be the last . . ."

"She's the first. And only. She'll honor the confidence."

Manfredi had been right. If his answer was yes, he would by necessity suspend his firm's activities and begin his travels to make contact with the offspring of Kessler and Von Tiebolt. His mother's curiosity would be aroused; she was not a woman to let her curiosity lie dormant. She would make inquiries, and if, by any chance—however remote—she unearthed information about the millions in Geneva and Heinrich Clausen's role in the massive theft, her reaction would be violent. Her memories of the paranoiac gangsters of the Third Reich were indelibly printed on her mind. If she made damaging disclosures public, the funds would be tied up in the international courts for years.

"Suppose she isn't persuaded?"

"You must be convincing. The letter is convincing, and we'll step in, if need be. Regardless, it's better to know her position at the outset."

What would that position be? Noel wondered. Althene was not your run-of-the-mill mother, as mothers were understood by this particular son. He knew very early in life that Althene was different. She did not fit into the mold of the wealthy Manhattan matron. The trappings were there—or had been. The horses, the boats, the weekends in Aspen and in the Hamptons, but not the frantic chase for ever-expanding acceptance and social control.

She'd done it all before. She'd lived in the turbulence that was the European thirties, a young, carefree American whose family had something left after the crash and were more comfortable away from their less-fortunate peers. She had known the Court of St. James's as well as the expatriate *salons* in Paris . . . and the dashing new inheritors of Germany. And out of those years had come a serenity shaped by love, exhaustion, loathing, and rage.

Althene was a special person, as much a friend as a mother, that friendship deep and without the need for constant reaffirmation. In point of fact, thought Holcroft, she was more friend than mother; she was never entirely comfortable in the latter role.

"I've made too many mistakes, my dear," she had said to him once, laughing, "to assume an authority based on biology."

Now he would ask her to face the memory of a man she had spent a great deal of her life trying to forget. Would she be frightened? That wasn't likely. Would she doubt the objectives set forth in the document given him by Ernst Manfredi? How could she, after reading the letter from Heinrich Clausen. Whatever her memories, his mother was a woman of intellect and perception. All men were subject to change, to remorse. She would have to accept that, no matter how distasteful it might be to her in this particular case.

It was the weekend; tomorrow was Sunday. His mother and stepfather spent the weekends at their house in the country, in Bedford Hills. In the morning he would drive up and have that talk.

And on Monday he would take the first steps on a trip that would lead him back to Switzerland. To an as yet unknown agency in Zurich. On Monday the hunt would begin.

Noel recalled his exchange with Manfredi. They were among the last words spoken before Holcroft left the train.

"The Kesslers had two sons. The oldest, Erich—named for the father—is a professor of history at the University of Berlin. The younger brother, Hans, is a doctor in Munich. From what we know, both are highly regarded in their respective communities. They're very close. Once Erich is told of the situation, he may insist on his brother's inclusion."

"Is that permitted?"

"There's nothing in the document that prohibits it. However, the stipend remains the same and each family has but one vote in all decisions."

"What about the Von Tiebolts?"

"Another story, I'm afraid. They may be a problem for you. After the war the records show that the mother and two children fled to Rio de Janeiro. Five or six years ago they disappeared. Literally. The police have no information. No address, no business associations, no listings in the other major cities. And that's unusual; the mother became quite successful for a time. No one seems to know what happened, or if people do, they're not willing to say."

"You said two children. Who are they?"

"Actually, there are three children. The youngest, a daughter, Helden, was born after the war, in Brazil, obviously conceived during the last days of the Reich. The oldest is another daughter, Gretchen. The middle child is Johann, the son."

"You say they disappeared?"

"Perhaps it's too dramatic a term. We're bankers, not investigators. Our inquiries were not that extensive, and Brazil is a very large country. *Your* inquiries must be exhaustive. The offspring of each man must be found and scrutinized. It's the first condition of the document; without compliance, the account will not be released."

Holcroft folded the document and put it back in his attaché case. As he did so, his fingers touched the edge of the single sheet of paper with the odd block lettering written by the survivors of Wolfsschanze thirty years ago. Manfredi was right: They were sick old men trying to play their last desperate roles in a drama of the future they barely understood. If they had understood, they would have appealed to the "son of Heinrich Clausen." Pleaded with him, not threatened him. The threat was the enigma. Why was it made? For what purpose? Again, perhaps, Manfredi was right. The strange paper had no meaning now. There were other things to think about.

Holcroft caught the eye of the stewardess chatting with two men at a table across the way and gestured for another scotch. She smiled pleasantly, nodded, and indicated that the drink would be there in moments. He returned to his thoughts.

The inevitable doubts surfaced. Was he prepared to commit what amounted to a year of his life to a project so immense that his own qualifications had to be examined before the children of Kessler and Von Tiebolt were examined—if, indeed, he could find the latter? Manfredi's words came back to him. *Do you really have a choice?* The answer to that question was both yes and no. The two million, which signified his own freedom, was a temptation difficult to reject, but he could reject it. His dissatisfactions were real, but professionally, things were going well. His reputation was spreading, his skills acknowledged by a growing number of clients who in turn told potential clients. What would happen if he suddenly stopped? What would be the effect should he abruptly withdraw from a dozen commissions for which he was competing? These too were questions to be considered deeply; he was not ruled by money alone.

Yet, as his mind wandered, Noel understood the uselessness of his thoughts. Compared to his . . . covenant . . . the questions were inconsequential. Whatever his personal circumstances, the distribution of millions to the survivors of an inhumanity unknown in history was long overdue; it was an obligation impossible to dismiss. A voice had cried out to him through the years, the voice of a man in agony who was the father he had never known. For reasons he was incapable of explaining to himself, he could not be deaf to that voice; he could not walk away from that man in agony. He would drive to Bedford Hills in the morning and see his mother.

Holcroft looked up, wondering where the stewardess was with his drink. She was at the dimly lit counter that served as the bar in the 747's lounge. The two men from the table had accompanied her; they were joined by a third. A fourth man sat quietly in a rear seat, reading a newspaper. The two men with the stewardess had been drinking heavily, while the third, in his search for camaraderie, pretended to be less sober than he was. The stewardess saw Noel looking at her and arched her eyebrows in mock desperation. She had poured his scotch, but one of the drunks had spilled it; she was wiping it up with a cloth. The drunks' companion suddenly lurched back against a chair, his balance lost. The stewardess dashed around the counter to help the fallen passenger; his friend laughed, steadying himself on an adjacent chair. The third man reached for a drink on the bar. The fourth man looked up in disgust, crackling his paper, the sound conveying his disapproval. Noel returned to the window not caring to be a part of the minor confusion.

Several minutes later the stewardess approached his

table. "I'm sorry, Mr. Holcroft. Boys will be boys, more so on the Atlantic run, I think. That was scotch on the rocks, wasn't it?"

"Yes. Thanks." Noel took the glass from the attractive girl and saw the look in her eyes. It seemed to say, *Thank you, nice person, for not coming on like those crashing bores.* Under different circumstances he might have pursued a conversation, but now he had other things to think about. His mind was listing the things he would do on Monday. Closing his office was not difficult in terms of personnel; he had a small staff: a secretary and two draftsmen he could easily place with friends—probably at higher salaries. But why in heaven's name would Holcroft, Incorporated, New York, close up shop just when its designs were being considered for projects that could triple its staff and quadruple its gross income? The explanation had to be both reasonable and above scrutiny.

Suddenly, without warning, a passenger on the other side of the cabin sprang from his seat, a hoarse, wild cry of pain coming from his throat. He arched his back spastically, as if gasping for air, clutched first his stomach, then his chest. He crashed into the wooden divider that held magazines and airline schedules and twisted maniacally, his eyes wide, the veins in his neck purple and distended. He lurched forward and sprawled to the deck of the cabin.

It was the third man, who had joined the two drunks at the bar with the stewardess.

The next moments were chaotic. The stewardess rushed to the fallen man, observed him closely, and followed procedure. She instructed the three other passengers in the cabin to remain in their seats, placed a cushion beneath the man's head, and returned to the counter and the intercom on the wall. In seconds a male flight attendant rushed up the circular staircase; the British Airways captain emerged from the flight deck. They conferred with the stewardess over the unconscious body. The male attendant walked rapidly to the staircase, descended, and returned within a few moments with a clipboard. It was obviously the plane's manifest.

The captain stood and addressed the others in the lounge. "Will you all please return to your seats below. There's a doctor on board. He's being summoned. Thank you very much."

As Holcroft sidestepped his way down the staircase, a stewardess carrying a blanket climbed quickly past him. Then he heard the captain issue an order over the intercom. "Radio Kennedy for emergency equipment. Medical. Male passenger, name of Thornton. Heart seizure, I believe."

The doctor knelt by the prone figure stretched out on the rear seat of the lounge and asked for a flashlight. The first officer hurried to the flight deck and returned with one. The doctor rolled back the eyelids of the man named Thornton, then turned and motioned for the captain to join him; he had something to say. The captain bent over; the doctor spoke quietly.

"He's dead. It's difficult to say without equipment, without tissue and blood analysis, but I don't think this man had a heart attack. I think he was poisoned. Strychnine would be my guess."

The customs inspector's office was suddenly quiet. Behind the inspector's desk sat a homicide detective from New York's Port Authority police, a British Airways clipboard in front of him. The inspector stood rigidly embarrassed to one side. In two chairs against the wall sat the captain of the 747 and the stewardess assigned to its first-class lounge. By the door was a uniformed police officer. The detective stared at the customs inspector in disbelief.

"Are you telling me that two people got off that plane, walked through sealed-off corridors into the sealed-off, guarded customs area, and *vanished?*"

"I can't explain it," said the inspector, shaking his head despondently. "It's never happened before."

The detective turned to the stewardess. "You're convinced they were drunk, miss?"

"Not now, perhaps," replied the girl. "I've got to have second thoughts. They drank a *great* deal; I'm certain of it; they couldn't have faked that. I served them. They appeared quite sloshed. Harmless, but sloshed."

"Could they have poured their drinks out somewhere? Without drinking them, I mean."

"Where?" asked the stewardess.

"I don't know. Hollow ashtrays, the seat cushions. What's on the floor?"

"Carpeting," answered the pilot.

The detective addressed the police officer by the door. "Get forensic on your radio. Have them check the carpet, the seat cushions, ashtrays. Left side of the roped-off area facing front. Dampness is enough. Let me know."

"Yes, sir." The officer left quickly, closing the door behind him.

"Of course," ventured the captain, "alcoholic tolerances vary."

"Not in the amounts the young lady described," the detective said.

"For God's sake, why is it important?" said the captain. "Obviously they're the men you want. They've vanished, as you put it. That took some planning, I daresay."

"Everything's important," explained the detective. "Methods can be matched with previous crimes. We're looking for anything. Crazy people. Rich, crazy people who jet around the world looking for thrills. Signs of psychosis, getting kicks while on a high—alcohol or narcotics, it doesn't matter. As far as we can determine, the two men in question didn't even know this Thornton; your stewardess here said they introduced themselves. Why did they kill him? And, accepting the fact that they did, why so brutally? It *was* strychnine, Captain, and take my word for it, it's a rough way to go."

The telephone rang. The customs inspector answered it; listened briefly, and handed it to the Port Authority detective. "It's the State Department. For you."

"State? This is Lieutenant Miles, NYPA police. Have you got the information I requested?"

"We've got it, but you won't like it. . . ."

"Wait a minute," Miles broke in. The door had opened and the uniformed officer had reappeared. "What have you got?" Miles asked the officer.

"The seat cushions and the carpet on the left side of the lounge are soaked."

"Then they were cold sober," said the detective, in a monotone. He nodded and returned to the telephone. "Go ahead, State. What won't I like?"

"Those passports in question were declared void more than four years ago. They belonged to two men from Flint, Michigan. Neighbors, actually; worked for the same company in Detroit. In June of 1973 they both went on a business trip to Europe and never came back."

"Why were the passports voided?"

"They disappeared from their hotel rooms. Three days later their bodies were found in the river. They'd been shot."

"*Jesus!* What river? Where?"

"The Isar. They were in Munich, Germany."

One by one the irate passengers of Flight 591 passed through the door of the quarantined room. Their names, addresses, and telephone numbers were checked off against the 747's manifest by a representative of British Airways. Next to the representative was a member of the Port Authority police, making his own marks on a duplicate list. The quarantine had lasted nearly four hours.

Outside the room the passengers were directed down a hallway into a large cargo area, where they retrieved their inspected luggage, and headed for the doors of the main terminal. One passenger, however, made no move to leave the cargo area. Instead, this man, who carried no luggage, but had a raincoat over his arm, walked directly to a door with thick, stenciled printing on the panel.

U. S. CUSTOMS. CONTROL CENTER
AUTHORIZED PERSONNEL ONLY

Showing identification, he stepped inside.

A gray-haired man in the uniform of a high-ranking customs official stood by a steel-framed window, smoking a cigarette. At the intrusion, he turned. "I've been waiting for you," he said. "There was nothing I could do while you were quarantined."

"I had the ID card ready in case you weren't here," replied the passenger, putting the identification back into his jacket pocket.

"Keep it ready. You may still need it; the police are all over the place. What do you want to do?"

"Get out to that aircraft."

"You think they're there?"

"Yes. Somewhere. It's the only explanation."

The two men left the room and walked rapidly across the cargo area, past the numerous conveyor belts, to a steel doorway marked NO ADMITTANCE. Using a key, the customs official opened it and preceded the younger man with the raincoat through the door. They were inside a long cinderblock tunnel that led to the field. Forty seconds later they reached another steel door, this one guarded by two men, one from U.S. Customs, the other from the Port Authority police. The gray-haired official was recognized by the former.

"Hello, Captain. Hell of a night, isn't it?"

"It's only begun, I'm afraid," said the official. "We may be involved, after all." He looked at the policeman. "This man's federal," he continued, angling his head at his companion. "I'm taking him to the five-ninety-one aircraft. There may be a narcotics connection."

The police officer seemed confused. Apparently his orders were to allow no one through the door. The customs guard interceded.

"Hey, come on. This man runs all of Kennedy Airport."

The policeman shrugged and opened the door.

Outside a steady rain fell from the black night sky as pockets of mist rolled in from Jamaica Bay. The man with the customs official put on his raincoat. His movements were swift; in the hand beneath the coat held over his arm had been a gun. It was now in his belt, the buttons at his waist unfastened.

The 747 glistened under floodlights, rain streaking down its fuselage. Police and maintenance crews were everywhere, distinguished from one another by the contrasting black and orange of their slickers.

"I'll build your cover with the police inside," said the customs official, gesturing at the metal steps that swept up from the back of the truck to a door in the fuselage. "Good hunting."

The man in the raincoat nodded, not really listening. His eyes were scanning the area. The 747 was the focal point; thirty yards from it in all directions were stanchions connected by ropes, policemen at midpoints between them. The man in the raincoat was within this enclosure; he could move about freely. He turned right at the end of the parallel ropes and proceeded toward the rear of the aircraft. He nodded to the police officers at their posts, slapping his identification open casually to those whose looks were questioning. He kept peering through the rain into the faces of those entering and leaving the plane. Three quarters around the plane, he heard the angry shout of a maintenance crewman.

"What the fuck are you *doing?* Get that winch secure!"

The target of the outburst was another crewman, standing on the platform of a fuel truck. This crewman had no rain slicker on; his white coverall was drenched. In the driver's seat of the truck sat another crewman, also without rain apparel.

That was *it,* thought the man in the raincoat. The killers had worn coveralls beneath their suits. But they had not taken into consideration the possibility of rain. Except for that mistake, the escape had been planned brilliantly.

The man walked over to the fuel truck, his hand on the gun concealed beneath his raincoat. Through the rain he stared at the figure beyond the truck window, in the driver's seat; the second man was above him, to his right on the platform, turned away. The face behind the window stared back in disbelief, and instantly lurched for the far side of the seat. But the man in the raincoat was too quick. He opened the door, pulled out his revolver and fired, the gunshot muted by a silencer. The man in the seat fell into the dashboard, blood streaming out of his forehead.

At the sound of the commotion below, the second man spun around on the steel platform of the truck and looked below.

"*You!* In the *lounge!* With the newspaper!"

"Get inside the truck," commanded the man in the raincoat, his words clear through the pounding rain, his gun concealed behind the door panel.

The figure on the platform hesitated. The man with the gun looked around. The surrounding police were preoccupied with their discomfort in the downpour, half blinded by the floodlights. None was observing the deadly scene. The man in the raincoat reached up, grabbed the white cloth of the surviving killer's coverall, and yanked him into the frame of the open door of the fuel truck.

"You failed. Heinrich Clausen's son still lives," he said calmly. Then he fired a second shot. The killer fell back into the seat.

The man in the raincoat closed the door and put his gun back into his belt. He walked casually away, directly underneath the fuselage toward the roped-off alleyway that led to the tunnel. He could see the customs official

emerging from the 747's door, walking rapidly down the
steps. They met and together headed for the door of the
tunnel.

"What happened?" asked the official.

"My hunting was good. Theirs wasn't. The question
is, what do we do about Holcroft?"

"That's not our concern. It's the Tinamou's. The Tinamou must be informed."

The man in the raincoat smiled to himself, knowing
his smile could not be seen in the downpour.

4

Holcroft got out of the taxi in front of his apartment on East Seventy-third Street. He was exhausted, the strain of the last three days heightened by the tragedy on board the flight. He was sorry for the poor bastard who'd had the heart attack, but furious at the Port Authority police who treated the incident as if it were an international crisis. Good Lord! *Quarantined* for damned near four hours! And all passengers in first class were to keep the police informed of their whereabouts for the next sixty days.

The doorman greeted him. "A short trip this time, Mr. Holcroft. But you got a lot of mail. Oh, and a message."

"A message?"

"Yes, sir," said the doorman, handing him a business card. "This gentleman came in asking for you last night. He was very agitated, you know what I mean?"

"Not exactly." Noel took the card and read the name: PETER BALDWIN, ESQ.; it meant nothing to him. WELLINGTON SECURITY SYSTEMS, LTD. THE STRAND, LONDON, W1A. There was a telephone number underneath. Holcroft had never heard of the British company. He turned the card over; on the back was scribbled ST. REGIS HOTEL. RM. 411.

"He insisted that I ring your apartment in case you'd gotten back and I didn't see you come in. I told him that was crazy."

"He could have telephoned me himself," said Noel, walking toward the elevator. "I'm in the book."

"He told me he tried, but your phone was out of order." The elevator door closed on the man's last words. Holcroft read the name again as the elevator climbed to the fifth floor. Peter Baldwin, Esq. Who was he? And since when was his phone out of order?

He opened his apartment door and reached for the light switch on the wall. Two table lamps went on simultaneously; Noel dropped his suitcase and stared in disbelief at the room.

Nothing was the same as it was three days ago! *Nothing.* Every piece of furniture, every chair, every table, every vase and ashtray, was moved into another position. His couch had been in the center of the room; it was now in the far-right corner. Each sketch and painting on the walls had been shifted around, none where it had been before! The stereo was no longer on the shelf; instead it was neatly arranged on a table. His bar, always at the rear of the living room, was now at the left of the door. His drafting board, usually by the window, was now by itself ten feet in front of him, the stool somewhere else—God knew where. It was the strangest sensation he had ever had. Everything familiar, yet not familiar at all. Reality distorted, out of focus.

He stood in the open doorway. Images of the room as it had been kept reappearing in front of his eyes, only to be replaced by what was in front of him now.

"What *happened?*" He heard his own words, unsure they were his at first.

He ran to the couch; the telephone was always by the couch, on a table at its right arm. But the couch had been moved, and the telephone had not been moved with it. He spun around toward the center of the room. Where was the table? It was not there; an armchair was where the table should be. The telephone was not there, either! *Where* was the telephone? Where was the table? Where the *hell* was the *telephone?*

It was by the window. There was his *kitchen* table by the *living-room* window, and the telephone was on top of it. The large center window that looked out at the apartment building across the wide courtyard below. The telephone wires had been taken out from under the wall-to-wall carpeting and moved to the window. It was crazy! Who would take the trouble to lift tacked-down carpeting and move telephone wires?

He raced to the table, picked up the phone, and pressed the intercom button that connected him to the switchboard in the lobby. He stabbed the signal button repeatedly; there was no answer. He kept his finger on it; finally, the harried voice of Jack the doorman answered.

"All right, all right. This is the lobby. . . ."

"Jack, it's Mr. Holcroft. Who came up to my apartment while I was away?"

"Who came what, sir?"

"Up to my *apartment!*"

"Were you robbed, Mr. Holcroft?"

"I don't know yet. I just know that everything's been moved around. Who was here?"

"Nobody. I mean, nobody *I* know of. And the other guys didn't say anything. I'm relieved at four in the morning by Ed, and he's off at noon. Louie takes over then."

"Can you call them?"

"Hell, I can call the police!"

The word was jarring. "Police" meant questions— *Where had he been? Whom had he seen?*—and Noel was not sure he wanted to give any answers.

"No, don't call the police. Not yet. Not until I see if anything's missing. It might be someone's idea of a joke. I'll call you back."

"I'll call the other guys."

Holcroft hung up. He sat on the wide windowsill and appraised the room. *Everything.* Not a single piece of furniture was where it had been before!

He was holding something in his left hand: the business card. PETER BALDWIN, ESQ.

". . . *he was very agitated, you know what I mean? . . . he insisted I ring your apartment . . . your phone was out of order. . . .*"

ST. REGIS HOTEL. RM. 411.

Noel picked up the phone and dialed. He knew the number well; he lunched frequently at the King Cole Grill.

"Yes? Baldwin here." The voice was British, the greeting abrupt.

"This is Noel Holcroft, Mr. Baldwin. You tried to reach me."

"Thank heavens! Where are you?"

"Home. In my apartment. I just got back."

"Back? From where?"

"I'm not sure that's any of your business."

"For God's sake, I've traveled over three thousand miles to see you! It's dreadfully important. Now where *were* you?"

The Englishman's breathing was audible over the

phone; the man's intensity seemed somehow related to fear. "I'm flattered you came all that distance to see me, but it still doesn't give you the right to ask personal questions. . . ."

"I have *every* right!" broke in Baldwin. "I spent twenty years with MI Six, and we have a great deal to talk about! You have no idea what you're doing. No one does but me."

"You *what? We* what?"

"Let me put it this way. Cancel Geneva. *Cancel* it, Mr. Holcroft, until we've talked!"

"Geneva? . . ." Noel felt suddenly sick to his stomach. How would this Englishman know about Geneva? How *could* he know?

A light flickered outside the window; someone in an apartment directly across the courtyard was lighting a cigarette. Despite his agitation, Holcroft's eyes were drawn to it.

"There's someone at the door," Baldwin said. "Stay on the phone. I'll get rid of whoever it is and be right back."

Noel could hear Baldwin put the telephone down, then the sound of a door opening and indistinguishable voices. Across the courtyard, in the window, a match was struck again, illuminating the long blond hair of a woman behind a sheer curtain.

Holcroft realized there was silence on the line; he could hear no voices now. Moments went by; the Englishman did not return.

"Baldwin? Baldwin, where are you? *Baldwin!*"

For a third time a match flared in the window across the way. Noel stared at it; it seemed unnecessary. He could see the glow of a cigarette in the blond woman's mouth. And then he saw what was in her other hand, silhouetted behind the sheer curtain: a telephone. She was holding a telephone to her ear and looking over at his window—looking, he was sure, at him.

"*Baldwin?* Where the hell *are* you?"

There was a click; the line went dead.

"*Baldwin!*"

The woman in the window slowly lowered the telephone, paused for a moment, and walked away, out of sight.

Holcroft stared at the window, then at the telephone in his hand. He waited until he got the active line, then redialed the St. Regis.

"I'm sorry, sir, room four-eleven's telephone seems to be out of order. We'll send someone up right away. May I have your number and we'll give it to Mr. Baldwin."

... your phone was out of order. ...

Something was happening that Noel did not understand. He knew only that he would not leave his name or number with the operator at the St. Regis. He hung up and looked again at the window across the courtyard. Whatever light there had been was gone. The window was dark; he could see only the white of the curtain.

He pushed himself away from the windowsill and wandered aimlessly about the room, around familiar possessions in unfamiliar locations. He was not sure what to do; he supposed he should see if anything was missing. Nothing seemed to be, but it was difficult to tell.

The telephone buzzed: the intercom from the lobby switchboard. He answered it.

"It's Jack, Mr. Holcroft. I just spoke to Ed and Louie. Neither of 'em know anything about anyone going up to your place. They're honest guys. They wouldn't screw around. None of us would."

"Thanks, Jack. I believe you."

"You want me to call the police?"

"No." Noel tried to sound casual. "I have an idea someone at the office was playing a joke. A couple of the fellows have keys."

"I didn't see anybody. Neither did Ed or—"

"It's okay, Jack," interrupted Holcroft. "Forget it. The night I left we had a party. One or two stayed over." It was all Noel could think of to say.

Suddenly it occurred to him that he had not looked in his bedroom. He went there now, his hand reaching for the light switch on the wall.

He expected it, but it was still a shock. The disorientation was now somehow complete.

Again, each piece of furniture had been moved to a different position. The bed was the first thing that struck his eye; it was oddly frightening. No part of it touched the wall. Instead, it was in the center of the room, iso-

lated. His bureau stood in front of a window; a small
writing desk was dwarfed against the expanse of the right
wall. As had happened minutes ago, when first he'd seen
the living room, the images of what his bedroom looked
like three days ago kept flashing before him, replaced by
the strangeness of what he now observed.

Then he saw it and gasped. Hanging down from the
ceiling, strapped together with dull black tape, was his
second telephone, the extension cord snaking up the wall
and across the ceiling to the hook that held it.

It was spinning slowly.

The pain shifted from his stomach to his chest; his
eyes were transfixed on the sight, on the suspended instrument revolving slowly in midair. He was afraid to
look beyond, but he knew he had to; he had to understand.

And when he did, his breath came back to him. The
phone was in the direct path of his bathroom door and
the door was open. He saw the curtains billowing in the
window above the basin. The steady stream of cold wind
was making the telephone spin.

He walked quickly into the bathroom to shut the
window. As he was about to pull the curtains, he saw a
brief flash of illumination outside; a match had been
struck in another window across the courtyard, the flare
startling in the darkness. He looked out.

There was the woman again! The blond-haired woman, her upper body silhouetted beyond another set of
sheer curtains. He stared at the figure, mesmerized by it.

She turned as she had turned before, and walked
away as she had walked away minutes ago. Out of sight.
And the dim light in the window went out.

What *was* happening? What did it mean? Things were
being orchestrated to frighten him. But by whom and
for what purpose? And what had happened to Peter
Baldwin, Esq., he of the intense voice and the command
to cancel Geneva? Was Baldwin a part of the terror, or
was he a victim of it?

Victim . . . *victim?* It was an odd word to use, he
thought. Why should there be any victims? And what did
Baldwin mean when he said he had "spent twenty
years with MI Six"?

MI Six? A branch of British intelligence. If he remembered correctly, MI *Five* was the section that dealt

with domestic matters; *Six* concerned itself with problems outside the country. The English CIA, as it were.

Good God! Did the British know about the Geneva document? Was British intelligence aware of the massive theft of thirty years ago? On the surface, it would appear so. . . . Yet that was not what Peter Baldwin had implied.

You have no idea what you're doing. No one does but me.

And then there was silence, and the line went dead.

Holcroft walked out of the bathroom and paused beneath the suspended telephone; it was barely moving now, but it had not stopped. It was an ugly sight, made macabre by the profusion of dull black tape that held the instrument together. As if the phone had been mummified, never to be used again.

He continued toward the bedroom door, then instinctively stopped and turned. Something had caught his eye, something he had not noticed before. The center drawer of the small writing desk was open. He looked closer. Inside the drawer was a sheet of paper.

His breathing stopped as he stared at the page below. It couldn't *be*. It was *insane*. The single sheet of paper was brownish yellow. With *age*. It was identical to the page that had been kept in a vault in Geneva for thirty years. The letter filled with threats written by fanatics who revered a martyr named Heinrich Clausen. The writing was the same; the odd Germanic printing of English words, the ink that was faded but still legible.

And what was legible was astonishing. For it had been written more than thirty years ago.

NOEL CLAUSEN-HOLCROFT
NOTHING IS AS IT WAS FOR YOU. NOTHING
CAN EVER BE THE SAME. . . .

Before he read further, Noel picked up an edge of the page. It crumbled under his touch.

Oh, God! It *was* written thirty years ago!

And that fact made the remainder of the message frightening.

THE PAST WAS PREPARATION, THE FUTURE IS
COMMITTED TO THE MEMORY OF A MAN AND HIS
DREAM. HIS WAS AN ACT OF DARING AND BRIL-

LIANCE IN A WORLD GONE MAD. NOTHING MUST
STAND IN THE WAY OF THAT DREAM'S FULFILL-
MENT.

WE ARE THE SURVIVORS OF WOLFSSCHANZE.
THOSE OF US WHO LIVE WILL DEDICATE OUR
LIVES AND BODIES TO THE PROTECTION OF THAT
MAN'S DREAM. IT WILL BE FULFILLED, FOR IT IS
ALL THAT IS LEFT. AN ACT OF MERCY THAT WILL
SHOW THE WORLD THAT WE WERE BETRAYED, THAT
WE WERE NOT AS THE WORLD BELIEVED US TO BE.

WE, THE MEN OF WOLFSSCHANZE, KNOW
WHAT THE BEST OF US WERE. AS HEINRICH
CLAUSEN KNEW.

IT IS NOW UP TO YOU, NOEL CLAUSEN-
HOLCROFT, TO COMPLETE WHAT YOUR FATHER
BEGAN. YOU ARE THE WAY. YOUR FATHER
WISHED IT SO.

MANY WILL TRY TO STOP YOU. TO THROW
OPEN THE FLOODGATES AND DESTROY THE
DREAM. BUT THE MEN OF WOLFSSCHANZE DO
SURVIVE. YOU HAVE OUR WORD THAT ALL THOSE
WHO INTERFERE WILL BE STOPPED THEMSELVES.

ANY WHO STAND IN YOUR WAY, WHO TRY
TO DISSUADE YOU, WHO TRY TO DECEIVE YOU
WITH LIES, WILL BE ELIMINATED.

AS YOU AND YOURS WILL BE SHOULD YOU
HESITATE. OR FAIL.

THIS IS OUR OATH TO YOU.

Noel grabbed the paper out of the drawer; it fell
apart in his hand. He let the fragments fall to the floor.

"Goddamned maniacs!" He slammed the drawer shut
and ran out of the bedroom. Where was the telephone?
Where the *hell* was the goddamned *telephone?* By the window—that was it; it was on the *kitchen* table by the fucking *window!*

"Maniacs!" he screamed again at no one. But not
really at no one: at a man in Geneva who had been on a
train bound for Zurich. Maniacs might have written that
page of garbage thirty years ago, but now, thirty years
later, other maniacs had delivered it! They had broken
into his home, invaded his privacy, touched his belongings.
. . . God knows what else, he thought, thinking of Peter
Baldwin, Esq. A man who had traveled thousands of

miles to see him, and talk with him . . . silence, a click, a dead telephone line.

He looked at his watch. It was almost one o'clock in the morning. What was it in Zurich? Six? Seven? The banks in Switzerland opened at eight. La Grande Banque de Genève had a branch in Zurich; Manfredi would be there.

The window. He was standing in front of the window where he had stood only minutes ago, waiting for Baldwin to come back on the phone. The *window*. Across the courtyard in the opposite apartment. The three brief flares of a match . . . the blond-haired woman in the window!

Holcroft put his hand in his pocket to make sure he had his keys. He did. He ran to the door, let himself out, raced for the elevator, and pushed the button. The indicator showed that the car was on the tenth floor; the arrow did not move.

God damn it!

He ran to the staircase and started down, taking the steps two at a time. He reached the ground floor and dashed out into the lobby.

"*Jesus,* Mr. Holcroft!" Jack stared at him. "You scared the shit out of me!"

"Do you know the doorman in the next building?" shouted Noel.

"Which one?"

"*Christ! That* one!" Holcroft gestured to the right.

"That's three-eighty. Yeah, sure."

"Come on with me!"

"Hey, wait a minute, Mr. Holcroft. I can't leave here."

"We'll only be a minute. There's twenty dollars in it for you."

"Only a minute. . . ."

The doorman at three-eighty greeted them, understanding quickly that he was to give accurate information to Jack's friend.

"I'm sorry, sir, but there's no one in that apartment. Hasn't been for almost three weeks. But I'm afraid it's been rented; the new tenants will be coming in. . . ."

"There *is* someone there!" said Noel, trying to control himself. "A blond-haired woman. I've *got* to find out who she is."

"A blond-haired woman? Kind of medium height, sort of good-looking, smokes a lot?"

"Yes, that's the one! Who is she?"

"You live in your place long, mister?"

"What?"

"I mean, have you been there a long time?"

"What's that got to do with anything?"

"I think maybe you've been drinking. . . ."

"What the hell are you talking about?! Who *is that woman?*"

"Not *is*, mister. *Was.* The blond woman you're talking about was Mrs. Palatyne. She died a month ago."

Noel sat in the chair in front of the window, staring across the courtyard. Someone was trying to drive him crazy. But why? It did not make sense! Fanatics, maniacs from thirty years ago, had sprung across three decades, commanding younger, unknown troops thirty years later. Again, *why?*

He had called the St. Regis. Room four-eleven's telephone was working, but it was continuously busy. And a woman he had seen clearly did not exist. But she did exist! And she was a part of it; he *knew* it.

He got out of the chair, walked to the strangely placed bar, and poured himself a drink. He looked at his watch; it was one-fifty. He had ten minutes to wait before the overseas operator would call him back; the bank could be reached at two A.M., New York time. He carried his glass back to the chair in front of the window. On the way, he passed his FM radio. It was not where it usually was of course; that was why he noticed it. Absently, he turned it on. He liked music; it soothed him.

But it was words, not music, that he heard. The *rat-tat-tatting* beneath an announcer's voice indicated one of those "all-news" stations. The dial had been changed. He should have known. *Nothing is as it was for you. . . .*

Something being said on the radio caught his attention. He turned quickly in the chair, part of his drink spilling onto his trousers.

". . . police have cordoned off the hotel's entrances. Our reporter, Richard Dunlop, is on the scene, calling in from our mobile unit. Come in, Richard. What have you learned?"

There was a burst of static followed by the voice of an excited newscaster.

"The man's name was Peter Baldwin, John. He was an Englishman. Arrived yesterday, or at least that's when he registered at the St. Regis; the police are contacting the airlines for further information. As far as can be determined, he was over here on vacation. There was no listing of a company on the hotel registry card."

"When did they discover the body?"

"About a half hour ago. A maintenance man went up to the room to check the telephone and found Mr. Baldwin sprawled out on the bed. The rumors here are wild and you don't know what to believe, but the thing that's stressed is the method of killing. Apparently, it was vicious, brutal. Baldwin was garroted, they said. A wire pulled through his throat. An hysterical maid from the fourth floor was heard screaming to the police that the room was drenched with—"

"Was robbery the motive?" interrupted the anchorman, in the interests of taste.

"We haven't been able to establish that. The police aren't talking. I gather they're waiting for someone from the British consulate to arrive."

"Thank you, Richard Dunlop. We'll stay in touch. . . . That was Richard Dunlop at the St. Regis Hotel, on Fifty-fifth Street in Manhattan. To repeat, a brutal murder took place at one of New York's most fashionable hotels this morning. An Englishman named Peter Baldwin . . ."

Holcroft shot out of the chair, lurched at the radio, and turned it off. He stood above it, breathing rapidly. He did not want to admit to himself that he had heard what he had just heard. It was not anything he had really considered; it simply was not possible.

But it *was* possible. It was real; it had happened. It was death. The maniacs from thirty years ago were not caricatures, not figures from some melodrama. They were vicious killers. And they were deadly serious.

Peter Baldwin, Esq., had told him to cancel Geneva. Baldwin had interfered with the dream, with the covenant. And now he was dead, brutally killed with a wire through his throat.

With difficulty, Noel walked back to the chair and sat down. He raised his glass to his lips and drank several long swallows of whiskey; the scotch did nothing for him. The pounding in his chest only accelerated.

A flare of a match! Across the courtyard, in the window! There she was! Silhouetted beyond the sheer curtains in a wash of dim light stood the blond-haired woman. She was staring across the way, staring at *him!* He got out of the chair, drawn hypnotically to the window, his face inches from the panes of glass. The woman nodded her head; she was slowly *nodding her head!* She was telling him something. She was telling him that what he perceived was the truth!

. . . *The blond woman you're talking about was Mrs. Palatyne. She died a month ago.*

A dead woman stood silhouetted in a window across the darkness and was sending him a terrible message. Oh, Christ, he was going *insane!*

The telephone rang; the bell terrified him. He held his breath and lunged at the phone; he could not let it ring again. It did awful things to the silence.

"Mr. Holcroft, this is the overseas operator. I have your call to Zurich. . . ."

Noel listened in disbelief at the somber, accented voice from Switzerland. The man on the line was the manager of the Zurich branch of La Grande Banque de Genève. A *directeur,* he said twice, emphasizing his position.

"We mourn profoundly, Mr. Holcroft. We knew Herr Manfredi was not well, but we had no idea his illness had progressed so."

"What are you talking about? What happened?"

"A terminal disease affects individuals differently. Our colleague was a vital man, an energetic man, and when such men cannot function in their normal fashions, it often leads to despondency and great depression."

"What *happened?*"

"It was suicide, Mr. Holcroft. Herr Manfredi could not tolerate his incapacities."

"*Suicide?*"

"There's no point in speaking other than the truth. Ernst threw himself out of his hotel window. It was mercifully quick. At ten o'clock, La Grande Banque will suspend all business for one minute of mourning and reflection."

"Oh, my *God. . . .*"

"However," concluded the voice in Zurich, "all of Herr Manfredi's accounts to which he gave his personal attention will be assumed by equally capable hands. We fully expect—"

Noel hung up the phone, cutting off the man's words. *Accounts . . . will be assumed by equally capable hands.* Business as usual; a man was killed, but the affairs of Swiss finance were not to be interrupted. And he *was* killed.

Ernst Manfredi did not *throw* himself out of a hotel in Zurich. He was *thrown* out. Murdered by the men of Wolfsschanze.

For God's sake, *why?* Then Holcroft remembered. Manfredi had dismissed the men of Wolfsschanze. He had told Noel the macabre threats were meaningless, the anguish of sick old men seeking atonement.

That had been Manfredi's error. He had undoubtedly told his associates, the other directors of La Grande Banque, about the strange letter that had been delivered with the wax seals unbroken. Perhaps, in their presence, he had laughed at the men of Wolfsschanze.

The match! The flare of light! Across the courtyard the woman in the window nodded! Again—as if reading his thoughts—she was confirming the truth. A dead woman was telling him he was right!

She turned and walked away; all light went out in the window.

"Come back! Come *back!*" Holcroft screamed, his hands on the panes of glass. "Who *are* you?"

The telephone beneath him buzzed. Noel stared at it, as if it were a terrible thing in an unfamiliar place; it was both. Trembling, he picked it up.

"Mr. Holcroft, it's Jack. I *think* I may know what the hell happened up at your place. I mean, I didn't think about it before, but it kinda hit me a few minutes ago."

"What was it?"

"A couple of nights ago these two guys came in. Locksmiths. Mr. Silverstein, on your floor, was having his lock changed. Louie told me about it, so I knew it was okay. Then I began to think. Why did they come at night? I mean, what with overtime and everything, why didn't they come in the daytime? So I just called Louie at home. He said they came *yesterday*. So who the hell were those other guys."

"Do you remember anything about them?"

"You're damned right I do! One of them in particular. You could pick him out in a crowd at the Garden! He had—"

There was a loud, sharp report over the line.

A *gunshot!*

It was followed by a crash. The telephone in the lobby had been dropped!

Noel slammed down the receiver and ran to the door, yanking it open with such force that it crashed into a framed sketch on the wall, smashing the glass. There was no time to consider the elevator. He raced down the stairs, his mind a blank, afraid to think, concentrating only on speed and balance, hoping to God he would not trip on the steps. He reached the landing and bolted through the lobby door.

He stared in shock. The worst had happened. Jack the doorman was arched back over the chair, blood pouring out of his neck. He had been shot in the throat.

He had interfered. He had been about to identify one of the men of Wolfsschanze and he had been killed for it.

Baldwin, Manfredi . . . an innocent doorman. Dead.

. . . *all those who interfere will be stopped. . . . Any who stand in your way, who try to dissuade you, who try to deceive you . . . will be eliminated.*

. . . *As you and yours will be should you hesitate. Or fail.*

Manfredi had asked him if he really had a choice. He did not any longer.

He was surrounded by death.

5

Althene Holcroft sat behind the desk in her study and glared at the words of the letter she held in her hand. Her chiseled, angular features—the high cheekbones, the aquiline nose, the wide-set eyes beneath arched, defined brows—were as taut, as rigid, as her posture in the chair. Her thin, aristocratic lips were tight; her breathing was steady, but each breath was too controlled, too deep, for normalcy. She read Heinrich Clausen's letter as one studying a statistical report that contradicted information previously held to be incontrovertible.

Across the room, Noel stood by a curving window that looked out on the rolling lawn and gardens behind the Bedford Hills house. A number of shrubs were covered with burlap; the air was cold, and the morning frost produced intermittent patches of light gray on the green grass.

Holcroft turned from the scene outside and looked at his mother, trying desperately to conceal his fear, to control the occasional trembling that came upon him when he thought about last night. He could not allow the terror he felt to be seen by his mother. He wondered what thoughts were going through her head, what memories were triggered by the sight of the handwritten words in blue ink put down by a man she once had loved, then had grown to despise. Whatever she was thinking, it would remain private until she chose to speak. Althene communicated only that which she cared to convey deliberately.

She seemed to sense his gaze and raised her eyes to his, but only briefly. She returned to the letter, allowing a briefer moment to brush away a stray lock that had fallen from the gray hair that framed her face. Noel wandered aimlessly toward the desk, glancing at the bookcases and photographs on the wall. The room reflected the owner, he mused. Graceful, even elegant; but, withal, there was a pervading sense of activity. The photographs showed men and women on horses at the hunt, in sailboats in rough weather, on skis in mountain snow. There was no denying it: There was an undercurrent of masculinity in this very feminine room. It was his mother's study, her sanctuary where she repaired for private moments of consideration. But it could have belonged to a man.

He sat down in the leather chair in front of the desk and lighted a cigarette with a gold Colibri, a parting gift from a young lady who had moved out of his apartment a month ago. His hand trembled again; he gripped the lighter as tightly as he could.

"That's a dreadful habit," said Althene, her eyes remaining on the letter. "I thought you were going to give it up."

"I have. A number of times."

"Mark Twain said that. At least be original."

Holcroft shifted his position in the chair, feeling awkward. "You've read it several times now. What do you think?"

"I don't *know* what to think," said Althene, placing the letter on the desk in front of her. "He wrote it; it's his handwriting, his way of expressing himself. Arrogant even in remorse."

"You agree it's remorse then?"

"It would appear so. On the surface, at any rate. I'd want to know a great deal more. I have a number of questions about this extraordinary financial undertaking. It's beyond anything conceivable."

"Questions lead to other questions, mother. The men in Geneva don't want that."

"Does it matter what they want? As I understand you, although you're being elliptical, they're asking you to give up a minimum of six months of your life and probably a good deal more."

Again, Noel felt awkward. He had decided not to show her the document from La Grande Banque. If she was adamant about seeing it, he could always produce it. If she was not, it was better that way; the less she knew, the better. He had to keep her from the men of Wolfsschanze. He had not the slightest doubt Althene would interfere.

"I'm not holding back any of the essentials," he said.

"I didn't say you were. I said you were elliptical. You refer to a man in Geneva you won't identify; you speak of conditions you only half describe, the oldest children of two families you won't name. You're leaving out a great deal."

"For your own good."

"That's condescending and, considering this letter, very insulting."

"I didn't mean to be either." Holcroft leaned forward. "No one wants that bank account even remotely connected with you. You've read that letter; you know what's involved. Thousands and thousands of people, hundreds of millions of dollars. There's no way to tell who might hold *you* responsible. You were the wife who told him the truth; you left him because he refused to accept it. When he finally realized that what you said *was* true, he did what he did. There may be men still alive who would kill you for that. I won't let you be put in that position."

"I see." Althene drew out the phrase, then repeated it as she rose from her chair and walked slowly across the room to the bay window. "Are you sure that's the concern the men in Geneva expressed?"

"They—he—implied it, yes."

"I suspect it was not the only concern."

"No."

"Shall I speculate on another?"

Noel stiffened. It was not that he underestimated his mother's perceptions—he rarely did that—but, as always, he was annoyed when she verbalized them before he had the chance to state them himself.

"I think it's obvious," he said.

"Do you?" Althene turned from the window and looked at him.

"It's in the letter. If the sources of that account were made public, there'd be legal problems. Claims would be made against it in the international courts."

"Yes." His mother looked away. "It's obvious, then. I'm amazed you were allowed to tell me anything."

Noel leaned back in the chair apprehensively, disturbed at Althene's words. "Why? Would you really do something?"

"It's a temptation," she answered, still gazing outside. "I don't think one ever loses the desire to strike back, to lash out at someone or something that's caused great pain. Even if that hurt changed your life for the better. God knows mine—ours—was changed. From a hell to a level of happiness I'd given up looking for."

"Dad?" asked Noel.

Althene turned. "Yes. He risked more than you'll ever know protecting us. I'd been the fool of the world and he accepted the fool—and the fool's child. He gave us more than love; he gave us our lives again. He asked only love in return."

"You've given him that."

"I'll give it till I die. Richard Holcroft is the man I once thought Clausen was. I was so wrong, so terribly wrong. . . . The fact that Heinrich has been dead these many years doesn't seem to matter; the loathing won't go away. I do want to strike back."

Noel kept his voice calm. He had to lead his mother away from her thoughts; the survivors of Wolfsschanze would not let her live. "You'd be striking back at the man you remember, not the man who wrote that letter. Maybe what you saw in him at first was really there. At the end, it came back to him."

"That would be comforting, wouldn't it?"

"I think it's true. The man who wrote that letter wasn't lying. He was in pain."

"He deserved pain, he caused so much; he was the most ruthless man I ever met. But on the surface, so different, so filled with purpose. And—oh, *God*—what that purpose turned out to be!"

"He changed, mother," interrupted Holcroft. "You were a part of that change. At the end of his life he wanted only to help undo what he'd done. He says it: 'Amends must be made.' Think what he did—what the three of them did—to bring that about."

"I can't dismiss it; I know that. Any more than I can dismiss the words. I can almost hear him say them, but it's a very young man talking. A young man filled with purpose, a very young, wild girl at his side." Althene paused, then spoke again, clearly. "Why did you show me the letter? Why did you bring it all back?"

"Because I've decided to go ahead. That means closing the office, traveling around a lot, eventually working out of Switzerland for a number of months. As the man in

Geneva said, you wouldn't have accepted all that without asking a lot of questions. He was afraid you'd learn something damaging and do something rash."

"At *your* expense?" asked Althene.

"I guess so. He thought it was a possibility. He said those memories of yours were strong. 'Indelibly printed' were his words."

"Indelibly," agreed Althene.

"His point was that there were no legal solutions; that it was better to use the money the way it was intended to be used. To make those amends."

"It's possible he was right. If it can be done. God knows it's overdue. Whatever Heinrich touched, very little of value and truth was the result." Althene paused, her face suddenly strained. "You were the one exception. Perhaps this is the other."

Noel got out of the chair and went to his mother. He took her by the shoulders and drew her to him. "That man in Geneva said you were incredible. You are."

Althene pulled back. "He said that? 'Incredible'?"

"Yes."

"Ernst Manfredi," she whispered.

"You *know* him?" asked Holcroft.

"It's a name that goes back many years. He's still alive then."

Noel did not answer her question. "How did you know it was he?"

"A summer afternoon in Berlin. He was there. He helped us get out. You and I. He got us on the plane, gave me money. Dear *God*. . . ." Althene disengaged herself from her son's arms and walked across the room, toward the desk. "He called me 'incredible' then, that afternoon. He said they would hunt me, find me. Find us. He said he would do what he could. He told me what to do, what to say. An unimpressive little Swiss banker was a giant that afternoon. My God, after all these years . . ."

Noel watched his mother, his astonishment complete. "Why didn't he say anything? Why didn't he *tell* me?"

Althene turned, facing her son but not looking at him. She was staring beyond him, seeing things he could not see. "I think he wanted me to find out for myself. This way. He was not a man to call in old debts indiscriminately." She sighed. "I won't pretend the questions are put to rest. I promise nothing. If I decide to take any action, I'll give you ample warning. But for the time being I won't interfere."

"That's kind of open ended, isn't it?"

"It's the best you'll get. Those memories are, indeed, indelibly printed."

"But for now you'll do nothing?"

"You have my word. It's not lightly given, nor will it be lightly taken back."

"What would change it?"

"If you disappeared, for one thing."

"I'll stay in touch."

Althene Holcroft watched her son walk out of the room. Her face—so tense, so rigid, only moments ago —was relaxed. Her thin lips formed a smile; her wide eyes were reflective, in them a look of quiet satisfaction and strength.

She reached for the telephone on her desk, pressed the single button *O*, and seconds later spoke.

"Overseas operator, please. I'd like to place a call to Geneva, Switzerland."

He needed a professionally acceptable reason to close up Holcroft, Incorporated. Questions of substance could not be asked. The survivors of Wolfsschanze were killers for whom questions were too easily construed as interference. He had to disappear legitimately. . . . But one did *not* disappear legitimately: One found plausible explanations that gave the appearance of legitimacy.

The *appearance* of legitimacy.

Sam Buonoventura.

Not that Sam wasn't legitimate: He was. He was one of the best construction engineers in the business. But Sam had followed the sun so long he had blind spots. He was a fifty-year-old professional drifter, a City College graduate from Tremont Avenue, in the Bronx, who had found a life of instant gratification in the warmer climes.

A brief tour of duty in the Army Corps of Engineers had convinced Buonoventura that there was a sweeter, more generous world beyond the borders of the United States, preferably south of the Keys. All one had to be was good—good in a job that was part of a larger job in which a great deal of money was invested. And during the fifties and sixties, the construction explosion in Latin America and the Caribbean was such that it might have been created for someone like Sam. He built a reputation among corporations and governments as the building tyrant who got things done in the field.

Once having studied blueprints, labor pools, and budgets, if Sam told his employers that a hotel or an airport or a dam would be operational within a given period of time, he was rarely in error beyond four percent. He was also an architect's dream, which meant that he did not consider himself an architect.

Noel had worked with Buonoventura on two jobs outside the country, the first in Costa Rica, where if it had not been for Sam, Holcroft would have lost his life. The engineer had insisted that the well-groomed, courteous architect from the classy side of Manhattan learn to use a handgun, not just a hunting rifle from Abercrombie & Fitch. They were building a postal complex in the back country, and it was a far cry from the cocktail lounges of the Plaza and the Waldorf, and from San José. The architect had thought the weekend exercise ridiculous, but courtesy demanded compliance. Courtesy, and Buonoventura's booming voice.

By the end of the following week, however, the architect was profoundly grateful. Thieves had come down from the hills to steal construction explosives. Two men had raced through the camp at night, they'd crashed into Noel's shack as he slept. When they realized the explosives were not there one man had run outside, shouting instructions to his accomplices.

"*¡Matemos el gringo!*"

But the *gringo* understood the language. He reached his gun—the handgun provided by Sam Buonoventura—and shot his would-be killer.

Sam had only one comment: "Goddamn. In some cultures I'd have to take care of you for the rest of your life."

Noel reached Buonoventura through a shipping company in Miami. He was in the Dutch Antilles, in the town of Willemstad, on the island of Curaçao.

"How the hell *are* you, Noley?" Sam shouted, over the phone. "Christ, it must be four, five years! How's your pistol arm?"

"Haven't used it since the *colinas,* and never expect to use it again. How are things with you?"

"These mothers got money to burn down here, so I'm lighting a few matches. You looking for work?"

"No. A favor."

"Name it."

"I'm going to be out of the country for a number of months on private business. I want a reason for not being in New York, for not being available. A reason that people won't question. I've got an idea, Sam, and wondered if you could help me make it work."

"If we're both thinking the same thing, sure I can."

They *were* thinking the same thing. It was not out of the ordinary for long-range projects in faraway places to employ consulting architects, men whose names would not appear on schematics or blueprints but whose skills would be used. The practice was generally confined to those areas where the hiring of native talent was a question of local pride. The inherent problem, of course, was that all too frequently the native talent lacked sufficient training and experience. Investors covered their risks by employing highly skilled outside professionals who corrected and amended the work of the locals, seeing the projects through to completion.

"Have you got any suggestions?" Noel asked.

"Hell, yes. Take your pick of half a dozen under-developed countries. Africa, South America, even some of the islands here in the Antilles and the Grenadines. The internationals are moving in like spiders, but the locals are still sensitive. The consulting jobs are kept separate and quiet; graft is soaring."

"I don't want a job, Sam. I want a cover. Someplace I can name, someone I can mention who'll back me up."

"Why not me? I'll be buried in this motherlode for most of the year. Maybe more. I've got two marinas and a full-scale yacht club to go to when the hotel's finished. I'm your man, Noley."

"That's what I was hoping."

"That's what I figured. I'll give you the particulars and you let me know where I can reach you in case any of your high-society friends want to throw a tea dance for you."

Holcroft placed his two draftsmen and his secretary in new jobs by Wednesday. As he had suspected, it was not difficult; they were good people. He made fourteen telephone calls to project-development executives at companies where his designs were under consideration, astonished to learn that of the fourteen, he was the leading contender in eight. Eight! If all came through, the fees would have totaled more than he had earned during the past five years.

But not two million dollars; he kept that in the back of his mind. And if it was not in the back of his mind, the survivors of Wolfsschanze were.

The telephone-answering service was given specific instructions. Holcroft, Incorporated, was unavailable at the time for architectural projects. The company was involved in an overseas commission of considerable magnitude. If the caller would leave his name and number . . .

For those who pressed for further information, a post-office box in Curaçao, Netherlands Antilles, under the name of Samuel Buonoventura, Limited, was listed. And, for the few who insisted on a telephone number, Sam's was to be given.

Noel had agreed to phone Buonoventura once a week; he would do the same with the answering service.

By Friday morning, he had an uneasy feeling about his decision. He was taking himself out of a garden he had cultivated to walk into an unfamiliar forest.

Nothing is as it was for you. Nothing can ever be the same.

Suppose he could not find the Von Tiebolt children. Suppose they were dead, their remains no more than graves in a Brazilian cemetery? They had disappeared five years ago in Rio de Janeiro; what made him think he could make them reappear? And if he could not, would the survivors of Wolfsschanze strike? He was afraid. But fear itself did not cover everything, thought Holcroft as he walked to the corner of Seventy-third Street and Third Avenue. There were ways to handle fear. He could take the Geneva document to the authorities, to the State Department, and tell them what he knew of Peter Baldwin and Ernst Manfredi and a doorman named Jack. He could expose the massive theft of thirty years ago, and grateful thousands over the world would see to it that he was protected.

That was the sanest thing to do, but somehow sanity and self-protection were not so important. Not now.

There was a man in agony thirty years ago. And that man was his rationale.

He hailed a cab, struck by an odd thought, one he knew was in the deep recesses of his imagination. It was the "something else" that drove him into the unfamiliar forest.

He was assuming a guilt that was not his. He was taking on the sins of Heinrich Clausen.

Amends must be made.

"Six-thirty Fifth Avenue, please," he said to the driver as he climbed into the cab. It was the address of the Brazilian Consulate.

The hunt had begun.

6

"Let me understand you, Mr. Holcroft," said the aging attaché, leaning back in his chair. "You say you wish to locate a family that you won't identify. You tell me this family immigrated to Brazil sometime in the forties and, according to the most recent information, dropped from sight several years ago. Is this correct?"

Noel saw the bemused expression on the attaché's face and understood. It was a foolish game perhaps, but Holcroft did not know any other one to play. He was not going to name the Von Tiebolts before he reached Brazil; he was not going to give anyone the chance to complicate further a search that had enough disadvantages at the start. He smiled pleasantly.

"I didn't quite say that. I asked how such a family might be found, given those circumstances. I didn't say I was the one looking."

"Then it's a hypothetical question? Are you a journalist?"

Holcroft considered the medium-level diplomat's question. How simple it would be to say yes; what a convenient explanation for the questions *he* would ask later. On the other hand, he'd be flying to Rio de Janeiro in a few days. There were immigration cards to be filled out, and a visa, perhaps; he did not know. A false answer now might become a problem later.

"No, an architect."

The attaché's eyes betrayed his surprise. "Then you'll visit Brasília, of course. It is a masterpiece."

"I'd like to very much."

"You speak Portuguese?"

"A bit of Spanish. I've worked in Mexico. And in Costa Rica."

"But we're straying," said the attaché, leaning forward in his chair. "I asked you if you were a journalist,

61

and you hesitated. You were tempted to say you were because it was expedient. Frankly, that tells me you are, indeed, the one looking for this family that has dropped from sight. Now, why not tell me the rest?"

If he was going to consider lying in his search through this unfamiliar forest, thought Noel, he'd better learn to analyze his minor answers first. Lesson one: preparation.

"There isn't that much to tell," he said awkwardly. "I'm taking a trip to your country and I promised a friend I'd look up these people he knew a long time ago." It was a variation on the truth and not a bad one, thought Holcroft. Perhaps that was why he was able to offer it convincingly. Lesson two: Base the lie in an aspect of truth.

"Yet your . . . *friend* has tried to locate them and was unable to do so."

"He tried from thousands of miles away. It's not the same."

"I daresay it isn't. So, because of this distance, and your friend's concern that there could be complications, shall we say, you'd prefer not to identify the family by name."

"That's it."

"No, it isn't. It would be far too simple a matter for an attorney to cable a confidential inquiry-of-record to a reciprocating law firm in Rio de Janeiro. It's done all the time. The family your friend wants to find is nowhere in evidence, so your *friend* wants you to trace them." The attaché smiled and shrugged, as if he had delivered a basic lecture in arithmetic.

Noel watched the Brazilian with growing irritation. Lesson three: Don't be led into a trap by pat conclusions casually stated. "You know something?" he said. "You're a very disagreeable fellow."

"I'm sorry you think so," replied the attaché sincerely. "I want to be of help. That's my function here. I've spoken to you this way for a reason. You are not the first man, God knows, nor will you be the last, to look for people who came to my country 'sometime in the forties.' I'm sure I don't have to amplify that statement. The vast majority of those people were Germans, many bringing to Brazil great sums of money transferred by compromised neutrals. What I'm trying to say is simply put: Be careful.

Such people as you speak of do not disappear without cause."

"What do you mean?"

"They have to, Mr. Holcroft. *Had* to. The Nuremberg Tribunals and the Israeli hunters aside, many possessed funds—in some cases, fortunes—that were stolen from conquered peoples, from their institutions, often from their governments. Those funds could be reclaimed."

Noel tensed the muscles of his stomach. There *was* a connection—abstract, even misleading, under the circumstances, but it was there. The Von Tiebolts were part of a theft so massive and complex it was beyond accounting procedures. But it could not be the reason they had vanished. Lesson four: Be prepared for unexpected coincidences, no matter how strained; be ready to conceal reactions.

"I don't think the family could be involved in anything like that," he said.

"But, of course, you're not sure, since you know so little."

"Let's say I'm sure. Now, all I want to know is how I go about finding them—or finding out what happened to them."

"I mentioned attorneys."

"No attorneys. I'm an architect, remember? Lawyers are natural enemies; they take up most of our time." Holcroft smiled. "Whatever a lawyer can do, I can do faster by myself. I do speak Spanish. I'll get by in Portuguese."

"I see." The attaché paused while he reached for a box of thin cigars on his desk. He opened it and held it out for Holcroft, who shook his head. "Are you sure? It's Havana."

"I'm sure. I'm also pressed for time."

"Yes, I know." The attaché reached for a silver table lighter on the desk, snapped it, and inhaled deeply; the tip of the cigar glowed. He raised his eyes abruptly to Noel. "I can't convince you to tell me the name of this family?"

"Oh, for Christ's sake . . ." Holcroft got up. He'd had enough; he'd find other sources.

"Please," said the Brazilian, "sit down, please. Just a minute or two longer. The time's not wasted, I assure you."

Noel saw the urgency in the attaché's eyes. He sat down. "What is it?"

"*La comunidad alemana.* I use the Spanish you speak so well."

"The German community? There's a German community in Rio—is that what you mean?"

"Yes, but it's not solely geographical. There's an outlying district—the German *barrio*, if you will—but that is not what I refer to. I'm speaking of what we call *la otra cara de los alemanes.* Can you understand that?"

"The 'other face' . . . what's underneath, below the German surface."

"Precisely. 'The underside,' you might say. What makes them what they are; what makes them do what they do. It's important that you understand."

"I think I do. I think you explained it. Most were Nazis getting out of the Nuremberg net, bringing in money that wasn't theirs; hiding, concealing identities. Naturally, such people would tend to stick together."

"Naturally," the Brazilian said. "But you'd think after so many years there'd be greater assimilation."

"Why? You work here in New York. Go down to the Lower East Side, or Mulberry Street or up to the Bronx. Enclaves of Italians, Poles, Jews. They've been here for decades. You're talking about twenty-five, thirty years. That's not much."

"There are similarities, of course, but it's not the same, believe me. The people you speak of in New York associate openly; they wear their heritages on their sleeves. It is not like that in Brazil. The German community pretends to be assimilated, but it is not. In commerce, yes, but in very little else. There is a pervading sense of fear and anger. Too many have been hunted for too long; a thousand identities are concealed daily from everyone but themselves. They have their own hierarchy. Three or four families control the community; their huge Germanic estates dot our countryside. Of course, they call them Swiss or Bavarian." Once more the attaché paused. "Do you begin to grasp what I'm saying? The consul general will not say it; my government will not permit it. But I am far down the ladder. It is left to me. *Do* you understand?"

Noel was bewildered. "Frankly, no. Nothing you've said surprises me. At Nuremberg they called it 'crimes against humanity.' That kind of thing leads to a lot of guilt, and guilt breeds fear. Of course such people in a country that isn't their own would stay close to each other."

"Guilt *does* breed fear. And fear in turn leads to suspicion. Finally, suspicion gives birth to violence. That's what you must understand. A stranger coming to Rio looking for Germans who have disappeared is undertaking a potentially dangerous search. *La otra cara de los alemanes.* They protect each other." The attaché picked up his cigar. "Give us the name, Mr. Holcroft. Let *us* look for these people."

Noel watched the Brazilian inhale the smoke from his precious Havana. He was not sure why, but he felt suddenly uneasy. *Don't be led into a trap by pat conclusions casually stated. . . .* "I can't. I think you're exaggerating, and obviously you won't help me." He stood up.

"Very well," said the Brazilian. "I'll tell you what you would find out for yourself. When you get to Rio de Janeiro, go to the Ministry of Immigration. If you have names and approximate dates, perhaps they can help you."

"Thanks very much," said Noel, turning toward the door.

The Brazilian walked rapidly out of the office into a large anteroom that served as a reception area. A young man sitting in an armchair quickly got to his feet at the sight of his superior.

"You may have your office back now, Juan."

"Thank you, Excellency."

The older man continued across the room, past a receptionist, to a pair of double doors. On the left panel was the great seal of the República Federal de Brasil; on the right was a plaque with gold printing that read OFÍCIO DO CÔNSUL GENERAL.

The consul general went inside to another, smaller anteroom that was his secretary's office. He spoke to the girl and walked directly to the door of his own office.

"Get me the embassy. The ambassador, please. If he's not there, locate him. Inform him that it's a confidential matter; he'll know whether he can talk or not."

Brazil's highest-ranking diplomat in America's major city closed the door, strode to his desk, and sat down. He picked up a sheaf of papers stapled together. The first several pages were photocopies of newspaper stories, accounts of the killing on British Airways flight 591 from London to New York, and the subsequent discovery of the two murders on the ground. The last two pages were copies of that aircraft's passenger manifest. The diplomat scanned the names: HOLCROFT, NOEL. DEP. GENEVA. BA #577. O. LON. BA #591. X. NYC. He stared at the information as if somehow relieved that it was still there.

His telephone hummed; he picked it up. "Yes?"

"The ambassador is on the line, sir."

"Thank you." The consul general heard an echo, which meant the scrambler was in operation. "Mr. Ambassador?"

"Yes, Geraldo. What's so urgent and confidential?"

"A few minutes ago a man came up here asking how he might go about locating a family in Rio he had not been able to reach through the usual channels. His name is Holcroft. Noel Holcroft, an architect from New York City."

"It means nothing to me," said the ambassador. "Should it?"

"Only if you've recently read the list of passengers on the British Airways plane from London last Saturday."

"Flight five-ninety-one?" The ambassador spoke sharply.

"Yes. He left that morning from Geneva on British Airways, and transferred at Heathrow to five-ninety-one."

"And now he wants to locate people in Rio? Who are they?"

"He refused to say. I was the 'attaché' he spoke with, naturally."

"Naturally. Tell me everything. I'll cable London. Do you think it's possible—" The ambassador paused.

"Yes," the consul general said softly. "I think it's very possible he is looking for the Von Tiebolts."

"Tell me everything," repeated the man in Washington. "The British believe those killings were the work of the Tinamou."

Noel felt a sense of *déjà vu* as he looked around the lounge of the Braniff 747. The colors were more vivid, the uniforms of the aircraft's personnel more fashionably cut. Otherwise, the plane seemed identical to that of British Airways flight 591. The difference was in attitude. This was the Rio Run, that carefree holiday that was to begin in the sky and continue on the beaches of the Gold Coast.

But this was to be no holiday, thought Holcroft, no holiday at all. The only climax awaiting him was one of discovery. The whereabouts or the nonwhereabouts of the family Von Tiebolt.

They'd been in the air for more than five hours. He had picked his way through a dismissable meal, slept through an even more dismissable film, and finally decided to go up to the lounge.

He had put off going upstairs. The memory of seven days ago was still discomforting. The unbelievable had happened in front of his eyes; a man had been killed not four feet from where he'd been sitting. At one point he could have reached over and *touched* the writhing figure. Death had been inches away, unnatural death, chemical death, murder.

Strychnine. A colorless crystalline alkaloid that caused paroxysms of unendurable pain. Why had it happened? Who was responsible and for what reason? The accounts were specific, the theories speculative.

Two men had been physically close to the victim in the lounge of Flight 591 from London. Either one could have administered the poison by way of the victim's drink; it was presumed one had. But again, why? According to the Port Authority police, there was no evidence that the two men had ever known Thornton. And the two men themselves—the suspected killers—had met *their* deaths by gunshot in a fuel truck on the ground. They had disappeared from the aircraft, from the sealed-off customs area, from the quarantined room, and themselves been murdered. Why? By whom?

No one had any answers. Only questions. And then even the questions stopped. The story faded from the newspapers and the broadcasts as dramatically as it had appeared, as though a blackout had been called. Again, why? Again, who was responsible?

"That was scotch on the rocks, wasn't it, Mr. Holcroft."

The *déjà vu* was complete. The words were the same but spoken by another. The stewardess above him, placing the glass on the round Formica table, was attractive—as the stewardess in Flight 591 had been attractive. The look in her eyes had that same quality of directness he remembered from the girl on British Airways. The words, even to the use of his name, were uttered in a similar tone, only the accent varied. It was all *too* much alike. Or was his mind—his eyes, his ears, his senses—preoccupied with the memory of seven days ago?

He thanked the stewardess, almost afraid to look at her, thinking that any second he would hear a scream beside him and watch a man in uncontrollable agony lunge out of his seat, twisting in spastic convulsions over the divider.

Then Noel realized something else, and it discomforted him further. He was sitting in the same seat he had occupied during those terrifying moments on Flight 591. In a lounge constructed identically with that lounge a week ago. It was not really unusual; he preferred the location and often sat there. But now it seemed macabre. His lines of sight were the same, the lighting no different now from the way it was then.

That was scotch on the rocks, wasn't it, Mr. Holcroft?
An outstretched hand, a pretty face, a glass.
Images, sounds.

Sounds. Raucous, drunken laughter. A man with too much alcohol in him, losing his balance, falling backward over the rim of the chair. His companion reeling in delight at the sight of his unsteady friend. A third man—the man who would be dead in moments—trying too hard to be a part of the revelry. Anxious to please, wanting to join. An attractive stewardess pouring whisky, smiling, wiping the bar on which two drinks had been reduced to one because one had been spilled, rushing around the counter to help a drunken passenger. The third anxious man, embarrassed perhaps, still wanting to play with the big boys, reaching. . . .

A *glass*. *The* glass! The single, remaining glass on the bar.

The third man had reached for that glass!

It was scotch on the rocks. The drink intended for the passenger sitting across the lounge at the small Formica table. Oh, my *God!* thought Holcroft, the images racing back and forth in sequence in his mind's eye. The drink on the bar—the drink a stranger named Thornton had taken—had been meant for *him!*

The strychnine had been meant for *him!* The twisting, horrible convulsions of agony were to be *his!* The terrible death assigned to *him!*

He looked down at the glass in front of him on the table; his fingers were around it.

That was scotch on the rocks, wasn't it? . . .

He pushed the drink aside. Suddenly he could no longer stay at that table, remain in that lounge. He had to get away; he had to force the images out of his mind. They were too clear, too real, too horrible.

He rose from the chair and walked rapidly, unsteadily, toward the staircase. The sounds of drunken laughter weaved in and out between an unrelenting scream of torment that was the screech of sudden death. No one else could hear those sounds, but they pounded in his head.

He lurched down the curving staircase to the deck below. The light was dim; several passengers were reading under the beams of tiny spotlights, but most were asleep.

Noel was bewildered. The hammering in his ears would not stop, the images would not go away. He felt the need to vomit, to expunge the fear that had settled into his stomach. Where was the toilet? In the galley . . . behind the galley? Beyond the curtain; that was it. Or was it? He parted the curtain.

Suddenly, his eyes were drawn down to his right, to the front seat of the 747's second section. A man had stirred in his sleep. A heavyset man whose face he had seen before. He did not recall where, but he was sure of it! A face creased in panic, racing by, close to his. What was it about the face? Something had made a brief but strong impression. What *was* it?

The *eyebrows;* that was it! Thick eyebrows, the coiled, matted hair an odd mixture of black and white. Salt-and-pepper eyebrows; *where* was it? Why did the sight of those strangely arresting brows trigger obscure memories of another act of violence? Where *was* it? He could not remember, and because he could not, he felt the blood rushing to his head. The pounding grew louder; his temples throbbed.

Suddenly, the man with the thick, coiled eyebrows woke up, somehow aware that he was being stared at. Their eyes locked; recognition was absolute.

And there was violence in that recognition. But of *what? When? Where?*

Holcroft nodded awkwardly, unable to think. The

pain in his stomach was knifelike; the sounds in his head were now cracks of thunder. For a moment he forgot where he was; then he remembered and the images returned. The sights and sounds of a killing that but for an accident would have claimed his life.

He had to get back to his seat. He had to control himself, to stop the pain and the thunder and the pounding in his chest. He turned and walked quickly beyond the curtain, past the galley, up the aisle to his seat.

He sat down in the semidarkness, grateful there was no one beside him. He pressed his head into the rim of the chair and closed his eyes, trying with all his concentration to rid his mind of the terrible sight of a grotesque face, screaming away the last few seconds of life. But he could not.

That face became *his* face.

Then the features blurred, as if the flesh were melting, only to be formed again. The face that now came into focus was no one he recognized. A strange, angular face, parts of which seemed familiar, but not as a whole.

Involuntarily, he gasped. He had never seen that face but suddenly he knew it. Instinctively. It was the face of Heinrich Clausen. A man in agony thirty years ago. The unknown father with whom he had his covenant.

Holcroft opened his eyes, which stung from the perspiration that had rolled down his face. There was another truth and he was not sure he wanted to recognize it. The two men who had tried to kill him with strychnine had themselves been murdered. They had interfered.

The men of Wolfsschanze had been aboard that plane.

7

The clerk behind the desk of the Pôrto Alegre Hotel pulled Holcroft's reservation from the file. A small yellow message envelope was stapled to the back of the card. The clerk tore it off and handed it to Noel.

"This came for you shortly past seven o'clock this evening, senhor."

Holcroft knew no one in Rio de Janeiro, and had told no one in New York where he was going. He ripped open the flap and drew out the message. It was from Sam Buonoventura. He was to return the overseas call as soon as possible, regardless of the hour.

Holcroft looked at his watch; it was nearly midnight. He signed the register and spoke as casually as he could, his mind on Sam.

"I have to telephone Curaçao. Will there be any trouble at this hour?"

The clerk seemed mildly offended. "Certainly not with our *telefonistas*, senhor. I cannot speak for Curaçao."

The origins of the difficulty notwithstanding, it was not until one-fifteen in the morning that he heard Buonoventura's rasping voice over the line.

"I think you've got a problem, Noley."

"I've got more than one. What is it?"

"Your answering service gave my number to this cop in New York, a Lieutenant Miles; he's a detective. He was hot as hell. Said you were supposed to inform the police if you left town, to say nothing about leaving the country."

Christ, he had forgotten! And now he understood just how vital those instructions were. The strychnine was meant for him! Had the police reached the same conclusion?

"What did you tell him, Sam?"

"Got hot myself. It's the only way to handle angry

71

cops. I told him you were off in the out-islands doing a survey for a possible installation Washington was interested in. A little bit north, we're not too far from the Canal Zone; it could mean anything. Nobody talks."

"Did he accept that?"

"Hard to tell. He wants you to call him. I bought you time, though. I said you radioed in this afternoon and I didn't expect to hear from you for three or four days, and I couldn't make contact. That's when he yelled like a cut bull."

"But did he buy it?"

"What else could he do? He thinks we're all fucking-A stupid down here, and I agreed with him. He gave me two numbers for you. Got a pencil?"

"Go ahead."

Holcroft wrote down the numbers—a Port Authority police telephone and Miles's home—thanked Buonoventura, and said he'd be in touch next week.

Noel had unpacked during the interminable wait for the Curaçao connection. He sat in a cane-backed chair in front of the window and looked out at the night-white beach and the dark waters beyond, reflecting the bright half moon. Below, on that isolated section of the street bordering the ocean walkway, were the curving, black-and-white parallel lines that signified the Copacabana, the golden coast of Guanabara. There was an emptiness about the scene that had nothing to do with its being deserted. It was too perfect, too pretty. He would never have designed it that way; there was an absence of character. He focused his eyes on the windowpanes. There was nothing to do now but think and rest and hope he could sleep. Sleep had been difficult for the past week; it would be more difficult now. Because he knew now what he had not known before: Someone had tried to kill him.

The knowledge produced an odd sensation. He could not believe that there was someone who wanted him dead. Yet someone had to have made that decision, had to have issued the order. Why? What had he done? Was it Geneva? His covenant?

We're dealing in millions. Those were not only the dead Manfredi's words; they were his warning. It was the only possible explanation. The information had got out, but there was no way to know how far it had spread, or who was affected by it, who infuriated. Or the identity of the unknown person—or persons—who wanted to stop the release of the Geneva account, to consign it to the litigations of the international courts.

Manfredi was right: The only moral solution was found in carrying out the intent of the document drawn up by three extraordinary men in the midst of the devastation their own monster had created. *Amends must be made.* It was the credo Heinrich Clausen believed in; it *was* honorable; it *was* right. In their misguided way, the men of Wolfsschanze understood.

Noel poured himself a drink, walked over to the bed, and sat down on the edge, staring at the telephone. Next to it were the two numbers written on a hotel message pad, given to him by Sam Buonoventura. They were his links to Lieutenant Miles, Port Authority police. But Holcroft could not bring himself to call. He had begun the hunt; he had taken the first step in his search for the family of Wilhelm von Tiebolt. Step, hell! It was a giant leap of four thousand air miles; he would not turn back.

There was so much to do. Noel wondered whether he was capable of doing it, whether he was capable of making his way through the unfamiliar forest.

He felt his eyelids grow heavy. Sleep was coming and he was grateful for it. He put down the glass and kicked off his shoes, not bothering with the rest of his clothes. He fell back on the bed and for several seconds stared at the white ceiling. He felt so alone, yet knew he wasn't. There was a man in agony, from thirty years ago, crying out to him. He thought about that man until sleep came.

Holcroft followed the translator into the dimly lit, windowless cubicle. Their conversation had been brief; Noel had sought specific information. The name was Von Tiebolt; the family, German nationals. A mother and two children—a daughter and a son—had immigrated to Brazil on or about June 15, 1945. A third child, another daughter, had been born several months later, probably in Rio de Janeiro. The records had to contain *some* information. Even if a false name was used, a simple cross-check of the weeks involved—two or three either way —would certainly unearth a pregnant woman with two children coming into the country. If there were more

than one, it was his problem to trace them. At least a
name, or names, would surface.

No, it was not an official inquiry. There were no
criminal charges; there was no seeking of revenge for
crimes going back thirty years. On the contrary, it was "a
benign search."

Noel knew that an explanation would be asked of
him, and he remembered one of the lessons learned at
the consulate in New York: *Base the lie in an aspect of
truth.* The family Von Tiebolt had relations in the
United States, went the lie. People who had immigrated
to America in the twenties and thirties. Very few were
left, and there was a large sum of money involved. Surely, the officials at the *Ministério do Imigração* would want
to help find the inheritors. It was entirely possible that
the Von Tiebolts would be grateful . . . and he, as the
intermediary, would certainly make known their cooperation.

Ledgers were brought out. Hundreds of photostats
from another era were studied. Faded, soiled copies of
documents, so many of which were obviously false papers purchased in Bern and Zurich and Lisbon. Passports.

But there were no documents relating to the Von
Tiebolts, no descriptions of a pregnant woman with two
children entering Rio de Janeiro during the month of June
or July in 1945. At least, none resembling the wife of
Wilhelm von Tiebolt. There were pregnant women, even
pregnant women with children, but none with children
that could have been Von Tiebolt's. According to Manfredi, the daughter, Gretchen, was twelve or thirteen
years old; the son, Johann, ten. Every one of the women
entering Brazil during those weeks was accompanied either by a husband or a false husband, and where there
were children, none—not *one*—was more than seven
years of age.

This struck Holcroft as being not only unusual but
mathematically impossible. He stared at the pages of
faded ink, at the often illegible entries made by harried
immigration officials thirty-odd years ago.

Something was wrong; his architect's eye was troubled. He had the feeling he was studying blueprints that
had not been finished, that were filled with minute alterations—tiny lines erased and changed, but very delicately,
so as not to disturb the larger design.

Erased and changed. *Chemically* erased, *delicately* changed. That was what bothered him! The birthdates! Page after page of miniature figures, digits subtly altered! A *3* became an *8*, a *1* a *9*, a *2* a *0*, the curve retained, a line drawn down, a zero added. Page after page in the ledgers, for the weeks of June and July of 1945, the birthdates of all the children entering Brazil had been changed so that none was born prior to 1938!

It was a painstakingly clever ruse, one that had to be thought out carefully, deliberately. Stop the hunt at the source. But do it in a way that appeared above suspicion. Small numbers faithfully—if hastily—recorded by unknown immigration personnel more than thirty years ago. Recorded from documents, the majority of which had been long since destroyed, for most were false. There was no way to substantiate, to confirm or deny the accuracy. Time and conspiracies had made that impossible. Of course there was no one resembling the Von Tiebolts! *Good Lord*, what a deception!

Noel pulled out his lighter; its flame would provide more light on a page where his eye told him there were numerous minute alterations.

"*Senhor!* That is forbidden!" The harsh command was delivered in a loud voice by the translator. "Those old pages catch fire easily. We cannot take such risks."

Holcroft understood. It explained the inadequate light, the windowless cubicle. "I'll bet you can't," he said, extinguishing his lighter. "And I suppose these ledgers can't be removed from this room."

"No, *senhor.*"

"And, of course, there are no extra lamps around, and you don't have a flashlight. Isn't that right?"

"*Senhor,*" interrupted the translator, his tone now courteous, even deferential. "We have spent nearly three hours with you. We have tried to cooperate fully, but as I'm sure you're aware, we have other duties to perform. So, if you have finished . . ."

"I think you made sure of that before I started," broke in Holcroft. "Yes, I'm finished. Here."

He walked in the bright afternoon sunlight, trying to make sense out of things, the soft ocean breezes caressing his face, calming his anger and his frustration. He strolled on the white boardwalk overlooking the immaculate sand of Guanabara Bay. Now and then he stopped and leaned against the railing, watching the grown-up children at their games. The beautiful people, sunning and stunning. Grace and arrogance coexisted with artifice. Money was everywhere, evidenced by the golden, oiled bodies, too often too perfectly formed, too pretty, all flaws concealed. But again, where was character? It was somehow absent on the Copacabana this afternoon.

He passed that section of the beach that fronted his hotel and glanced up at the windows, trying to locate his room. For a moment he thought he had found it, then realized he was wrong. He could see two figures behind the glass, beyond the curtains.

He returned to the railing and lit a cigarette. The lighter made him think about the thirty-year-old ledgers so painstakingly doctored. Had they been altered just for him? Or had there been others over the years looking for the Von Tiebolts? Regardless of the answer, he had to find another source. Or other sources.

La comunidad alemana. Holcroft recalled the words of the attaché in New York. He remembered the man's saying there were three or four families who were the arbiters of the German community. It followed that such men had to know the most carefully guarded secrets. *Identities are concealed every day. . . . A stranger coming to Rio looking for Germans who have disappeared is undertaking a potentially dangerous search . . .* "la otra cara de los alemanes." *They protect each other.*

There was a way to eliminate the danger, Noel thought. It was found in the explanation he had given the translator at the Ministry of Immigration. He traveled a great deal, so it was plausible that someone somewhere had approached him, knowing he was flying to Brazil, and asked him to locate the Von Tiebolts. It had to be a person who dealt in legitimate confidentiality, a lawyer or a banker. Someone whose own reputation was above reproach. Without analyzing it deeply, Holcroft knew that whoever he decided upon would be the key to his explanation.

An idea for a candidate struck him, the risks apparent, the irony not lost. Richard Holcroft, the only father he had ever known. Stockbroker, banker, naval officer . . . father. The man who had given a wild young mother and her child a chance to live again. Without fear, without the stain.

Noel looked at his watch. It was ten minutes past five—past three in New York. Midafternoon on a Monday. He did not believe in omens, but he had just come upon one. Every Monday afternoon Richard Holcroft went to the New York Athletic Club, where old friends played gentle squash and sat around thick oak tables in the bar and reminisced. Noel could have him paged, talk to him alone—ask for help. Help that was to be rendered confidentially, for confidentiality was not only the essence of the cover but the basis of his protection. Someone, *anyone*, had contacted Richard Holcroft—man of stature— and asked him to locate a family named Von Tiebolt in Brazil. Knowing his son was going to Rio, he quite logically asked his son to make inquiries. It was a confidential matter; it would not be discussed. No one could turn away the curious with greater authority than Dick Holcroft.

But Althene was not to be told. That was the hardest part of the request. Dick adored her; there were no secrets between them. But his father—damn it, *step*father —would not refuse him if the request was based in genuine need. He never had.

He crossed the smooth marble floor of the hotel lobby toward the bank of elevators, oblivious of sights and sounds, his concentration on what he would say to his stepfather. As a result, he was startled when an obese American tourist tapped his shoulder.

"They calling you, Mac?" The man pointed toward the front desk.

Behind the counter the clerk was looking at Noel. In his hand was the familiar yellow message envelope; he gave it to a bellhop, who started across the lobby.

The single name on the slip of paper was unknown to him: CARARRA. There was a telephone number below, but no message. Holcroft was bewildered. The lack of a message was unusual; it was not the Latin way of doing things. Senhor Cararra could phone again; he had to reach New York. He had to build another cover.

Yet, in his room, Holcroft read the name again: CARARRA. His curiosity was aroused. Who was this Cararra that he expected to be called back on the basis of a name alone, a name the man knew meant nothing to Holcroft? In South American terms it was discourteous to the point of being insulting. His stepfather could wait a few minutes while he found out. He dialed the number.

Cararra was not a man but a woman, and from the sound of her low, strained voice she was a frightened woman. Her English was passable but not good; it did not matter. Her message was as clear as the fear she conveyed.

"I cannot talk now, senhor. Do not call this number again. It is not necessary."

"You left it with the operator. What did you expect me to do?"

"It was a . . . *êrro.*"

"*Yerro?* Mistake?"

"Yes. A mistake. I will call you. *We* will call."

"What about? Who are you?"

"*Mas tarde!*" The voice descended to a harsh whisper and was abruptly gone with the click of the line.

Mas tarde . . . mas tarde. Later. The woman would call him again. Holcroft felt a sudden hollowness in his stomach, as sudden as the abrupt disappearance of the frightened whisper. He could not recall when he had heard a woman's voice so filled with fear.

That she was somehow connected with the missing Von Tiebolts was the first thought that came to his mind. But in what way? And how in God's name would she know about *him?* The feeling of dread came over him again . . . and the image of the horrible face contorted in death, thirty thousand feet in the air. He was being observed; strangers were watching him.

The whine of the telephone receiver interrupted his thoughts; he had forgotten to hang up. He depressed the button, released it, and made the call to New York. He needed his protection quickly; he knew that now.

He stood by the window, staring out at the beach-front, waiting for the operator to call him back. There was a flash of light from the street below. The chrome of a car grille had caught the rays of the sun and reflected them skyward. The car had passed that section of the boardwalk where he had been standing only minutes ago. Standing and absently glancing up at the hotel windows, trying to spot his room.

The *windows.* . . . The angle of *sight.* Noel moved

closer to the panes and studied the diagonal line from the spot below—where he had been standing—to where he stood now. His architect's eye was a practiced eye; angles did not deceive him. Too, the windows were not that close to one another, befitting the separation of rooms in an oceanfront hotel on the Copacabana. He looked up at *this* window, thinking it was not his room because he saw figures inside, behind the glass. But it *was* his room. And there *had* been people inside.

He walked to his closet and stood looking at his clothes. He trusted his memory for detail as much as he trusted his eye for angular lines. He pictured the closet where he had changed clothes that morning. He had fallen asleep in the suit he had worn from New York. His light-tan slacks had been on the far right, almost against the closet wall. It was habit: trousers on the right, jackets on the left. The slacks were still on the right, but not against the wall. Instead, they were several inches toward the center. His dark-blue blazer was *in* the center, *not* on the left side.

His clothes had been searched.

He crossed to the bed and his open attaché case. It was his office when he traveled; he knew every millimeter of space, every compartment, the position of every item in every slot. He did not have to look long.

His attaché case had been searched as well.

The telephone rang, the sound an intrusion. He picked it up and heard the voice of the Athletic Club's operator, but he knew he could not now ask for Richard Holcroft; he could not involve him. Things were suddenly too complicated. He had to think them through.

"New York Athletic Club. Hello? Hello? . . . Hello, Rio operator? There's no one on the line, Rio. Hello? New York Athletic Club. . . ."

Noel replaced the receiver. He had been about to do something *crazy*. His room had been searched! In his need for a cover in Rio de Janeiro, he had been about to lead someone directly to the one person closest to his mother, once the wife of Heinrich Clausen. What had he been *thinking* of?

And then he realized that nothing was wasted. Instead, another lesson had been learned. *Carry out the lie logically, then reexamine it, and use the most credible part.* If he could invent a reason for such a man as

Richard Holcroft to conceal the identity of those seeking the Von Tiebolts, he could invent the man himself.

Noel was breathing hard. He had almost committed a terrible error, but he was beginning to know what to look for in the unfamiliar forest. The paths were lined with traps; he had to keep his guard up and move cautiously. He could not permit himself a mistake like the one he had nearly made. He had come very close to risking the life of the father that was, for one he had never known.

Very little of value or truth ever came from anything he touched. His mother's words, and like Manfredi's, meant as a warning. But his mother—unlike Manfredi—was wrong. Heinrich Clausen was as much a victim as he was a villain of his time. The anguished letter he had written while Berlin was falling confirmed it, and what he had done confirmed it. Somehow his son would prove it.

La comunidad alemana. Three, four families in the German community, the arbiters who made irreversible decisions. One of them would be his source. And he knew exactly where to look.

The old, heavy-set man with thick jowls and steel-gray hair, cut short in the fashion of a Junker, looked up from the huge dining-room table at the intruder. He ate alone, no places set for family or guests. It seemed strange, for as the door was opened by the intruder, the voices of other people could be heard; there were family and guests in the large house, but they were not at the table.

"We have additional information on Clausen's son, Herr Graff," said the intruder, approaching the old man's chair. "You know about the Curaçao communication. Two other calls were made this afternoon. One to the woman, Cararra, and the second to a men's club in New York."

"The Cararras will do their job well," said Graff, his fork suspended, the puffed flesh around his eyes creased. "What is this club in New York?"

"A place called the New York Athletic Club. It is—"

"I know what it is. A wealthy membership. Whom was he calling?"

"The call was placed to the location, not to a person. Our people in New York are trying to find out."

The old man put down his fork. He spoke softly, insultingly. "Our people in New York are slow, and so are you."

"I beg your pardon?"

"Undoubtedly among the members will be found the name of Holcroft. If so, Clausen's son has broken his word; he's told Holcroft about Geneva. That is dangerous. Richard Holcroft is an old man, but he is not feeble. We always knew that if he lived long enough, he might be a stumbling block." Graff shifted his large head and looked at the intruder. "The envelope arrived in Sesimbra; there is no excuse. The events of the other night had to be clear to the son. Cable the Tinamou. I don't trust his associate here in Rio. Use the eagle code and tell him what I believe. Our people in New York will have another task. The elimination of a meddling old man. Richard Holcroft must be taken out. The Tinamou will demand it."

8

Noel knew what he was looking for: a bookstore that was more than a place to buy books. In every resort city there was always one major shop that catered to the reading requirements of a specific nationality. In this case, its name was A Livraria Alemão: the German Bookshop. According to the desk clerk, it carried all the latest German periodicals, and Lufthansa flew newspapers in daily. That was the information Holcroft sought. Such a store would have accounts; someone there would know the established German families in Rio. If he could get just one or two names. . . . It was a place to start.

The store was less than ten minutes from the hotel. "I'm an American architect," he said to the clerk, who was halfway up a ladder, rearranging books on the top shelf. "I'm down here checking out the Bavarian influence on large residential homes. Do you have any material on the subject?"

"I didn't know it was a subject," replied the man in fluent English. "There's a certain amount of Alpine design, chalet-style building, but I wouldn't call it Bavarian."

Lesson six, or was it seven? Even if the lie is based in an aspect of truth, make sure the person you use it on knows less than you do.

"Alpine, Swiss, Bavarian. They're pretty much the same thing."

"Really? I thought there were considerable differences."

Lesson eight or nine. Don't argue. Remember the objective.

"Look, to tell you the truth, a rich couple in New York are paying my way here to bring back sketches. They were in Rio last summer. They rode around and

82

spotted some great homes. They described them as Bavarian."

"Those would be in the northwest countryside. There are several marvelous houses out there. The Eisenstat residence, for example; but then, I think they're Jewish. There's an odd mixture of Moorish, if you can believe it. And, of course, there's the Graff mansion. That's almost too much, but it's really spectacular. To be expected, I imagine. Graff's a millionaire many times over."

"What's the name again? Graff?"

"Maurice Graff. He's an importer; but then, aren't they all?"

"Who?"

"Oh, come now, don't be naïve. If he wasn't a general, or a muckedy-muck in the High Command, I'll piss port wine."

"You're English."

"I'm English."

"But you work in a German bookstore."

"Ich spreche gut Deutsch."

"Couldn't they find a German?"

"I suppose there are advantages hiring someone like myself," said the Britisher cryptically.

Noel feigned surprise. "Really?"

"Yes," replied the clerk, scaling another rung on the ladder. "No one asks me questions."

The clerk watched the American leave and stepped quickly down from the ladder, sliding it across the shelf track with a shove of his hand. It was a gesture of accomplishment, of minor triumph. He walked rapidly down the book-lined aisle and turned so abruptly into an intersecting stack that he collided with a customer examining a volume of Goethe.

"Verzeihung," said the clerk under his breath, not at all concerned.

"Schwesterchen," said the man with the thick black-and-white eyebrows.

At the reference to his lack of masculinity, the clerk turned. "You!"

"The friends of Tinamou are never far away," replied the man.

"You followed him?" asked the clerk.

"He never knew. Make your call."

The Englishman continued on his way to the door of an office at the rear of the store. He went inside, picked up the telephone, and dialed. It was answered by the aide of the most powerful man in Rio.

"Senhor Graff's residence. Good afternoon."

"Our man at the hotel deserves a large tip," said the clerk. "He was right. I insist on talking to Herr Graff. I did precisely as we agreed, and I did it superbly. I've no doubt he'll be calling. Now, Herr Graff, please."

"I'll pass along your message, butterfly," said the aide.

"You'll do no such thing! I have other news I'll tell only to him."

"What does it concern? I don't have to tell you he's a busy man."

"Shall we say a countryman of mine? Do I make myself clear?"

"We know he's in Rio; he's already made contact. You'll have to do better than that."

"He's still here. In the store. He may be waiting to talk to me."

The aide spoke to someone nearby. The words, however, were distinct. "It's the actor, mein Herr. He insists on speaking to you. Everything went as scheduled during the past hour, but there seems to be a complication. His countryman is in the bookshop."

The phone passed hands. "What is it?" asked Maurice Graff.

"I wanted you to know that everything went exactly as we anticipated. . . ."

"Yes, yes, I understand that," interrupted Graff. "You do excellent work. Now, what's this about the *Engländer?* He's there?"

"He followed the American. He was no more than ten feet from him. He's still here, and I expect he'll want me to tell him what's happening. Should I?"

"No," replied Graff. "We are perfectly capable of running things here without interference. Say to him that we're concerned he'll be recognized; that we suggest he remain out of sight. Tell him I do not approve of his methods. You may say you heard it from me personally."

"*Thank* you, Herr Graff! It will be a pleasure."

"Yes, I know it will."

* * *

Graff handed the telephone back to his aide. "The Tinamou must not let this happen," he said. "It starts again."

"What, mein Herr?"

"All over again," continued the old man. "The interference, the silent observations, one upon the other. Authority becomes divided, everyone's suspect."

"I don't understand."

"Of course you don't. You weren't there." Graff leaned back in his chair. "Send a second cable to the Tinamou. Tell him that we request he order his wolf back to the Mediterranean. He's taking too many risks. We object, and cannot be responsible under the circumstances."

It took several phone calls and the passage of twenty-four hours, but word that Graff would see him finally came, shortly past two o'clock the next afternoon. Holcroft leased a car at the hotel and drove northwest out of the city. He stopped frequently, studying the tourist map provided by the rental agency. He finally found the address, and swung through the iron gates into the ascending drive that led to the house at the top of the hill.

The road leveled off into a large parking area of white concrete, bordered by green shrubbery that was broken up by flagstone paths leading through groves of fruit trees on either side.

The clerk at the bookstore had been right. The Graff estate was spectacular. The view was magnificent: plains nearby, mountains in the distance, and far to the east the hazy blue of the Atlantic. The house itself was three stories high. A series of balconies rose on both sides of the central entrance: a set of massive double doors—oiled mahogany, hinged with large, pitted triangles of black iron. The effect *was* Alpine, as if a geometric design of many Swiss chalets were welded into one and set down on a tropical mountain.

Noel parked the car to the right of the front steps and got out. There were two other automobiles in the parking area—a white Mercedes limousine and a low-slung, red Maserati. The Graff family traveled well. Holcroft gripped his attaché case and camera and started up the marble steps.

* * *

"I'm flattered our minor architectural efforts are appreciated," said Graff. "It's natural, I suppose, for transplanted people to create a touch of their homeland in new surroundings. My family came from the *Schwarzwald.* ... The memories are never far away."

"I appreciate your having me out here, sir." Noel put the five hastily drawn sketches back into his attaché case and closed it. "I speak for my client as well, of course."

"You have everything you need?"

"A roll of film and five elevation sketches are more than I had hoped for. Incidentally, the gentleman who showed me around will tell you the photographs were limited to the exterior structural detail."

"I don't understand you."

"I wouldn't want you to think I was taking pictures of your private grounds."

Maurice Graff laughed softly. "My residence is very well protected, Mr. Holcroft. Besides, it never crossed my mind that you were examining the premises for purposes of theft. Sit down, please."

"Thank you." Noel sat opposite the old man. "These days some people might be suspicious."

"Well, I won't mislead you. I did call the Pôrto Alegre Hotel to see if you were registered. You were. You are a man named Holcroft from New York whose reservation was made by a reputable travel agency that obviously knows you, and you use credit cards cleared by computers. You entered Brazil with a valid passport. What more did I need? The times are technically too complicated for a man to pretend to be someone he's not, wouldn't you agree?"

"Yes, I guess I would," replied Noel, thinking that it was the moment perhaps to shift to the real purpose of his visit. He was about to speak, but Graff continued, as if filling an awkward silence.

"How long will you be in Rio?" he asked.

"Only a few more days. I have the name of your architect, and naturally I'll consult with him when he's free to see me."

"I'll have my secretary telephone; there'll be no delay. I have no idea how such financial arrangements are made—or, indeed, if there are any—but I'm quite sure he'd let you have copies of the plans if they would be helpful to you."

Noel smiled, the professional in him aroused. "It's a question of selective adaptation, Mr. Graff. My calling him would be as much a matter of courtesy as anything else. I might ask where certain materials were purchased, or how specific stress problems were solved, but that'd be it. I wouldn't ask for the plans, and I think he'd be reluctant to say yes if I did."

"There would be *no* reluctance," said Graff, his bearing and intensity a reflection of a military past.

. . . *If he wasn't a general, or a muckedy-muck in the High Command, I'll piss port wine.* . . .

"It's not important, sir. I've got what I came for."

"I see." Graff shifted his heavy frame in the chair. It was the movement of a weary old man toward the end of a long afternoon. Yet the eyes were not weary; they were strangely alert. "An hour's conference would be sufficient, then?"

"Easily."

"I'll arrange it."

"You're very kind."

"Then you can return to New York."

"Yes." It was the moment to mention the Von Tiebolts. Now. "Actually, there's one other thing I should do while I'm here in Rio. It's not terribly important, but I said I'd try. I'm not sure where to begin. The police, I imagine."

"That sounds ominous. A crime?"

"Quite the contrary. I meant whichever department of the police it is that could help locate some people. They're not in the telephone directory. I even checked unlisted numbers; they don't have one."

"Are you sure they're in Rio?"

"They were when last heard from. And I gather the other cities in Brazil were checked out, again through the telephone companies."

"You intrigue me, Mr. Holcroft. Is it so important these people be found? What did they do? But then you said there was no crime."

"None. I know very little. A friend of mine in New York, an attorney, knew I was coming here and asked me to do what I could to locate this family. Apparently it was left some money by relatives in the Midwest."

"An inheritance?"

"Yes."

"Then perhaps legal counsel here in Rio . . ."

"My friend sent what he termed 'inquiries of record' to several law firms down here," said Noel, remembering the words of the attaché in New York. "There weren't any satisfactory responses."

"How did he explain that?"

"He didn't. He was just annoyed. I guess the money wasn't enough for three attorneys to get involved."

"Three attorneys?"

"Yes," replied Noel, astonished at himself. He was filling a gap instinctively, without *thinking*. "There's the lawyer in Chicago—or St. Louis—my friend's firm in New York, and the one down here in Rio. I don't imagine what's confidential to an outsider is confidential between attorneys. Perhaps splitting a fee three ways wasn't worth the trouble."

"But your friend is a man of conscience." Graff arched his brows in appreciation. Or something else, Holcroft thought.

"I'd like to think so."

"Perhaps I can help. I have friends."

Holcroft shook his head. "I couldn't ask you. You've done enough for me this afternoon. And, as I said, it's not that important."

"Naturally," said Graff, shrugging. "I wouldn't care to intrude in confidential matters." The German looked over at the windows, squinting. The sun was settling above the western mountains; shafts of orange light streamed through the glass, adding a rich hue to the dark wood of the study.

"The name of the family is Von Tiebolt," said Noel, watching the old man's face. But whatever he expected to find, nothing could have prepared him for what he saw.

Old Graff's eyes snapped open, their glance shooting over at Holcroft, filled with loathing. "You are a *pig*," said the German, his voice so low it could barely be heard. "This was a trick, a devious ruse to come into my house! To come to me!"

"You're wrong, Mr. Graff. You can call my client in New York. . . ."

"*Pig! . . .*" the old man screamed. "The Von Tiebolts! *Verräter!* Below filth! Cowards! *Schweinhunde!* How *dare* you!"

Noel watched, mesmerized and helpless. Graff's face

was discolored with rage; the veins in his neck were at the surface of his flesh, his eyes red and furious, his hands trembling, gripping the arms of the chair.

"I don't understand," said Holcroft, getting to his feet.

"You understand . . . you *garbage!* You are looking for the Von Tiebolts! You want to give them life again!"

"They're *dead?*"

"Would to the Almighty they *were!*"

"Graff, listen to me. If you know something—"

"*Get out of my house!*" The old man struggled up from the chair and screamed at the closed door of the study. "Werner! *Komm' her!*"

Graff's aide burst through the door. "*Mein Herr? Was ist—*"

"Take this impostor away! Get him out of my house!"

The aide looked at Holcroft. "This way. *Quickly!*"

Noel reached down for his attaché case and walked swiftly toward the door. He stopped and turned to look once more at the enraged Graff. The old German stood like a bloated, grotesque manikin, yet he could not control his trembling.

"Get out! You are *contemptible!*"

The final, searing accusation shattered Noel's self-control. It was not he who was contemptible; it was the figure of arrogance in front of him, this swollen image of indulgence and brutality. This monster who betrayed, then destroyed, a man in agony thirty years ago . . . and thousands like him. This *Nazi.*

"You're in no position to call me names."

"We'll see who's in what position. Get *out!*"

"I'll get out, General, or whatever the hell you are. I can't get out fast enough, because now I understand. You don't know me from the last corpse you bastards burned, but I mention one name and you can't stand it. You're torn apart because you know—and I know—that Von Tiebolt saw through you thirty years ago. When the bodies piled up. He saw what you *really* were."

"We did not conceal what we were! The world knew. There was no deception on our part!"

Holcroft stopped and swallowed involuntarily. In his burst of anger, he had to seek justice for the men who had cried out to him from the grave; he had to strike back at this symbol of the once-awesome might and de-

* * *

cay that had stolen a father from him. He could not help himself.

"Get this clear," said Noel. "I'm going to find the Von Tiebolts, and you're not going to stop me. Don't think you can. Don't think you've got me marked. You haven't. I've got *you* marked. For exactly what you are. You wear your Iron Cross a little too obviously."

Graff had regained control. "Find the Von Tiebolts, by all means. We'll be there!"

"I'll find them. And when I do, if anything happens to them, I'll know who did it. I'll brand you for what you are. You sit up here in this castle and bark your orders. You're still pretending. You were finished years ago— before the war was over—and men like Von Tiebolt knew it. They understood, but you never did. You never will."

"Get *out!*"

A guard raced into the room; hands grabbed Noel from behind. An arm plunged over his right shoulder and down across his chest. He was yanked briefly off his feet and pulled backward out of the room. He swung his attaché case and felt the impact on the large, weaving body of the man dragging him through the door. He rammed his left elbow into the stomach of that unseen body and kicked viciously, jabbing his heel into his attacker's shin bone. The response was immediate; the man yelped; the grip across Noel's chest was momentarily lessened. It was enough.

Holcroft shot his left hand up, grabbing the cloth of the extended arm, and pulled forward with all his strength. He angled his body to the right; his right shoulder jammed into the chest that rose behind him. His assailant stumbled. Noel rammed a last shoulder block into the elevated chest, throwing his attacker into an antique chair against the wall. Man and delicate wood met in a crushing impact; the frame of the chair collapsed under the weight of the body. The guard was stunned, his wide eyes blinking, his focus temporarily lost.

Holcroft looked down at the man. The guard was large, but his bulk was the most threatening part of him. And the bulk was just that; like old Graff, a mountain of flesh packed under a tight-fitting jacket.

Through the open door Holcroft could see Graff start

for the telephone on his desk. The aide he had called Werner took an awkward step toward Noel.

"Don't," said Holcroft. He walked across the large hallway toward the front entrance. On the opposite side of the foyer several men and women stood in an open archway. None made a move toward him; none even raised his voice. The German mentality was consistent, thought Noel, not unhappy with the realization. These minions were awaiting orders.

"Do as I've instructed," said Graff into the telephone, his voice calm, with no trace of the fury he had exhibited only minutes ago. He was now the general officer issuing commands to an attentive subordinate. "Wait until he's halfway down the hill, then throw the gate switch. It's vital that the American thinks he has escaped." The old German hung up and turned to his aide. "Is the guard hurt?"

"Merely stunned, mein Herr. He's walking around, shaking off the effects of the blow."

"Holcroft is angry," mused Graff. "He's filled with himself, exhilarated, consumed with purpose. That's good. Now he must be frightened, made to tremble at the unexpected, at the sheer brutality of the moment. Tell the guard to wait five minutes and then take up pursuit. He must do his job well."

"He has his orders; he's an expert marksman."

"Good." The former *Wehrmachtsgeneral* walked slowly to the window and squinted into the final rays of the sun. "Soft words, lover's words . . . and then sharp, hysterical rebukes. The embrace, and the knife. One must follow the other in rapid succession until Holcroft has no judgment left. Until he can no longer distinguish between ally and enemy, knowing only that he must press forward. When finally he breaks, we'll be there and he'll be ours."

9

Noel slammed the huge door behind him and walked down the marble steps to the car. He swung the automobile into reverse, so that his hood faced the downhill drive out of the Graff estate, pressed the accelerator and headed for the exit.

Several things occurred to him. The first was that the afternoon sun had descended behind the western mountains, creating pockets of shadows on the ground. Daylight was disappearing; he needed his headlights. Another concern was that Graff's reaction to the mention of the Von Tiebolts had to mean two things: The Von Tiebolts were alive, and they were a threat. But a threat to what? To whom? And where were they?

A third was more of a feeling than a specific thought. It was his reaction to the physical encounter he had just experienced. Throughout his life he had taken whatever size and strength he possessed as a matter of course. Because he was large and relatively well coordinated, he never felt the need to seek physical challenge except in competition against himself, in bettering a tennis game or besting a ski slope. As a result, he avoided fights; they struck him as unnecessary.

It was this general attitude that had made him laugh when his stepfather had insisted he join him at the club for a series of lessons in self-defense. The city was turning into a jungle; Holcroft's son was going to learn how to protect himself.

He took the course, and promptly forgot everything he had learned when it was over. If he had actually absorbed *anything*, he had done it subconsciously.

He *had* absorbed something, reflected Noel, pleased with himself. He remembered the glazed look in the eyes of the guard.

The last thought that crossed his mind as he turned

into the downhill drive was also vague. Something was wrong with the front seat of the car. The furious activity of the last minutes had blurred his usually acute eye for such things, but something about the checkered cloth of the seat cover bothered him. . . .

Terrible sounds interrupted his concentration: the barking of dogs. Suddenly, the menacing faces of enormous long-haired black shepherds lunged at the windows on both sides of the car. The dark eyes glistened with hatred and frustration; the fur-lined, saliva-soaked jaws slapped open and shut, emitting the shrill, vicious sounds of animals reaching a quarry but unable to sink their teeth into flesh. It was a pack of attack dogs—five, six, seven—at all windows now, their paws scratching against the glass. An animal leaped up on the hood, its face and teeth against the windshield.

Beyond the dog, at the base of the hill, Holcroft saw the huge gate beginning to move, the movement magnified in the beams of his headlights. It was starting the slow arc that would end with its closing! He pressed the accelerator against the floor, gripped the wheel until his arms were in pain, and drove at full speed, swerving to his left, through the stone pillars, missing the steel gate by inches. The dog on the hood flew off to the right in midair, yelping in shock.

The pack on the hill had pulled up behind the gate in the darkening twilight. The explanation had to be that a high-frequency whistle—beyond human ears—had caused them to stop. Perspiring, Noel held the pedal against the floorboard and sped down the road.

He came to a fork in the countryside. Did he take the right, or the left? He could not recall; absently he reached for his map on the seat.

That was what had bothered him! The map was no longer there. He took the left fork, reaching below the seat to see if the map had fallen to the floor. It had not. It had been removed from the car!

He arrived at an intersection. It was not familiar; or, if it was, the darkness obscured any familiarity. He turned right, out of instinct, knowing he had to keep going. He kept the car at high speed, looking for anything that he could relate to the drive out from Rio. But the darkness was full now; he saw nothing he remembered. The road made a wide, sweeping curve to the right and then there was a sharp, steep incline of a hill. He recalled no curve, remembered no hill. He was lost.

The top of the hill flattened out for approximately a hundred yards. On his left was a lookout, bordered by a parking area enclosed by a chest-high wall fronting the cliff. Along the wall were rows of telescopes with round casings, the type activated by coins. Holcroft pulled over and stopped the car. There were no other automobiles, but maybe one would come. Perhaps if he looked around he could get his bearings. He got out of the car and walked to the wall.

Far below in the distance were the lights of the city. Between the cliff and the lights, however, there was only darkness. . . . No, not total darkness; there was a winding thread of light. A road? Noel was next to one of the telescopes. He inserted a coin and peered through the sight, focusing on the weaving thread of light he presumed was a road. It was.

The lights were spaced far apart; they were street lamps, welcome but out of place in a path cut out of the Brazilian forests. If he could reach the beginning of that road. . . . The telescope would move no farther to his right. Goddamn it! Where did the road begin? It *had* to be. . . .

Behind him he heard the sound of an engine racing up the hill he had just climbed. Thank God! He would stop the car, if he had to stand in the middle of the road to do it. He ran from the wall, across the concrete, toward the tarred pavement.

He reached the edge and froze. The car lunging over the final incline into the lookout area was a white Mercedes limousine. The same car that stood gleaming in the afternoon sun on top of another hill. Graff's car.

It stopped abruptly, tires screeching. The door opened and a man got out. In the reflecting spill of the headlights he was recognizable: Graff's guard!

He reached into his belt. Holcroft stood paralyzed. The man raised a gun, aiming at him. It was unbelievable! It could not be happening!

The first gunshot was thunderous; it shook the silence like a sudden cracking of the earth. A second followed. The road several feet away from Noel exploded in a spray of rock and dust. Whatever instincts remained beyond his paralysis, his *disbelief,* commanded him to run, to save himself. He was going to die! He was about to be killed in a deserted tourist lookout above the city of Rio de Janeiro! It was insane!

His legs were weak; he forced himself to race toward the rented car. His feet *ached;* it was the strangest sensation he had ever felt. Two more gunshots filled the night; there were two more explosions of tar and concrete.

He reached the car and fell below the door panel for protection. He reached up for the handle.

Another gunshot, this one louder, the vibration deafening. Accompanying the detonation was another kind of explosion, one that rang with the violent smashing of glass. The car's rear window had been blown out.

There was nothing else to do! Holcroft pulled the door open and leaped inside. In panic he turned the ignition key. The engine roared; his foot pressed the accelerator against the floor. He jammed the gearshift into drive; the car bolted forward in the darkness. He spun the wheel; the car swerved, narrowly missing impact with the wall. His instincts ordered him to switch on the headlights. In a blur he saw the downhill road, and in desperation he aimed for it.

The descent was filled with curves. He took them at high speed, sliding, skidding, barely able to hold the car in control, his arms aching. His hands were wet with sweat; they kept slipping. Any second he fully believed he would crash; any moment now he would die in a final explosion.

He would never remember how long it took, or precisely how he found the winding road with the intermittent streetlights, but at last it was there. A flat surface heading left, heading *east,* the road into the city.

He was in dense countryside; tall trees and thick forests bordered the asphalt, looming up like the sides of an immense canyon.

Two cars approached from the opposite direction; he wanted to cry with relief at the sight of them. He was approaching the outskirts of the city. He was into the suburbs. The streetlights were close together now, and suddenly there were cars everywhere, turning, blocking, passing. He never knew he could be so grateful to see traffic.

He came to a traffic light; it was red. He was again grateful—for its actually being there, and the brief rest it brought him. He reached into his shirt pocket for his cigarettes. *God*, he wanted a cigarette!

A car pulled alongside him on his left. He stared once more in disbelief. A man beside the driver—a man he had never seen before in his life—had rolled down his window and was raising a pistol. Around the barrel was a perforated cylinder—a silencer. The unknown man was aiming the gun at him!

Holcroft recoiled, ducking his head, spinning his neck, yanking the gearshift, plunging the accelerator to the floor. He heard the terrible spit and the crash of glass behind him. The rented car sprang forward into the intersection. Horns blew crazily; he swerved in front of an approaching automobile, turning at the last second to avoid a collision.

The cigarette had fallen from his lips, burning a hole in the seat.

He sped into the city.

The telephone was moist and glistening with sweat in Noel's hand. "Are you *listening* to me?" he shouted.

"Mr. Holcroft, calm down, *please*." The voice of the attaché at the American Embassy was disbelieving. "We'll do everything we can. I have the salient facts and we'll pursue a diplomatic inquiry as rapidly as possible. However, it *is* past seven o'clock; it'll be difficult reaching people at this hour."

"Difficult to *reach* people? Maybe you didn't *hear* me. I was damn near killed! Take a look at that car! The windows were blown out!"

"We're sending a man over to your hotel to take possession of the vehicle," said the attaché matter-of-factly.

"I've got the keys. Have him come up to my room and get them."

"Yes, we'll do that. Stay where you are and we'll call you back."

The attaché hung up. *Christ!* The man sounded as if he had just heard from an irritating relative and was anxious to get off the phone so he could go to dinner!

Noel was frightened beyond any fear he had ever known. It gripped him and panicked him and made breathing difficult. Yet in spite of that sickening, all-pervasive fear, something was happening to him that he did not understand. A minute part of him was angry, and he felt that anger growing. He did not want it to grow; he was afraid of it, but he could not stop it. Men had attacked him and he wanted to strike back.

He had wanted to strike back at Graff, too. He had wanted to call him by his rightful name: monster, liar, corrupter . . . *Nazi.*

The telephone rang. He spun around as if it were an alarm, signifying another attack. He gripped his wrist to steady the trembling and walked quickly to the bedside table.

"Senhor Holcroft?"

It was not the man at the Embassy. The accent was Latin.

"What is it?"

"I must speak with you. It is very important that I speak with you right away."

"Who is this?"

"My name is Cararra. I am in the lobby of your hotel."

"Cararra? A woman named Cararra called me yesterday."

"My sister. We are together now. We must both speak with you now. May we come up to your room?"

"No! I'm not seeing anyone!" The sounds of the gunshots, the explosions of concrete and glass—they were all still too sharp in his mind. He would not be an isolated target again.

"Senhor, you *must!*"

"I *won't!* Leave me alone or I'll call the police."

"They can't help you. We can. We wish to help you. You seek information about the Von Tiebolts. We have information."

Noel's breathing stopped. His eyes strayed to the mouthpiece of the telephone. It was a trap. The man on the phone was trying to trap him. Yet, if that were so, why did he announce the trap?

"Who sent you here? Who told you to call me? Was it Graff?"

"Maurice Graff does not talk to people like us. My sister and I, we are beneath his contempt."

You are contemptible! Graff held most of the world

in contempt, thought Holcroft. He breathed again and
tried to speak calmly. "I asked you who sent you to me.
How do you know I'm interested in the Von Tiebolts?"

"We have friends at Immigration. Clerks, not important people. But they listen; they observe. You will
understand when we speak." The Brazilian's words suddenly accelerated; the phrases tumbled awkwardly. Too
awkwardly to be studied or rehearsed. *"Please,* senhor.
See us. We have information and it is information you
should *have.* We want to help. By helping you, we help
ourselves."

Noel's brain raced. The lobby of the Pôrto Alegre
was always crowded, and there was a certain truth in the
bromide that there was safety in numbers. If Cararra and
his sister really knew something about the Von Tiebolts,
he had to see them. But not in an isolated situation, not
alone. He spoke slowly.

"Stay by the reception desk, at least ten feet in front
of it, with both hands out of your pockets. Have your
sister on your left, her right hand on your arm. I'll be
down in a little while, but not in the elevator. And you
won't see me first. I'll see you."

He hung up, astonished at himself. Lessons *were* being learned. They were basic, no doubt, to those abnor-
mal men who dealt in a clandestine world, but new to
him. Cararra would not have his hand gripped around a
gun in his pocket; his sister—or whoever she was—
would not be able to reach into a purse without his
noticing. They would have their attentions on the doorways, not the elevators, which of course he would use.
And he would know who they were.

He walked out of the elevator in a crowd of tourists.
He stood briefly with them, as if one of the party, and
looked at the man and woman by the front desk. As instructed, Cararra's hands were at his side, his sister's right
hand linked to her brother's arm, as if she were afraid to
be set adrift. And he *was* her brother; there was a distinct similarity in their features. Cararra was in his early
thirties, perhaps; his sister, several years younger. Both
dark—skin, hair, eyes. Neither looked at all imposing;
their clothes were neat but inexpensive. They were out of
place among the furs and evening gowns of the hotel's
guests, aware of their awkward status, their faces embarrassed, their eyes frightened. Harmless, thought Hol-

croft. Then he realized he was making too fast a judgment.

They sat in a back booth of the dimly lit cocktail lounge, the Cararras across the table from Noel. Before they'd gone inside, Holcroft had remembered that the embassy was supposed to call him back. He told the desk that if the call came, it was to be relayed to him in the lounge. But only the embassy—no one else.

"Tell me first how you learned I was looking for the Von Tiebolts," said Noel after their drinks arrived.

"I told you. A clerk at Immigration. The word was passed discreetly, last Friday, among the sections, that an American would be coming in asking about a German family named Von Tiebolt. Whoever took the request was to call in another, a man from the *policía do administração.* That's the secret police."

"I know what it is. He called himself, a 'translator.' I want to know why *you* were told."

"The Von Tiebolts were our friends. Very close friends."

"Where are they?"

Cararra exchanged a brief look with his sister. The girl spoke.

"Why do you look for them?" she asked.

"I made that clear at Immigration. It's nothing out of the ordinary. They were left some money by relatives in the United States."

Brother and sister again looked at each other, and again the sister spoke. "Is it a large amount of money?"

"I don't know," replied Holcroft. "It's a confidential matter. I'm merely a go-between."

"A what?" Again the brother.

"*Un tercero,*" answered Noel, looking at the woman. "Why were you so frightened on the telephone yesterday? You left your number, and when I called you back, you told me I shouldn't have. Why?"

"I made a . . . mistake. My brother said it was a bad mistake. My name, the telephone number—it was wrong to leave them."

"It would anger the Germans," explained Cararra. "If they were watching you, intercepting your messages, they would see that we called you. It would be dangerous to us."

"If they're watching me now, they know you're here."

"We talked it over," continued the woman. "We made our decision; we must take the risk."

"What risk?"

"The Germans despise us. Among other things, we are Portuguese Jews," said Cararra.

"They think like that even now?"

"Of course they do. I said we were close to the Von Tiebolts. Perhaps I could clarify. Johann was my dearest friend; he and my sister were to be married. The Germans would not permit it."

"Who could stop them?"

"Any number of men. With a bullet in the back of Johann's head."

"Good *Christ*, that's crazy!" But it was not crazy, and Holcroft knew it. He had been a target high in the hills; gunshots still rang in his ears.

"For certain Germans such a marriage would be the final insult," said Cararra. "There are those who say the Von Tiebolts were traitors to Germany. These people still fight the war three decades later. Great injustices were done to the Von Tiebolts here in Brazil. They deserve whatever can be done for them. Their lives were made most difficult for causes that should have died years ago."

"And you figured I could do something for them? What made you think that?"

"Because powerful men wanted to stop you; the Germans have a great deal of influence. Therefore you, too, were a powerful man, someone the Graffs in Brazil wanted to keep from the Von Tiebolts. To us that meant you intended no harm to our friends, and if no harm, you meant well. A powerful American who could help them."

"You say the 'Graffs in Brazil.' That's Maurice Graff, isn't it? Who is he? What is he?"

"The worst of the Nazis. He should have been hanged at Nürnberg."

"You know Graff?" asked the woman, her eyes on Holcroft.

"I went out to see him. I used a client in New York as an excuse, said he wanted me to look over Graff's house. I'm an architect. At one point, I mentioned the Von Tiebolts, and Graff went out of his mind. He began screaming and ordered me out. When I drove down the hill, a pack of attack dogs came after the car. Later,

Graff's guard followed me. He tried to kill me. In traffic, the same thing happened again. Another man shot at me from a car window."

"Mother of God!" Cararra's lips parted in shock.

"We should not be seen with him," said the woman, gripping her brother's arm. Then she stopped, studying Noel closely. "If he's telling the truth."

Holcroft understood. If he was to learn anything from the Cararras, they had to be convinced he was exactly who he said he was. "I'm telling the truth. I've also told it to the American Embassy. They're sending someone over to take the car as evidence."

The Cararras looked at each other; then both turned to Holcroft. His statement was the proof they needed; it was in their eyes.

"We believe you," said the sister. "We must hurry."

"The Von Tiebolts are alive?"

"Yes," said the brother. "The Nazis think they are somewhere in the southern mountains, around the Santa Catarina colonies. They're old German settlements; the Von Tiebolts could change their names and melt in easily."

"But they're not there."

"No. . . ." Cararra seemed to hesitate, unsure of himself.

"Tell me where they are," pressed Noel.

"Is it a good thing you bring to them?" asked the girl, concern in her voice.

"Far better than anything you can imagine," replied Holcroft. "*Tell* me."

Once again, brother and sister exchanged glances. Their decision was made. Cararra spoke. "They are in England. As you know, the mother is dead. . . ."

"I didn't know," said Noel. "I don't know anything."

"They go by the name of Tennyson. Johann is known as John Tennyson; he is a journalist for a newspaper—the *Guardian*. He speaks several languages and covers the European capitals for the paper. Gretchen, the oldest, is married to a British naval officer. We don't know where she lives, but her husband's name is Beaumont; he is a commander in the Royal Navy. Of Helden, the youngest daughter, we know nothing. She was always a little distant, a bit headstrong."

"Helden? It's an odd name."

"It fits her," said Cararra's sister softly.

"The story is that her birth certificate was filled out by a doctor who did not speak German, who did not understand the mother. According to Senhora von Tiebolt, she gave the child's name as 'Helga,' but the hospital staff was rushed. They wrote down 'Helden.' In those days, one did not argue with what was written on papers. The name stayed with her."

"Tennyson, Beaumont. . . ." Holcroft repeated the names. "England? How did they get out of Brazil and over to England without Graff finding out? You say the Germans have influence. Passports were needed; transportation had to be arranged. How did they do it?"

"Johann . . . John . . . he's a remarkable man, a brilliant man."

"*A homen talentoso,*" added his sister, her strained features softening with the words. "I love him very much. After five years we still love each other."

"Then you've heard from him? From them?"

"Every now and then," said Cararra. "Visitors from England get in touch with us. Never anything written on paper."

Noel stared at this man riddled with fear. "What kind of world do you live in?" he asked incredulously.

"One where your own life can be taken," answered Cararra.

It was true, thought Noel, as a knot of pain formed in his stomach. A war that was lost thirty years ago was still being fought by those who had lost it. It had to be stopped.

"Mr. Holcroft?" The greeting was tentative, the stranger standing by the table not sure he had the right party.

"Yes, I'm Holcroft," said Noel warily.

"Anderson, American Embassy, sir. May I speak with you?"

The Cararras rose as one from the table and sidestepped out of the booth. The embassy man stepped back as Cararra approached Holcroft.

Cararra whispered, "*Adeus, senhor.*"

"*Adeus,*" the woman whispered also, reaching out to touch Noel's arm.

Without looking at the man from the embassy, brother and sister walked rapidly out of the lounge.

* * *

Holcroft sat beside Anderson in the embassy car. They had less than an hour to get to the airport; if the ride took any longer, he would miss the Avianca flight to Lisbon, where he could transfer to a British Airways plane for London.

Anderson had agreed—reluctantly, petulantly—to drive him.

"If it'll get you out of Rio," Anderson had drawled, "I'll go like a greased pig in a slaughterhouse and pay the speeding tickets from my per diem. You're trouble."

Noel grimaced. "You don't believe a word I've said, do you?"

"Goddamn it, Holcroft, do I have to tell you again? There's no car at the hotel; no window's been blown out. There's no record of your even renting a car!"

"It was there! I rented it! I saw Graff!"

"You *called* him. You didn't *see* him. To repeat, he says he got a call from you—something about looking at his house—but you never showed up."

"That's a lie! I was there! After I left, two men tried to kill me. One of them I saw . . . hell, I *fought* with . . . inside his place!"

"You're juiced, man."

"Graff's a fucking Nazi! After thirty years, he's *still* a Nazi, and you people treat him like he's some kind of statesman."

"You're damn right," said Anderson. "Graff's very special material. He's protected."

"I wouldn't brag about it."

"You've got it all backward, Holcroft. Graff was at a place called Wolfsschanze in Germany in July in 1944. He's one of the men who tried to kill Hitler."

10

There was no blinding sunlight outside his hotel window
now; no golden, oiled bodies of grown-up children playing
in the white sands of the Copacabana. Instead, the London streets were mottled with drizzle, and gusts of
wind swept between the buildings and through the alleys.
Pedestrians rushed from doorways to bus queues, train
stations, pubs. It was that hour in London when Englishmen felt sprung from the coils of daylight drudgery; making a living was not living. In Noel's experience no other
city in the world took such pleasure at the end of the
workday. There was a sense of controlled exhilaration
in the streets, even with the rain and the wind.

He turned from the window and went to the bureau
and his silver flask. It had taken nearly fifteen hours of
flying to reach London, and now that he was here, he was
not sure how to proceed. He had tried to think on the
planes, but the events in Rio de Janeiro were so stunning,
and the information gathered so contradictory, that he
felt lost in a maze. His unfamiliar forest was too dense.
And he had just begun.

Graff, a survivor of Wolfsschanze? One of the *men of
Wolfsschanze?* It wasn't possible. The men of Wolfs-
schanze were committed to Geneva, to the fulfillment of
Heinrich Clausen's dream, and the Von Tiebolts were an
integral part of that dream. Graff wanted to destroy the
Von Tiebolts, as he had ordered the death of Heinrich
Clausen's son on a deserted lookout above Rio and from a
car window in a city street at night. He was no part of
Wolfsschanze. He could not be.

The Cararras. They were complicated, too. What in
heaven's name prevented them from leaving Brazil? It was
not as though the airports or the piers were closed to
them. He believed what they had told him, but there were

too many elementary questions that needed answers. No matter how he tried to suppress the idea, there was something contrived about the Cararras. What *was* it?

Noel poured himself a drink and picked up the telephone. He had a name and a place of work: John Tennyson; the *Guardian*. Newspaper offices did not close down at the end of the day. He would know in minutes if the initial information given him by the Cararras was true. If there was a John Tennyson writing for the *Guardian*, then Johann von Tiebolt had been found.

If so, the next step according to the Geneva document was for John Tennyson to take him to his sister Gretchen Beaumont, wife of Commander Beaumont, Royal Navy. She was the person he had to see; she was the oldest surviving issue of Wilhelm von Tiebolt. The key.

"I'm terribly sorry, Mr. Holcroft," said the polite voice over the phone at the *Guardian*'s news desk, "but I'm afraid we can't give out the addresses or telephone numbers of our journalists."

"But John Tennyson does work for you." It was not a question; the man had already stated that Tennyson was not in the London office. Holcroft merely wanted a direct confirmation.

"Mr. Tennyson is one of our people on the Continent."

"How can I get a message to him? Immediately. It's urgent."

The man at the desk seemed to hesitate. "That would be difficult, I think. Mr. Tennyson moves around a great deal."

"Come on, I can go downstairs, buy your paper, and see where his copy's filed from."

"Yes, of course. Except that Mr. Tennyson does not use a byline. Not in daily dispatches; only in major retrospectives. . . ."

"How do *you* get in touch with him when you need him?" broke in Holcroft, convinced the man was stalling.

Again there was the hesitation, a clearing of the throat. *Why?* "Well . . . there's a message pool. It could take several days."

"I don't *have* several days. I've got to reach him right away." The subsequent silence was maddening. The man at the *Guardian* had no intention of offering a solution. Noel tried another trick. "Listen, I probably shouldn't say this . . . it's a confidential matter . . . but there's money involved. Mr. Tennyson and his family were left a sum of money."

"I wasn't aware that he was married."

"I mean *his* family. He and his two sisters. Do you know them? Do you know if they live in London? The oldest is—"

"I know nothing of Mr. Tennyson's personal life, sir. I suggest you get in touch with a solicitor." Then, without warning, he hung up.

Bewildered, Holcroft replaced the phone. Why such a deliberate lack of cooperation? He had identified himself, given the name of his hotel, and for several moments the man at the *Guardian* seemed to listen, as if he might offer help. But no offers came, and suddenly the man had ended their conversation. It was all very strange.

The telephone rang; he was further bewildered. No one knew he was at this hotel. On the immigration card he'd filled out on the phone he had purposely listed the Dorchester as his London residence, not the Belgravia Arms, where he was staying. He did not want anyone— especially anyone from Rio de Janeiro—to be able to trace his whereabouts. He picked up the receiver, trying to suppress the pain in his stomach.

"Yes?"

"Mr. Holcroft, this is the front desk, sir. We've just learned that your courtesy basket was not delivered in time. We're dreadfully sorry. Will you be in your room for a while, sir?"

For God's sake, thought Noel. Millions upon millions were being held in Geneva, and a desk clerk was concerned about a basket of fruit. "Yes, I'll be here."

"Very good, sir. The steward will be there shortly."

Holcroft replaced the phone, the pain in his stomach subsiding. His eyes fell on the telephone directories on the bottom shelf of the bedside table. He picked one up and turned the pages to the letter *T*.

There was an inch and a half of Tennysons, about fifteen names, no John but three *J*'s. He'd start with those. He lifted up the phone and made the first call.

"Hello, John?"

The man on the line was Julian. The other two *J*'s were women. There was a Helen Tennyson, no Helden. He dialed the number. An operator told him the phone was disconnected.

He turned to the directory with the letter *B*. There were six Beaumonts in London, none indicating any rank or affiliation with the Royal Navy. But there was nothing to lose; he picked up the phone and started dialing.

Before he finished the fourth call, there was a knock at the door; his basket of English courtesy had arrived. He swore at the interruption; put the phone down, and walked to the door, reaching into his pocket for some change.

Two men stood outside, neither in steward's uniform, both in overcoats, each with hat in hand. The taller of the two was in his fifties, straight gray hair above a weathered face; the younger man was about Noel's age, with clear blue eyes, curly reddish hair, and a small scar on his forehead.

"Yes?"

"Mr. Holcroft?"

"Yes."

"Noel Holcroft, United States citizen, passport number F-two-zero-four-seven-eight—"

"I'm Noel Holcroft. I've never memorized my passport number."

"May we come in, please?"

"I'm not sure. Who are you?"

Both men held black identification cases in their hands; they opened them unobtrusively. "British Military Intelligence, Five branch," the older man said.

"Why do you want to see me?"

"Official business, sir. May we step inside?"

Noel nodded uncertainly, the pain returning to his stomach. Peter Baldwin, the man who had ordered him to "cancel Geneva," had been with MI Six. And Baldwin had been killed by the men of Wolfsschanze because he had interfered. Did these two British agents know the truth about Baldwin? Did they know Baldwin had *called* him? Oh, *God*, telephone numbers could be traced through hotel switchboards! They *had* to know! . . . Then Holcroft remembered: Baldwin had *not* called him; he had come to his apartment. Noel had called *him*.

You don't know what you're doing. I'm the only one who does.

If Baldwin was to be believed, he had said nothing to

anyone. If so, where was the connection? Why was British Intelligence interested in an American named Holcroft? How did it know where to find him? *How?*

The two Englishmen entered. The younger, red-haired man crossed rapidly to the bathroom, looked inside, then turned and went to the window. His older associate stood by the desk, his eyes scanning the walls, the floor, and the open closet.

"All right, you're inside," Noel said. "What is it?"

"The Tinamou, Mr. Holcroft," said the gray-haired man.

"The what?"

"I repeat. The Tinamou."

"What the hell is that?"

"According to any standard encyclopedia, the Tinamou is a ground-dwelling bird whose protective coloring makes him indistinguishable from his background; whose short bursts of flight take him swiftly from one location to another."

"That's very enlightening, but I haven't the vaguest idea what you're talking about."

"We think you do," said the younger man by the window.

"You're wrong. I've never heard of a bird like that, and don't know any reason why I should have. Obviously, you're referring to something else, but I don't make the connection."

"Obviously," interrupted the agent by the desk, "we're not referring to a bird. The Tinamou is a man; the name is quite applicable, however."

"It means nothing to me. Why should it?"

"May I give you some advice?" The older man spoke crisply, with an edge to his voice.

"Sure. I probably won't understand it anyway."

"You'd do far better cooperating with us than not. It's possible you're being used, but frankly we doubt it. However, if you help us now, we're prepared to assume that you *were* being used. I believe that's eminently fair."

"I was right," said Holcroft. "I don't understand you."

"Then let me clear up the details and perhaps you will. You've been making inquiries about John Tennyson, born Johann von Tiebolt, immigrant to the UK roughly six years ago. He is currently employed as a multilingual correspondent for the *Guardian*."

"The man at the *Guardian* desk," interrupted Noel. "He called you—or had someone call. That's why he stalled, why he went on the way he did, then cut me off. And that goddamned fruit; it was to make sure I didn't go out. What *is* this?"

"May we ask why you're trying to find John Tennyson?"

"No."

"You've stated, both here and in Rio de Janeiro, that a sum of money is involved. . . ."

"*Rio de!* . . . Jesus!"

"That you're an 'intermediary,'" continued the Englishman. "That was the term you used."

"It's a confidential matter."

"We think it's an international one."

"Good God, why?"

"Because you're trying to deliver a sum of money. If the ground rules are followed, it amounts to three quarters of the full payment."

"For what?"

"For an assassination."

"*Assassination?*"

"Yes. In the data banks of half the civilized world, the Tinamou has a single description: 'assassin.' 'Master assassin,' to be precise. And we have every reason to believe that Johann von Tiebolt, alias John Tennyson, is the Tinamou."

Noel was stunned. His mind raced furiously. An assassin! Good God! Was that what Peter Baldwin had been trying to tell him? That one of the Geneva inheritors was an assassin?

No one knows but me. Baldwin's words.

If they were true, under no condition could he reveal his real reason for wanting to find John Tennyson. Geneva would explode in controversy; the massive account would be frozen, thrown into the international courts, his covenant destroyed. He could not allow that to happen; he knew it now.

Yet it was equally vital that his reasons for seeking Tennyson be above suspicion, beyond any relationship to —or cognizance of—the Tinamou.

The Tinamou! An assassin! It was potentially the most damaging news possible. If there was any truth in what MI Five believed, the bankers in Geneva would suspend all discussions, close the vaults, and wait for another generation. Yet any decision to abort the covenant would be for appearance's sake. If Tennyson *was* this Tinamou, he could be exposed, caught, severed from all association with the Geneva account, and the covenant would remain intact. Amends *would* be made. According to the conditions of the document, the older *sister* was the key—she was the eldest surviving child—not the brother.

An assassin! Oh, *God!*

First things first. Holcroft knew he had to dispel the convictions of the two men in his room. He walked unsteadily to a chair, sat down, and leaned forward.

"Listen to me," he said, his voice weak in astonishment. "I've told you the truth. I don't know anything about any Tinamou, any assassin. My business is with the Von Tiebolt *family*, not a particular member of the family. I was trying to find Tennyson because I was told he was Von Tiebolt and worked at the *Guardian*. That's all there is to it."

"If so," said the red-haired man, "perhaps you'll explain the nature of your business."

Base the lie in an aspect of truth.

"I'll tell you what I can, which isn't a great deal. Some of it I pieced together myself from what I learned in Rio. It *is* confidential, and it *does* concern money." Noel took a deep breath, and reached for his cigarettes. "The Von Tiebolts were left an inheritance—don't ask me by whom, because I don't know, and the lawyer won't say."

"What's the name of this lawyer," asked the gray-haired man.

"I'd have to get his permission to tell you," answered Holcroft, lighting his cigarette, wondering whom in New York he could call from an untraceable pay phone in London.

"We may ask you to do that," said the older agent. "Go on, please."

"I found out in Rio that the Von Tiebolts were despised by the German community there. I have an idea—and it's only an idea—that somewhere along the line they opposed the Nazis in Germany, and someone, perhaps an anti-Nazi German—or Germans—left them the money."

"In America?" asked the red-haired man.

Noel sensed the trap and was prepared for it. *Be*

consistent. "Obviously, whoever left the Von Tiebolts money has been living there for a long time. If he, or they, came to the United States after the war, that could presume they had a clean bill of health. On the other hand, they could be relatives who came to the States years ago. I honestly don't know."

"Why were you chosen as the intermediary? You're not a lawyer."

"No, but the lawyer's a friend of mine," replied Holcroft. "He knows I travel a lot, knew I was going to Brazil for a client. . . . I'm an architect. He asked me to call around, gave me some names, including Rio's Immigration people."

Keep it simple; avoid complication.

"That was asking quite a bit of you, wasn't it?" The red-haired agent's disbelief was in his question.

"Not really. He's done me favors; I can do him one." Noel drew on his cigarette. "This is crazy. What started out as a simple . . . well, it's just crazy."

"You were told Johann von Tiebolt was John Tennyson and that he worked in London, or was based in London," said the older man, his hands in his overcoat pockets, looking down at Noel. "So, as a favor, you decided to make the trip from Brazil to the UK to find him. As a *favor.* . . . Yes, Mr. Holcroft, I'd say it was crazy."

Noel glared up at the gray-haired man. He remembered Sam Buonoventura's words: *I got hot myself. . . . It's the only way to handle angry cops.*

"Now just a minute! I didn't make a special trip from Rio to London for the Von Tiebolts. I'm on my way to Amsterdam. If you check my office in New York, you'll find that I'm doing some work in Curaçao. For your benefit, it's Dutch, and I'm going to Amsterdam for design conferences."

The look in the older man's eyes seemed to soften. "I see," he said quietly. "It's quite possible we drew the wrong conclusions, but I think you'll agree the surface facts led us to them. We may owe you an apology."

Pleased with himself, Noel suppressed the urge to smile. He had adhered to the lessons, handled the lie with his guard up.

"It's okay," he replied. "But now I'm curious. This Tinamou. How do you know it's Von Tiebolt?"

"We're not certain," replied the gray-haired agent.

"We were hoping you'd provide that certainty. I think we were wrong about that."

"You certainly were. But why Tennyson? I guess I should tell the lawyer in New York. . . ."

"No," interrupted the Englishman. "Don't do that. You must not discuss this with anyone."

"It's a little late for that, isn't it?" Holcroft said, gambling. "The 'matter' *has* been discussed. I'm under no obligation to you, but I do have an obligation to that lawyer. He's a friend."

The MI-Five men looked at each other, their mutual concern in the exchange.

"Beyond an obligation to a friend," the older man said, "I suggest that you have a far greater responsibility. One that can be substantiated by your own government. This is a highly classified, intensely sensitive investigation. The Tinamou is an international killer. His victims include some of the world's most distinguished men."

"And you believe he's Tennyson?"

"The evidence is circumstantial, but very, very strong."

"Still, not conclusive."

"Not conclusive."

"A few minutes ago you sounded positive."

"A few minutes ago we tried to trap you. It's merely a technique."

"It's damned offensive."

"It's damned effective," said the red-haired man with the scar on his forehead.

"What's the circumstantial evidence against Tennyson?"

"Will you hold it in the strictest confidence?" asked the older agent. "That request can be transmitted by the highest law-enforcement officials in your country, if you wish."

Holcroft paused. "All right, I won't call New York; I won't say anything. But I want information."

"We don't bargain." The younger man spoke offensively, cut off by a look from his associate.

"It's not a question of a bargain," said Noel. "I said I'd reach *a* member of the family, and I think I should. Where can I contact Tennyson's sisters? One's married to a commander in the navy named Beaumont. The lawyer in New York knows that; he'll try to find her if I don't. It might as well be me."

"Far better that it's you," agreed the gray-haired man. "We're convinced that neither woman is aware of her brother's activities. As near as we can determine, the family are estranged from one another. How seriously, we don't know, but there's been little or no communication. Frankly, your showing up is a complication we'd rather not be burdened with. We don't want alarms raised; a controlled situation is infinitely preferable."

"There won't be any alarms," said Noel. "I'll deliver my message and go about my business."

"To Amsterdam?"

"To Amsterdam."

"Yes, of course. The older sister is married to Commander Anthony Beaumont; she's his second wife. They live near Portsmouth, several miles north of the naval base, in a suburb of Portsea. He's in the telephone directory. The younger girl recently moved to Paris. She's a translator for Gallimard Publishers, but she's not at the address listed with the company. We don't know where she lives."

Holcroft rose from the chair and walked between the two men to the desk. He picked up the hotel pen and wrote on a page of stationery.

"Anthony Beaumont . . . Portsmouth. . . . Gallimard Publishers. . . . How do you spell 'Gallimard'?"

The red-haired agent told him.

Noel finished writing. "I'll make the calls in the morning and send a note to New York," he said, wondering to himself how long it would take to drive to Portsmouth. "I'll tell the lawyer I reached the sisters but was unable to contact the brother. Is that all right?"

"We couldn't persuade you to drop the entire matter?"

"No. I'd have to say why I dropped it, and you don't want that."

"Very well. It's the best we can hope for, then."

"Now, tell me why you think John Tennyson is this Tinamou. You owe me that."

The older man paused. "Perhaps we do," he said. "I reemphasize the classified nature of the information."

"Whom would I tell it to? I'm not in your line of work."

"All right," said the gray-haired man. "As you say, we owe you. But you should know that the fact that you've been told gives us a certain insight. Very few people have been."

Holcroft stiffened; it wasn't difficult to convey his anger. "And I don't imagine too many have had men like you knock on their doors and been accused of paying off assassins. If this were New York, I'd haul you into court. You *do* owe me."

"Very well. A pattern was uncovered, at first too obvious to warrant examination until we studied the man. For several years, Tennyson consistently appeared in or near areas where assassinations took place. It was uncanny. He actually reported the events for the *Guardian*, filing his stories from the scene. A year or so ago, for example, he covered the killing of that American in Beirut, the embassy fellow who was, of course, CIA. Three days before, he'd been in Brussels; suddenly he was in Tehran. We began to study him, and what we learned was astonishing. We believe he's the Tinamou. He's utterly brilliant and, quite possibly, utterly mad."

"What did you find out?"

"For starters, you know about his father. One of the early Nazis, a butcher of the worst sort. . . ."

"Are you sure about that?" Noel asked the question too rapidly. "What I mean is, it doesn't necessarily follow. . . ."

"No, I suppose it doesn't," said the gray-haired agent. "But what does follow is, to say the least, unusual. Tennyson is a manic overachiever. He completed two university degrees in Brazil at the age at which most students would have been matriculating. He has mastered five languages; speaks them fluently. He was an extremely successful businessman in South America; he amassed a great deal of money. These are hardly the credentials of a newspaper correspondent."

"People change; interests change. That *is* circumstantial. Pretty damned weak, too."

"The circumstances of his employment, however, lend strength to the conjecture," said the older man. "No one at the *Guardian* remembers when or how he was employed. His name simply appeared on the payroll computers one day, a week before his first copy was filed from Antwerp. No one had ever heard of him."

"Someone had to hire him."

"Yes, someone did. The man whose signature appeared on the interview and employment records was killed in a most unusual train accident that took five lives on the underground."

"A subway in London. . . ." Holcroft paused. "I remember reading about that."

"A trainman's error, they called it, but that's not good enough," added the red-haired man. "That man had eighteen years' experience. It was bloody well murder. Courtesy of the Tinamou."

"You can't be sure," said Holcroft. "An error's an error. What were some of the other . . . coincidences? Where the killings took place."

"I mentioned Beirut. There was Paris, too. A bomb went off under the French minister of labor's car in the rue du Bac, killing him instantly. Tennyson was in Paris; he'd been in Frankfort the day before. Seven months ago, during the riots in Madrid, a government official was shot from a window four stories above the crowds. Tennyson was in Madrid; he'd flown in from Lisbon just hours before. There are others; they go on."

"Did you ever bring him in and question him?"

"Twice. Not as a suspect, obviously, but as an expert on the scene. Tennyson is the personification of arrogance. He claimed to have analyzed the areas of social and political unrest, and followed his instincts, knowing that violence and assassination were certain to erupt in those places. He had the cheek to lecture us; said we should learn to anticipate and not so often be caught unawares."

"Could he be telling the truth?"

"If you mean that as an insult, it's noted. In light of this evening, perhaps we deserve it."

"Sorry. But when you consider his accomplishments, you've got to consider the possibility. Where is Tennyson now?"

"He disappeared four days ago in Bahrain. Our operatives are watching for him from Singapore to Athens."

The two MI-Five men walked into the empty elevator. The red-haired agent turned to his colleague.

"What do you make of him?" he asked.

"I don't know," was the soft-spoken reply. "We've

given him enough to send him racing about; perhaps we'll learn something. He's far too much of an amateur to be a legitimate contact. Those paying for a killing would be fools to send the money with Holcroft. The Tinamou would reject it if they did."

"But he was lying."

"Quite so. Quite poorly."

"Then he's being used."

"Quite possibly. But for what?"

11

According to the car-rental agency, Portsmouth was roughly seventy miles from London, the roads clearly marked, the traffic not likely to be heavy. It was five past six. He could be in Portsea before nine, thought Noel, if he settled for a quick sandwich instead of dinner.

He had intended to wait until morning, but a telephone call made to confirm the accuracy of the MI-Five information dictated otherwise. He reached Gretchen Beaumont, and what she told him convinced him to move quickly.

Her husband, the commander, was on sea duty in the Mediterranean; tomorrow at noon she was going on "winter holiday" to the south of France, where she and the commander would spend a weekend together. If Mr. Holcroft wished to see her about family matters, it would have to be tonight.

He told her he would get there as soon as possible, thinking as he hung up that she had one of the strangest voices he had ever heard. It was not the odd mixture of German and Portuguese in her accent, for that made sense; it was in the floating, hesitant quality of her speech. Hesitant or vacuous—it was difficult to tell. The commander's wife made it clear—if haltingly so—that in spite of the fact that the matters to be discussed were confidential, a naval aide would be in an adjoining room. Her concerns gave rise to an image of a middle-aged, self-indulgent *Hausfrau* with an overinflated opinion of her looks.

Fifty miles south of London, he realized that he was making better time than he had thought possible. There was little traffic, and the sign on the road, reflected in the headlights, read PORTSEA—15 M.

It was barely ten past eight. He could slow down and try to collect his thoughts. Gretchen Beaumont's directions had been clear; he'd have no trouble finding the residence.

For a vacuous-sounding woman, she had been very specific when it came to giving instructions. It was somehow contradictory in light of the way she spoke, as if sharp lines of reality had suddenly, abruptly, shot through clouds of dreamlike mist.

It told him nothing. He was the intruder, the stranger who telephoned and spoke of a vitally important matter he would not define—except in person.

How *would* he define it? How could he explain to the middle-aged wife of a British naval officer that she was the key that could unlock a vault containing seven hundred and eighty million dollars?

He was getting nervous; it was no way to be convincing. Above all, he had to be convincing; he could not appear afraid or unsure or artificial. And then it occurred to him that he could tell her the truth—as Heinrich Clausen saw the truth. It was the best lever he had; it was the ultimate conviction.

Oh, God! Please make her understand!

He made the two left turns off the highway and drove rapidly through the peaceful, tree-lined suburban area for the prescribed mile and a half. He found the house easily, parked in front, and got out of the car.

He opened the gate and walked up the path to the door. There was no bell; instead there was a brass knocker, and so he tapped it gently. The house was designed simply. Wide windows in the living room, small ones on the opposite, bedroom side; the facade, old brick above a stone foundation—solid, built to last, certainly not ostentatious and probably not expensive. He had designed such houses, usually as second homes on the shore for couples still unsure they could afford them. It was the ideal residence for a military man on a military budget. Neat, trim, and manageable.

Gretchen Beaumont opened the door herself. Whatever image she had evoked on the telephone vanished at the sight of her; it disappeared in a rush of amazement, with the impact of a blow to his stomach. Simply put, the woman in the doorway was one of the most beautiful he had ever seen in his life. The fact that she was a woman was almost secondary. She was like a statue, a sculptor's ideal, refined over and over again in clay before chisel was put to stone. She was of medium height, with long blond hair that framed a face of finely boned, perfectly proportioned features. Too perfect, too much in the sculptor's mind . . . too cold. Yet the coldness was lessened by her large, wide eyes; they were light blue and inquisitive, neither friendly nor unfriendly.

"Mr. Holcroft?" she asked in that echoing, dreamlike voice that gave evidence of Germany and Brazil.

"Yes, Mrs. Beaumont. Thank you so much for seeing me. I apologize for the inconvenience."

"Come in, please."

She stepped back to admit him. In the doorway he had concentrated on her face, on the extraordinary beauty that was in no way diminished by the years; it was impossible now not to notice the body, emphasized by her translucent dress. The body, too, was extraordinary, but in a different way from the face. There was no coldness, only heat. The sheer dress clung to her skin, the absence of a brassiere apparent, accentuated by a flared collar, unbuttoned to the midpoint between her large breasts. On either side, in the center of the swelling flesh, he could see her nipples clearly, pressing against the soft fabric as if aroused.

When she moved, the slow, fluid motion of her thighs and stomach and pelvis combined into the rhythm of a sensual dance. She did not walk; she glided—an extraordinary body screaming for observation as a prelude to invasion and satisfaction.

Yet the face was cold and the eyes distant; inquisitive but distant. And Noel was perplexed.

"You've had a long trip," she said, indicating a couch against the far wall. "Sit down, please. May I offer you a drink?"

"I'd appreciate it."

"What would you care for?" She held her place in front of him, momentarily blocking his short path to the couch, her light-blue eyes looking intently into his. Her breasts were revealed clearly—so close—beneath the sheer fabric. The nipples were taut, rising with each breath; again in that unmistakable rhythm of a sexual dance.

"Scotch, if you have it," he said.

"In England, that's whiskey, isn't it?" she asked, walking toward a bar against the wall.

"It's whiskey," he said, sinking into the soft pillows of

the couch, trying to concentrate on Gretchen's face. It was difficult for him, and he knew she was trying to make it difficult. The commander's wife did not have to provoke a sexual reaction; she did not have to dress for the part. But dress for it she had, and provoke she did. Why?

She brought over his scotch. He reached for it, touching her hand as he did so, noting that she did not withdraw from the contact but, instead, briefly pressed his curved fingers with her own. She then did a very strange thing; she sat down on a leather hassock only feet away and looked up at him.

"Won't you join me?" he asked.

"I don't drink."

"Then perhaps you'd prefer that I don't."

She laughed throatily. "I have no moral objections whatsoever. It would hardly become an officer's wife. I'm simply not capable of drinking or of smoking, actually. Both go directly to my head."

He looked at her over the rim of the glass. Her eyes remained eerily on his, unblinking, steady, still distant, making him wish she'd look away.

"You said on the phone that one of your husband's aides would be in an adjoining room. Would you like us to meet?"

"He wasn't able to be here."

"Oh? I'm sorry."

"Are you?"

It was *crazy*. The woman was behaving like a courtesan unsure of her standing, or a high-priced whore evaluating a new client's wallet. She leaned forward on the hassock, picking at an imaginary piece of lint on the throw rug beneath his feet. The gesture was foolish, the effect too obvious. The top of her dress parted, exposing her breasts. She could not have been unaware of what she was doing. He had to respond; she expected it. But he would not respond in the way she anticipated. A father had cried out to him; nothing could interfere. Even an unlikely whore.

An unlikely whore who was the key to Geneva.

"Mrs. Beaumont," he said, placing his glass awkwardly on the small table next to the couch, "you're a very gracious woman and I'd like nothing better than to sit here for hours and have a few drinks, but we've got to talk. I asked to see you because I have extraordinary news for you. It concerns the two of us."

"The two of *us?*" said Gretchen, emphasizing the pronoun. "By all means talk, Mr. Holcroft. I've never met you before; I don't know you. How can this news concern the two of us?"

"Our fathers knew each other years ago."

At the mention of the word "father," the woman stiffened. "I have no father."

"You had; so did I," he said. "In Germany over thirty years ago. Your name's Von Tiebolt. You're the oldest child of Wilhelm von Tiebolt."

Gretchen took a deep breath and looked away. "I don't think I want to listen further."

"I know how you feel," replied Noel. "I had the same reaction myself. But you're wrong. *I* was wrong."

"Wrong?" she asked, brushing away the long blond hair that swung across her cheek with the swift turn of her head. "You're presumptuous. Perhaps you didn't live the way we lived. Please don't tell me I'm wrong. You're in no position to do that."

"Just let me tell you what I've learned. When I'm finished, you can make your own decision. Your knowing is the important thing. And your support, of course."

"Support of what? Knowing what?"

Noel felt oddly moved, as if what he was about to say were the most important words of his life. With a normal person the truth would be sufficient, but Gretchen Beaumont was not a normal person; her scars were showing. It would take more than truth; it would take enormous conviction.

"Two weeks ago I flew to Geneva to meet with a banker named Manfredi. . . ."

He told it all, leaving out nothing save the men of Wolfsschanze. He told it simply, even eloquently, hearing the conviction in his own voice, feeling the profound commitment in his mind, the stirrings of pain in his chest.

He gave her the figures: seven hundred and eighty million for the survivors of the Holocaust, and the descendants of those survivors still in need. Everywhere. Two million for each of the surviving eldest children, to be used as each saw fit. Six months—possibly longer—of a collective commitment.

Finally, he told her of the pact in death the three fathers made, taking their lives only after every detail in Geneva was confirmed and iron bound.

When he had finished, he felt the perspiration rolling down his forehead. "It's up to us now," he said. "And a man in Berlin—Kessler's son. The three of us have to finish what they started."

"It all sounds so incredible," she said quietly. "But I really don't see why it should concern me."

He was stunned at her calm, at her complete equanimity. She had listened to him in silence for nearly half an hour, heard revelations that had to be shattering to her, yet she displayed no reaction whatsoever. *Nothing.* "Haven't you understood a word I've said?"

"I understand that you're very upset," said Gretchen Beaumont in her soft, echoing voice. "But I've been very upset for most of my life, Mr. Holcroft. I've been that way because of Wilhelm von Tiebolt. He is nothing to me."

"He *knew* that, can't you see? He tried to make up for it."

"With money?"

"More than money."

Gretchen leaned forward and slowly reached out to touch his forehead. With her fingers extended, she wiped away the beads of perspiration. Noel remained still, unable to break the contact between their eyes.

"Did you know that I was Commander Beaumont's second wife?" she asked.

"Yes, I heard that."

"The divorce was a difficult time for him. And for me, of course, but more so for him. But it passed for him; it will not pass for me."

"What do you mean?"

"I'm the intruder. The foreigner. A breaker of marriages. He has his work; he goes to sea. I live among those who don't. The life of a naval officer's wife is a lonely one in usual circumstances. It can become quite difficult when one is ostracized."

"You must have known there'd be a degree of that."

"Of course."

"Well, if you knew it? . . ." He left the question suspended, not grasping the point.

"Why did I marry Commander Beaumont? Is that what you mean to ask?"

He did not want to ask *anything!* He was not interested in the intimate details of Gretchen Beaumont's life. Geneva was all that mattered; the covenant, everything. But he needed her cooperation.

"I assume the reasons were emotional; that's generally why people get married. I only meant that you might have taken steps to lessen the tension. You could live farther away from the naval base, have different friends." He was rambling, awkwardly, a little desperately. He wanted only to break through her maddening reserve.

"My question's more interesting. Why did I marry Beaumont?" Her voice floated again; it rose quietly in the air. "You're right; it's emotional. Quite basic."

She touched his forehead again, her dress parting once more as she leaned forward, her lovely, naked breasts exposed again. Noel was tired and aroused and angry. He *had* to make her understand that her private concerns were meaningless beside Geneva! To do that, he had to make her like him; yet he could not touch her.

"Naturally it's basic," he said. "You love him."

"I loathe him."

Her hand was now inches from his face, her fingers a blur at the corner of his eyes—a blur because their eyes were locked; he dared not shift them. And he dared not touch her.

"Then why did you marry him? Why do you stay with him?"

"I told you. It's basic. Commander Beaumont has a little money; he's a highly respected officer in the service of his government, a dull, uninteresting man more at home on a ship than anywhere else. All this adds up to a very quiet, very secure niche. I am in a comfortable cocoon."

There was the lever! Geneva provided it. "Two million dollars could build a very secure cocoon, Mrs. Beaumont. A far better shelter than you have here."

"Perhaps. But I would have to leave this one in order to build it. I'd have to go outside—"

"Only for a while."

"And what would happen?" she continued, as if he had not interrupted. "Outside? Where I'd have to say yes or no. I don't want to think about that; it would be so difficult. You know, Mr. Holcroft, I've been unhappy most of my life, but I don't look for sympathy."

She was infuriating! He felt like slapping her. "I'd like to return to the situation in Geneva," he said.

She settled back into the hassock, crossing her legs. The sheer dress rose above her knees, the soft flesh of her thigh revealed. The pose was seductive; her words were not.

"But I have returned to it," she said. "Perhaps awkwardly, but I'm trying to explain. As a child I came out of Berlin. Always running, until my mother and my brother and I found a sanctuary in Brazil that proved to be a hell for us. I've floated through life these past years. I've followed—instincts, opportunities, men—but I've followed. I haven't led. I've made as few decisions as possible."

"I don't understand."

"If you have business that concerns my family, you'll have to talk to my brother, Johann. He makes the decisions. He brought us out of South America after my mother died. He is the Von Tiebolt you must reach."

Noel suppressed his desire to yell at her. Instead, he exhaled silently, a sense of weariness and frustration sweeping over him. Johann von Tiebolt was the one member of the family he had to avoid, but he could not tell Gretchen Beaumont why. "Where is he?" he asked rhetorically.

"I don't know. He works for the *Guardian* newspaper, in Europe."

"Where in Europe?"

"Again, I have no idea. He moves around a great deal."

"I was told he was last seen in Bahrain."

"Then you know more than I do."

"You have a sister."

"Helden. In Paris. Somewhere."

All the children will be examined . . . decisions made.

Johann had been examined and a judgment had been made—rightly or wrongly—that disqualified him from Geneva. He was a complication they could not afford: he would draw attention where none could be permitted. And this strange, beautiful woman on the hassock—even if she felt differently—would be rejected by Geneva as incompetent. It was as simple as that.

Paris. Helden von Tiebolt.

Absently, Noel reached for his cigarettes, his thoughts now on an unknown woman who worked as a translator for a publishing house in Paris. He was only vaguely aware of the movement in front of him, so complete was his concentration. Then he noticed and he stared at Gretchen Beaumont.

The commander's wife had risen from the hassock and unfastened the buttons of her dress to the waist. Slowly, she parted the folds of silk. Her breasts were released; they sprang out at him, the nipples taut, stretched, swollen with tension. She raised her skirt with both her hands, bunching it above her thighs, and stood directly in front of him. He was aware of the fragrance that seemed to emanate from her—a delicate perfume with a sensuousness as provoking as the sight of her exposed flesh. She sat down beside him, her dress now above her waist, her body trembling. She moaned and reached for the back of his neck, drawing his face to hers, his lips to hers. Her mouth opened as she received his mouth; she sucked, breathing rapidly, her warm breath mixed with the juices that came from her throat. She put her hand on his trousers and groped for his penis . . . hard, soft, hard. *Harder.* She became suddenly uncontrollable; her moans were feverish. She pressed into him. Everywhere.

Her parted lips slid off his mouth and she whispered. "Tomorrow I go to the Mediterranean. To a man I loathe. Don't say anything. Just give me tonight. Give me *tonight!*"

She moved away slightly, her mouth glistening, her eyes so wide they seemed manic. Slowly, she rose above him, her white skin everywhere. The trembling subsided. She slid a naked leg over his and got to her feet. She pulled his face into her waist and reached for his hand. He stood up, embracing her. She held his hand in hers, and together they walked toward the door of the bedroom. As they went inside, he heard the words, spoken in that eerie, echoing monotone.

"Johann said a man would come one day and talk of a strange arrangement. I was to be nice to him and remember everything he said."

12

Holcroft awoke with a start, for several seconds not sure where he was; then he remembered. Gretchen Beaumont had led him into the bedroom with that incredible statement. He had tried to press her, tried to learn what else her brother had said, but she was in no state to answer clearly. She was in a frenzy, needing the sex desperately; she could concentrate on nothing else.

They had made love maniacally, she the aggressor, writhing on the bed at fever pitch, beneath him, above him, beside him. She'd been insatiable; no amount of exploration and penetration could gratify her. At one point she had screamed, clasping her legs around his waist, her fingers digging into his shoulders long after he was capable of response. And then his exhaustion had caught up with him. He'd fallen into a deep but troubled sleep.

Now he was awake, and he did not know what had interrupted that sleep. There'd been a noise, not loud, but sharp and penetrating, and he did not know what it was or where it came from.

Suddenly, he realized he was alone in the bed. He raised his head. The room was dark, the door closed, a dim line of light at the bottom.

"Gretchen? . . ." There was no reply; no one else was in the room.

He threw the covers off and got out of the bed, steadying his weakened legs, feeling drained, disoriented. He lurched for the door and yanked it open. Beyond, in the small living room, a single table lamp was on, its light casting shadows against the walls and the floor.

There was the noise again! A metallic sound that echoed throughout the house, but it did not come from inside the house. He ran to a living-room window and peered through the glass. Under the spill of a streetlamp he could see the figure of a man standing by the hood of his rented car, a flashlight in his hand.

Before he knew what was happening, he heard a muffled voice from somewhere else outside, and the beam of light shot up at the window. At him. Instinctively, he pulled his hand up to shield his eyes. The light went out, and he saw the man race toward a car parked diagonally across the street. He had not noticed that car, his concentration so complete on his own and on the unknown man with the flashlight. Now he tried to focus on this automobile; there was a figure in the front seat. He could not distinguish anything but the outline of the head and shoulders.

The running man reached the door on the street side, pulled it open, and climbed in behind the wheel. The engine roared; the car shot forward, then skidded into a U-turn before it sped away.

Briefly, in the wash of light from the streetlamp, Noel saw the person in the seat next to the driver. For less than a second the face in the window was no more than twenty yards away, racing by.

It was Gretchen Beaumont. Her eyes stared ahead through the windshield, her head nodding as if she were talking rapidly.

Several lights went on in various houses across from the Beaumont residence. The roar of the engine and the screeching of the tires had been a sudden, unwelcome instrusion on the peaceful street in Portsea. Concerned faces appeared in the windows, peering outside.

Holcroft stepped back. He was naked, and he realized that being seen naked in Commander Beaumont's living room in the middle of the night while Commander Beaumont was away would not be to anyone's advantage, least of all his own.

Where had she gone? What was she doing? What was the sound he had heard?

There was no time to think about such things; he had to get away from the Beaumont house. He turned from the window and ran back to the bedroom, adjusting his eyes to the dim light, trying to find a light switch or a lamp. He remembered that in the frenzy of their lovemaking, Gretchen had swung her hand above his head into the shade of the bedside light, sending it to the floor. He knelt down, groping until he found it. It was on its

side, the bulb protected by the linen shade surrounding
it. He snapped it on. Light filled the room, its spill washing up from the floor. There were elongated shadows and
patches of darkness, but he could see his clothes draped
over an armchair, his socks and shorts by the bed.

He stood up and dressed as rapidly as he could. Where
was his jacket? He looked about, remembering vaguely
that Gretchen had slipped it off his arms and dropped it
near the door. Yes, there it was. He walked across the
room toward it, glancing briefly at his reflection in the
large mirror above the bureau.

He froze, his eyes riveted on a photograph in a silver
frame on the bureau. It was of a man in naval uniform.

The *face*. He had seen it before. Not long ago. Weeks
. . . days, perhaps. He was not sure where from, but he
was certain he knew that face. He walked to the bureau
and studied the photograph.

It was the eyebrows! They were odd, different; they
stood out as an entity in themselves . . . like an in-
congruous cornice above an undefined tapestry. They
were heavy, a thick profusion of black-and-white hair
interwoven . . . salt and pepper. Eyes that blinked open
suddenly, eyes that stared up at him. He remembered!

The plane to Rio de Janeiro! And something else.
The face from that moment on the plane to Brazil
prodded another memory—a memory of violence. But a
blurred, racing figure was all he recalled.

Noel turned the silver frame over and clawed at the
surface until he loosened the backing. He slid it out of
the groove and removed the photograph. He saw minute indentations on the glossy surface; he turned it over.
There was writing. He held it up to catch the light
and, for a moment, stopped breathing. The words were
German: NEUAUFBAU ODER TOD.

Like the face in the picture, he'd seen these words
before! But they were meaningless to him; German words
that meant nothing . . . yet he had seen them!

Bewildered, he folded the photograph and stuffed it
into his trouser pocket.

He opened a closet door, shoved the silver frame between folded clothes on the shelf, picked up his
jacket, and went into the living room. He knew he
should get out of the house as fast as he could, but his

curiosity about the man in the photograph consumed him. He had to know *something* about him.

There were two doors, in the near and far walls of the living room. One was open and led to the kitchen; the other was closed. He opened it and walked into the commander's study. He turned on a light; photographs of ships and men were everywhere, along with citations and military decorations. Commander Beaumont was a career officer of no mean standing. A bitter divorce followed by a questionable marriage might have created messy personal problems for the man, but the Royal Navy had obviously overlooked them. The latest citation was only six weeks old: for outstanding leadership in coastal patrols off the Balearic Islands during a week of gale-force seas.

A cursory look at the papers on the desk and in the drawers added nothing. Two bank books showed accounts in four figures, neither more than three thousand pounds; a letter from his former wife's solicitor demanded property in Scotland; there were assorted copies of ships' logs and sailing schedules.

Holcroft wanted to stay in that room a while longer, to look more thoroughly for clues to the strange man with the odd eyebrows, but he knew he dared not. He had already tested the situation beyond reason; he had to get out.

He left the house and looked across the way, up to the windows that only minutes ago had been filled with lights and curious faces. There were no lights now, no faces; sleep had returned to Portsea. He walked rapidly down the path and swung the gate open, annoyed that the hinges squeaked. He opened the door of the rented car, and quickly got behind the wheel. He turned the key in the ignition.

Nothing. He turned it again. And again and again. Nothing!

He released the hood and raced to the front of the car, not worried about the noise; worried about something far more serious. There was no reason for the rented car's battery to be worn down, but even if it were, there would still be a faint click in the ignition. The light of the street-lamp spread over the exposed engine, showing him what he was afraid he might find.

The wires were cut, severed at their source with a surgeon's precision. No amount of simple splicing would start the car; it would have to be towed away.

And whoever was responsible knew that an American would be without means of travel in an unfamiliar area in the middle of the night. If there were taxis in this outlying suburb, it was doubtful they'd be available at that hour; it was past three o'clock. Whoever immobilized the car wanted him to stay where he was; it had to follow that others would come after him. He had to run. As far and as fast as he could . . . reach the highway . . . hitch a ride north, out of the area.

He closed the hood. The sharp, metallic noise echoed throughout the street. He was grateful it had done so before.

He started up the block toward the traffic light; it was not operating now. Crossing the intersection, he began walking faster, then broke into a run. He tried to pace himself; there was a mile and a half before he reached the highway. He was sweating, and he could feel the knot in his stomach forming again.

He saw the lights before he heard the furious pitch of the engine. Up ahead, directly ahead on the straight road, the glare of headlights came out of the darkness, drawing closer so rapidly that the automobile had to be traveling at tremendous speed.

Noel saw an opening to his right, a space between a line of waist-high privet hedge, an entrance to another path to another doorway. He dived through it and rolled into the dirt beneath the shrubbery, wondering if he'd been seen. It was suddenly very important for him not to be involved with Gretchen Beaumont. She was a dismissable enigma, an unhappy, highly erotic . . . beautiful woman. But in herself a threat to Geneva, as was her brother.

The approaching car raced by. He had not been seen. Then the sound of the roaring motor was replaced by the screeching of tires. Holcroft crawled halfway through the break in the hedge, his face turned to his left, his eyes focused on the block behind him.

The car had stopped directly in front of the Beaumont house. Two men leaped from the car and raced up the path. Noel could hear the squeaking of the gate hinges. There was no point in remaining where he was; it was the moment to run. Now he heard the tapping of the door knocker a hundred yards away.

He moved to his right on his hands and knees, along the sidewalk, by a privet hedge, until he was in the shadows between the streetlamps. He got to his feet and ran.

He kept running straight ahead, up the dark, tree-lined street, block after block, corner after corner, hoping to God he would recognize the first turn to the highway when he came to it. He cursed cigarettes as his breath became shorter and turned into pain-filled gasps; sweat poured down his face and the pounding in his chest became intolerable. The rapid cracks of his own footsteps on the pavement frightened him. It was the sound of a man running in panic in the middle of the night, and that man in panic was himself.

Footsteps. *Racing* footsteps. They were his, but *more* than his! Behind him, steady, heavy, gaining on him. There was someone running after him! Someone running in silence, not calling his name, not demanding that he stop! . . . Or was his hearing playing tricks on him? The hammering in his chest vibrated throughout his entire body; were his footsteps echoing in his ears? He dared not turn, *could* not turn. He was going too fast—into light, into shadow.

He came to the end of yet another block, to another corner, and turned right, knowing it was not the first of the turns that would take him to the highway, but turning anyway. He had to know if there was someone behind him. He raced into the street.

The footsteps *were* there, the rhythm different, not his own, closer, ever closer, shortening the distance between them. He could stand it no longer; and he could run no faster. He twisted his waist, trying to look over his shoulder.

It was there; *he* was there! The figure of a man silhouetted in the light of a streetlamp on the corner. A stocky man, running in silence, shortening the gap, only yards away.

His legs aching, Noel hammered his feet on the surface in a final burst of speed. He turned again, his panic complete.

And his legs gave out, tangled in the chaos and the terror of the chase. He plunged headlong onto the street, his face scraping the asphalt, his extended hands icelike and stinging. He twisted over on his back, instinctively raising his feet to ward off his assailant—the silent, racing figure that shot out of the darkness and was suddenly over him.

Everything was a blur; only the thrashing outlines of arms and legs silhouetted in the darkness penetrated his sweat-filled eyes. And then he was pinned. An enormous weight was crushing his chest, a forearm—like a heavy iron bar—was across his throat, choking off all sound.

The last thing he saw was a hand raised high, a dark claw in the night sky, a curved hand that held an object in it. And then there was nothing. Only a huge chasm filled with wind. He was falling toward unseen depths in darkness.

He felt the cold first. It made him shiver. Then the dampness; it was everywhere. He opened his eyes to distorted images of grass and dirt. He was surrounded by wet grass and mounds of cold earth. He rolled over, grateful to see the night sky; it was lighter to his left, darker to his right.

His head ached; his face stung; his hands were in pain. Slowly he raised himself and looked around. He was in a field, a long flat stretch of ground that appeared to be a pasture. In the distance he could see the faint outlines of a wire fence—barbed wire strung between thick posts ten or twenty yards apart. It *was* a pasture.

He smelled cheap whiskey or rancid wine.

His clothes were drenched with it, his shirt sopping wet, sending the awful fumes into his nostrils. His *clothes* . . . his wallet, his money! He rose unsteadily to his feet and checked his pockets, both hands stinging as he plunged them into the moist cloth.

His wallet, his money clip with the bills in it, his watch—all were there. He had not been robbed, only beaten unconscious and taken away from the area where the Beaumonts lived. It was crazy!

He felt his head. A bump had formed, but the skin was not broken. He had been hit with some kind of padded blackjack or pipe. He took several awkward steps; he could move, and that was all that mattered. And he could see more clearly now; it would be morning soon.

Beyond the fence there was a slight rise in the

ground, forming a ridge that extended as far as he could see in both directions. Along the ridge he saw highway lights. He started across the field, toward the fence and the ridge and the highway, hoping to convince a driver to give him a ride. As he climbed over the fence, a thought suddenly occurred to him. He checked his pockets again.

The photograph was gone!

A milk truck stopped and he climbed in, watching the smile of the driver fade abruptly as the stench filled the cab. Noel tried to make light of it—a predicament brought on by an innocent American's having been taken in by some very sharp British sailors in Portsmouth—but the driver found nothing amusing. Holcroft got out at the first town.

It was an English village, the Tudor architecture of the square marred by a profusion of delivery trucks in front of a roadside stop.

"There's a telephone inside," said the milkman. "And a gents' room, too. A wash would do you no harm."

Noel walked into the sight and sounds of the early-morning truckers, the smell of hot coffee somehow reassuring. The world went on; deliveries were made and small comforts accepted without particular notice. He found the washroom, and did what he could to minimize the effects of the night. Then he sat in a booth next to the pay telephone on the wall and had black coffee, waiting for an angry trucker to conclude an argument with an angrier dispatcher on the other end of the line. When the call was finished, Noel got out of the booth and went to the phone. Gretchen Beaumont's telephone number in his hand. There was nothing to do but try to find out what happened, try to reason with her, if, indeed, she had returned.

He dialed.

"Beaumont residence." A male voice was on the line.

"Mrs. Beaumont, please."

"May I ask who's calling?"

"A friend of the commander. I heard Mrs. Beaumont was leaving today to join him. I'd like her to take a message to him."

"Who is this, please?"

Noel replaced the receiver. He did not know who had answered the phone; he knew only that he needed help. Professional help. It was possibly dangerous for Geneva to seek it, but it was necessary. He would be cautious—very cautious—and learn what he could.

He rummaged through his jacket pockets for the card given him by the MI-Five man at the Belgravia Arms. There was only a name—Harold Payton-Jones—and a telephone number. The clock on the wall read ten minutes to seven; Noel wondered if anyone would answer the phone. He placed the call to London.

"Yes?"

"This is Holcroft."

"Oh, yes. We wondered if you'd ring up."

Noel recognized the voice. It was the gray-haired intelligence agent from the hotel. "What are you talking about?" Noel said.

"You've had a difficult night," the voice said.

"You *expected* me to call! You were there. You were watching!"

Payton-Jones did not respond directly. "The rented car's at a garage in Aldershot. It should be repaired by noon. The name's easily remembered; it's Boot's. Boot's Garage, Aldershot. There'll be no charge, no bill, no receipt."

"Wait a minute! What the hell is this? You had me followed! You had no right to do that."

"I'd say it was a damned good thing we did."

"You were in that car at three o'clock this morning! You went into Beaumont's house!"

"I'm afraid we weren't and we didn't." The MI-Five man paused briefly. "And if you believe that, then you didn't get a very good look at them, did you?"

"No. Who were they?"

"I wish we knew. Our man got there closer to five."

"Who ran after me? Who bashed my head in and left me in that goddamned field?"

Again the agent paused. "We don't know anything about that. We knew only that you had left. In a hurry, obviously, your car immobilized."

"It was a setup! I was the pigeon!"

"Quite so. I'd advise you to be more cautious. It's both tasteless and dangerous to take advantage of the wife of a commander in the Royal Navy while her husband's at sea."

"Bullshit! The commander's no more at sea than I

am! He was on a plane to Rio less than two weeks ago.
I saw him! He's got something to do with the Von Tiebolts."

"Most assuredly," replied Payton-Jones. "He married
the oldest daughter. As to his being on an aircraft two
weeks ago, it's preposterous. He's been in the Mediterranean for the past three months."

"No! I *saw* him! Listen to me. There was a photograph in the bedroom. I took it. It was him! And
something else. There was writing on the back. In German."

"What did it say?"

"I don't know. I don't speak German. But it's goddamned unusual, don't you think?" Holcroft stopped. He
had not meant to go this far. In his anger, he had lost
his control! *Goddamn it!*

"What's unusual?" asked the agent. "German is Mrs.
Beaumont's native tongue; the family's spoken it for years.
An endearing phrase, words of devotion to or from her
new husband? Not unusual at all."

"I guess you're right," said Noel, backing off. Then he
realized he had retreated too quickly. The MI-Five man
was suspicious; Noel could sense it in his next words.

"On second thought, perhaps you should bring the
photograph to us."

"I can't. I don't have it."

"I thought you said you took it."

"I don't have it now. I . . . I just don't have it."

"Where are you, Holcroft? I think you should drop in
and see us."

Without consciously making the decision, Noel
pressed down the lever, severing the connection. The act
preceded the thought, but once it was done, he understood clearly why he did it. He could not ally himself
with MI Five, he could not solidify any relationship whatsoever. On the contrary, he had to get as far away from
British Intelligence as was possible. There could be no
association at *all*. MI Five had *followed* him. After they
had told him they would leave him alone, they had gone
back on their word.

The survivors of Wolfsschanze had spelled it out:
*There are those who may learn of the work in Geneva . . .
who will try to stop you, deceive you . . . kill you.*

Holcroft doubted that the British would kill him, but

they *were* trying to stop him. If they succeeded, it was as good as killing him. The men of Wolfsschanze did not hesitate. *Peter Baldwin, Esq. Ernst Manfredi. Jack.* All dead.

The men of Wolfsschanze would kill him if he failed. And that was the terrible irony. He did not *want* to fail. Why couldn't they understand that? Perhaps more than the survivors of Wolfsschanze, he wanted to see Heinrich Clausen's dream realized.

He thought of Gretchen Beaumont, follower of instincts, opportunities, and men. And of her brother, the arrogant, brilliant multilingual newspaperman who was suspected of being an assassin. Neither would be remotely acceptable to Geneva.

There was one child left. Helden von Tiebolt—now Helden Tennyson—currently living in Paris. Address unknown. But he had a name. "Gallimard."

Paris.

He had to get to Paris. He had to elude MI Five.

13

There was a man in London, a stage designer, who'd had a brief vogue as a decorator among the wealthy on both sides of the Atlantic. Noel suspected that Willie Ellis was more often hired for his outrageous personality and his talents as a raconteur than for any intrinsic abilities as an interior decorator. He had worked with Willie on four occasions, vowing each time never to do it again but knowing each time that he probably would. For the truth was that Noel liked Willie immensely. The mad Englishman was not all artifice and elegance. Underneath, in quiet moments, there was a thinking, talented man of the theater who knew more about the history of design than anyone Holcroft had ever met. He could be fascinating.

When he was not outrageous.

They had kept in touch over the years, and whenever Noel was in London, there was always time for Willie. He had thought there would be no time this trip, but that was changed now. He needed Willie. He got the number from London information and dialed.

"Noel, my friend, you're out of your mind! No one's up but those stinking birds and street cleaners."

"I'm in trouble, Willie. I need help."

Ellis knew the small village where Holcroft was calling from and promised to be there as soon as he could, which he estimated would be something close to an hour. He arrived thirty minutes late, cursing the idiots on the road. Noel climbed into the car, taking Willie's outstretched hand as well as his characteristic abuse.

"You're an absolute mess and you smell like a barmaid's armpit. Keep the window open and tell me what the hell happened."

Holcroft kept the explanation simple, giving no names

137

and obscuring the facts. "I have to get to Paris, and there are people who want to stop me. I can't tell you much more than that except to say that I haven't done anything wrong, anything illegal."

"The first is always relative, isn't it? And the second is generally subject to interpretation and a good barrister. Shall I assume a lovely girl and an irate husband?"

"That's fine."

"That keeps me clean. What stops you from going to the airport and taking the next plane to Paris?"

"My clothes, briefcase, and passport are at my hotel in London. If I go there to get them, the people who want to stop me will find me."

"From the looks of you, they're quite serious, aren't they?"

"Yes. That's about it, Willie."

"The solution's obvious," said Ellis. "I'll get your things and check you out. You're a wayward colonial I found in a Soho gutter. Who's to argue with my preferences?"

"There may be a problem with the front desk."

"I can't imagine why. My money's coin of the realm, and you'll give me a note; they can match signatures. We're nowhere near as paranoid as our cousins across the sea."

"I hope you're right, but I've got an idea the clerks have been reached by the people who want to find me. They may insist on knowing where I am before they let you have my things."

"Then I'll tell them," said Willie, smiling. "I'll leave them a forwarding address and a telephone number where your presence can be confirmed."

"What?"

"Leave it to me. By the way, there's some cologne in the glove compartment. For Christ's sake, use it."

Ellis made arrangements for the whiskey-soaked clothes to be picked up by the cleaners and returned by midafternoon, then left the Chelsea flat for the Belgravia Arms.

Holcroft showered, shaved, put the soiled clothes in a hamper outside the door, and called the car-rental agency. He reasoned that if he went for the car in Aldershot, MI

Five would be there. And when he drove away, the British would not be far behind.

The rental agency was not amused, but Holcroft gave them no choice. If they wanted the automobile back, they would have to pick it up themselves. Noel was sorry, but there was an emergency; the bill could be sent to his office in New York.

He had to get out of England with as little notice as possible. Undoubtedly, MI Five would have the airports and the Channel boats watched. Perhaps the solution was to be found in a last-minute ticket on a crowded plane to Paris. With any luck, he'd reach Orly Airport before MI Five knew he had left England. The shuttles to Paris were frequent, the customs procedures lax. Or he could buy two tickets—one to Amsterdam, one to Paris—go through the KLM gates, then on some pretext come back outside and rush to the Paris departure area, where Willie held his luggage.

What was he *thinking* of? Ruses, evasions, deceptions. He was a criminal without a crime, a man who could not tell the truth, because in that truth was the destruction of so much.

He began to perspire again, and the pain returned to his stomach. He felt weak and disoriented. He lay down on Willie's couch in Willie's bathrobe and closed his eyes. The image of melting flesh came back into focus. The face emerged; he heard the cry clearly, and he fell asleep, the plaintive sound in his ears.

He woke suddenly, aware that someone was above him, looking down at him. Alarmed, he whipped over on his back, then sighed in relief at the sight of Willie standing by the couch.

"You've had some rest, and it shows. You look better, and God knows you smell better."

"Did you get my things?"

"Yes, and you were right. They were anxious to know where you were. When I paid the bill, the manager came out and behaved like a rep-company version of Scotland Yard. He's mollified, if confused. He's also got a telephone number where you're currently in residence."

"In residence?"

"Yes. I'm afraid your reputation hasn't been vastly improved, unless you've had a change of heart. The number's for a hospital in Knightsbridge that doesn't get a *P* from National Health. It specializes in venereal diseases. I know a doctor there quite well."

"You're too much," said Noel, standing. "Where are my things?"

"In the guest room. I thought you'd want to change."

"Thanks." Holcroft started toward the door.

"Do you know a man named Buonoventura?" Ellis asked.

Noel stopped. He had sent Sam a three-word cablegram from the airport in Lisbon: BELGRAVIA ARMS LONDON. "Yes. Did he call?"

"Several times. Quite frantically, I gather. The hotel switchboard said the call came from Curaçao."

"I know the number," said Holcroft. "I have to get in touch with him. I'll put the call on my credit card."

It was five minutes before he heard Sam's rasping voice and less than five seconds before he realized it was not fair to ask the construction engineer to lie any longer.

"Miles isn't fooling around anymore, Noley. He told me he's getting a court order for your return to New York. He's going to serve it on the owners down here, figuring they're American. He knows they can't force you to go back, but he says they'll know you're wanted. It's a little rough, Noley, because you're not on any payroll."

"Did he say why?"

"Only that he thinks you have information they need."

If he could get to Paris, Noel thought, he would want Buonoventura to be able to reach him, but he did not want to burden him with an address. "Listen, Sam. I'm leaving for Paris later today. There's an American Express office on the Champs-Elysées, near the avenue George Cinq. If anything comes up, cable me there."

"What'll I tell Miles if he calls again? I don't want to get my ass burned."

"Say you reached me and told me he was trying to find me. Tell him I said I'd get in touch with him as soon as I could. That's all you know." Noel paused. "Also tell him I had to get to Europe. Don't volunteer, but if he presses, let him know about the American Express office. I can phone for messages."

"There's something else," said Sam awkwardly.

"Your mother called, too. I felt like a goddamned idiot lying to her; you shouldn't lie to your mother, Noley."

Holcroft smiled. A lifetime of deviousness had not taken the basic Italian out of Sam. "When did she call?"

"Night before last. She sounds like a real lady. I told her I expected to hear from you yesterday; that's when I started phoning."

"I'll call her when I get to Paris," said Noel. "Anything else?"

"Isn't that enough?"

"Plenty. I'll be in touch in a few days, but you know where to cable me."

"Yeah, but if your mother calls, I'm going to let her know, too."

"No sweat. And thanks, Sam. I owe you."

He hung up, noticing that Willie Ellis had gone into the kitchen, where he had turned on the radio. One of Willie's attributes was that he was a gentleman. Noel sat by the phone for several moments, trying to figure things out. His mother's call was not surprising. He had not spoken with her since that Sunday morning in Bedford Hills nearly two weeks ago.

Miles was something else again. Holcroft did not think of the detective as a person; he had no face or voice. But Miles had arrived at certain conclusions; he was certain of that. And those conclusions tied him to three deaths connected with British Airways Flight 591 from London to New York. Miles was not letting go; if he persisted, he could create a problem Noel was not sure he could handle. The detective could ask for international police cooperation. And if he did, attention would be drawn to the activities of a United States citizen who had walked away from a homicide investigation.

Geneva would not tolerate that attention; the covenant would be destroyed. Miles had to be contained. But *how?*

His unfamiliar forest was lined with traps; every protective instinct he possessed told him to turn back. Geneva needed a man infinitely more cunning and experienced than he. Yet he could not turn back. The survivors of Wolfsschanze would not permit it. And deep in his own consciousness he knew he did not want to. There was the face that came into focus in the darkness. He had to find

his father and, in the finding, show the world a man in
agony who was brave enough and perceptive enough to
know that amends must be made. And brilliant enough
to make that credo live.

Noel walked to the kitchen door. Ellis was at the sink,
washing teacups.

"I'll pick up my clothes in a couple of weeks, Willie.
Let's go to the airport."

Ellis turned, concern in his eyes. "I can save you
time," he said, reaching for a china mug on a shelf. "You'll
need some French money until you can convert. I keep a
jarful for my bimonthly travels to the fleshpots. Take what
you need."

"Thanks." Holcroft took the mug, looking at Willie's
exposed arms beneath rolled-up sleeves. They were as
powerful and muscular as any two arms he'd ever seen.
It struck Noel that Willie could break a man in half.

The madness started at Heathrow and gathered momentum at Orly.

In London he bought a ticket on KLM to Amsterdam, on the theory that the story he gave MI Five
had been checked out and considered plausible. He suspected it had been both, for he saw a bewildered man in a
raincoat watch him in astonishment as he raced out of
the KLM departure gates back to Air France. There
Willie was waiting for him with a ticket for a crowded
plane to Paris.

Immigration procedure at Orly was cursory, but the
lines were long. As he waited, Noel had time to study
the milling crowds in the customs area and beyond the
swinging doors that led to the terminal proper. Beyond
those doors he could see two men; there was something
about them that caught his attention. Perhaps it was their
somber faces, joyless expressions that did not belong in a
place where people greeted one another. They were talking quietly, their heads immobile, as they watched the passengers walk out of customs. One held a piece of paper
in his hand; it was small, shiny. A photograph? Yes. A
photograph of *him*.

These were not the men of Wolfsschanze. The men
of Wolfsschanze knew him by sight; and the men of
Wolfsschanze were never seen. MI Five had reached its
agents in Paris. They were waiting for him.

"Monsieur." The customs clerk stamped Holcroft's passport routinely. Noel picked up his luggage and started toward the exit, feeling the panic of a man about to walk into an unavoidable trap.

As the doors parted, he saw the two men turn away to avoid being noticed. They were not going to approach him; they were going to . . . *follow* him.

The realization gave painful birth to an unclear strategy. Painful because it was so alien to him, unclear because he was not sure of the procedures. He only knew that he had to go from point *A* to point *B* and back again to *A*, losing his pursuers somewhere in the vicinity of *B*.

Up ahead in the crowded terminal he saw the sign: LIGNES AÉRIENNES INTÉRIEURES.

France's domestic airline shuttled about the country with splendid irregularity. The cities were listed in three columns: ROUEN, LE HAVRE, CAEN . . . ORLÉANS, LE MANS, TOURS . . . DIJON, LYON, MARSEILLES.

Noel walked rapidly past the two men, as if oblivious of all but his own concerns. He hurried to the Intérieures counter. There were four people ahead of him.

His turn came. He inquired about flights south. To the Mediterranean. To Marseilles. He wanted a choice of several departure times.

There was a flight that landed at five cities in a southwest arc from Orly to the Mediterranean, the clerk told him. The stops were Le Mans, Nantes, Bordeaux, Toulouse, and Marseilles.

Le Mans. The flight time to Le Mans was forty minutes. Estimated driving time, three, three and a half hours. It was now twenty minutes to four.

"I'll take that one," Noel said. "It gets me to Marseilles at just the right time."

"Pardon, monsieur, but there are more direct flights."

"I'm being met at the airport. No point in being early."

"As you wish, monsieur. I will see what is available. The flight leaves in twelve minutes."

Five minutes later, Holcroft stood by the departure gate, the *Herald Tribune* opened in front of him. He looked over the top of the page. One of the two somber-faced Britishers was talking with the young lady who had sold him his ticket.

Fifteen minutes later the plane was airborne. Twice

Noel wandered up the aisle to the lavatory, looking at the passengers in the cabin. Neither of the two men was on the aircraft; no one else seemed remotely interested in him.

At Le Mans he waited until the departing passengers got off the plane. He counted; there were seven of them. Their replacements began coming on board.

He grabbed his suitcase from the luggage rack, walked quickly to the exit door and down the metal steps to the ground. He went inside the terminal and stood by the window.

No one came out of the plane; no one was following him.

His watch read seventeen minutes to five. He wondered if there was still time to reach Helden von Tiebolt. Again he had the essence of what he needed—a name and a place of work. He walked to the nearest telephone, thankful for Willie's jar of franc notes and coins.

In his elementary French, he spoke to the operator. *"S'il vous plaît, le numéro de Gallimard à Paris . . ."*

She was there. Mademoiselle Tennyson did not have a telephone at her desk, but if the caller would hold on, someone would get her on the line. The woman at the Gallimard switchboard spoke better English than most Texans.

Helden von Tiebolt's voice had that same odd mixture of Portuguese and German as her sister's but it was not nearly so pronounced. Too, there was a trace of the echo Noel remembered so vividly in Gretchen's speech, but not the halting, once-removed quality. Helden von Tiebolt—Mademoiselle Tennyson—knew what she wanted to say and said it.

"Why should I meet with you? I don't know you, Mr. Holcroft."

"It's urgent. Please, believe me."

"There's been an excess of urgencies in my life. I'm rather tired of them."

"There's been nothing like this."

"How did you find me?"

"People . . . people you don't know, in England, told me where you worked. But they said you didn't live at the address listed with your employer, so I had to call you here."

"They were so interested they inquired where I lived?"

"Yes. It's part of what I have to tell you."

"Why were they interested in me?"

"I'll tell you when I see you. I *have* to tell you."

"Tell me now."

"Not on the phone."

There was a pause. When the girl spoke, her words were clipped, precise . . . afraid. "Why exactly do you wish to see me? What can there be that's so urgent between us?"

"It concerns your family. *Both* our families. I've seen your sister. I've tried to locate your brother—"

"I've spoken to neither in over a year," interrupted Helden Tennyson. "I can't help you."

"What we have to talk about goes back over *thirty* years."

"No!"

"There's money involved. A great deal of money."

"I live adequately. My needs are—"

"Not only for *you*," pressed Noel, cutting her off. "For thousands. Everywhere."

Again there was the pause. When she spoke, she spoke softly. "Does this concern events . . . people going back to the war?"

"Yes." Was he getting through to her at last?

"We'll meet," said Helden.

"Can we arrange it so we . . . we—" He was not sure how to phrase it without frightening her.

"So we won't be seen by those watching for us? Yes."

"How?"

"I've had experience. Do exactly as I say. Where are you?"

"At the Le Mans airport. I'll rent a car and drive up to Paris. It'll take me two or three hours."

"Leave the car in a garage and take a taxi to Montmartre. To the Sacré-Coeur cathedral. Go inside to the far end of the church, to the chapel of Louis the Ninth. Light a candle and place it first in one holder, then change your mind and place it in another. You'll be met by a man who will take you outside, up to the square, to a table at one of the street cafés. You'll be given instructions."

"We don't have to be *that* elaborate. Can't we just meet at a bar? Or a restaurant?"

"It's not for your protection, Mr. Holcroft, but mine. If you're not who you imply you are, if you're not *alone*, I won't see you. I'll leave Paris tonight and you'll never find me."

14

The granite, medieval splendor of Sacré-Coeur rose in the night sky like a haunting song of stone. Beyond the enormous bronze doors, an infinite cavern was shrouded in semidarkness, flickering candles playing a symphony of shadows on the walls.

From near the altar, he could hear the strains of a *Te Deum Laudamus*. A visiting choir of monks stood in isolated solemnity, singing quietly.

Noel entered the dimly lit circle beyond the apse that housed the chapels of the kings. He adjusted his eyes to the dancing shadows and walked along the balustrades that flanked the entrances to the small enclosures. The rows of scattered candles provided just enough light for him to read the inscription: LOUIS IX. Louis the Pious, Louis the Just, Son of Aquitaine, Ruler of France, Arbiter of Christendom.

Pious. . . . Just. . . . Arbiter.

Was Helden von Tiebolt trying to tell him something?

He inserted a coin in the prayer box, removed a thin tapered candle from its receptacle, and held it to the flame of another nearby. Following instructions, he placed it in a holder, then seconds later removed it and inserted it in another several rows away.

A hand touched his arm, fingers gripped his elbow, and a voice whispered into his ear from the shadows behind him.

"Turn around slowly, monsieur. Keep your hands at your side."

Holcroft did as he was told. The man stood not much over five feet six or seven, with a high forehead and thinning dark hair. He was in his early thirties, Noel guessed, and pleasant-looking, the face pale, even soft. If there was anything particularly noticeable about him, it was his clothes; the dim light could not conceal the fact that they were expensive.

An aura of elegance emanated from the man, heightened by the mild fragrance of cologne. But he acted neither elegantly nor softly. Before Noel knew what was happening, the man's hands were jabbed into both sides of his chest, and strong fingers spanned the cloth in rapid movements, descending to his belt and the pockets of his trousers.

Holcroft jerked backwards.

"I said, be still!" the man whispered.

In the candlelight, by the chapel of Louis IX, in the cathedral of Sacré-Coeur, on the top of Montmartre, Noel was checked for a weapon.

"Follow me," said the man. "I will walk up the street to the square; stay quite far behind. I will join two friends at an outside table at one of the street cafés, probably Bohème. Walk around the square; take your time; look at the artists' work; do not hurry. Then come to the table and sit with us. Greet us as if we are familiar *faces*, not necessarily *friends*. Do you understand?"

"I understand."

If this was the way to reach Helden von Tiebolt, so be it. Noel stayed a discreet distance behind the man, the fashionably cut overcoat not hard to follow among the less elegant clothes of the tourists.

They reached the crowded square. The man stood for a moment, lighting a cigarette, then proceeded across the street to a table beyond the sidewalk, behind a planter filled with shrubbery. As he had said, there were two people at the table. One was a man dressed in a ragged field jacket, the other a woman in a black raincoat, a white scarf around her neck. The scarf contrasted with her very dark, straight hair, as dark as the black raincoat. She wore tortoise-shell glasses, framed intrusions on a pale face with no discernible makeup. Noel wondered if the plain-looking woman was Helden von Tiebolt. If she was, there was little resemblance to her sister.

He started his stroll around the square, pretending interest in the artworks on display everywhere. There were canvases with bold dashes of color and heavy, un-thought-out lines, and bulging wide eyes of charcoal-rendered children . . . cuteness and swiftness and artificiality. There was little of merit; nor was there meant to be. This was the tourist marketplace, the bazaar where the bizarre was for sale.

Nothing had changed in the Montmartre, thought Holcroft, as he threaded his way around the last turn toward the café.

He walked by the planter and nodded at the two men and the woman seated at the table beyond. They nodded back; he proceeded to the entrance, walked in, and returned to the "familiar faces, not necessarily friends." He sat down in the empty chair; it was beside the dark-haired woman with the tortoise-shell glasses.

"I'm Noel Holcroft," he said to no one in particular.

"We know," answered the man in the field jacket, his eyes on the crowds in the square.

Noel turned to the woman. "Are you Helden von—? Excuse me, Helen Tennyson?"

"No, I've never met her," replied the dark-haired woman, looking intently at the man in the field jacket. "But I will take you to her."

The man in the expensive overcoat turned to Holcroft. "You alone?"

"Of course. Can we get started? Helden . . . Tennyson . . . said I'd be given instructions. I'd like to see her, talk for a while, and then find a hotel. I haven't had much sleep during the past few days." He started to get up from the table.

"Sit down!" The woman spoke sharply.

He sat, more out of curiosity than in response to command. And then he had the sudden feeling that these three people were not testing him; they were frightened. The elegantly dressed man was biting the knuckle of his index finger, staring at something in the middle of the square. His companion in the field jacket had his hand on his friend's arm, his gaze leveled in the identical direction. They were looking at someone, someone who disturbed them profoundly.

Holcroft tried to follow their line of sight, tried to peer between the crisscrossing figures that filled the street in front of the café. He stopped breathing. Across the street were the two men he thought he had eluded at Le Mans. It didn't make sense! No one had followed him off the plane.

"It's *them*," he said.

The elegantly dressed man turned his head swiftly; the man in the field jacket was slower, his expression disbelieving; the dark-haired woman studied him closely.

"Who?" she asked.

"Those two men over there, near the entrance to the restaurant. One's in a light topcoat, the other's carrying a raincoat over his arm."

"Who are they?"

"They were at Orly this afternoon; they were waiting for me. I flew to Le Mans to get away from them. I'm almost sure they're British agents. But how did they know I was *here*? They weren't on the plane. No one followed me; I'd *swear* to it!"

The three exchanged glances; they believed him, and Holcroft knew why. He had picked out the two Englishmen himself, volunteered the information before being confronted with it.

"If they're British, what do they want with you?" asked the man in the field jacket.

"That's between Helden von Tiebolt and myself."

"But you think they *are* British?" pressed the man in the jacket.

"Yes."

"I hope you're right."

The man in the overcoat leaned forward. "What do you mean you flew to Le Mans? What happened?"

"I thought I could throw them off. I was convinced I *had*. I bought a ticket to Marseilles. I made it clear to the girl at the counter that I had to get to Marseilles, and then picked a flight that had stops. The first was Le Mans, and I got off. I saw them *questioning* her. I never said anything *about* Le Mans!"

"Don't excite yourself," said the man in the field jacket. "It only draws attention."

"If you think they haven't spotted me, you're crazy! But how did they *do* it?"

"It's not difficult," said the woman.

"You rented a car?" asked the elegantly dressed man.

"Of course. I had to drive back to Paris."

"At the airport?"

"Naturally."

"And naturally, you asked for a map. Or at least directions, no doubt mentioning Paris. I mean, you were not driving to Marseilles."

"Certainly, but lots of people do that."

"Not so many, not at an airport that has flights to Paris. And none with your name. I can't believe you have false papers."

Holcroft was beginning to understand. "They checked," he said in disgust.

"One person on a telephone for but a few minutes," said the man in the field jacket. "Less, if you were reported having left the plane at Le Mans."

"The French would not miss the opportunity of selling an empty seat," added the man in the elegant coat. "Do you see now? There are not so many places that rent cars at airports. The make, the color, the license, would be given. The rest is simple."

"Why simple? In all Paris, to find *one car?*"

"Not *in* Paris, monsieur. On the road *to* Paris. There is but one main highway; it is the most likely to be used by a foreigner. You were picked up outside of Paris."

Noel's astonishment was joined by a sense of depression. His ineptness was too apparent. "I'm sorry. I'm really sorry."

"You did nothing intentionally," said the elegant man, his concentration back on the Englishmen, who were now seated in the first booth of the restaurant in the middle of the square. He touched the arm of the man in the field jacket. "They've sat down."

"I see."

"What are we going to do?" asked Holcroft.

"It's being done," answered the dark-haired woman. "Do exactly what we tell you to do."

"*Now,*" said the man in the expensive coat.

"Get up!" ordered the woman. "Walk with me out into the street and turn right. Quickly!" Bewildered, Holcroft rose from his chair and left the café, the woman's fingers clasped around his arm. They stepped off the curb.

"To the right!" she repeated.

He turned to his right.

"Faster!" she said.

He heard a crash of glass behind them, then angry shouts. He turned and looked back. The two Englishmen had left the booth, colliding with a waiter. All three were covered with wine.

"Turn right again!" commanded the woman. "Into the doorway!"

He did as he was told, shouldering his way past a crowd of people in the entrance of yet another café. Once inside, the woman stopped him; he whirled around instinctively and watched the scene in the square.

The Englishmen were trying to disengage themselves from the furious waiter. The man in the topcoat was throwing money on the table. His companion had made better progress; he was under the trellis, looking frantically to his left—in the direction Holcroft and the girl had taken.

Noel heard shouts; he stared in disbelief at the source. Not twenty feet from where the agents stood was a dark-haired woman in a shiny black raincoat, wearing thick tortoise-shell glasses and a white scarf around her neck. She stood yelling at someone loudly enough to draw the attention of everyone around her.

Including the Englishmen.

She stopped abruptly and began running up the crowded street, toward the south end of Montmartre. The British agents took up the chase. Their progress was slowed unexpectedly by a number of young people in jeans and jackets who seemed to be purposely blocking the Englishmen. Furious shouts erupted; then he could hear the shrill whistles of the *gendarmes*.

Montmartre became pandemonium.

"Come! *Now!*" The dark-haired woman—the one at his side—grabbed Noel's arm again, and again propelled him into the street. "Turn left!" she ordered, pushing him through the crowds. "Back where we were."

They approached the table behind the planter box. Only the man in the expensive overcoat remained; he stood up as they drew near.

"There may be others," he said. "We don't know. Hurry!"

Holcroft and the woman continued running. They reached a side street no wider than a large alley; it was lined with small shops on both sides, the dimly lit storefronts providing the only light in the block.

"This way!" said the woman, now holding Noel's hand, running beside him. "The car is on the right. The first one by the corner!"

It was a Citroën; it looked powerful but undistinguished. There were layers of dirt on the body, the wheels were filthy and caked with mud. Even the windows had a film of dust on them.

"Get in the front! Drive," commanded the woman, handing him a key. "I'll stay in the back seat."

Holcroft climbed in, trying to orient himself. He started the engine. The vibrations caused the chassis to tremble. It had an outsized motor, designed for a heavier car, guaranteeing enormous speed for a lighter one.

"Go straight toward the bottom of the hill!" said the woman behind him. "I'll tell you where to turn."

The next forty-five minutes were blurred into a series of plunges and sudden turns. The woman issued directions at the last second, forcing Noel to turn the wheel violently in order to obey. They sped into a highway north of Paris from a twisting entrance road that caused the Citroën to lurch sideways, careening off the mound of grass that was the center island. Holcroft held the wheel with all his strength, first straightening the car and then weaving between two nearly parallel cars ahead.

"Faster!" screamed the dark-haired woman in the back seat. "Can't you go *faster?*"

"Jesus! We're over ninety-five!"

"Keep looking in your mirrors! I'll watch the side roads! And go *faster!*"

They drove for ten minutes in silence, the wind and the steady high-pitched hum of the tires maddening. It was *all* maddening, thought Noel as he shifted his eyes from the windshield to the rearview mirror to the side-view mirror, which was caked with dirt. What were they *doing?* They were out of Paris; whom were they running from *now?* There was no time to think; the woman was screaming again.

"The next exit; that's the one!"

He barely had time to brake and turn the car into the exit. He screeched to a halt at the stop sign.

"Keep going! To the left!"

The split seconds of immobility were the only pause in the madness. It began again: the accelerated speed over the dark country roads, the sudden turns, the commands barked harshly in his ear.

The moonlight that had washed over the splendor

of Sacré-Coeur now revealed stretches of rock-hewn farmland. Barns and silos loomed in irregular silhouettes; small houses with thatched roofs appeared and disappeared.

"There's the road!" yelled the woman.

It was a dirt road angling off the tarred surface over which they traveled; the trees would have concealed it if one did not know where or when to look. Noel slowed the Citroën and turned in. The entire car shook, but the voice behind him did not permit more cautious driving.

"Hurry! We have to get over the hill so our lights won't be seen!"

The hill was steep, the road too narrow for more than one vehicle. Holcroft pressed the accelerator; the Citroën lurched up the primitive road. They reached the crest of the hill, Noel gripping the steering wheel as if it were uncontrollable. The descent was rapid; the road curved to the left and flattened out. They were level again.

"No more than a quarter of a mile now," said the woman.

Holcroft was exhausted; the palms of his hands were soaked. He and the woman were in the loneliest, darkest place he could imagine. In a dense forest, on a road unlisted on any map.

Then he saw it. A small thatched house on a flat plot of ground dug out of the forest. There was a dim light on inside.

"Stop here," was the command, but it was not rendered in the harsh voice that had hammered into his ears for nearly an hour.

Noel stopped the car directly in front of the path that led to the house. He took several deep breaths and wiped the sweat from his face, closing his eyes briefly, wishing the pain would leave his head.

"Please turn around, Mr. Holcroft," said the woman, no stridency in her tone.

He did so. And he stared through the shadows at the woman in the back seat. Gone were the shining black hair and the thick-rimmed glasses. The white scarf was still there, but now it was partially covered by long blond hair that cascaded over her shoulders, framing a face—a very lovely face—he had seen before. Not *this* face, but one like it; delicate features modeled lovingly in clay before a chisel was put to stone. This face was not cold and the eyes were not distant. There was vulnerability and in-volvement. She spoke quietly, returning his stare through the shadows.

"I am Helden von Tiebolt, and I have a gun in my hand. Now, what do you want of me?"

15

He looked down and saw a tiny reflection of light off the barrel of the automatic. The gun was pointed at his head, the bore only inches away, her fingers curved around the trigger.

"The first thing I want," he said, "is for you to put that thing away."

"I'm afraid I can't do that."

"You're the last person on earth I'd want to see hurt. You've got nothing to fear from me."

"Your words are reassuring, but I've heard such words before. They were not always true."

"Mine are." He looked into her eyes through the dim light, holding his gaze steady. The tenseness of her expression diminished. "Where are we?" Noel asked. "Was all that craziness necessary? The riot in Montmartre, racing around the country like maniacs. What are you running from?"

"I might ask the same question of you. You're running, too. You flew to Le Mans."

"I wanted to avoid some people. But I'm not afraid of them."

"I also avoid people, and I *am* afraid of them."

"Who?" The specter of the Tinamou intruded on Noel's thoughts; he tried to push it away.

"You may or may not be told, depending upon what you have to say to me."

"Fair enough. Right now you're the most important person in my life. That may change when I meet your brother, but right now, it's you."

"I can't imagine why. We've never met. You said you wanted to see me over matters that could be traced back to the war."

" 'Traced back to your father' would be more specific."

"I never knew my father."

"Both our fathers. Neither of us knew them."

He told her what he had told her sister, but he did not mention the men of Wolfsschanze; she was frightened enough. And he heard his words again, as if echoes from last night, in Portsea. It *was* only last night, and the woman he spoke to now was like the woman then—but only in appearance. Gretchen Beaumont had listened in silence; Helden did not. She interrupted him quietly, continuously, asking questions he should have asked himself.

"Did this Manfredi show you proof of his identity?"

"He didn't have to; he had the papers from the bank. They were legitimate."

"What are the names of the directors?"

"The directors?"

"Of the Grande Banque de Genève. The overseers of this extraordinary document."

"I don't know."

"You should be told."

"I'll ask."

"Who will handle the legal aspects of this agency in Zurich?"

"The bank's attorneys, I imagine."

"You imagine?"

"Is it important?"

"It's six months of your life. I'd think it would be."

"*Our* lives."

"We'll see. I'm not the oldest child of Wilhelm von Tiebolt."

"I told you when I called you from Le Mans," said Holcroft, "that I'd met your sister."

"And?" asked Helden.

"I think you know. She's not capable. The directors in Geneva won't accept her."

"There's my brother, Johann. He's next in age."

"I know that. I want to talk about him."

"Not now. Later."

"What do you mean?"

"I mentioned on the phone that there had been an excess of urgencies in my life. There has also been an excess of lies. I'm an expert in that area; I know a liar when I hear his words. You don't lie."

"Thank you for that." Noel was relieved; they had a basis for *talking*. It was his first concrete step. In a way, in spite of everything, he felt exhilarated. She lowered the gun to her lap.

"Now we must go inside. There's a man who wants to speak with you."

Holcroft's exhilaration crashed with her words. He could not share Geneva with anyone but a member of the Von Tiebolt family. "No," he said, shaking his head. "I'm not talking with anyone. What I've discussed with you is between us. No one else."

"Give him a chance. He must know that you don't mean to hurt me. Or hurt others. He must be convinced that you are not part of something else."

"Part of what?"

"He'll explain."

"He'll ask questions."

"Say only what you wish to say."

"No! You don't understand. I can't say *anything* about Geneva, and neither can you. I've tried to explain—"

He stopped. Helden raised the automatic. "The gun is still in my hand. Get out of the car."

He preceded her up the short path to the door of the house. Except for the dim light in the windows, it was dark. The surrounding trees filtered the moonlight to such a degree that only muted rays came through the branches, so weak they seemed to disintegrate in the air.

Noel felt her hand reaching around his waist, the barrel of the gun in the small of his back.

"Here's a key. Open the door. It's difficult for him to move around."

Inside, the small room was like any other one might imagine in such a house deep in the French countryside, with one exception: Two walls were lined with books. Everything else was simple to the point of primitiveness— sturdy furniture of no discernible design, a heavy old-fashioned desk, several unlit lamps with plain shades, a wood floor, and thick, plastered walls. The books were somehow out of place.

In the far corner of the room sat an emaciated man in a wheelchair. He was between a floor lamp and a short table, the light over his left shoulder, a book in his lap. His hair was white and thin, combed carefully over his head. Holcroft guessed he was well into his seventies. In spite of his gaunt appearance, the face was strong, the eyes behind the steel-rimmed spectacles alert. He was dressed in a cardigan sweater buttoned to the throat, and a pair of corduroy trousers.

"Good evening, Herr Oberst," said Helden. "I hope we didn't keep you waiting too long."

"Good evening, Helden," replied the old man, putting the book to one side. "You're here and obviously safe. That's all that matters."

Noel watched, mesmerized, as the gaunt figure put his hands on the arms of the wheelchair and rose slowly. He was extremely tall, over six feet two or three. He continued speaking in an accent obviously German and just as obviously aristocratic.

"You're the young man who telephoned Miss Tennyson," he said, not asking a question. "I'm known simply as *Oberst*—colonel—which was not my rank, but I'm afraid it will have to do."

"This is Noel Holcroft. He is an American, and he is the man." Helden took a step to her left, revealing the gun in her hand. "He is here against his will. He did not want to talk with you."

"How do you do, Mr. Holcroft?" The colonel nodded, offering no hand. "May I ask why you're reluctant to speak to an old man?"

"I don't know who you are," replied Noel as calmly as he could. "Further, the matters I've discussed with Miss ... Tennyson ... are confidential."

"Does she agree?"

"Ask her." Holcroft held his breath. In seconds he would know how convincing he had been.

"They are," said Helden, "if they are true. I *think* they are true."

"I see. But you must be convinced, and I am the devil's advocate without a brief." The old man lowered himself back into the wheelchair.

"What does that mean?" asked Noel.

"You won't discuss these confidential matters, yet I must ask questions, the answers to which could allay our anxieties. You see, Mr. Holcroft, you have no reason to be afraid of me. On the contrary, we may have a great deal to fear from you."

"Why? I don't know you; you don't know me. Whatever it is you're involved with has nothing to do with me."

"We must *all* be convinced of that," said the old man.

"Over the telephone you spoke to Helden of urgency, of a great deal of money, of concerns that go back more than thirty years."

"I'm sorry she told you that," interrupted Noel. "Even that's too much."

"She said very little else," continued the colonel. "Only that you saw her sister, and that you're interested in her brother."

"I'll say it again. It's confidential."

"And finally," said the old man, as if Holcroft had not spoken, "that you wished to meet secretly. At least, you implied as much."

"For my own reasons," said Noel. "They're none of your business."

"Aren't they?"

"No."

"Let me summarize briefly, then." The colonel pressed the fingers of his hands together, his eyes on Holcroft. "There's urgency, a great sum of money, matters traced back three decades, interest in the offspring of a ranking member of the Third Reich's High Command, and—most important, perhaps—a clandestine meeting. Doesn't all this suggest something?"

Noel refused to be drawn into speculation. "I have no idea what it suggests to you."

"Then I'll be specific. A trap."

"A trap?"

"Who are you, Mr. Holcroft? A disciple of ODESSA? Or a soldier of the Rache, perhaps?"

"The ODESSA? . . . or the . . . what?" asked Holcroft.

"The *Rache*," replied the old man sharply, pronouncing the word with phonetic emphasis.

"The '*Rah-kuh*'? . . ." Noel returned the cripple's penetrating stare. "I don't know what you're talking about."

Oberst glanced at Helden, then pulled his eyes back to Holcroft. "You've heard of neither?"

"I've heard of the ODESSA. I don't know anything about the . . . '*Rah-kuh*' . . . or whatever you call it."

"Recruiters and killers. Yet both recruit. Both kill. The ODESSA and the Rache. The pursuers of children."

"Pursuers of children?" Noel shook his head. "You'll have to be clearer, because I haven't the vaguest idea what you're saying."

Again, the old man looked at Helden. What passed between them Holcroft could not decipher, but Oberst turned back to him, the hard eyes boring in as if studying a practiced liar, watching for signs of deception—or recognition. "I'll put it plainly to you," he said. "Are you one of those who seek out the children of Nazis? Who pursue them wherever they can be found, killing them for revenge—for crimes they never committed—making *examples* of the innocent? *Or* forcing them to join you. Threatening them with documents portraying their parents as monsters, promising to expose them as offspring of psychopaths and murderers if they refuse to be recruited —destroying what lives they have for the insanity of your cause? These are the people who seek the children, Mr. Holcroft. Are you one of them?"

Noel closed his eyes in relief. "I can't tell you how wrong you are. I won't tell you any more than that, but you're so wrong it's incredible."

"We have to be sure."

"You can be. I'm not involved in things like that. I've never heard of those kind of things before. People like that are sick."

"Yes, they're sick," agreed Oberst. "Don't mistake me. The Wiesenthals of this world search out the real monsters, the unpunished criminals who still laugh at Nürnberg, and we can't object; that's another war. But the persecution of the children must stop."

Noel turned to Helden. "Is this what you're running from? After all these years, they're still after you?"

The old man answered. "Acts of violence take place every day. Everywhere."

"Then why doesn't anyone know about it?" demanded Holcroft. "Why aren't there stories in the newspapers? Why are these things kept quiet?"

"Would . . . 'anyone,' as you put it, really care?" asked the colonel. "For the children of Nazis?"

"For God's sake, they were *kids*." Again Noel looked at Helden. "Is what I saw tonight part of this? You have to *protect* each other? Is it so widespread?"

"We're called the 'children of hell,' " said the Von Tiebolt daughter simply. "Damned for what we are and damned for what we're not."

"I don't *understand* it," protested Holcroft.

"It's not vital that you do." The old soldier once

again got up slowly, trying, thought Noel, to rise to his former imposing height. "It's only important that we be convinced you are from neither army. Are you satisfied, Helden?"

"Yes."

"There's nothing more you wish me to know?"

The woman shook her head. "I'm satisfied," she repeated.

"Then so am I." The colonel extended his hand to Noel. "Thank you for coming. As Helden will explain, my existence is not widely known; nor do we want it to be. We would appreciate your confidence."

Holcroft took the hand, surprised at the old man's firm grip. "If I can count on yours."

"You have my word."

"Then you have mine," Noel said.

They drove in silence, headlights knifing the darkness. Holcroft was behind the wheel, Helden in the front seat, beside him, directing him by nodding wearily, pointing to the turns. There was no screaming now; there were no harsh commands barked at the last second. Helden seemed as exhausted from the events of the night as was he. But the night was not over; they had to talk.

"Was all that necessary?" he asked. "Was it so important for him to see me?"

"Very much so. He had to be convinced you weren't part of the ODESSA. Or the Rache."

"What exactly are they? He spoke as if I should know, but I don't. I didn't really understand him."

"They're two extremist organizations, sworn enemies of each other. Both fanatic, both after us."

"Us?"

"The children of Party leaders. Wherever we are; wherever we've scattered to."

"Why?"

"The ODESSA seeks to revive the Nazi party. The disciples of ODESSA are everywhere."

"Seriously? They're for real?"

"Very real. And very serious. The ODESSA's recruiting methods range from blackmail to physical force. They're gangsters."

"And this . . . 'Rah-kuh'?"

"*Rache*. The German word for 'vengeance.' In the

beginning it was a society formed by the survivors of the concentration camps. They hunted the sadists and the killers, those thousands who were never brought to trial."

"It's a Jewish organization, then?"

"There are Jews in the Rache, yes, but now they're a minority. The Israelis formed their own groups and operated out of Tel Aviv and Haifa. The Rache is primarily Communist; many believe it was taken over by the KGB. Others think Third World revolutionaries gravitated to it. The 'vengeance' they spoke of in the beginning has become something else. The Rache is a haven for terrorists."

"But why are they after *you?*"

Helden looked at him through the shadows. "To recruit us. Like everyone else, we have our share of revolutionaries. They're drawn to the Rache; it represents the opposite of what they're running from. For most of us, however, it's no better than the Party at its worst. And on those of us who won't be recruited, the Rache uses its harsher tactics. We're the scapegoats, the fascists they're stamping out. They use our names—often our corpses —to tell people Nazis still live. Not unlike the ODESSA, it's frequently 'recruit or kill.' "

"It's *insane,*" said Noel.

"Insane," agreed Helden. "But very real. We say nothing; we're not anxious to call attention to ourselves. Besides, who would care? We're Nazi children."

"The ODESSA, the Rache. . . . No one I know knows anything about them."

"No one you know has any reason to."

"Who's Oberst?"

"A great man who must remain in hiding for the rest of his life because he had a conscience."

"What do you mean?"

"He was a member of the High Command and saw the horrors. He knew it was futile to object; others had, and they were killed. Instead, he remained, and used his rank to countermand order after order, saving God knows how many lives."

"There's nothing dishonorable in that."

"He did it the only way he could. Quietly, within the bureaucracy of command, without notice. When it was over, the Allies convicted him because of his status in the Reich; he spent eighteen years in prison. When what he did finally came out, thousands of Germans despised him. They called him a traitor. What was left of the Officer Corps put a price on his head."

Noel, remembering Helden's words, said, "Damned for what he was and damned for what he wasn't."

"Yes," she answered, pointing suddenly to a turn in the road she'd nearly missed.

"In his own way," said Noel, turning the wheel, "Oberst is like the three men who wrote the Geneva document. Didn't it occur to you?"

"It occurred to me."

"You must have been tempted to tell him."

"Not really. You asked me not to."

He looked at her; she was looking straight ahead, through the windshield. Her face was tired and drawn, her skin pale, accentuating the dark hollows beneath her eyes. She seemed alone, and that aloneness was not to be intruded upon lightly. But the night was *not* over. They had things to say to each other; decisions had to be made.

For Noel was beginning to think that this youngest child of Wilhelm von Tiebolt would be the one selected to represent the Von Tiebolt family in Geneva.

"Can we go someplace where it's quiet? I think a drink would do us both good."

"There's a small inn about four or five miles from here. It's out of the way; no one will see us."

As they swung off the road, Noel's eyes were drawn to the rearview mirror. Headlights shone in the glass. It was an odd turn off the Paris highway, odd in the sense that there were no signs; an unmarked exit. The fact that a driver behind them had a reason to take this particular exit at this particular time seemed too coincidental for comfort. Holcroft was about to say something when a strange thing happened.

The lights in the mirror went out. They simply were not there any longer.

The inn had once been a farmhouse: part of the grazing field was now a graveled parking lot bordered by a post-and-rail fence. The small dining room was through an archway off the bar. Two other couples were inside; the people were distinctly Parisian, and just as obviously having discreet dinners with companions they could not see in Paris. Eyes shot up at the newcomers, no signs of welcome in the glances. A fireplace filled with flaming logs was at the far end of the room. It was a good place to talk.

They were shown to a table to the left of the fire. Two brandies were ordered and delivered.

"It's nice here," said Noel, feeling the warmth of the flames and the alcohol. "How did you find it?"

"It's on the way to the colonel's. My friends and I often stop here to talk among ourselves."

"Do you mind if I ask you questions?"

"Go ahead."

"When did you leave England?"

"About three months ago. When the job was offered."

"Were you the Helen Tennyson in the London directory?"

"Yes. In English, the name 'Helden' seems to require an explanation, and I was tired of having to give one. It's not the same in Paris. The French don't have much curiosity about names."

"But you don't call yourself 'Von Tiebolt.' " Holcroft saw the flash of resentment on her face.

"No."

"Why 'Tennyson'?"

"I think that's rather obvious. 'Von Tiebolt' is extremely German. When we left Brazil for England, it seemed a reasonable change."

"Just a change? Nothing else?"

"No." Helden sipped her brandy and looked at the fire. "Nothing else."

Noel watched her; the lie was in her voice. She was not a good liar. She was hiding something, but to call her on it now would only provoke her. He let the lie pass. "What do you know about your father?"

She turned back to him. "Very little. My mother loved him, and from what she said, he was a better man than his years in the Third Reich might indicate. But then, you've confirmed that, haven't you? At the end, he was a profoundly moral man."

"Tell me about your mother."

"She was a survivor. She fled Germany with nothing but a few pieces of jewelry, two children, and a baby inside her. She had no training, no skills, no profession, but she could work, and she was . . . convincing. She started selling in dress shops, cultivated customers, used her flair for clothes—and she had that—as the basis for her own business. Several businesses, actually. Our home in Rio de Janeiro was quite comfortable."

"Your sister told me it was . . . a sanctuary that turned into a kind of hell."

"My sister is given to melodramatics. It wasn't so bad. If we were looked down upon, there was a certain basis for it."

"What was that?"

"My mother was terribly attractive. . . ."

"So are her daughters," interrupted Noel.

"I imagine we are," said Helden matter-of-factly. "It's never concerned me. I haven't had to use it—whatever attractiveness I may have. But my mother did."

"In Rio?"

"Yes. She was kept by several men. . . . *We* were kept, actually. There were two or three divorces, but she wouldn't marry the husbands involved. She broke up marriages, extracting money and business interests as she did. When she died, we were quite well off. The German community considered her a pariah. And, by extension, her children."

"She sounds fascinating," said Holcroft, smiling. "How did she die?"

"She was killed. Shot through the head while she was driving one night."

The smile faded abruptly. Images returned: a deserted lookout high above the city of Rio; the sounds of gunfire and the explosions of cement; the shattering of glass. . . . *Glass.* A car window blown out with the spit of silenced gunshot; a heavy black pistol leveled at his head. . . .

Then the words came back to him, spoken in the booth of a cocktail lounge. Words Holcroft had believed were ridiculous, the products of unreasonable fear.

The Cararras, brother and sister. The sister, dearest friend and fiancée of Johann von Tiebolt.

He and my sister were to be married. The Germans would not permit it.

Who could stop them?

Any number of men. With a bullet in the back of Johann's head.

The Cararras. Dear friends and suppliants for the

ostracized Von Tiebolts. It suddenly struck Noel that if Helden knew how the Cararras had helped him, she might be more cooperative. The Cararras had risked their lives to send him to the Von Tiebolts. She would have to respond to that confidence with her own.

"I think I should tell you," he said. "In Rio it was the Cararras who contacted me. They told me where to start looking for you. They were the ones who told me your new name was Tennyson."

"Who?"

"Your friends, the Cararras. Your brother's fiancée."

"The Cararras? In Rio de Janeiro?"

"Yes."

"I've never heard of them. I don't know any Cararras."

16

The tactic blew up in his face with the impact of a back-fired rifle. Suddenly Helden was wary of him, apprehensive of saying anything further about her family.

Who were the Cararras?

Why had they told him things that were not true?

Who sent them to him? Her brother had no fiancée, nor any best friend whom she could recall.

He did not claim to understand; he could only speculate as truthfully as possible. No one else had come forward. For reasons known only to them, the Cararras had created a relationship that did not exist; still, it made no sense to call them enemies of the Von Tiebolts. They had reached him for the purpose of *helping* the two sisters and the brother who had been driven from Brazil. There were those in Rio—a powerful man named Graff, for one—who would pay a great deal of money to locate the Von Tiebolts. The Cararras, who had much to gain and very little to lose, had not told him.

"They wanted to help," Noel said. "They weren't lying about that. They said you'd been persecuted; they did want to help you."

"It's possible," said Helden. "Rio is filled with people who are still fighting the war, still hunting for those they call traitors. One is never sure who is a friend and who is an enemy. Not among the Germans."

"Did you know Maurice Graff?"

"I knew who he was, of course. Everyone did. I never met him."

"I did," Noel said. "*He* called the Von Tiebolts traitors."

"I'm sure he did. We were pariahs, but not in the nationalistic sense."

"What sense, then?"

The girl looked away again, lifting the brandy glass to her lips. "Other things."

"Your mother?"

"Yes," replied Helden. "It was my mother. I told you, the German community despised her."

Again Holcroft had the feeling she was telling him only part of the truth. He would not pursue it now. If he gained her confidence, she would tell him later. She *had* to tell him; whatever it was might have an affect on Geneva. Everything affected Geneva now.

"You said your mother broke up marriages," he said. "Your sister used almost the same words about herself. She said she was shunned by the officers and their wives in Portsmouth."

"If you're looking for a pattern, I won't try to dissuade you. My sister is quite a bit older than I. She was closer to my mother, watched her progress, saw the advantages that came mother's way. It wasn't as if she was oblivious of such things. She knew the horror of Berlin after the war. At the age of thirteen she slept with soldiers for food. American soldiers, Mr. Holcroft."

It was all he had to know about Gretchen Beaumont. The picture was complete. A whore, for whatever reasons, at fourteen. A whore—for whatever other reasons—at forty-five-plus. The bank's directors in Geneva would rule her out on grounds of instability and incompetence.

But Noel knew there were stronger grounds. The man Gretchen Beaumont said she loathed, but lived with. A man with odd, heavy eyebrows who had followed him to Brazil.

"What about her husband?"

"I barely know him."

She looked away again at the fire. She was frightened; she *was* hiding something. Her words were too studiedly nonchalant. Whatever it was she would not talk about had something to do with Beaumont. There was no point in evading the subject any longer. Truth between them had to be a two-way matter; the sooner she learned that, the better for both of them.

"Do you know anything about him? Where he came from? What he does in the navy?"

"No, nothing. He's a commander on a ship; that's all I know."

"I think he's more than that, and I think you know it. Please don't lie to me."

At first, her eyes flashed with anger; then, just as rapidly, the anger subsided. "That's a strange thing to say. Why would I lie to you?"

"I wish I knew. You say you barely know him, but you seem scared to death. *Please.*"

"What are you driving at?"

"If you know something, tell me. If you've heard about the document in Geneva, tell me what you've heard."

"I know nothing. I've heard nothing."

"I saw Beaumont two weeks ago on a plane to Rio. The same plane I took from New York. He was following me."

He could see fear in Helden's eyes. "I think you're wrong," she said.

"I'm not. I saw his photograph in your sister's house. His house. It was the same man. I stole that photograph and it was stolen from me. After someone beat the *hell* out of me for it."

"Good *lord.* . . . You were beaten for his *photograph?*"

"Nothing else was missing. Not my wallet or my money or my watch. Just his picture. There was writing on the back of it."

"What did it say?"

"I don't know. It was in German, and I can't read German."

"Can you remember any of the words?"

"One, I think. The last word. T-O-D. *Tod.*"

" '*Ohne dich sterbe ich.*' Could that be it?"

"I don't know. What does it mean?"

" 'Without you I die.' It's the sort of thing my sister would think of. I told you, she's melodramatic." She was lying again; he knew it!

"An endearment?"

"Yes."

"That's what the British said, and I didn't believe them either. Beaumont was on that plane. That picture was taken from me because there was some kind of message on it. For Christ's sake, what's going *on?*"

"I don't know!"

"But you know *something.*" Noel tried to control himself. Their voices were low, almost whispers, but their argument carried over to the other diners. Holcroft reached across the table and covered her hand. "I'm asking you again. You know something. Tell me."

He could feel a slight tremble in her hand. "What I know is so confusing it would be meaningless. It's more what I sense than what I know, really." She took her hand from his. "A number of years ago Anthony Beaumont was a naval attaché in Rio de Janeiro. I didn't know him well, but I remember him coming to the house quite often. He was married at the time, but interested in my sister—a diversion, I suppose you might call it. My mother encouraged it. He was a high-ranking naval officer; favors could be had. But my sister argued violently with my mother. She despised Beaumont and would have nothing to do with him. Yet only a few years later we moved to England and she married him. I've never understood."

Noel leaned forward, relieved. "It may not be as difficult to understand as you think. She told me she married him for the security he could give her."

"And you believed her?"

"Her behavior would seem to confirm what she said."

"Then I can't believe you met my sister."

"She was your sister. You look alike: both beautiful."

"It's my turn to ask you a question. Given that beauty, do you really think she would settle for a naval officer's salary and the restricted life of a naval officer's wife? I can't. I never have."

"What do you think, then?"

"I think she was forced to marry Anthony Beaumont."

Noel leaned back in the chair. If she was right, the connection was in Rio de Janeiro. With her mother, perhaps. With her mother's murder.

"How could Beaumont force her to marry him? And why?"

"I've asked myself both questions a hundred times. I don't know."

"Have you asked her?"

"She refuses to talk to me."

"What happened to your mother in Rio?"

"I told you: She manipulated men for money. The Germans despised her, called her immoral. Looking back, it's hard to refute."

"Was that why she was shot?"

"I guess so. No one really knows; the killer was never found."

"But it could be the answer to the first question, couldn't it? Isn't it possible that Beaumont knew something about your mother that was so damaging he could blackmail your sister?"

Helden turned her palms up in front of her. "What could possibly *be* so damaging? Accepting everything that was said about my mother as being true, why would it have any effect on Gretchen?"

"That would depend on what it was."

"There's nothing conceivable. She's in England now. She's her own person, thousands of miles away. Why should she be concerned?"

"I have no idea." Then Noel remembered. "You used the words 'children of hell.' Damned for what you were, and damned for what you weren't. Couldn't that apply to your sister as well?"

"Beaumont isn't interested in such things. It's an entirely different matter."

"Is it? You don't know that. It's your opinion he forced her to marry him. If it isn't something like that, what is it?"

Helden looked away, deep in thought now, not in a lie. "Something much more recent."

"The document in Geneva?" he asked. Manfredi's warning repeated in his ears, the specter of Wolfsschanze in his mind.

"How did Gretchen react when you told her about Geneva?" asked Helden.

"As if it didn't matter."

"Well? . . ."

"It could have been a diversion. She was too casual—just as you were too casual when I mentioned Beaumont a few minutes ago. She could have expected it and steeled herself."

"You're guessing."

It was the moment, thought Noel. It would be in her eyes—the rest of the truth she would not talk about. Did it come down to Johann von Tiebolt?

"Not really guessing. Your sister said that her brother told her a man would 'come one day and talk of a strange arrangement.' Those were her words."

Whatever he was looking for—a flicker of recognition, a blink of fear—it was not there. There was *something*, but nothing he could relate to. She looked at him as if she herself were trying to understand. Yet there was a fundamental innocence in her look, and that was what *he* could not understand.

"'A man would come one day.' It doesn't make sense," she said.

"Tell me about your brother."

She did not answer for several moments. Instead, her eyes strayed to the red tablecloth; her lips parted in astonishment. Then, as if she were coming out of a trance, she said, "Johann? What's there to say?"

"Your sister told me he got the three of you out of Brazil. Was it difficult?"

"There were problems. We had no passports, and there were men who tried to stop us from obtaining them."

"You were immigrants. At least, your mother, brother, and sister were. They had to have papers."

"Whatever papers there were in those days were burned as soon as they served their purpose."

"Who wanted to stop you from leaving Brazil?"

"Men who wanted to bring Johann to trial."

"For what?"

"After mother was killed, Johann took over her business interests. She never allowed him to do much when she was alive. Many people thought he was ruthless, even dishonest. He was accused of misrepresenting profits, withholding taxes. I don't think any of it was true; he was simply faster and brighter than anyone else."

"I see," said Noel, recalling MI-Five's evaluation—"overachiever." "How did he avoid the courts and get you out?"

"Money. And all-night meetings in strange places with men he never identified. He came home one morning and told Gretchen and me to pack just enough things for a short overnight trip. We drove to the airport and were flown in a small plane to Recife, where a man met us. We were given passports; the name on them was Tennyson. The next thing Gretchen and I knew we were on a plane for London."

Holcroft watched her closely. There was no hint of a lie. "To start a new life under the name of Tennyson," he said.

"Yes. Completely new. We'd left everything behind us." She smiled. "I sometimes think with very little time to spare."

"He's quite a man. Why haven't you stayed in touch? You obviously don't hate him."

Helden frowned, as if she were unsure of her own answer. "Hate him? No. I resent him, perhaps, but I don't hate him. Like most brilliant men, he thinks he should take charge of everything. He wanted to run my life, and I couldn't accept that."

"Why is he a newspaperman? From all I've learned about him, he could probably own one."

"He probably will one day, if that's what he wants. Knowing Johann, I suspect it's because he thought that writing for a well-known newspaper would give him a certain prominence. Especially in the political field, where he's very good. He was right."

"Was he?"

"Certainly. In a matter of two or three years, he was considered one of the finest correspondents in Europe."

Now, thought Noel. MI Five meant nothing to him; Geneva was everything. He leaned forward.

"He's considered something else, too. . . . I said in the Montmartre that I would tell you—and *only* you— why the British questioned me. It's your brother. They think I'm trying to reach him for reasons that have nothing to do with Geneva."

"What reasons?"

Holcroft kept her eyes engaged. "Have you ever heard of a man they call the Tinamou?"

"The assassin? Certainly. Who hasn't?"

There was nothing in her eyes. Nothing but vague bewilderment. "I, for one," said Noel. "I've read about killers for hire and assassination conspiracies but I've never heard of the Tinamou."

"You're an American. His exploits are more detailed in the European press than in yours. But what has he got to do with my brother?"

"British Intelligence thinks he may *be* the Tinamou."

The expression on Helden's face was arrested in shock. So complete was her astonishment that her eyes were suddenly devoid of life, as noncommittal as a blind man's. Her lips trembled and she tried to speak, unable to find the words. Finally, the words came. They were barely audible.

"You can't be *serious*."

"I assure you, I am. What's more to the point, the British are."

"It's outrageous. Beyond anything I've ever heard! On what basis can they possibly *reach* such a conclusion?"

Noel repeated the salient points analyzed by MI Five.

"My *God*," said Helden when he had finished. "He covers all of Europe, as well as the Middle East! Certainly the English could check with his editors. He doesn't *choose* the places they send him to. It's preposterous!"

"Newspapermen who write interesting copy, who file stories that sell papers, are given a very free hand when it comes to the places they cover. That's the case with your brother. It's almost as though he knew he'd gain that prominence you spoke of; knew that in a few short years he'd be given a flexible schedule."

"You can't *believe* this."

"I don't know what to believe," said Holcroft. "I only know that your brother could jeopardize the situation in Geneva. The mere fact that he's under suspicion by MI Five could be enough to frighten the bankers. They don't want that kind of scrutiny where the Clausen account is concerned."

"But it's unjustified!"

"Are you sure?"

Helden's eyes were angry. "Yes, I'm sure. Johann may be a number of things, but he's no killer. The viciousness starts again: The Nazi child is hounded."

Noel remembered the first statement made by the gray-haired MI-Five man: *For starters, you know about the father.* . . . Was it possible Helden was right? Did MI Five's suspicions come from memories and hostilities that went back thirty years to a brutal enemy? *Tennyson is the personification of arrogance.* . . . It was possible.

"Is Johann political?"

"Very, but not in the usual sense. He doesn't stand for any particular ideology. Instead, he's highly critical of them all. He attacks their weaknesses, and he's vicious about hypocrisy. That's why a lot of people in government can't stand him. But he's no assassin!"

If Helden was right, Noel thought, Johann von Tie-bolt could be an enormous asset to Geneva, or, more specifically, to the agency that was to be established in Zurich. A multilingual journalist whose judgments were listened to, who had experience in finance . . . could be eminently qualified to dispense millions throughout the world.

If the shadow of the Tinamou could be removed from Johann von Tiebolt, there was no reason for the directors of La Grande Banque de Genève ever to learn of MI Five's interest in John Tennyson. The second child of Wilhelm von Tiebolt would be instantly acceptable to the bankers. He might not be the most personable man alive, but Geneva was not sponsoring a personality contest. He could be an extraordinary asset. But first the Tinamou's shadow *had* to be removed, British Intelligence suspicions laid to rest.

Holcroft smiled. *A man would come one day and talk of a strange arrangement. . . .* Johann von Tiebolt— John Tennyson—was waiting for him!

"What's funny?" said Helden, watching him.

"I have to meet him," answered Noel, ignoring the question. "Can you arrange it?"

"I imagine so. It'll take a few days. I don't know where he is. What will you say to him?"

"The truth; maybe he'll reciprocate. I've got a damn good idea he knows about Geneva."

"There's a telephone number he gave me to call if I ever needed him. I've never used it."

"Use it now. Please."

She nodded. Noel understood that there were questions left unanswered. Specifically, a man named Beaumont, and an event in Rio de Janeiro that Helden would not discuss. An event connected to the naval officer with the heavy black-and-white eyebrows. And it was possible that Helden knew nothing about that connection.

Perhaps John Tennyson did. He certainly knew a lot more than he told either sister.

"Does your brother get along with Beaumont?" asked Holcroft.

"He despises him. He refused to come to Gretchen's wedding."

What *was* it? wondered Noel. Who was the enigma that was Anthony Beaumont?

17

Outside the small inn, in the far corner of the parking area, a dark sedan rested in the shadow of a tall oak tree. In the front seat were two men, one in the uniform of the English navy, the other in a charcoal-gray business suit, his black overcoat opened, the edge of a brown leather holster visible beneath his unbuttoned jacket.

The naval officer was behind the wheel. His blunt features were tense. The eyebrows of black-and-white hair arched just noticeably every now and then, as if prodded by a nervous tic.

The man beside him was in his late thirties. He was slender but he was not thin; his was the tautness that comes with discipline and training. The breadth of his shoulders, the long muscular neck, and the convex line of a chest that stretched his tailored shirt were evidence of a body honed to physical precision and strength. Each feature of his face was refined and each coordinated with the whole. The result was striking, yet cold, as if the face were chiseled in granite. The eyes were light blue, almost rectangular, their gaze steady and noncommittal; they were the eyes of a confident animal, quick to respond, the response unpredictable. The sculptured head was covered by a glistening crown of blond hair that reflected the light of the distant parking-lot lamps; above this face, his hair had the appearance of pale-yellow ice. The man's name was Johann von Tiebolt, for the past five years known as "John Tennyson."

"Are you satisfied?" asked the naval officer, obviously apprehensive. "There's no one."

"There *was* someone," replied the blond man. "Considering the precautions taken since Montmartre, it's not entirely surprising there's no one now. Helden and the other children are quite effective."

"They run from idiots," said Beaumont. "The Rache is filled with Marxist subhumans."

"When the time comes, the Rache will serve its purpose. Our purpose. But it's not the Rache I'm concerned with. I want to know who tried to kill him." Tennyson turned in the shadows, his cold eyes glaring. He slammed his hand on the top of the leather dashboard. "Who tried to *kill Clausen's son?*"

"I swear to you, I've told you everything we know! Everything we've learned. It was *not* a mistake on our part."

"It was a mistake because it nearly happened," replied Tennyson, his voice quiet again.

"It was Manfredi; it *had* to be Manfredi," continued Beaumont. "It's the only explanation, Johann. . . ."

"My name is John. Remember that."

"Sorry. It *is* the only explanation. We don't know what Manfredi said to Holcroft on that train in Geneva. It's possible he tried to convince him to walk away. And when Holcroft refused, he sent out the orders for his execution. They failed in the station because of me. I think you should remember that."

"You won't let me forget it," interrupted Tennyson. "You may be right. He expected to control the agency in Zurich; that could never be. So the removal of assets totaling seven hundred and eighty million dollars became too painful an exercise."

"Just as the promise of two million is an irresistible temptation to Holcroft, perhaps."

"Two million he banks only in his mind. But his death will come at *our* hands, no one else's."

"Manfredi acted alone, believe that. His executioners have no one to take orders from now. Since the hotel room in Zurich, there've been no further attempts."

"That's a statement Holcroft would find impossible to accept. . . . There they *are*." Tennyson sat forward. Through the windshield, across the parking area, he could see Noel and Helden coming out of the door. "Do the colonel's children meet here frequently?"

"Yes," answered Beaumont. "I learned of it from an ODESSA agent who followed them one night."

The blond man coughed a quiet laugh; his words were scathing. "ODESSA! Caricatures, who weep in cellars over too many steins of beer! They're laughable."

"They're persistent."

"And they, too, will be useful," said Tennyson, watching Noel and Helden get into the car. "As before, they will be the lowest foot soldiers, fed to the enemy's cannon. First seen, first sacrificed. The perfect diversion for more serious matters."

The Citroën's loud, outsized engine was heard. Holcroft backed the car out of its slot, then drove through the entrance posts onto the country road.

Beaumont turned on the ignition. "I'll stay a fair distance behind. He won't spot me."

"No, don't bother," said Tennyson. "I'm satisfied. Take me to the airport. You've made the arrangements?"

"Yes. You'll be flown on a Mirage to Athens. The Greeks will get you back to Bahrain. It's all military transport, UN-courier status, Security Council immunity. The pilot of the Mirage has your papers."

"Well done, Tony."

The naval officer smiled, proud of the compliment. He pressed the accelerator; the sedan roared out of the parking lot into the darkness of the country road. "What will you do in Bahrain?"

"Make my presence known by filing a story on an oil-field negotiation. A prince of Bahrain has been most cooperative. He has had no choice. He made an arrangement with the Tinamou. The poor man lives in terror that the news will get out."

"You're extraordinary."

"And you're a devoted man. You always have been."

"After Bahrain, what?"

The blond man leaned back in the seat and closed his eyes. "Back to Athens and on to Berlin."

"Berlin?"

"Yes. Things are progressing well. Holcroft will go there next. Kessler's waiting for him."

There was a sudden burst of static from a radio speaker beneath the dashboard. It was followed by four short, high-pitched hums. Tennyson opened his eyes; the four hums were repeated.

"There are telephone booths on the highway. Get me to one. Quickly!"

The Englishman pressed the accelerator to the floor; the sedan sped down the road, reaching seventy miles an hour in a matter of seconds. They came to an intersection. "If I'm not mistaken, there's a petrol station around here."

"Hurry!"

"I'm sure of it," said Beaumont, and there it was, at the side of the road, dark, no light in the windows. "Damn, it's closed!"

"What did you expect?" asked Tennyson.

"The phone's inside. . . ."

"But there *is* a phone?"

"Yes. . . ."

"Stop the car."

Beaumont obeyed. The blond man got out and walked to the door of the station. He took out his pistol and broke the glass with the handle.

A dog leaped up at him, barking and growling, fangs bared, jaws snapping. It was an old animal of indeterminable breed, stationed more for effect than for physical protection. Tennyson reached into his pocket, pulled out a perforated cylinder, and spun it on to the barrel of his pistol. He raised the gun and fired through the shattered glass into the dog's head. The animal fell backward. Tennyson smashed the remaining glass by the latch above the doorknob.

He let himself in, adjusted his eyes to the light, and stepped over the dead animal to the telephone. He reached an operator and gave her the Paris number that could connect him to a man who would, in turn, transfer his call to a telephone in England.

Twenty seconds later he heard the breathless, echoing voice. "I'm sorry to disturb you, Johann, but we have an emergency."

"What is it?"

"A photograph was taken. I'm very concerned."

"What photograph?"

"A picture of Tony."

"Who took it?"

"The American."

"Which means he recognized him. Graff was right: Your devoted husband can't be trusted. His enthusiasm outweighs his discretion. I wonder where Holcroft saw him?"

"On the plane, perhaps. Or through the doorman's description. It doesn't matter. Kill him."

"Yes, of course." The blond man paused, then spoke thoughtfully. "You have the bank books?"

"Yes."

"Deposit ten thousand pounds. Let the transfer be traced through Prague."

"KGB? Very good, Johann."

"The British will suffer another defection. Friendly diplomats will argue among themselves, each accusing the other of a lack of candor."

"*Very* good."

"I'll be in Berlin next week. Reach me there."

"So soon Berlin?"

"Yes, Kessler's waiting. *Neuaufbau oder Tod.*"

"*Oder der Tod,* my brother."

Tennyson hung up and stared through the night light at the dead animal on the floor. He had no more feeling for the clump of lifeless fur than for the man waiting in the car. Feelings were kept for more important things, not for animals and misfits—regardless of how devoted either might be.

Beaumont was a fool, a judgment contained in a dossier sent from Scotland to Brazil years ago. But he had a fool's energy and a fool's sense of surface accomplishment. He had actually become an outstanding naval officer. This son of a *Reichsoberführer* had climbed the ladder of Her Majesty's Royal Navy to the point where he was given vital responsibility. Too much for his intellect; that intellect needed to be directed. In time, they had projected that Beaumont might become a power within the Admiralty, an expert consulted by the Foreign Office. It was an optimum situation; extraordinary advantages could be handed to them through Beaumont. He had remained a *Sonnenkind;* he was permitted to live.

But no more. With the theft of a photograph, Beaumont was finished, for in that theft was the threat of scrutiny. There could be no scrutiny whatsoever; they were too close, and there was still too much to accomplish. If Holcroft gave the photograph to the wrong people in Switzerland, told them of Beaumont's presence in New York or Rio, military authorities might be alerted. Why was this outstanding officer so interested in the Geneva document? The question could not arise. This son of the *Reichsoberführer* had to be removed. In a way, it was a pity. The commander would be missed; at times he'd been invaluable.

Gretchen knew that value. Gretchen was Beaumont's teacher, his guide . . . his intellect. She was enormously proud of her work, and now she called for Beaumont's death. So be it. They'd find another to take his place.

They were everywhere, thought Johann von Tiebolt as he walked to the door. Everywhere. *Die Sonnenkinder*. The Children of the Sun, never to be confused with the damned. The damned were wandering refuse, entitled to nothing.

Die Sonnenkinder. Everywhere. In all countries, in all governments, in armies and navies, in industry and trade unions, commanding intelligence branches and the police. All quietly waiting. Grown-up children of the New Order. *Thousands*. Sent out by ship and plane and submarine to all points of the civilized world. So *far* above the average—confirmed every day by their progress everywhere. They were the proof that the concept of racial superiority was undeniable. Their strain was pure, their excellence unquestioned. And the purest of all, the most excellent of all, was the Tinamou.

Von Tiebolt opened the door and stepped outside. Beaumont had driven the sedan fifty yards down the country road, headlights out. The commander went by the book; his training was apparent in everything he did—except when his enthusiasm overrode his discretion. That enthusiasm would now cost him his life.

Tennyson walked slowly toward the sedan. He wondered absently how it all had begun for Anthony Beaumont. The son of the *Reichsoberführer* had been sent to a family in Scotland; beyond that Tennyson had never inquired. He had been told of Beaumont's tenacity, his stubbornness, his singleness of purpose, but not of how he had been sent out of Germany. It was not necessary to know. There'd been thousands; all records were destroyed.

Thousands. Selected genetically, the parents studied, families traced back several generations for organic and psychological frailties. Only the purest were sent out, and everywhere these children were watched closely, guided, trained, indoctrinated—but told nothing until they grew up. And even then, not all. Those who failed to live up to their birthright, who showed weakness or gave evidence of being compromised, were never told, only weeded out.

Those that remained were the true inheritors of the Third Reich. They were in positions of trust and authority everywhere. Waiting . . . waiting for the signal from Switzerland, prepared to put the millions to immediate use.

Millions funneled judiciously, *politically*. One by one, nations would fall in line, shaped internally by the *Sonnenkinder*, who would have at their disposal extraordinary sums to match and consolidate their influence. Ten million here, forty million there, one hundred million where it was necessary.

In the free world the election processes would be bought, the electorates having fewer and fewer choices, only echoes. It was nothing new; successful experiments had already taken place. Chile had cost less than twenty-seven million, Panama no more than six. In America, Senate and congressional seats were to be had for a few hundred thousand. But when the signal came from Switzerland, the millions would be dispensed scientifically, the art of demographics employed. Until the Western world was led by the grown-up children of the Reich. *Die Sonnenkinder*.

The Eastern bloc would be next, the Soviet Union and its satellites succumbing to the blandishments of their own emerging bourgeoisie. When the signal came, promises would be made and people's collectives everywhere would suddenly realize there was a better way. Because, suddenly, extraordinary funds would be available; austerity could be replaced by the simple dislocation of loyalties.

The Fourth Reich would be born, not confined to the borders of one or two countries but spread all over the world. The Children of the Sun would be the rightful masters of the globe. *Die Sonnenkinder*.

Some might say it was preposterous, inconceivable. It was not; it was happening. Everywhere.

But mistakes were made, thought Tennyson, as he approached the sedan. They were inevitable, and just as inevitable was the fact that they had to be corrected. Beaumont was a mistake. Tennyson put the pistol back in his holster; it would not stay there long.

He walked around the car to the driver's window; it was rolled down, the commander's face turned in concern. "What was it? Is anything wrong?"

"Nothing that can't be fixed. Move over, I'll drive. You can direct me."

"Where to?"

"They said there's a lake somewhere in the vicinity, not more than eight or ten kilometers away. It was difficult to hear; it was a bad connection."

"Only lake near here is just east of Saint-Gratien. It's nearer twelve to fifteen."

"That must be the one. There are forests?"

"Profuse."

"That's the one," said Tennyson, getting into the car as Beaumont moved over on the seat. "I know the headlight codes. You tell me where to go; I'll concentrate on the lamps."

"Seems odd."

"Not odd. Complicated. They may pick us up along the way. I'll know what to look for. Quickly, now. Which direction do we go?"

"Turn around, to begin with. Head back to that dreadful road; then turn left."

"Very well." Tennyson started the engine.

"What *is* it?" Beaumont asked. "It must be a bloody emergency. I've heard a four-dash signal only once before, and *that* was our man at Entebbe."

"He wasn't our man. Tony. He was our puppet."

"Yes, of course. The Rache terrorist. Still, he was our *connection*, if you know what I mean."

"Yes, I know. Turn here? Left?"

"That's it. Well, for God's sake, *tell* me! What the devil's going on?"

Tennyson steadied the car and accelerated. "Actually, it may concern you. We're not sure, but it's a possibility."

"*Me?*"

"Yes. Did Holcroft ever spot you? See you more than once? Be aware that you were following him?"

"*Spot* me? Never! Never, never, *never!* I *swear* it."

"In Geneva? Think."

"Certainly not."

"In New York?"

"I was never within a mile of him! Impossible."

"On the plane to Rio de Janeiro?"

Beaumont paused. "No. . . . He came through a curtain; he was quite drunk, I think. But he took no notice, no notice at all. I saw him; he didn't see me."

That was it, thought Tennyson. This devoted child of the Reich believed what he had to believe. There was no point in discussing the matter any further.

"Then it's all a mistake, Tony. A wasted half hour. I talked with your wife, my dear sister. She said you were much too discreet for such a thing to have happened."

"She was right. She's *always* right, as you well know. Remarkable girl. Regardless of what you may think, ours was not purely a marriage of convenience."

"I know that, Tony. It makes me very happy."

"Take the next right. It goes north, toward the lake."

It was cold in the forest, colder by the water. They parked at the end of a dirt road and walked up the narrow path to the edge of the lake. Tennyson carried a flashlight he had taken from the glove compartment of the sedan. In Beaumont's hand was a narrow shovel; they had decided to build a small pit fire to ward off the chill.

"Will we be here that long?" Beaumont asked.

"It's possible. There are other matters to discuss, and I'd like your advice. This is the east shore of the lake?"

"Oh, yes. A good rendezvous. No one here this time of year."

"When are you due back at your ship?"

"Have you forgotten? I'm spending the weekend with Gretchen."

"Monday, then?"

"Or Tuesday. My exec's a good chap. He simply assumes I'm prowling around on business. Never questions if I'm a day or so late."

"Why should he? He's one of us."

"Yes, but there are patrol schedules to be observed. Can't muck them up."

"Of course not. Dig here, Tony. Let's have the fire not too near the water. I'll go back and watch for the signals."

"Good."

"Make the hole fairly deep. We wouldn't want the flames too obvious."

"Righto."

Fire. Water. Earth. Burned clothing, charred flesh, smashed and scattered bridgework. John Tennyson walked back over the path and waited. Several minutes later he removed his pistol from the holster and took a long-bladed hunting knife from his overcoat pocket. It would be a messy job, but necessary. The knife, like the shovel, had been in the trunk of the sedan. They were emergency tools, and always there.

A mistake had been revealed. It would be rectified by the Tinamou.

18

Holcroft sipped coffee and looked out at the cold, bright Paris morning. It was the second morning since he had seen Helden, and she was no nearer reaching her brother than she was the night before last.

"He'll call me; I know he will," she had told him over the phone minutes ago.

"Suppose I go out for a while?" he had asked.

"Don't worry. I'll reach you."

Don't worry. It was an odd remark for her to make, considering where he was and how he got there—how *they* got there.

It had been an extension of the madness. They had left the country inn and driven back to Montmartre, where a man had come out of a doorway and relieved them of the Citroën; they had walked through the crowded streets, past two sidewalk cafés where successive nods meant they could return to Noel's rented car.

From Montmartre she had directed him across Paris, over the Seine, into Saint-Germain-des-Prés, where they had stopped at a hotel; he had registered and paid for the night. It was a diversion; he did not go to his room. Instead, they had proceeded to a second hotel on the rue Chevalle, where a soft-drink sign provided him with a name for the registry: N. Fresca.

She had left him in the lobby, telling him she would call him when she had news of her brother.

"Explain something," he had said. "Why are we doing all this? What difference does it make where I stay or whether or not I use my own name?"

"You've been seen with me."

Helden. Strange name, strange woman. An odd mixture of vulnerability and strength. Whatever pain she had endured over the years she refused to turn into self-pity. She recognized her heritage; understood that the children of Nazis were hounded by the ODESSA and the Rache and they had to live with it: damned for what they were and damned for what they were not.

Geneva could help these children; *would* help them. Noel had settled that for himself. He identified with them easily. But for the courage of an extraordinary mother, he could be one of them.

But there were other, more immediate concerns. Questions that affected Geneva. Who was the elusive Anthony Beaumont? What did he stand for? What really happened to the Von Tiebolts in Brazil? How much did Johann von Tiebolt know about the covenant?

If anyone had the answers it was Johann . . . John Tennyson.

Holcroft walked back to the window; a flock of pigeons flew over a nearby roof, fanning up into the morning wind. The Von Tiebolts. Three weeks ago he had never heard the name, but now his life was inextricably involved with theirs.

Helden. Strange name, strange girl. Filled with complications and contradictions. He had never met anyone like her. It was as if she were from another time, another place, fighting the legacies of a war that had passed into history.

The Rache. The ODESSA . . . *Wolfsschanze*. All fanatics. Adversaries in a bloodbath that had no meaning now. It was over, *had* been over for thirty years. It was dead history, finished.

The pigeons swooped down again, and in their mass attack on the rooftop, Noel suddenly saw something —understood something—he had not before. It had been there since the other night—since his meeting with Herr Oberst—and he had not perceived it.

It was *not* over. The war itself had been revived. By Geneva!

There will be men who will try to stop you, deceive you, kill you. . . .

The ODESSA. The Rache. *These* were Geneva's enemies! Fanatics and terrorists who would do anything to destroy the covenant. Anyone else would have exposed the account by appealing to the international courts; neither the ODESSA nor the Rache could do that. Helden was wrong—at least, partially wrong. Whatever interest both had in the children of party leaders was suspended to fight the cause of Geneva! To stop *him*. They had learned about the account in Switzerland—somehow, somewhere —and were committed to blocking it. If to succeed meant killing him, it was not a decision of consequence; he was expendable.

It explained the strychnine on the plane—a horrible death that was meant for him. The terror tactics of the Rache. It clarified the events in Rio de Janeiro—gunshots at a deserted lookout and a shattered car window in the night traffic. Maurice Graff and the psychopathic followers of Brazil's ODESSA. They knew—they *all* knew—about Geneva!

And if they did, they also knew about the Von Tiebolts. That would explain what had happened in Brazil. It was never the *mother;* it was Johann von Tiebolt. He was running from Graff's ODESSA; the protective brother saving what was left of the family, spiriting himself and his two sisters out of Rio.

To live and fulfill the covenant in Geneva.

A man will come one day and talk of a strange arrangement. . . . And in that "strange arrangement" was the money and the power to destroy the ODESSA—and the Rache—for certainly these were legitimate objectives of the covenant.

Noel understood clearly now. He and John Tennyson and a man named Kessler in Berlin would control Geneva; they would direct the agency in Zurich. They would rip out the ODESSA wherever it was; they would crush the Rache. Among the amends that had to be made was the stilling of fanatics, for fanatics were the fathers of murder and genocide.

He wanted to call Helden, to tell her that soon she could stop running—they could *all* stop running—stop hiding, stop living in fear. He wanted to tell her that. And he wanted to see her again.

But he had given his word not to call her at Gallimard, not to try to reach her for any reason. It was maddening; *she* was maddening, yet he could not break his word.

The telephone. He had to call the American Express office on the Champs-Elysées. He had told Sam Buonoventura he would check for messages there.

It was a simple matter to get messages by telephone; he had done so before. No one had to know where he was. He put down his coffee and went to the phone, suddenly remembering that he had a second call to make. His mother. It was too early to call her in New York; he'd reach her later in the day.

"I'm sorry, monsieur," said the clerk at the American Express office. "You must sign for the cables in person. I'm very sorry."

Cables! Noel replaced the phone, annoyed but not angry. Getting out of the hotel room would be good for him, would take his mind off the anticipated call from Helden.

He walked along the rue Chevalle, a cold wind whipping his face. A taxi took him across the river, into the Champs-Elysées. The air and the bright sunlight were invigorating; he rolled the window down, feeling the effects of both. For the first time in days he felt confident; he knew where he was going now. Geneva was closer, the blurred lines between enemies and friends more defined.

Whatever was waiting for him at the American Express office seemed inconsequential. There was nothing he could not handle in New York or London. His concerns were now in Paris. He and John Tennyson would meet and talk and draw up plans, the first of which would be to go to Berlin and find Erich Kessler. They knew who their enemies were; it was a question of eluding them. Helden's friends could help.

As he got out of the taxi, he looked over at the tinted-glass window of the American Express office, and was struck by a thought. Was the refusal to read him his messages over the phone a trap? A means of getting him to show himself? If so, it was a bit obvious, and no doubt a tactic of British Intelligence.

Noel smiled. He knew exactly what to say if the British picked him up: John Tennyson was no more an assassin than he was, and probably far less of one than a number of MI-Five personnel.

He might even go a step further and suggest that the Royal Navy take a good, long look at one of its more decorated officers. All the evidence pointed to the probability that Commander Anthony Beaumont was a member of the ODESSA, recruited in Brazil by a man named Graff.

* * *

He felt he was falling through space, plunging downward, unable to catch his breath. His stomach was hollow and pain shot through his lower chest. He was gripped by combined feelings of grief and fear . . . and anger. The cablegram read:

YOUR FATHER DIED FOUR DAYS AGO STOP UNABLE
TO CONTACT YOU STOP PLEASE RESPOND BY
TELEPHONE BEDFORD HILLS STOP

MOTHER

There was a second cable, from Lieutenant David Miles, New York Police Department.

THE RECENT DEATH OF RICHARD HOLCROFT
MAKES IT IMPERATIVE YOU CONTACT ME IM-
MEDIATELY STOP PROFESSIONALLY I RECOM-
MEND YOU SPEAK TO ME BEFORE REACHING ANY-
ONE ELSE STOP

There were the same two telephone numbers Buonoventura had given him in Rio de Janeiro, and six—*six*—follow-up inquiries listed by day and hour since the original message had been received at the American Express office. Miles had checked twice a day to see if his message had been picked up.

Noel walked up the Champs-Elysées, trying to collect his thoughts, trying to control his grief.

The only father he had ever known. "Dad" . . . "my *father*," Richard Holcroft. Always said with affection, with love. And always with warmth and humor, for Richard Holcroft was a man of many graces, not the least of which was an ability to laugh at himself. He had guided his son—stepson—no, *goddamn it*, his *son!* Guided but never interfered, except when interference was the only alternative.

Oh, God, he was *dead!*

What caused the sharp bolts of pain—pain he understood was part of the fear and the anger—was implied in Miles's cable. Was he somehow responsible for Richard Holcroft's death? Oh, *Christ!* Was that death related to a vial of strychnine poured into a drink thirty thousand feet over the Atlantic? Was it woven into the fabric of *Geneva?*

Had he somehow sacrificed the father he had known all his life for one he never knew?

He reached the corner of the avenue George V. Across the broad intersection that teemed with traffic he saw a sign above awnings that stretched the length of the sidewalk café: FOUQUET'S. It was all familiar to him. To his left was the Hôtel George V. He had stayed there, briefly, a year ago, courtesy of an extremely wealthy hotelman, who had delusions, later proved to be just that, of duplicating its exterior in Kansas City.

Holcroft had struck up a friendship with the assistant manager. If the man was still there, perhaps he'd let him use a telephone. If telephone calls *were* traced back to the George V, it would be a simple matter to learn about them. And a simpler matter to leave misleading information regarding his whereabouts.

Anticipate.

"But, of course, it's my pleasure, Noel. It's so good to see you again. I am chagrined you do not stay with us, but at these prices, I don't blame you. Here, use my office."

"I'll charge the calls to my credit card, of course."

"I'm not worried, my friend. Later, an *apéritif*, perhaps?"

"I'd like that," said Noel.

It was ten-forty-five, Paris time. Quarter to six in New York. If Miles was as anxious as his message implied, the hour was insignificant. He picked up the phone and placed the call.

Noel looked at Miles's message again.

THE RECENT DEATH OF RICHARD HOLCROFT . . .
PROFESSIONALLY I RECOMMEND YOU SPEAK TO
ME BEFORE REACHING ANYONE ELSE . . .

The recommendation had an ominous tone; the "anyone else" had to mean his mother.

He put the paper down on the desk and reached into his pocket for Althene's cablegram.

YOUR FATHER DIED FOUR DAYS AGO . . . UNABLE
TO CONTACT YOU . . .

The guilt he felt at not having been with her nearly matched the guilt and the fear and the anger that consumed him when he considered the possibility that he was responsible for the death. Possibility? He *knew* it, he *felt* it.

He wondered—painfully—if Miles had reached Althene. And if he had, what had he said to her?

The telephone rang.

"Is this Noel Holcroft?"

"Yes. I'm sorry you had trouble reaching me. . . ."

"I won't waste time going into that," interrupted Miles, "except to say you've violated federal laws."

"*Wait* a minute," broke in Noel angrily. "What am I guilty of? You found me. I'm not hiding."

"*Finding* you after trying to locate you for damn near a week is called flagrantly ignoring and disregarding the law. You were not to leave the City of New York without telling us."

"There were pressing personal matters. I left word. You haven't got a case."

"Then let's try 'obstruction of justice.' "

"What?"

"You were in the lounge of that British seven-forty-seven, and you and I both know what happened. Or, should I say, what *didn't* happen?"

"What are you talking about?"

"That drink was meant for you, not Thornton."

Holcroft knew it was coming, but his knowing it did not lessen the impact. Still, he was not about to agree without a protest. "That's the craziest goddamn thing I've ever heard," he said.

"Come on! You're a bright, upstanding citizen from a bright, upstanding family, but your behavior for the past five days has been stupid and less than candid."

"You're insulting me, but you're not saying anything. You mentioned in your message—"

"We'll get to that," interrupted the detective. "I want you to know whose side you're on. You see, I want you to cooperate, not fight."

"Go ahead."

"We traced you to Rio. We spoke to—"

"You *what?*" Had Sam turned on him?

"It wasn't hard. Incidentally, your friend Buonoventura doesn't know. His cover for you didn't wash. He said you were in a boat out of Curaçao, but Dutch immigration didn't have you in the territory. We got a list of the overseas telephone numbers he called and checked the airlines. You were on Braniff out of New York, and you stayed at a Pôrto Alegre Hotel in Rio."

The amateur could not match the professional. "Sam said you called a couple of times."

"Sure did," agreed Miles. "You left Rio and we wanted to find out where you went; we knew he'd get in touch with you. Didn't you get my message at the hotel in London?"

"No."

"I'll take your word. Messages get lost."

But that message had not been lost, thought Noel. It had been stolen by the men of Wolfsschanze. "I know where I stand now. Get to the point."

"You don't *quite* know," Miles replied. "We talked to the embassy in Rio, to a man named Anderson. He said you told him quite a story. How you were trapped, chased, shot at. He said he didn't believe a word of it; considered you a troublemaker and was glad to get you out of Brazil."

"I know. He drove me to the airport."

"Do you want to tell me about it?" asked the detective.

Noel stared at the wall. It would be so easy to unburden himself, to seek official protection. The faceless Lieutenant Miles was a symbol of authority. But he was the wrong symbol in the wrong place at the wrong time. "No. There's nothing you can do. It's been resolved."

"Has it?"

"Yes."

Neither spoke for several seconds. "All right, Mr. Holcroft. I hope you change your mind, because I think I can help you. I think you *need* help." Miles paused. "I now make a formal request for your return to the City of New York. You are considered a prime witness in a homicide and intrinsic to our jurisdictional interrogations."

"Sorry. Not now."

"I didn't think you would. So let me try informally. It concerns your father."

The terrible news was coming, and he could not help himself. He said the words quietly. "He was killed, wasn't he?"

"I didn't hear that. You see, if I did, I'd have to go to

my superior and report it. Say you said it without provocation. You drew a conclusion that couldn't possibly be based on anything I said to you. I'd have to request extradition."

"Get off it, Miles! Your telephone message wasn't subtle! 'The recent death,' et cetera; 'professionally speaking, I recommend,' et cetera! What the hell am I supposed to think?"

Again, there was a pause from the New York end. "Okay. It's checkmate. You've got a case."

"He was murdered, wasn't he?"

"We think so."

"What have you said to my mother?"

"Nothing. It's not my jurisdiction. She doesn't even know my name. And that answers my next question. You haven't talked to her yet."

"Obviously. Tell me what happened."

"Your father was in what can best be described as a very unusual accident. He died an hour later, at the hospital, as a result of the injuries."

"What was the accident?"

"An old man from the Bronx lost control of his car near the Plaza Hotel. The car went wild, jumped the curb, and plunged into a crowd of people on the sidewalk. Three were killed instantly. Your father was thrown against the wall; actually, he was pinned, almost crushed."

"You're saying the car aimed for him!"

"Hard to tell. There was mass confusion, of course."

"Then what *are* you saying?"

Miles hesitated. "That the car aimed for him."

"Who was the driver?"

"A seventy-two-year-old retired accountant with an inflamed heart, a pacemaker, no family at all, and a license that expired several years ago. The 'pacer' was shorted in the accident; the man died on the way to the hospital."

"What was his connection to my father?"

"So far, no definite answers. But I've got a theory. Do you want to hear it?"

"Of course!"

"Will you come back to New York?"

"Don't press me. What's your theory?"

"I think the old guy was recruited. I think there was someone else in that car, probably in the back seat, hold-

ing a gun to his head. During the confusion, he smashed
the pacer and got away. I think it was an execution made
to look like a freak accident in which more than the target got killed."

Noel held his breath. There had been another "freak
accident." A subway in London had gone out of control,
killing five people. And among those killed was the only
man who could shed light on John Tennyson's employment at the *Guardian*.

It was bloody well murder. . . .

The thought of a connection was appalling. "Aren't
you reaching, Miles?" Holcroft asked.

"I said it was a theory, but not without some support. When I saw the name Holcroft on the accident report, I did a little digging. The old man from the Bronx
has an interesting history. He came to this country in
'forty-seven, supposedly a penniless Jewish immigrant, a
victim of Dachau. Only he wasn't penniless, as half a
dozen bankbooks show, and his apartment is a fortress.
Besides which, he made thirteen trips to Germany and
back since he got here."

Beads of perspiration broke out on Noel's forehead.
"What are you trying to say?"

"I don't think that old guy was ever near Dachau.
Or if he was, he was part of the management. Almost no
one knew him in his apartment building; no one ever saw
him in a synagogue. I think he was a Nazi."

Holcroft swallowed. "How does that connect him to
my father?"

"Through you. I'm not sure how yet, but through
you."

"Through me?" Noel felt the acceleration of his
heartbeat.

"Yes. In Rio, you told Anderson that someone
named Graff was a Nazi and tried to kill you. Anderson
said you were crazy on both points, but I don't. I believe
you."

"I was mad as hell. I didn't *mean* to tie one into the
other. It was a misunderstanding. . . ." Noel sought desperately to find the words. "Graff's paranoid, a hot-tem-
pered German, so I called him a Nazi, that's all. He
thought I was making sketches, taking pictures of his
grounds. . . ."

"I said I *believed* you, Holcroft," broke in the detective. "And I've got my reasons."

"What are they?" Noel knew he could barely be heard; he was suddenly afraid. His father's death was a warning. The Rache. The ODESSA. Whichever, it was another *warning*. His mother had to be protected!

Miles was talking, but Holcroft could not hear the detective; his mind raced in panic. Miles had to be stopped! He could not be allowed near Geneva!

"Those men on the plane who tried to kill you were German," Miles explained. "They used passports taken off two Americans killed in Munich five years ago, but they were German; the dental work gave them away. They were shot at Kennedy Airport; their bodies were found in a fuel truck. The bullets that killed them came from a German Heckler and Koch nine-millimeter pistol. The silencer was made in Munich. Guess where that little old man traveled when he went to Germany—at least on the six trips we were able to trace."

"Munich," whispered Noel.

"That's right. Munich. Where it all began and where it's still going on. A bunch of Nazis are fighting among each other thirty years after that goddamn war is over, and you're right in the middle of it. I want to know *why*."

Noel felt drained, swept by exhaustion and fear. "Leave it alone. There's nothing you can do."

"There's something I might be able to *prevent*, goddammit! Another murder."

"Can't you understand?" said Holcroft, in pain. "I can say it because he *was* my father. Nothing can be resolved in New York. It can only be resolved over here. Give me time; for the love of God, give me *time*. I'll get back to you."

"How long?"

"A month."

"Too much. Cut it in half. You've got two weeks."

"Miles, *please* . . ."

There was a click on the line; the connection in New York was severed.

Two weeks. Oh, God, it wasn't possible!

But it *had* to be possible. In two weeks he had to be in a position to stop Miles from going further. He could do that with the resources in Geneva. A philanthropic agency with assets of seven hundred and eighty million dollars would be listened to—quietly, in confidence. Once the account was freed, arrangements could be made, understandings reached, cooperation given and received. The ODESSA would be exposed, the Rache destroyed.

All this would happen *only* when three acceptable offspring presented themselves to the bank in Geneva. It *would* happen, Noel was convinced of that, but until then he had to protect his mother. He had to reach Althene and convince her that for the next few weeks she had to disappear.

What could he say to her? She'd never obey him. She'd never listen to him if she believed for an instant her husband had been murdered. What in God's name could he *say* to her?

"Allo? Allo, monsieur?" The voice of the operator floated out from the telephone. "Your call to New York—"

Holcroft hung up so quickly he jarred the instrument's bell. He could not talk to his mother. Not now. In an hour or so, not now. He had to think. There was so much to think about, so much to do.

He was going mad.

19

"He'll go mad," said the blond-haired man into the telephone at Hellenikon Airport, in Athens. "He must have heard the news by now. It will be a strain that may tear him apart; he won't know what to do. Tell our man in Paris to stay close to him for the next twenty-four hours. He must not return to America."

"He won't," said Gretchen Beaumont, thousands of miles away.

"You can't be sure. The psychological stresses are building properly; our subject's in a delicate frame of mind. However, he can be guided. He's waiting for me; he sees me now as his answer to so many things, but the string must be drawn tighter. I want him to go to Berlin first. For a day or two. To Kessler."

"Shall we use his mother? We could plant the idea with her."

"No. Under no circumstances must she be touched. It would be far too dangerous."

"Then how will you suggest Berlin?" asked Gretchen Beaumont, in England.

"I won't," answered John Tennyson, in Athens. "I will convince our sister to lead him to that conclusion. She's trying to reach me, of course."

"Be careful with her, Johann."

"I will."

Holcroft walked along the concrete bank of the Seine, unaware of the biting winds that came off the river. An hour ago he had been filled with confidence; now he felt lost. He knew only that he had to keep moving, clear his head, make decisions.

He had to reevaluate some matters, too. An hour ago the one man he believed he could count on was Helden's brother. That judgment was suspect now. A runaway car

on a New York street that took the life of the only father
he had ever known was too similar to an unexplained disaster in a London subway.

*The man was killed in a most unusual accident that
took five lives . . .* MI Five.

*An execution . . . . a freak accident in which more
than the target got killed.* David Miles, NYPD.

The meeting with Tennyson was suddenly *not* the
answer to everything; the shadow of the Tinamou had
appeared again. *A man would come one day and talk of a
strange arrangement.* Tennyson was waiting for him, but
perhaps he was waiting for the wrong reasons. Perhaps he
had sold out their covenant for a higher price.

If he had, he was as responsible for Richard Holcroft's death as surely as if his foot had been on the
accelerator and his hands on the wheel. Should that be
the case, Tennyson would not leave the meeting alive.
The son would kill for the father; he owed Richard Holcroft that.

Noel stopped and put his hands on the concrete wall,
astonished at himself . . . at his thoughts. He was actually
projecting himself into the role of a killer! His covenant
was extracting a cost more terrible than anything he had
considered.

He would confront Tennyson with the facts as they
had been given to him. He would watch the son of Wilhelm von Tiebolt closely. The truth or the lie: It would
be in Tennyson's words, in his eyes. Holcroft hoped to
God he would recognize it.

One step at a time. His mind was clearing. Each
move had to be considered carefully; yet that caution
could not slow him down.

First things first, and first there was the indisputable
fact that he could no longer move freely, carelessly. The
most deadly warning of all had been given him: the killing
of a loved one. He accepted that warning in fear and in
rage. The fear would make him careful; the rage would
give him a degree of courage. It *had* to; he was depending
on it.

Next was his mother. What could he say that she
would accept without being suspicious? Whatever it was,
she had to believe him. If she thought for an instant that
her husband's death was the work of men spawned by the
Third Reich, she would raise her voice in fury. And her

first cry would be her last. What could he say to her that would sound plausible?

He started walking again, absently, his eyes unfocused. As a result, he collided with a short man strolling in the opposite direction.

"Excuse me. *Pardon, monsieur,*" Noel said.

The Frenchman had been glancing at a newspaper; he shrugged, and smiled pleasantly. *"Rien."*

Noel stopped. The Frenchman reminded him of someone. The round, pleasant face, the spectacles.

Ernst Manfredi.

His mother had respected Manfredi, still owed the Swiss banker a great debt. Perhaps he could speak to Althene through Ernst Manfredi, invent an explanation given him by the banker. Why not? The words would not be contradicted; Manfredi was dead.

It was Manfredi who had been concerned for his old friend Althene *Clausen. He* had been frightened for her. He had been afraid that during the coming weeks, while the extraordinary account in Geneva was being released, Clausen's name would surface. There would be those who remembered a headstrong young woman who left her husband in revulsion, whose words became the basis for Heinrich Clausen's moral conversion. A conversion that resulted in the theft of hundreds of millions. Dormant hostilities might be aroused, revenge sought against that woman.

It was *Manfredi's* fear that she had to respect. The old banker knew more than either of them, and if he had thought it best that she disappear for a while, until the impact of the account's release was diminished, she should take his advice. A sick old man about to end his life did not draw frivolous conclusions.

The explanation made sense; it was consistent with their conversation in Bedford Hills three weeks ago. His mother would see that consistency. She would listen to the "words" of Ernst Manfredi.

Instinctively, Noel glanced over his shoulder to see if anyone was following him. It had become a habit. Fear made him careful; rage gave him a certain strength. He wanted very much to see an enemy. He was getting used to his unfamiliar forest.

He headed back to the hotel. He had rushed out of the George V in panic and bewilderment, avoiding the assistant manager, needing the cold air of the streets to clear his head. Now he would accept an aperitif and ask to make another transatlantic call. To his mother.

He walked faster, stopping abruptly twice, turning quickly. Was anyone there?

It was possible. A dark-green Fiat had slowed down a block behind. *Good.*

He crossed the street rapidly, went into the front entrance of a sidewalk café, and emerged seconds later from an exit that led out to the avenue George V. He walked up the block, stopping at a newsstand for a paper.

He could see the green Fiat careening around the corner near the café. It stopped abruptly. The driver parked at the curb and lowered his head. *Good.* It was suddenly made clear to Noel what he would do after the aperitif and the call to Althene.

He would see Helden. He needed a gun.

Von Tiebolt stared at the mouthpiece of the pay phone in the Athens airport, his lips parted in shock.

"What did you say?" he asked.

"It's true, Johann," said Helden in Paris. "British Intelligence thinks you may be the Tinamou."

"How *extraordinary.*" The astonished blond man drew out the word. "And outrageous!"

"That's what I said to Holcroft. I told him you were being hounded for the things you write . . . and because of who you are. Who *we* are."

"Yes, I imagine so." Von Tiebolt could not concentrate on his sister's reasoning; he gripped the receiver in anger. An error had been made somewhere; steps had to be taken immediately to correct it. What had led MI Five to *him?* Every track had been covered! But then, he could produce the Tinamou at will; it was his final strategy. No one was more trusted than the suspect who produced the hunted killer. This was the ultimate tactic of his creation. He might have to employ it sooner than he thought.

"Johann, are you there?"

"Yes, sorry."

"You *must* meet Holcroft as soon as possible."

"Of course. I'll be in Paris in four or five days. . . ."

"Not until then?" interrupted Helden. "He's very anxious."

"It's quite impossible."

"There's so much more to tell you. . . ." She told him of the account in Geneva; of the agency in Zurich that would dispense hundreds of millions; of the American son of Heinrich Clausen; of Erich Kessler in Berlin; of the Von Tiebolts in Rio. Finally, haltingly, she repeated the words uttered by their sister: *A man will come one day and talk of a strange arrangement.* "Did you say that?" she asked her brother.

"Yes. There's a great deal you've never been told. I didn't know when or how it would happen, only that it would. I spoke to Gretchen earlier. This Holcroft saw her the other night. I'm afraid she wasn't much help to him. We have a commitment as profound and as moving as anything in recent history. Amends must be made. . . ."

"That's what Holcroft said," broke in Helden.

"I'm sure he did."

"He's frightened. He tries not to show it, but he is."

"He should be. It's an enormous responsibility. I have to learn what he knows in order to help."

"Then come to Paris now."

"I can't. It's only a few days."

"I'm worried. If Noel's what he says he is, and I see no reason to doubt him—"

" 'Noel'?" asked the brother, with mild surprise.

"I like him, Johann."

"Go on."

"If he's the one that's to bring the three of you to the directors of La Grande Banque, then nothing can happen in Geneva without him."

"So?"

"Others know that. I think they know about the account in Switzerland. Terrible things have happened. They've tried to stop him."

"Who?"

"My guess would be the Rache. Or the ODESSA."

"That's doubtful," said John Tennyson. "Neither is capable of keeping such extraordinary news quiet. Take a newspaperman's word for it."

"The Rache kills; so does the ODESSA. Someone tried to kill Noel."

Tennyson smiled to himself; errors had been made, but the primary strategy was working. Holcroft was being pounded on all sides. When everything came together in

Geneva, he'd be exhausted, completely malleable. "He must be very cautious, then. Teach him the things you know, Helden. As much as you can. The tricks we've all learned from one another."

"He's seen some of those tricks," said the girl, a soft, compassionate laugh in her voice. "He hates using them."

"Better than ending up dead." The blond man paused. The transition had to be casual. "Gretchen mentioned a photograph, a picture of Beaumont. She thinks Holcroft took it."

"He did. He's convinced he saw Beaumont on the plane from New York to Rio. He thinks he was following him. It's part of what he'll tell you."

So it *was* the plane, thought Tennyson. The American was more observant than Beaumont had wanted to believe. Beaumont's disappearance would be explained in a matter of days, but it would be difficult to explain the photograph in Holcroft's possession if he showed it to the wrong people in Switzerland. The fanatic commander had left too obvious a trail, from Rio to the Admiralty. They had to get the photograph back. "I don't know what to say to that, Helden. I never liked Beaumont. I never trusted him. But he's been in the Mediterranean for months. I don't see how he could have left his ship and turned up on a plane out of New York. Holcroft's wrong." Tennyson paused again. "However, I think Noel should bring the photograph with him when we meet. He shouldn't be carrying it around. Nor should he talk about Beaumont. Tell him that. It could lead people to Gretchen. To us. Yes, I think it would be a good idea if he brought the photograph with him."

"He can't do that. It was stolen from him."

The blond man froze. It was *impossible*. None of *them* had taken the photograph! No *Sonnenkind*. He'd be the first to know. Someone *else*? He lowered his voice. "What do you mean, 'stolen from him'?"

"Just that. A man chased him, beat him unconscious, and took the picture. Nothing else, just the photograph."

"What man?"

"He didn't know. It was night; he couldn't see. He woke up in a field miles away from Portsmouth."

"He was attacked in Portsmouth?"

"About a mile from Gretchen's house, as I gather."

Something *was* wrong. Terribly wrong. "Are you sure Holcroft wasn't lying?"

"Why should he?"

"What *exactly* did he tell you?"

"That he was chased by a man in a black sweater. The man hit him with a blunt weapon and took the photograph out of his pocket when he was unconscious. Just the photograph. Not his money or anything else."

"I see." But he did *not* see! And it was the unseen that disturbed him. He could not convey his fears to Helden; as always, he had to appear in total control. Yet he had to search out this unseen, unknown disturbance. "Helden, I'd like you to do something . . . for all of us. Do you think you could arrange to take a day off from work?"

"I imagine so. Why?"

"I think we should try and find out who it is that has so much interest in Holcroft. Perhaps you might suggest a drive in the country, to Fontainebleau or Barbizon."

"But why?"

"I have a friend in Paris; he often does odd jobs for me. I'll ask him to follow you, very discreetly, of course. Perhaps we'll learn who else takes the trip."

"One of our people could do it."

"No, I don't think so. Don't involve your friends. Herr Oberst should not be a part of this."

"All right. We'll start out around ten in the morning. From his hotel. The Douzaine Heures, rue Chevalle. How will I know the man?"

"You won't. He'll pick you up. Say nothing to Holcroft; it would upset him needlessly."

"Very well. You'll call me when you get to Paris?"

"The minute I arrive, *meine Schwester.*"

"*Danke, mein Bruder.*"

Tennyson replaced the phone. There was a last call to make before he boarded the plane to Berlin. Not to Gretchen, now; he did not want to speak with her. If Beaumont's actions proved to be as disastrous as they appeared, if in his recklessness he had impeded the cause of Wolfsschanze, then all the strings that led to him and through him to Geneva would have to be severed. It was not an easy decision to make. He loved Gretchen as few men on earth loved their sisters; in a way that the world disapproved of because the world did not understand. She took care of his needs, satiated his hungers, so that there were never any outside complications. His mind was free to concentrate on his extraordinary mission in life. But that, too, might have to end. Gretchen, his sister, his lover, might have to die.

Holcroft listened to Althene's last words, stunned at her equilibrium, astonished that it had been so easy. The funeral had been yesterday.

"You do what you must, Noel. A good man died needlessly, foolishly, and that's the obscenity. But it's over; there's nothing either of us can do."

"There's something you can do for me."

"What's that?"

He told her of Manfredi's death—as the Swiss believed it had happened. An old man wracked with pain, preferring a quick end to prolonged suffering and infirmity. "The last thing he did as a banker was to meet with me in Geneva."

Althene was silent for a moment, reflecting on a friend who once meant a great deal to her. "It was like him to fulfill an agreement as important as the one he brought to you. He wouldn't leave it to others."

"There was something else; it concerned you. He said you'd understand." Holcroft held the telephone firmly and spoke as convincingly as he could. He expressed Manfredi's "concerns" about those who might remember a headstrong woman many believed responsible for the conversion of Heinrich Clausen, and for his decision to betray the Reich. He explained that it was entirely possible that there remained fanatics who might still seek revenge. Manfredi's old friend Althene Clausen should not risk being a target; she should go away for a while, where no one could find her in the event Clausen's name surfaced. "Can you understand, mother?"

"Yes," answered Althene. "Because he said it to me once before, several hundred years ago. On a warm afternoon in Berlin. He said they would look for us then, too. He was right; he's right now. The world is filled with lunatics."

"Where will you go?"

"I'm not sure. Take a trip, perhaps. It's a very good

time for it, isn't it? People are so embarrassingly solicitous about death."

"I'd rather you went someplace where you were out of sight. Just for a few weeks."

"It's easy to be out of sight. I have a certain expertise in that. For two years after we left Berlin, you and I kept moving. Until Pearl Haror, actually. The Bund's activities were too varied for comfort in those days; it took its orders from the Wilhelmstrasse."

"I didn't know that," said Holcroft, moved.

"There's a great deal— No matter. Richard put an end to it all. He made us stop running, stop hiding. I'll let you know where I am."

"How?"

His mother paused. "Your friend in Curaçao, Mr. Buonoventura. He was positively reverential. I'll let him know."

Holcroft smiled. "All right. I'll call Sam."

"I never did tell you about those days, did I? Before Richard came into our lives. I really must; you might be interested."

"I'd be very interested. Manfredi was right. You are incredible."

"No, dear. Merely a survivor."

As always, they said rapid goodbyes; they were friends. Noel walked out of the assistant manager's office. He started across the George V lobby, toward the bar, where his friend was waiting with aperitifs, then decided to take a short detour. He crossed to the huge window to the left of the entrance and peered out between the folds of the red velvet drapes. The green Fiat was still down the street.

Noel continued across the lobby toward the bar. He would spend a quarter of an hour in pleasant conversation with the assistant manager, during which he would impart some very specific, if erroneous, information, and ask a favor or two.

And then there was Helden. If she did not call him by five o'clock, he would telephone her at Gallimard. He had to see her; he wanted a gun.

"Four or five *days?*" exploded Holcroft into the phone. "I don't want to wait four or five days. I'll meet him anywhere! I can't waste time."

"He said he wouldn't be in Paris until then and suggested you go on to Berlin in the meantime. It would only take you a day or so."

"He knew about Kessler?"

"Perhaps not by name, but he knew about Berlin."

"Where was he?"

"At the airport in Athens."

Noel remembered. *He disappeared four days ago in Bahrain. Our operatives are watching for him from Singapore to Athens:* British Intelligence would have its confrontation with John Tennyson imminently, if it had not taken place already. "What did he say about the British?"

"He was furious, as I knew he would be. It's not unlike Johann to write an article that would embarrass the Foreign Office. He was outraged."

"I trust he won't. The last thing any of us want is a newspaper story. Can you call him back? Can *I* call him? He could fly in tonight. I could pick him up at Orly."

"I'm afraid not. He was catching a plane. There's only a number in Brussels; it's where he picks up his messages. It took him nearly two days to get mine."

"Goddammit!"

"You're overwrought."

"I'm in a hurry."

"Noel . . ." Helden began haltingly. "I don't have to work tomorrow. Could we meet? Perhaps go for a drive? I'd like to talk."

Holcroft was startled. He wanted to see *her.* "Why wait until tomorrow? Let's have dinner."

"I can't. I have a meeting tonight. I'll be at your hotel at ten o'clock tomorrow morning. In the afternoon you can fly to Berlin."

"Are you meeting your friends?"

"Yes."

"Helden, do something for me. I never thought I'd ask this of anyone, but . . . I want a gun. I don't know how to go about getting one, what the laws are."

"I understand. I'll bring it. Until morning."

"See you tomorrow." Holcroft hung up and looked at his open attaché case on the hotel chair. He could see the cover of the Geneva document. It reminded him of the threat from the men of Wolfsschanze. *Nothing is as it was for you. . . .* He knew now how completely true that was.

He had borrowed a gun in Costa Rica. He had killed a man who was about to kill him, and he never wanted to see a gun in his hand again, for as long as he lived. That, too, was changed. Everything was changed, because a man he never knew had cried out to him from the grave.

20

"Do you like mountain trout?" asked Helden, as she handed him the automatic in the front seat of his rented car.

"Trout's fine," he said, laughing.

"What's funny?"

"I don't know. You hand me a gun, which isn't the most normal thing for a person to do, and at the same time you ask me what I'd like for lunch."

"One has nothing to do with the other. I think it might be a good idea if you took your mind off your problems for a few hours."

"I thought you wanted to talk about them."

"I do. I also wanted to know you better. When we met the other night, you asked all the questions."

"Before I asked those questions, you did all the yelling."

Helden laughed. "I'm sorry about that. It was hectic, wasn't it?"

"It was crazy. You have a nice laugh. I didn't know you laughed."

"I do quite frequently. At least twice a month, regularly as clockwork."

Holcroft glanced at her. "I shouldn't have said that. I don't imagine you find much to laugh at."

She returned his look; a smile was on her lips. "More than you think, perhaps. And I wasn't offended. I'm sure you think me rather solemn."

"Our talk the other night wasn't designed for a barrel of laughs."

"No, it wasn't." Helden turned, both hands on her knees beneath the pleated white skirt on the seat. There was a gamine quality about her Noel had not noticed before. It was reinforced by her words. "Do you ever think about them?" she asked.

"Who?"

"Those fathers you and I never knew. What they did was so incredible, such an act of daring."

"Not just one act. Hundreds . . . thousands of them. Each different, each complicated, going on for months. Three years of manipulations."

"They must have lived in terror."

"I'm sure they did."

"What drove them?"

"Just what . . ." Noel stopped, not knowing why he did so. "Just what Heinrich Clausen wrote in his letter to me. They were shocked beyond anything we can imagine when they learned about the 'rehabilitation camps.' Auschwitz, Belsen—it blew their minds. It seems incredible to us now, but remember, that was 'forty-three. There were conspiracies of silence."

Helden touched his arm; the contact was brief, but it was firm. "You call him Heinrich Clausen. You can't say 'father,' can you?"

"I *had* a father." Noel stopped. It was not the moment to talk at length about Richard Holcroft; he had to control himself. "He's dead. He was killed five days ago in New York."

"Oh, *God*. . . ." Helden stared at him; he could feel the intensity of her concern. "Killed? Because of Geneva?" she asked.

"I don't know."

"But you think so."

"Yes." He gripped the wheel and was silent. A shell was forming, and it was an awful thing.

"I'm sorry, Noel. I don't know what else to say. I wish I could comfort you somehow, but I don't know how."

He looked at her, at her lovely face and at the clear brown eyes filled with concern. "With all your problems, just saying that is enough. You're a nice person, Helden. I haven't met too many people like you."

"I could say the same . . . nice person."

"We've both said it. Now, what about that trout? If we're going to take a few hours off, why not tell me where we're going?"

"To Barbizon. There's a lovely restaurant in the center of the town. Have you ever been to Barbizon?"

"Several times," said Noel, his eyes suddenly on the small rectangular mirror outside the window.

There was a dark-green Fiat behind them. He had no idea whether it was the same car that had waited for him yesterday on the avenue George V, but he intended to find out—without alarming Helden. He slowed down; the Fiat did not pass. Instead, it veered into the right lane, allowing another car to come between them.

"Is something wrong?" asked Helden.

Holcroft depressed the accelerator. The automobile lurched slightly at the slower speed. "No, not really. I had trouble with this damn thing yesterday. It needs a carburetor adjustment, I think. Every now and then there's an air lock. It passes if you nurse it."

"You sound very efficient."

"I'm a fair mechanic. You don't take jobs in Mexico and points south unless you are." He stepped on the pedal and held it down; the car sped forward.

He could see the green Fiat in the rearview mirror now. It swerved to the left, passing the intervening car, then returned to the right lane, behind them. The question was answered. They were being followed.

His fear was making him cautious. Whoever was in that Fiat was indirectly involved with Richard Holcroft's death; he was certain of it. And he was going to trap that man.

"There. Everything's fine now," he said to Helden. "The air lock's passed. Lunch in Barbizon sounds like a hell of a good idea. Let's see if I remember the way."

He did not. On purpose. He took several wrong turns, covering his mistakes with laughter, insisting the whole French countryside had been changed around. It became a silly game with a deadly serious objective: He had to see the face of the man in the Fiat. In Paris that face had been obscured behind a windshield and a cloud of cigarette smoke; he had to be able to recognize it in a crowd.

The Fiat's driver, however, was no amateur. If he was bewildered by Noel's aimless turns and shifting speeds, he gave no indication of it, staying a discreet distance behind them, never allowing the gap between them to become too close. There was a disabled car on a narrow road south of Corbeil-Essonnes; it was a good excuse to stop. Holcroft pulled alongside to see if he could help; the driver of the Fiat had no choice. He drove swiftly past the two parked cars. Noel looked up. The man was fair, his hair light brown; and there was something else: splotches, or pockmarks, on the man's cheek.

He would know that face again. That was all that mattered.

The driver of the disabled car thanked Holcroft, indicating that help was on the way.

Noel nodded and started up again, wondering if he'd see the green Fiat soon. Would it be in a side road, waiting for him, or would it simply emerge from nowhere and appear in the rearview mirror?

"That was a very nice thing to do," said Helden.

"We ugly Americans do nice things every once in a while. I'll get back on the highway."

If the green Fiat was in a side road, he did not see it. It was simply there, in his mirror, on the highway. They got off at the Seine-et-Marne exit and drove into Barbizon. The green Fiat stayed far behind, but it was there.

Their lunch was a strange mixture of ease and awkwardness: brief starts and abrupt stops; short conversations begun, suddenly suspended at midpoint, the purpose unremembered. Yet the ease was in their being together, physically close to each other. Holcroft thought she felt it as surely as he did.

This sense of closeness was confirmed by something Helden did, obviously without thinking about it: She touched him repeatedly. She would reach over briefly and touch his sleeve, or, more briefly, his hand. She would touch him for emphasis, or because she was asking a question, but she touched him as if it were the most natural thing in the world for her to do. And it was natural for him to accept her touch and return it.

"Your brother didn't discuss Beaumont?" he asked.

"Yes, he did. He was very angry. Everything about Beaumont angers him. He thinks you were wrong about seeing him on the plane, though. He wanted you to bring the photograph. I told him you didn't have it. He was furious."

"About the photograph?"

"Yes. He said it might be dangerous. It could lead 'people,' he said, to Gretchen, to you. To Geneva."

"I think the answer's simpler. The Royal Navy's no

different from any other military organization. The officers protect each other."

"My promiscuous sister, you mean?"

Holcroft nodded; he really did not want to discuss Gretchen Beaumont, not with Helden. "Something like that."

She touched his fingers. "It's all right, Noel. I don't sit in judgment where my sister's concerned." Then she took away her hand, embarrassed. "What I mean is, I have no right. . . . No, I don't mean that, either. I mean where you are concerned, I have no right. . . ."

"I think we both know what you mean," interrupted Holcroft, covering her hand with his. "Feel free to have a right. I think I like it."

"You make me feel foolish."

"Do I? It's the last thing I want to make you feel." He pulled back his hand, and followed her glance out the window. She was looking at the small stone pond on the terrace, but his attention did not remain where hers did. His gaze rose to several groups of tourists strolling in the Barbizon street beyond the gates of the restaurant. The man with the light-brown hair and pockmarked face was standing motionless on the far sidewalk. A cigarette was in his mouth, what appeared to be an artist's brochure in his hands. But the man was not looking at the brochure. His head was raised slightly, his eyes angled over at the entrance of the restaurant.

It was time to make his move, thought Noel. His rage was rekindled; he wanted that man.

"I've got an idea," he said as casually as he could. "I saw a poster by the door that—in my schoolboy French —I think said *Fête d'Hiver*. Someplace called Montereau-something-or-other. Isn't that a kind of carnival?"

"The *fête* is, not the village. It's about seven or eight miles south of here, I think."

"What is it? The carnival, I mean."

"*Fêtes d'hiver*? They're quite common and usually run by the local churches. As a rule, they're associated with a saint's day. It's like a flea market."

"Let's go."

"Really?"

"Why not? It might be fun. I'll buy you a present."

Helden looked at him quizzically. "All right," she said.

*   *   *

The bright afternoon sunlight bounced off the side-view mirror in harsh reflections, causing Holcroft to squint and blink repeatedly, trying to rid his eyes of blind spots. The dark-green Fiat appeared now and then. It was far behind them, but never out of sight for very long.

He parked the car behind a church, which was the focal point of the small town. Together he and Helden walked around the rectory to the front and into the crowds.

The village square was typically French, the cobble-stone streets spreading out like irregular spokes from an imperfect wheel, old buildings and winding sidewalks everywhere. Stalls were set up in no discernible order, their awnings in various stages of disrepair, crafts and foodstuffs of all descriptions piled on counters. Shiny platters and a profusion of oilcloth caught the rays of sun; shafts of light shot through the crowd. This *fête* was not aimed at the tourist trade. Foreigners belonged to the spring and summer months.

The man with the pockmarked face was standing in front of a stall halfway across the square. He was munching on a piece of pastry, his eyes darting in Hol-croft's direction. The man did not know he had been spotted; Noel was certain of that. He was far too casual, too intent on eating. He had his targets under surveillance; all was well. Holcroft turned to Helden, at his side.

"I see the present I want to get you!" he shouted.

"Don't be silly. . . ."

"Wait here! I'll be back in a few minutes."

"I'll be over there"—she pointed to her right—"at the pewter display."

"Fine. See you soon."

Noel began edging his way through the crowd. If he could weave enough, slouch enough, and make sufficiently quick movements, he could reach the edge of the mass of colliding bodies without the light-haired man's seeing him. Once on the cobblestone sidewalk beyond the crowd, he could inch his way around to within yards of the pastry stall.

He reached the sidewalk; the man had not seen him get there. He had ordered another piece of pastry and was eating it absently, rising on the balls of his feet, peer-ing anxiously over the heads of the crowd. Abruptly, he seemed to relax and settle back, his attention only half on his targets. He had spotted Helden; apparently he was convinced that if he could see her, her companion would not be far away.

Noel feigned a suddenly lame ankle and limped around the border of the crowd, his new injury allowing him to bend over in pain. There was no way the man could see him now.

Noel was directly behind the pastry stall, no more than ten yards from it. He watched the man closely. There was something primitive about him as he stood there motionless, eating deliberately, every now and then stretching to make sure his quarry was still in sight. It struck Holcroft that he was watching a predator. He could not see its eyes, but somehow he knew they were cold and alert. The thought made him angry, raising images in his mind of such a man seated behind a driver, a gun perhaps at the driver's head, waiting for Richard Holcroft to emerge on a New York sidewalk. It was the sense of ice-cold, deadly manipulation that enraged him.

Noel lunged into the crowd, his right hand gripping the automatic in his pocket, his left extended in front of him, fingers taut. When Noel touched him, it would be a grip the light-haired man would never forget.

Suddenly he was blocked. *Blocked!* As he parted the shoulders of a man and a woman in front of him, a third figure met him head on, cross-checking him with its body, its face turned away. He was being stopped deliberately!

"Get out of my way! Goddammit, let go of me!"

He could see that his shouts, or his English, or both, had alarmed the light-haired man, just feet away, who spun in place, dropping his pastry. His eyes were wild; his face was flushed. He spun again and forced his way through the crowd, away from Noel.

"Get out of—!" Holcroft could feel it before he saw it. Something had sliced through his jacket, ripping the lining above his left pocket. He looked down, his eyes unbelieving. A knife had been thrust at his side; had he not twisted his body, it would have penetrated!

He grabbed the wrist holding the knife, pushing it away, afraid to let go, crashing his shoulder up into the chest of the man who held it. Still the man kept his face hidden. Who *was* he? There was no time to think or wonder; he had to get the terrible knife away!

Noel screamed. He bent over, his enemy's wrist vised in both his hands, the blade thrusting about in the crowded space, his whole body writhing, twisting into those surrounding him. He yanked the fist with the blade extending from it, then smashed it down with his full weight, falling to the street as he did so. The blade fell away, clattering on the stone.

Something crashed into his neck. Suddenly dazed, he still knew what it was; he had been hit with an iron pipe. He lay curled up in terror and confusion, but he could not stay down! Instinct made him lurch up; fear made him hold his place, waiting for an attack, prepared to fend it off. And rage made him seek out his attackers.

They were gone. The body that belonged to the unseen face was gone. The knife on the ground was gone! And all around him people backed away, staring at him as if he were deranged.

My God! he thought, with a terrible awareness. If they would kill him, they would kill Helden! If the man with the pockmarked face was protected by killers, and those killers knew he had spotted their charge, they would assume that Helden had spotted him, too. They would go after her! They would kill *her*, because she was part of his trap!

He broke his way through the circle of onlookers, and dodged a hundred angry arms and hands in the direction he instinctively remembered she'd indicated only minutes before. A stall that was selling some kind of pitchers, or plates, or . . . pitchers, plates, *pewter.* That was it! A stall with pewter. Where was it?

It was there, but she was not. She was nowhere to be seen. He ran up to the counter of the stall and shouted.

"A woman! A blond woman was here!"

"*Pardon? Je ne parle pas—*"

"*Une femme. . . . Aux cheveux blonds. Elle a été ici!*"

The vendor shrugged and continued polishing a small bowl.

"*Où est elle?*" shouted Holcroft.

"*Vous êtes fou! Fou!*" yelled the stallkeeper. "*Voleur! Police!*"

"*Non! S'il vous plaît! Une femme aux—*"

"*Ah,*" broke in the vendor. "*Une blonde. Dans ce sens.*" He gestured to his left.

Holcroft pushed himself away from the stall and

raced into crowds again. He pulled at overcoats and jackets, making a path for himself. Oh, Christ, he had *killed* her! His eyes searched everywhere, every corridor, every pair of eyes, every thatch of hair. She was nowhere.

"*Helden!*"

Suddenly, a fist hammered into his right kidney, and an arm shot over his shoulder, locking itself around his neck, choking the air out of his throat. He slammed his right elbow into the body of his assailant, now behind him, now dragging him backward through the crowd. Gasping for air, he jammed his left elbow into the hard, twisting figure holding him, then his right again. He had caught his attacker in the rib cage; the lock around his throat loosened for an instant, and that instant was enough. He spun to his left, his fingers digging into the forearm around his neck, and pulled downward, throwing his assailant over his hip. Both men fell to the ground.

Noel saw the face! Beneath the unruly crop of red hair was the small scar on the forehead, and beneath it the angry blue eyes. The man was the younger of the two MI-Five agents who had questioned him in his London hotel. Noel's rage was complete; the madness based in a terrible error had gone unchecked. British Intelligence had intruded, and that intrusion might well have cost Helden her life.

But *why?* Why here in an obscure French village? He had no answers. He knew only that this man whose throat he now clutched was his enemy, as dangerous to him as the Rache or the ODESSA.

"Get *up!*" Holcroft struggled to his feet and pulled at the man. His mistake was in momentarily releasing the agent. Without warning, a paralyzing blow hammered into his stomach. His eyes spun out of focus, and for several moments he was aware only of being yanked through a sea of astonished faces. Suddenly he was slammed against the wall of a building; he could *hear* the impact of his head on the hard surface.

"You goddamn fool! What the devil do you think you're doing? You were nearly killed back there!"

The MI-Five man did not scream, but he might as well have, so intense was his tone. Noel focused his eyes; the agent had him pinned. The man's forearm was again pressed against his throat.

"You son of a bitch!" He could barely whisper the words. "You're the ones who tried to kill me. . . ."

"You're a certifiable lunatic, Holcroft! The Tinamou wouldn't *touch* you. I've got to get you out of here."

"The Tinamou? Here?"

"Let's go!"

"*No!* Where's Helden?"

"Certainly not with us! Do you think we're crazy?"

Noel stared at the man; he was telling the truth. It was all insane. "Then someone's taken her! She's gone!"

"If she's gone, she went willingly," said the agent. "We tried to warn you. Leave it alone!"

"No, you're wrong! There was a man—with pockmarks on his face . . ."

"The Fiat?"

"Yes! Him. He was following us. I went after him and his men caught me. They tried to kill me!"

"Come with me," ordered the agent, grabbing Holcroft's arm and propelling him down the sidewalk.

They reached a dark narrow alleyway between two buildings. No ray of sunlight penetrated; everything was in shadow. The alley was lined with garbage cans. Beyond the third garbage can on the right Noel could see a pair of legs. The rest of the figure was hidden by the receptacle.

The agent pushed Noel into the alley; four or five steps were all that were needed to get a clear view of the upper part of the body.

At first glance, the man with the pockmarked face appeared to be drunk. In his hand he clutched a bottle of red wine; it had spilled into the crotch of his trousers. But it was a different red from the stain that had spread over his chest.

The man had been shot.

"There's your killer," said the agent. "Now will you listen to us? Go back to New York. Tell us what you know and leave it alone."

Noel's mind churned; mists of confusion enveloped him. There was violent death in the skies, death in New York, death in Rio, death here in a small French village. The Rache, the ODESSA, the survivors of Wolfsschanze. . . .

Nothing is as it was for you. . . .

He turned to the MI-Five man, his voice no more than a whisper. "Don't you understand? I *can't* . . . ."

There was a sudden skirmish at the end of the alleyway. Two figures raced by, one propelling the other. Commands were shouted—guttural, harsh, the words not distinguishable but the violence clear. Cries for help were cut short by the sound of flesh against flesh, vicious slaps repeated again and again. And then the blurred figures were gone, but Holcroft could hear the scream.

"Noel! *Noel!* . . ."

It was Helden! Holcroft found his mind again and knew what he had to do. With all his strength, he slammed his shoulder into the side of the agent, sending him crashing over the garbage can that concealed the dead body of the man with the pockmarked face.

He ran out of the alley.

21

The screams continued, how far away he could not tell, so boisterous were the crowds in the village square. Music issued from a number of concertinas and cornets. Pockets of space were formed for couples, skipping, twirling, turning, in countryside dances. The *fête d'hiver* was now a carnival.

"*Noel! Noel. . . .*"

Up the curving sidewalk to the left of the square—the cries came from that direction! Holcroft ran wildly, colliding with a pair of lovers embracing against a wall. There.

"*Noel!*"

He was on a side street lined with three-story buildings. He raced down it, hearing the scream again, but no words, no name, only a scream cut short by the impact of a blow that produced a cry of pain.

Oh, *God*, he had to find—

A *door!* A door was partially open; it was the entrance to the fourth building on the right. The scream had come from there!

He ran to it, remembering as he drew near that he had a gun in his pocket. He reached in and pulled it out, thinking as he held it awkwardly in his hand that he had never really looked at the weapon. He did so now, and for an instant he stopped and stared at it.

He knew little about handguns, but he knew this one. It was a Budischowsky TP-70 Autoloading Pistol, the same type of gun Sam Buonoventura had lent him in Costa Rica. The coincidence gave him no confidence; rather, it made him sick. This was not his world.

He checked the safety and pulled the door open, staying out of sight. Inside was a long, narrow, dimly lit corridor. On the left wall, spaced perhaps twelve feet from each other, were two doors. From what he remembered of this type of structure he had to presume that there were identically spaced doors on the right wall; he could not see them from where he stood.

He darted into the entrance, the gun held steady in front of him. There were the two doors on the right wall. Four doors. Behind one of them Helden was a captive. But which one? He walked to the first door on the left and put his ear to it.

There was a scratching sound, erratic, unfamiliar. He had no idea what it was. Cloth, fabric . . . the tearing of cloth? He put his hand on the knob and twisted it; the door swung free and he opened it, his weapon in firing position.

Across the dark room was an old woman on her knees, scrubbing the floor. She was in profile, her gaunt features sagging, her arm working in circles on the soft wood. She was so old she neither saw him nor heard him. He closed the door.

A black ribbon was nailed to the door on the right. A death had taken place behind that door; a family was in mourning. A death behind *that door*. The thought was too unnerving; he listened.

This was it! A struggle was going on. Heavy breathing, movement, tension; inside that room there was desperation. Helden was behind that door!

Noel stepped back, his automatic leveled, his right foot raised. He took a deep breath, and, as if his foot were a battering ram, he drove it into the wood to the left of the knob. The force of the blow sent the door crashing inward.

Inside, on a filthy bed, were two naked teenagers, a dark-haired boy on top of a fat, fair-skinned girl, the girl's legs spread up toward the ceiling, the boy lying between them, both hands on her breasts. At the sound of the crash and the sight of the stranger, the girl screamed. The boy spun off her, rolling onto the floor, his mouth open in shock.

The crash! The sound of the crash was an alarm. Holcroft ran into the corridor and raced to the next door on the left. There was no time to be concerned about anything but finding Helden. He slammed his shoulder into the door, twisting the knob awkwardly with his left hand, his right gripping the handle of the gun. There was no need for force; the door gave way.

Noel stood in the door frame, for an instant feeling ashamed. Against the wall by a window was a blind man. He was an old man and he was trembling at the unseen, unknown violence that had invaded his dark privacy.

"*Nom de Dieu . . .*" he whispered, holding his hands in front of him.

The sound of racing footsteps came from the hallway, footsteps that grew louder—the sound of a man not simply running but running frantically, leather slapping against wood. Holcroft turned quickly, in time to see the figure of the MI-Five agent rush past. There was a crash of glass from somewhere outside. Noel lurched out of the blind man's room, looking to the left, where the crash had come from; there was sunlight streaming through an open door at the end of the corridor. Its panes of glass had been painted black; he had not seen it in the dim light.

How did the agent know a door was there? Why had he kicked it open and raced outside? Did the MI-Five man think *he* had gone out that way? Instinct told him the agent would not give him that much credit; he was an amateur, a lunatic. No, he was after someone else.

It could be only Helden! But Helden was behind the door across from the blind man's room; it was the only place left. It *had* to be. The agent was wrong!

Holcroft kicked the door in front of him; the lock broke, the door swung open, and he rushed inside.

It was empty, had been empty a very long time. Layers of dust were everywhere . . . and there were no footprints. No one had been inside that room for weeks.

The MI-Five man had been right. The amateur had not known something that the professional had perceived.

Noel ran out of the empty room, down the dark corridor, through the shattered door, and out into a courtyard. On the left was a heavy wooden door that led back to the side street. It was open, and Holcroft raced through it. He could hear sounds of the carnival from the square, but they were not the only sounds. Far down the deserted street to his right he could hear a scream, cut off now as it had been cut off before. He ran in the direction of the scream, in Helden's direction, but he could see no one.

"Get *back!*" The command came from a recessed doorway.

There was a gunshot; above him stone shattered and he could hear the sickening whine of a ricocheting bullet.

Noel threw himself to the ground, onto the hard, irregular surface of the cobblestones. As he broke his fall, his finger touched the trigger of his gun. It fired, the explosion next to his face. In panic, he rolled over and over toward the recessed doorway. Hands grabbed him, pulling his body into the shadows. The man from British Intelligence, the young man with the scar on his forehead, yanked him back against the stone entranceway.

"I repeat! You're a goddamned fool! I should kill you myself and save them the trouble." The agent was crouched against the wall; he inched his face to the edge.

"I don't *believe* you," said Noel. "I don't believe *any* of this. Where is she?"

"The bastard's holding her across the way, about twenty yards down. My guess is he's got a radio and has contacted a car."

"They're going to *kill* her!"

"Not now they won't. I don't know why, but that's not what they have in mind. Perhaps because she's his sister."

"Get off that! It's *wrong:* it's crazy! I told her; she reached him. He's no more this Tinamou than you are. And he's mad as hell. He'll probably write something for his paper, make you, the Foreign Office, the whole damned British government, look like assholes!"

The MI-Five agent stared at Holcroft. His look was that of a man studying the ravings of a psychopath, equal parts curiosity, revulsion, and astonishment. "He *what? You* what?"

"You heard me."

"My *God.* . . . Whoever you are, whatever you're involved with, you're not remotely connected with any of this."

"I told you that in London," said Noel, struggling to sit up, trying to find his breath again. "Did you think I was lying?"

"We knew you were lying; we just didn't know why. We thought you were being used by men wanting to reach Von Tiebolt."

"For what?"

"Make a blind contact, neither side exposing itself. It

was a fair cover: money in America, left for the family."

"But for *what?*"

"Later! You want the girl, I want the bastard who's got her. Listen to me." The agent gestured at the automatic in Noel's hand. "Do you know how to use that?"

"I once had to use a gun like it. I'm no expert."

"You don't have to be; you'll have a large target. If I'm right, they've got a car cruising the area."

"Don't you?"

"No, I'm alone. Now listen to me. If a car drives up, it'll have to stop. The second it does I'm going to dash over to that doorway across the street. As I'm running, cover me by shooting directly at the car. Aim for the windscreen. Hit the tires, the radiator. I don't care what, but try to get the windscreen. Shoot it up; immobilize the damned car, if you can; and pray to God that the locals stay away at that fucking wingding in the square."

"Suppose they don't, suppose someone—"

"Try not to hit him, you ass!" broke in the Englishman. "And keep your fire to the right side of the car. *Your* right. Expose yourself as little as possible."

"The *right* side of the car?"

"Yes, unless you want to hit the girl, which, frankly, I don't give a piss about. But I want *him*. Of course, if I'm wrong, none of this applies, and we'll have to think of something else."

The agent's face was pressed against the stone. He inched it forward, peering down the street. The unfamiliar forest belonged to such men, not to well-intentioned architects. "You weren't wrong back in that old building," Noel said. "You knew there was another way out."

"A second exit. No one worth his pecker would allow himself to be trapped inside."

Once more the professional was right. Noel could hear the screeching of tires; an automobile careened around an unseen corner and drew rapidly closer. The agent stood up, gesturing for Noel to follow. He looked around the edge of the entranceway, his forearm angled across his chest, his pistol in his hand.

There was a second screech of tires; the automobile came to a stop. The agent shouted at Holcroft as he leaped from the doorway, firing his pistol twice at the car, and raced across the street.

"Now!"

It was a brief nightmare, made intensely real by the shattering sounds and the frantic movement. Noel was actually *doing* it. He could see the automatic in front of him, at the end of *his* arm, being held in *his* hand. He could feel the vibrations that traveled through his body each time he squeezed the trigger. *The right side of the car. Your right. Unless—* He tried desperately to be accurate. Amazed, he saw the windshield shatter and crack; he heard bullets enter the door; he heard the screams of a human being . . . and then he saw that human being fall out of the door and onto the cobblestones beside the car. It was the driver; his arms were extended in front of him; blood poured out of his head and he did not move.

Across the street he could see the MI-Five man come out of a doorway, crouching, his pistol out in front of him. Then he heard the command:

"Release her! You can't get out!"

"Nie und nimmer!"

"Then she can go with you! I don't give a piss! . . . Spin to your right, miss! *Now!*"

Two explosions, one right after the other; a woman's scream echoed throughout the street. Noel's mind went wildly out of focus. He raced across the pavement, afraid to think, afraid to see what he might see, to find what he dared not find, for his own sanity.

Helden was on her knees, trembling, her breathing a series of uncontrollable sobs. She stared at the dead man, splayed on the pavement to her left. But she was *alive;* that was all he cared about. Noel ran to her and fell down beside her, pulling her shivering head into his chest.

"Him. . . . *Him,*" Helden whispered, pushing Noel away. "Quickly."

"What?" Noel followed her look.

The MI-Five agent was trying to crawl; his mouth opened and closed; he was trying to speak and no sound emerged. And over the front of his shirt was a spreading stain of red.

A small crowd had gathered at the entrance to the square. Three or four men stepped forward tentatively.

"Get him," said Helden. "Get him quickly."

She was capable of thinking and he was not; she was able to make a decision and he was immobile. "What are we going to do? Where are we going to go?" was all he could say, not even sure the words were his.

"These streets, the alleys. They connect. We have to get him away."

"*Why?*"

Helden's eyes bored into his. "He saved my life. He saved yours. *Quickly!*"

He could only do as he was ordered; he could not think for himself. He got to his feet and ran to the agent, bending over him, their faces inches apart. He saw the angry blue eyes that floated in their sockets, the mouth that struggled to say something but could not.

The man was dying.

Noel lifted the agent to his feet; the Englishman could not stand, so he picked him up, astonished at his own strength. He turned and saw Helden lurching toward the automobile at the curb; the motor was still running. Noel carried the agent over to the shot-up car.

"I'll drive," Helden said. "Put him in the back seat."

"The windshield! You can't see!"

"You can't carry him very far."

The next minutes were as unreal to Holcroft at the sight of the gun still in his hand. Helden made a swift U-turn, careening over the sidewalk, swerving out to the middle of the street. Sitting beside her, Noel realized something in spite of the panic. He realized it calmly, almost dispassionately: He was beginning to adjust to this terrible new world. His resistance was wearing down, confirmed by the fact that he *had* acted; he had *not* run away. People had tried to kill him. They had tried to kill the girl beside him. Perhaps that was enough.

"Can you find the church?" he asked, now amazed at his own control.

She looked at him briefly. "I think so. Why?"

"We couldn't drive this car even if you could see. We have to find ours." He gestured through the cracked glass of the windshield; steam was billowing from the hood. "The radiator was punctured. Find the church."

She did, mostly by instinct, driving up the narrow streets and alleys that connected the irregular spokes that spread out from the village square. The last few blocks were frightening. People were running beside the car, shouting excitedly. For several moments Noel thought it was the shattered windshield, riddled with bullet holes, that drew the villagers' attention; it was not. Figures rushed by toward the hub of the square, the word had spread.

Des gens assassinées! La tuerie!

Helden swung into the street that passed the church
rectory and fronted the entrance to the parking lot. She
turned in and drove up beside the rented car. Holcroft
looked in the rear seat. The MI-Five man was angled back
in the corner, still breathing, his eyes on Noel. He moved
his hand, as if to draw Noel closer.

"We're switching cars," said Holcroft. "We'll get you
to a doctor."

"Listen . . . to me first, you ass," whispered the Englishman. His eyes strayed to Helden. "Tell him."

"Listen to him, Noel," she said.

"What is it?"

"Payton-Jones—you have the number?"

Holcroft remembered. The name on the card given
him by the middle-aged, gray-haired intelligence agent in
London was Harold Payton-Jones. He nodded. "Yes."

"Call him. . . ." The MI-Five man coughed. "Tell him
what happened . . . everything."

"You can tell him yourself," said Noel.

"You're a piss ant. Tell Payton-Jones there's a complication we don't know about. The man we thought was
sent by the Tinamou, Von Tiebolt's man . . ."

"My brother's *not* the Tinamou," cried Helden.

The agent looked at her through half-closed lids.
"Maybe you're right, miss. I didn't think so before, but
you may be. I only know that the man who followed you
in the Fiat works for Von Tiebolt."

"He followed us to protect us! To find out who was
after Noel."

Holcroft spun in the seat and stared at Helden. "You
know about him?"

"Yes," she replied. "Our lunch today was Johann's
idea."

"Thanks a lot."

"*Please.* You don't understand these things. My
brother does. I do."

"Helden, I tried to trap that man! He was killed!"

"What? Oh, my *God* . . ."

"That's the complication," whispered the agent,
speaking to Noel. "If Von Tiebolt's not the Tinamou, what
is he? Why was his man shot? Those two men, why did
they try to take *her*? Kill *you*? Who were they? This
car . . . trace it." The Englishman gasped; Noel reached

over the seat but the agent waved him away. "Just listen. Find out who they were, who owns this car. They're the complication."

The MI-Five man was barely able to keep his eyes open now; his whisper could hardly be heard. It was obvious that he would die in moments. Noel leaned over the seat.

"Would the complication have anything to do with a man named Peter Baldwin?"

It was as though an electric shock had jolted the dying man. His eyelids sprang open; the pupils beneath came briefly back from death. *"Baldwin? . . ."* The whisper echoed and was eerily plaintive.

"He called me in New York," said Holcroft. "He told me not to do what I was doing, not to get involved. He said he knew things that no one else knew. He was killed an hour later."

"He was telling the *truth!* Baldwin was telling the truth!" The agent's lips began to tremble; a trickle of blood emerged from the corner of his mouth. "We never believed him; he was trading off *nothing!* We were sure he was *lying. . . ."*

"Lying about what?"

The MI-Five man stared at Noel; then, with effort, shifted his gaze to Helden. "There isn't time. . . ." He struggled pathetically to look again at Holcroft. "You're clean. You must be . . . you wouldn't have said what you just said. I'm going to trust you, both of you. Reach Payton-Jones . . . as fast as you can. Tell him to go back to the Baldwin file. Code Wolfsschanze. . . . It's Wolfsschanze."

The agent's head fell forward. He was dead.

22

They sped north on the Paris highway as the late-afternoon sun washed the countryside with rays of orange and cold yellow. The winter sun was the same everywhere: It was a constant. And Holcroft was grateful for it.

Code Wolfsschanze. It's Wolfsschanze.

Peter Baldwin had known about Geneva. He had tried to tell MI Five, but the doubters in British Intelligence had not believed him.

He was trading off nothing!

What was he trading *for?* What was the bargain he sought? Who *was* Peter Baldwin?

Who *had been* Peter Baldwin?

Who was Von Tiebolt . . . Tennyson?

If Von Tiebolt's not the Tinamou, what is he? Why was his man shot? Why did they try to take her? Kill you?

Why?

At least one problem was put to rest: John Tennyson was *not* the Tinamou. Whatever else the son of Wilhelm von Tiebolt was—and it might well be dangerous to Geneva—he was not the assassin. But then, who was he? What had he done to become involved with killers? Why were men after him—and, by extension, his sister?

The questions kept Noel's mind from dwelling on the last hours. He could not think about them; he would explode if he did. Three men killed—one by him. Killed by gunfire in the back street of a remote French village during a carnival. Madness.

"What do you think 'Wolfsschanze' stands for?" asked Helden.

"I know what it stands for," he said.

She turned, surprised.

He told her—everything he knew about the survivors

230

of Wolfsschanze. There was no point in concealing facts now. When he had finished, she was silent. He wondered if he had pushed her too far. Into a conflict she wanted no part of. She had said to him only a few days ago that if he did not do as she instructed, if he was not who he said he was, she would leave Paris and he would never find her. Would she do that now? Was the threat of Wolfsschanze the final burden she could not accept?

"Are you afraid?" he asked.

"That's a foolish question."

"I think you know what I mean."

"Yes." She leaned her head back on the seat. "You want to know if I'll run away."

"I guess that's it. Will you?"

She did not reply for several moments; nor did he press her. When she spoke, there was the echoing sadness in her voice—so like her sister's and yet so different. "I can't run away any more than you can. Morality and fear aside, it's simply not practical, is it? They'd find us. They'd kill us."

"That's pretty final."

"It's realistic. Besides, I'm tired of running. I have no energy left for it. The Rache, the ODESSA, now Wolfsschanze. Three hunters who stalk each other as well as us. It's got to end. Herr Oberst is right about that."

"I came to the same conclusion yesterday afternoon. It occurred to me that if it weren't for my mother, I'd be running with you."

"Heinrich Clausen's son," said Helden reflectively.

"And someone else's." He returned her look. "Do we agree? We don't get in touch with this Payton-Jones?"

"We agree."

"MI Five'll look for us. They have no choice. They had a man on us; they'll find out he was killed. There'll be questions."

"Which we can't answer. We were followed; we did not follow."

"I wonder who they were? The two men," he said.

"The Rache, I would think. It's their style."

"Or the ODESSA."

"Possibly. But the German spoken by the one who took me was odd. The dialect wasn't recognizable. He was not a Münchner, and certainly not a Berliner. It was strange."

"How do you mean?"

"It was very guttural, but still soft, if that makes sense."

"Not too much. Then you think they were from the Rache?"

"Does it matter? We've got to protect ourselves from both. Nothing has changed. At least, not for me." She reached over and touched his arm. "I'm sorry for you, though."

"Why?"

"Because now you are running with us. You're one of the children now—*die verwünschte Kinder*. The damned. And you've had no training."

"It seems to me I'm getting it in a hurry."

She withdrew her hand. "You should go to Berlin."

"I know. We've got to move quickly. Kessler has to be reached and brought in; he's the last of the"—Holcroft paused—"the issue."

She smiled sadly at the word. "There's you and my brother; you're both knowledgeable, both ready to move. Kessler must be made ready, too. . . . Zurich is the issue. And the solution to so much."

Noel glanced at her. It did not take much to perceive what she was thinking. Zurich meant resources beyond imagination; surely a part of them would be used to curb, if not eliminate, the fanatics of the ODESSA and the Rache. Holcroft knew that she knew he had witnessed their horrors for himself; a one-third vote was hers for the asking. Her brother would agree.

"We'll make Zurich work," he said. "You can stop running soon. We can all stop."

She looked at him pensively. Then she moved over on the seat next to him and put her hand through his arm and held it. She laid her head on his shoulder, her long blond hair falling over his jacket.

"I called for you and you came to me," she said in her odd, floating voice. "We nearly died this afternoon. A man gave his life for us."

"He was a professional," replied Noel. "Our lives may have been incidental to him. He was after information, after a man he thought could give it to him."

"I know that. I've seen such men before, such professionals. But at the last, he was decent; many aren't.

They sacrifice others too easily in the name of profession-alism."

"What do you mean?"

"You're not trained; you would have done as he told you. You could have been used for bait, to draw fire. It would have been easier for him to let you take the bullets, and then me. I wasn't important to him. In the confusion he might have saved his own life and gotten his man. But he saved us."

"Where shall we go in Paris?"

"Not Paris," said Helden. "Argenteuil. There's a small hotel on the river. It's lovely."

Noel raised his left hand from the wheel and let it fall on the hair that cascaded down his jacket. "You're lovely," he said.

"I'm frightened. The fear has to go away."

"Argenteuil?" he mused. "A small hotel in Argen-teuil. You seem to know a lot of places for someone who's been in France for only a few months."

"You have to know where they don't ask questions. You're taught quickly; you learn quickly. Take the Billan-court exit. Please hurry."

Their room overlooked the Seine, with a small bal-cony beyond the glass doors directly above the river. They stood for a few minutes in the night air, his arm around her, both of them looking down at the dark waters. Nei-ther spoke; comfort was in their touch.

There was a knock on the door. Helden tensed; he smiled and reassured her.

"Relax. While you were washing up I ordered a bottle of brandy."

She returned his smile and breathed again. "You should really let me do that. Your French is quite im-possible."

"I can say 'Remy Martin,'" he said, releasing her. "Where I went to school it was the first thing we learned." He went inside toward the door.

Holcroft took the tray from the waiter and stood for a moment watching Helden. She had closed the doors to the balcony and was staring out the windows at the night sky. She was a private woman, a lonely woman, and she was reaching out to him. He understood that.

He wished he understood other things. She was beautiful; it was the simple truth, and needed no elaboration. Nor could she be unaware of that beauty. She was highly intelligent, again an attribute so obvious no further comment was necessary. And beyond that intelligence she was familiar with the ways of her shadow world. She was street-smart in a larger sense, in an international sense; she moved swiftly, decisively. There had to have been dozens of times when she used sex to get an advantage, but he suspected it was used in cold calculation: Buyer beware, there is nothing but a body for you to take; my thoughts are mine; you'll share none of them.

She turned from the glass doors; her eyes were soft, her expression warm and yet still distant, still observing. "You look like an impatient maître d' waiting to escort me to my table."

"Right this way, mademoiselle," said Noel, carrying the tray to the small bureau across the room and placing it on top. "Would the lady care for a table by the water?" He moved a small chaise in front of the glass doors and faced her, smiling and bowing. "If the lady would care to be seated, brandy will be served, and the fireworks will begin. The torchbearers on the boats await only your presence."

"But where will you sit, my attractive *garçon?*"

"At your feet, lady." He leaned over and kissed her, holding her shoulders, wondering if she would withdraw or push him away.

Whatever he expected, he was not prepared for what happened. Her lips were soft and moist, parted as if swollen, moving against his, inviting him into her mouth. She reached up with both her hands and cupped his face, her fingers gently caressing his cheeks, his eyelids, his temples. Still her lips kept moving, revolving in desperate circles, pulling him into her. They stood together. He could feel her breasts pressed against his shirt, her legs against his, pushing into him, matching strength for strength, arousing him.

Then a strange thing happened. She began to tremble; her fingers crept around his neck and dug into his flesh, holding him fiercely, as if she were afraid he might move away. He could hear the sobs that came from her throat, feel the convulsions that gripped her. He moved his hands to her waist and gently pulled his face from hers, forcing her to look at him.

She was crying. She stared at him for a moment; pain was in her eyes, a hurt so deep Noel felt he was an intruder watching a private agony.

"What is it? What's the matter?"

"Make the fear go away," she whispered plaintively. She reached for the buttons on her blouse and undid them, exposing the swell of her breasts. "I can't be alone. Please, make it go *away*."

He pulled her to him, cradling her head against his chest, her hair beneath his face soft and lovely, as she was soft and lovely.

"You're not alone, Helden. Neither am I."

They were naked beneath the covers, his arm around her, her head on his chest. With his free hand, he kept lifting the strands of her long blond hair, letting them fall to cover her face.

"I can't see when you do that," she said, laughing.

"You look like a sheep dog."

"Are you my shepherd?"

"I have a staff."

"That's dreadful. You have a dirty mouth." She reached up with her index finger and tapped his lips. He caught her finger between his teeth and growled. "You can't frighten me," she whispered, raising her face above his, depressing his tongue playfully. "You're a cowardly lion. You make noises, but you won't bite."

He took her hand. "Cowardly lion? *The Wizard of Oz?*"

"Of course," she answered. "I loved *The Wizard of Oz*. I saw it dozens of times in Rio. It's where I began to learn English. I wanted so to be called Dorothy. I even named my little dog Toto."

"It's hard to think of you as a little girl."

"I was, you know. I didn't spring full flower. . . ." She stopped and laughed. She had raised herself above him; her breasts were in front of his face. His hand instinctively reached for the left nipple. She moaned and covered his hand, holding it where it was as she lowered herself back down on his chest. "Anyway, I *was* a little girl. There were times when I was very happy."

"When?"

"When I was alone. I always had a room to myself; mother made sure of that. It was always in the back of the house or the apartment; or, if we were in a hotel, it was separate, away from my brother and sister. Mother said I was the youngest and should not be disturbed by the hours they kept."

"I imagine that could get pretty lonely. . . ."

"Oh, no! Because I was never alone. My friends were in my mind, and they would sit in chairs and on my bed and we'd talk. We would talk for hours, telling each other our secrets."

"What about school? Didn't you have flesh-and-blood friends?"

Helden was silent for a moment. "A few, not many. As I look back, I can't blame them. We were all children. We did as our parents told us to do. Those of us who had a parent left."

"What did the parents tell them?"

"That I was a Von Tiebolt. The little girl with the silly first name. My mother was . . . well, my mother. I think they thought my stigma was contagious."

She may have been branded with a stigma, thought Noel, but her mother was not the cause of it. Maurice Graff's ODESSA had more important things on its mind. Millions upon millions siphoned off their beloved Reich to be used by traitors such as Von Tiebolt for a massive apology.

"Things got better when you grew up, didn't they?"

"Better? Certainly. You adjust, you mature, you understand attitudes you didn't as a child."

"More friends?"

"Closer ones, perhaps, not necessarily more. I was a poor mixer. I was used to being by myself; I understood why I was not included at parties and dinners. At least, not in the so-called respectable households. The years curtailed my mother's social activities, shall we say, but not her business interests. She was a shark; we were avoided by our own kind. And of course the Germans were never really accepted by the rest of Rio, not during those years."

"Why not? The war was over."

"But not the embarrassments. The Germans were a

constant source of embarrassment then. Illegal monies, war criminals, Israeli hunters . . . it went on for years."

"You're such a beautiful woman, it's difficult to think of you . . . let's say, isolated."

Helden raised herself and looked at him. She smiled, and with her right hand pushed her hair back, holding it at the base of her neck. "I was very stern-looking, my darling. Hair straight, wrapped in a bun, large glasses and dresses always a size too large. You wouldn't have looked at me twice. . . . Don't you believe me?"

"I wasn't thinking about that."

"What then?"

"You just called me 'my darling.' "

She held his eyes. "Yes, I did, didn't I? It seemed quite natural. Do you mind?"

He reached for her, his answer his touch.

She sat back on the chaise, her slip serving as a negligee; she sipped the brandy. Noel was on the floor beside her, leaning against the small couch, his shorts and open shirt taking the place of a bathrobe. They held hands and watched the lights of the boats shimmering on the water.

He turned his head and looked at her. "Feeling better?"

"Much better, my darling. You're a very gentle man. I haven't known many in my life."

"Spare me."

"Oh, I don't mean that. For your information, I'm known among Herr Oberst's ranks as *Fräulein Eiszapfen.*"

"What's that?"

" 'Icicle.' 'Mademoiselle Icicle.' At work, they're convinced I'm a lesbian."

"Send them to me."

"I'd rather not."

"I'll tell them you're a faggot in drag who uses whips and bicycle chains. They'll run at the sight of you."

"That's very sweet." She kissed him. "You're warm and gentle and you laugh easily. I'm terribly fond of you, Noel Holcroft, and I'm not sure that's such a good thing."

"Why?"

"Because we'll say good-bye and I'll think of you."

Noel reached up and held the hand that still touched

his face; he was suddenly alarmed. "We just said hello. Why good-bye?"

"You have things to do. I have things to do."

"We both have Zurich."

"*You* have Zurich. I have my life in Paris."

"They're not mutually exclusive."

"You don't know that, my darling. You don't know anything about me. Where I live, how I live."

"I know about a little girl who had a room to herself and saw *The Wizard of Oz* dozens of times."

"Think kindly of her. She will of you. Always."

Holcroft took her hand from his face. "What the hell are you trying to say? Thanks for a lovely evening, now good-bye?"

"No, my darling. Not like that. Not now."

"Then what *are* you saying?"

"I'm not sure. Perhaps I'm just thinking out loud. . . . We have days, weeks, if you wish them."

"I wish them."

"But promise me you'll never try to find where I live, never try to reach me. I'll find you."

"You're married!"

Helden laughed. "No."

"Then, living with someone."

"Yes, but not in the way you think."

Noel watched her closely. "What am I supposed to say to that?"

"Say that you'll promise."

"Let me understand you. Outside of where you work, there's no place I can reach you. I can't know where you live, or how to get in touch with you?"

"I'll leave a number of a friend. In an emergency she'll reach me."

"I thought I was a friend."

"You are. But in a different way. Please, don't be angry. It's for your own protection."

Holcroft remembered three nights ago. In the midst of her own anxieties, Helden had been worried about him, worried that he had been sent by the wrong people. "You said in the car that Zurich was the solution to so much. Is it the answer for you? Could Zurich change the way you live?"

She hesitated. "It's possible. There's so much to do. . . ."

"And so little time," completed Holcroft. He touched her cheek, forcing her to look at him. "But before the money's released, there's the bank in Geneva and specific conditions that have to be met."

"I understand. You've explained them, and I'm sure Johann knows about them."

"I'm not so sure. He's laid himself open to a lot of speculation that could knock him out of the box."

"Knock him where?"

"Disqualify him. Frighten the men in Geneva; make them close the vaults. We'll get to him in a minute. I want to talk about Beaumont. I think I know what he is, but I need your help to confirm it."

"How can I help?"

"When Beaumont was in Rio, did he have any connection with Maurice Graff?"

"I have no idea."

"Can we find out? Are there people in Rio who would know?"

"Not that I know."

"God damn it, we've got to learn. Learn everything we can about him."

Helden frowned. "That will be difficult."

"Why?"

"Three years ago, when Gretchen said she was going to marry Beaumont, I was shocked; I told you that. I was working at the time for a small research firm off Leicester Square—you know, one of those dreadful places that you send five pounds to and they get you all the information you want on a subject. Or a person. They're superficial, but they do know how to use sources." Helden paused.

"You checked on Beaumont?" asked Noel.

"I tried to. I didn't know what I was looking for, but I tried. I went back to his university records, got all the available information about his naval career. Everything was filled with approvals and recommendations, awards and advancements. Why, I can't tell you—except that there seemed to me to be an inconsistency. I went farther back to find out what I could about his family in Scotland."

"What was the inconsistency?"

"Well, according to the naval records, his parents were quite ordinary. I got the impression they were rather poor. Owners of a greengrocery or a florist shop in a town called Dunheath, south of Aberdeen, on the North Sea. Yet, when he was at university—Cambridge, by the way —he was a regular student."

"Regular? . . . What should he have been?"

"On scholarship, I would think. There was need, and he was qualified, yet there were no applications for a scholarship. It seemed odd."

"So you went back to the family in Scotland. What did you learn?"

"That's the point. Next to nothing. It was as if they had disappeared. There was no address, no way to reach them. I sent off several inquiries to the town clerk and the postal service—obvious places people never think of. The Beaumonts were apparently an English family who simply arrived in Scotland one day shortly after the war, stayed for a few years, then left the country."

"Could they have died?"

"Not according to the records. The navy always keeps them up to date in case of injury or loss of life. They were still listed as living in Dunheath, but they had left. The postal service had no information at all."

It was Holcroft's turn to frown. "That sounds crazy."

"There's something more." Helden pushed herself up against the curve of the chaise. "At Gretchen's wedding, there was an officer from Beaumont's ship. His second-in-command, I think. The man was a year or two younger than Beaumont, and obviously his subordinate, but there was a give-and-take between them that went beyond friendship, beyond that of officer to officer."

"What do you mean, 'give-and-take'?"

"It was as if they were always thinking exactly alike. One would start a sentence, the other might finish it. One would turn in a particular direction, the other would comment on what the first was looking at. Do you know what I mean? Haven't you seen people like that? Men like that?"

"Sure. Brothers who are close, or lovers. And often military men who've served a long time together. What did you do?"

"I checked on that man. I used the same sources, sent out the same inquiries, as I had with Beaumont. What came back was extraordinary. They *were* alike; only the names were different. Their academic and military records were almost identical, superior in every way. They both came from obscure towns, their parents undistinguished and certainly not well off. Yet each had gone to a major university without financial aid. And each had become an officer without any prior indication that he was seeking a military career."

"What about the family of Beaumont's friend? Were you able to locate them?"

"No. They were listed as living in a mining town in Wales, but they weren't. They hadn't been there in years, and no one had any information about them."

What Helden had learned was consistent with Noel's theory that Anthony Beaumont was an ODESSA agent. What was important now was to take Beaumont—and any "associates"—out of the picture. They could not be allowed to interfere further with Geneva. Perhaps he and Helden were wrong: Perhaps they should reach Payton-Jones and let Beaumont become his problem. But there were side issues to consider, among which was the danger of British Intelligence's reopening the Peter Baldwin file, going back to Code Wolfsschanze.

"What you've told me fits in with what I've been thinking," Noel said. "Let's go back to your brother. I have an idea what happened in Rio. Will you talk about it now?"

Helden's eyes widened. "I don't know what you mean."

"Your brother learned something in Rio, didn't he? He found out about Graff and the Brazilian ODESSA. That was why he was hounded, why he had to get out. It wasn't your mother, or your brother's business dealings, or anything like that. It was Graff and the ODESSA."

Helden slowly let out her breath. "I never heard that, believe me."

"Then what was it? Tell me, Helden."

Her eyes pleaded with him. "Please, Noel. I owe you so much; don't make me pay like this. What happened to Johann in Rio has nothing to do with you. Or with Geneva."

"You don't know that. *I* don't know that. I just know that you have to tell me. I have to be prepared. There's so much I don't understand." He gripped her hand. "Listen to me. This afternoon I broke into a blind man's room. I smashed the door in; the sound was awful

—sudden and loud. He was an old man and, of course, he couldn't see me. He couldn't see the fear in my own eyes. His hands shook and he whispered a prayer in French. . . .

"For a moment I wanted to go to that man and hold his hands and tell him I knew how he felt. You see, he *didn't* see the fear in my eyes. I'm frightened, Helden. I'm not the sort of person who crashes into people's rooms, and shoots guns, and gets shot at. I can't turn back, but I'm scared. So you've got to help me."

"I want to; you know that."

"Then tell me what happened in Rio. What happened to your brother?"

"It's simply not important," she said.

"*Everything's* important." Noel stood up and crossed to the chair where he had thrown his jacket. He showed Helden the torn lining. "Look at this. Someone in that crowd this afternoon tried to put a knife in me. I don't know about you, but that's never happened to me before; it's just not something I know anything about. It petrifies me . . . and it makes me goddamned angry. And five days ago in New York, the man I grew up with—the only man I ever called my father—walked out on a sidewalk and was killed by an 'out-of-control car' that *aimed* for him and crushed him against a building! His death was a warning. For *me!* So don't talk to me about the Rache, or the ODESSA, or the men of Wolfsschanze. I'm beginning to learn all about those sick sons of bitches, and I want every last one of them put away! With the money in Zurich, we can do that. Without it, no one'll listen to us. It's an economic fact of life. You don't dismiss people who have seven hundred and eighty million dollars. You *listen* to people like that." Holcroft let the jacket fall to the floor. "The only way we'll get to Zurich is to satisfy the bank in Geneva, and the only way to reach Geneva is to use our heads. There's no one really on our side; there's just us. The Von Tiebolts, the Kesslers . . . and one Clausen. Now, what happened in Rio?"

Helden looked down at the torn jacket, then back at Noel.

"Johann killed someone."

"Who?"

"I don't know—I really don't. But it was someone important."

23

Holcroft listened to her, watching for false notes. There were none. She was telling him what she knew, and it was not a great deal.

"About six weeks before we left Brazil," Helden explained, "I drove home one night after a seminar at the university; we lived out in the countryside then. There was a dark-colored limousine in front, so I parked behind it. As I walked up to the porch, I heard yelling from inside. There was a terrible fight and I couldn't imagine who it was; I didn't recognize the one screaming. He kept yelling things like 'killer,' 'murderer,' 'it was you' . . . things like that. I ran inside and found Johann standing in the hallway in front of the man. He saw me, and told the man to be still. The man tried to strike Johann, but my brother is very powerful; he held the man's arms and pushed him out the door. The last words the man screamed were to the effect that others also knew; that they would see Johann hanged as a murderer, and if that didn't happen, they'd kill him themselves. He fell on the steps, still screaming, then he ran to the limousine, and Johann went after him. He said something to him through the window; the man spat in my brother's face and drove off."

"Did you ask your brother about it?"

"Naturally. But Johann wouldn't discuss it other than to say the man was mad. He had lost a great deal of money in a business venture and had gone crazy."

"You didn't believe him?"

"I wanted to, but then the meetings began. Johann would be out until all hours, away for days; he behaved quite abnormally. Then, only weeks later, we flew to Recife with a new name and a new country. Whoever was killed was very rich, very powerful. He had to be to have friends like that."

"You have no idea who the man was inside your house that night?"

"No. I'd seen him before, but I couldn't remember where, and Johann wouldn't tell me. He ordered me never to bring up the matter again. There were things I should not be told."

"You accepted that?"

"Yes. Try to understand. We were children of Nazis, and we knew what that meant. It was often best not to ask questions."

"But you had to know what was going on."

"Oh, we were taught; make no mistake about it," said Helden. "We were trained to elude the Israelis; they could force information from us. We learned to spot a recruiter from the ODESSA, a maniac from the Rache; how to get away, how to use a hundred different tricks to throw them off."

Noel shook his head in amazement. "Your everyday training for the high-school glee club. It's crazy."

"That's a word you could use three weeks ago," she said, reaching for his hand. "Not now. Not after today."

"What do you mean?"

"In the car I said I felt sorry for you because you had no training."

"And I said I thought I was getting it in a hurry."

"But so little, and so late. Johann told me to teach you what I could. I want you to listen to me, Noel. Try to remember everything I tell you."

"What?" Holcroft felt the strength of her grip and saw the concern in her eyes.

"You're going to Berlin. I want you back."

With those words she began. There were moments when Noel thought he might smile—or, worse, laugh—but her intensity kept him in check; she was deadly serious. That afternoon three men had been killed. He and Helden might easily have been the fourth and the fifth victims. So he listened and tried to remember. Everything.

"There's no time to get false papers; they take days. You have money; buy an extra seat on the plane. Stay alert, and don't let anyone sit next to you; don't get hemmed in. And don't eat or drink anything you didn't bring with you."

His mind briefly raced back to a British 747 and a vial of strychnine. "That's a suggestion I won't forget."

"You might. It's so easy to ask for coffee or even a glass of water. Don't."

"I won't. What happens when I get to Berlin?"

"To any city," she corrected. "Find a small hotel in a crowded district where the main business is pornography, where there's prostitution, narcotics. Front desks never ask for identification in those areas. I know someone who'll give us the name of a hotel in Berlin. . . ."

Her words poured forth, describing tactics, defining methods, telling him how to invent his own variations. . . .

False names were to be used, rooms switched daily, hotels changed twice a week. Phone calls were to be placed from public booths, never from hotel rooms, never from residences. A minimum of three changes of outer clothing, including hats and caps and dissimilar glasses, were to be carried; shoes were to have rubber soles. These were best for running with a minimum of sound, for stopping and starting quickly, and walking silently. If questioned, he was to lie indignantly but not arrogantly, and never in a loud tone of voice. That kind of anger triggered hostility, and hostility meant delay and further questions. While flying from airport to airport, a gun was to be dismantled, its barrel separated from the handle, the firing pin removed. These procedures generally satisfied the European customs clerks: Inoperable weapons did not concern them; contraband did. But if they objected, he was to let them confiscate the gun; another could be purchased. If they let the weapon through, he was to reassemble it immediately, in the toilet stall of a men's room.

The street. . . . He knew something about the streets and crowds, he told Helden. One never knew enough, she replied, telling him to walk as close to the curb as possible, to be ready to dash out among the traffic at any sign of hostility or surveillance.

"Remember," she said, "you're the amateur, they're the professionals. Use that position; turn your liability into an asset. The amateur does the unexpected, not because he's clever or experienced but because he doesn't know any better. Do the unexpected rapidly, obviously, as if confused. Then stop and wait. A confrontation is often the last thing surveillance wants. But if he does want it, you might as well know it. Shoot. You should have a silencer; we'll get you one in the morning. I know where."

He turned, stunned, unable to speak. She saw the astonishment in his eyes. "I'm sorry," she said, leaning forward, smiling sadly and kissing him.

They talked through most of the night, the teacher and the pupil, lover and lover. Helden was obsessed; she would invent situations and then demand that he tell her what he would do in the hypothetical circumstances.

"You're on a train, walking through a narrow corridor; you're carrying important papers. A man comes toward you from the opposite direction; you know him; he's the enemy. There are people behind you; you can't go back. What do you do?"

"Does the man—the enemy—want to hurt me?"

"You don't know. What do you do? Quickly!"

"Keep going, I guess. Alert, expecting the worst."

"No, my darling! The *papers*. You've got to protect them! You trip; you fall to the floor!"

"Why?"

"You'll draw attention to yourself; people will help you up. The enemy won't make his move in that situation. You create your own diversion."

"With *myself*," said Noel, seeing the point.

"Exactly."

It went on, and on, and on, until the teacher and the pupil were exhausted. They made quiet love and held each other in the comfort of their warmth, the world outside a faraway thing. Finally, Helden fell asleep, her head on his chest, her hair covering her face.

He lay awake for a while, his arm across her shoulders, and wondered how a girl who'd been entranced by *The Wizard of Oz* had grown up to become so skilled a practitioner in arts of deception and escape. She was from another world, and he had entered that world with alarming speed.

They awoke too late for Helden to go to work.

"It's just as well," she said, reaching for the phone. "We have shopping to do. My supervisor will accept a second day of illness. I think she's in love with me."

"I think I am too," said Noel, letting his fingers trace the curve of her neck. "Where do you live?"

She looked at him, smiling as she gave the number to the operator. Then she covered the mouthpiece. "You'll not extract vital information by appealing to my baser instincts. I'm trained, remember?" She smiled again.

And was maddening again. "I'm serious. Where do you *live?*"

The smile disappeared. "I can't tell you." She removed her hand from the telephone and spoke rapidly in French to the Gallimard switchboard.

An hour later they drove into Paris, first stopping at his hotel, to pick up his things, then moving on to a district profuse with secondhand-clothing stores. The teacher once more asserted her authority; she chose the garments with a practiced eye. The clothes she selected for the pupil were nondescript, difficult to spot in a crowd.

A mackinaw and a brown topcoat were added to his raincoat. A battered country walking hat; a dark fedora, its crown battered; a black cap whose visor fell free of the snap. All were well worn. But not the shoes; they were new. One pair with thick crêpe soles; a second, less informal, whose leather soles were the base for a layer of rubber attached by a shoemaker down the street.

The shoe-repair shop was four blocks away from a shabby storefront. Helden went in alone, instructing him to remain outside. She emerged ten minutes later with a perforated cylinder, the silencer for his automatic.

He was being outfitted with uniforms and the proper weapon. He was being processed and sent into combat after the shortest period of basic training one could imagine. He had seen the enemy. Alive and following him . . . and then dead in the streets and alleyways of a village called Montereau-faut-Yonne. Where was the enemy now?

Helden was confident they had lost him for a while. She thought the enemy might pick him up at the airport, but once in Berlin, he could lose that enemy again.

He *had* to. She wanted him back; she would be waiting.

They stopped at a small café for lunch and wine. Helden made a final phone call and returned to the booth with the name of a hotel in Berlin. It was in the *Hurenviertel*, that section of the city where sex was an open commodity.

She held his hand, her face next to his; in minutes

he would go out on the street alone and hail a taxi for Orly Airport.

"Be careful, my darling."

"I will."

"Remember the things I've told you. They may help."

"I'll remember."

"The hardest thing to accept is that it's all real. You'll find yourself wondering, why me? why this? Don't think about it; just accept it."

Nothing is as it was for you. Nothing can ever be the same.

"I have. I've also found you."

She glanced away, then turned back to. him. "When you get to Berlin, near the hotel, pick up a whore in the street. It's a good protective device. Keep her with you until you make contact with Kessler."

The Air France 707 made its final approach into Tempelhof Airport. Noel sat on the right side of the plane, in the third seat on the aisle, the space next to him unoccupied.

You have money; buy an extra seat . . . and don't let anyone sit next to you; don't get hemmed in.

The ways of survival, spoken by a survivor, thought Holcroft. And then he remembered that his mother had called herself a survivor. Althene had taken a certain pride in the term, her voice four thousand miles away, over the telephone.

She had told him she was taking a trip. It was her way of going into hiding for several weeks, the methods of evasion and concealment learned more than thirty years ago. God, she *was* incredible! Noel wondered where she would go, what she would do. He would call Sam Buonoventura, in Curaçao, in a few days. Sam might have heard from her by then.

The customs inspection at Tempelhof was swift. Holcroft walked into the terminal, found the men's room, and reassembled his gun.

As instructed, he took a taxi to the *Tiergarten* park. Inside the cab, he opened his suitcase, changed into the worn brown topcoat and the battered walking hat. The car stopped; he paid the fare, got out, and walked into the park, sidestepping strollers, until he found an empty bench, and sat down. He scanned the crowds; no one stopped or hesitated. He got up quickly and headed for an exit. There was a taxi stand nearby; he stood in line, glancing around unobtrusively to see if he could spot the enemy. It was difficult now to single out anything or anyone specifically; the late-afternoon shadows were becoming longer and darker.

His turn came. He gave the driver the names of two intersecting streets. The intersection was three blocks north and four blocks west of the hotel. The driver grinned and spoke in thickly accented but perfectly understandable English.

"You wish a little fun? I have friends, *Herr Amerikaner*. No risk of the French sickness."

"You've got me wrong. I'm doing sociological research."

"*Wie?*"

"I'm meeting my wife."

They drove in silence through the streets of Berlin. With each turn they made, Noel watched for a car somewhere behind them that made the same turn. A few did, but none for any length of time. He recalled Helden's words: *They often use radios. Such a simple thing as a change of coat or the wearing of a hat will throw them off. Those receiving instructions will look for a man in a jacket and no hat, but he is not there.*

Were there unseen men watching for a certain taxi and a certain passenger wearing certain clothing? He would never know; he knew only that no one appeared to be following him now.

During the twenty-odd minutes it took to reach the intersection, night had come. The streets were lined with gaudy neon signs and suggestive posters. Young fair-haired cowboys coexisted with whores in slit skirts and low-cut blouses. It was another sort of carnival, thought Holcroft, as he walked south for the prescribed three blocks, toward the corner where he would turn left.

He saw a prostitute in a doorway, applying lipstick to her generous mouth. She was in that indeterminate age bracket so defiantly obscured by whores and chic suburban housewives—somewhere between thirty-five and forty-eight, and losing the fight. Her hair was jet black, framing her pallid white skin, her eyes deep, hollowed with shadows. Beyond, on the next block, he could see the shabby hotel's marquee, one letter shorted out in its neon sign.

He approached her, not entirely sure what to say. His lacking German was not his only impediment: He had never picked up a whore in the streets.

He cleared his throat. "Good evening, Fräulein? Can you speak English?"

The woman returned his look, coolly at first, appraising his cloth topcoat. Then her eyes dropped to the suitcase in his right hand, the attaché case in his left. She parted her lips and smiled; the teeth were yellow. *"Ja, mein American friend. I speak good. I show you a good time."*

"I'd like that. How much?"

"Twenty-five deutsche marks."

"I'd say the negotiations are concluded. Will you come with me?" Holcroft took his money clip from his pocket, peeled off three bills, and handed them to the woman. "Thirty deutsche marks. Let's go to that hotel down the street."

"Wohin?"

Noel gestured at the hotel in the next block. "There," he said.

"Gut," said the woman, taking his arm.

The room was like any room in a cheap hotel in a large city. If there was a single positive feature, it was to be found in the naked light bulb in the ceiling. It was so dim it obscured the stained, broken furniture.

"Dreissig Minuten," announced the whore, removing her coat and draping it over a chair with a certain military élan. "You have one half hour, no more. I am, as you Americans say, a businessman. My time is valuable."

"I'm sure it is," said Holcroft. "Take a rest or read something. We'll leave in fifteen or twenty minutes. You'll stay with me and help me make a phone call." He opened the attaché case and found the paper with the information on Erich Kessler. There was a chair against the wall; he sat down and started to read in the dim light.

"Ein Telephonanruf?" said the woman. "You pay thirty marks for me to do nothing for you but help you *mit dem Telephon?*"

"That's right."

"That is . . . *verrückt!*"

"I don't speak German. I may have trouble reaching the person I've got to call."

"Why do we wait here, then? There is *Telephon* by the corner."

"For appearances, I guess."

The whore smiled. "I am your *Deckung.*"

"What?"

"You take me up to a room, no one asks questions."

"I wouldn't say that," replied Noel uneasily.

"It's not my business, mein Herr." She came over to his chair. "But as long as we're here . . . why not have a little fun? You paid. I'm not so bad. I once looked better, but I'm not so bad."

Holcroft returned her smile. "You're not so bad at all. But no thanks. I've got a lot on my mind."

"Then you do your work," said the whore.

Noel read the information given to him by Ernst Manfredi a lifetime ago in Geneva.

Erich Kessler, Professor of History, Free University of Berlin. Dahlen district. Speaks fluent English. Contacts: University telephone— 731–426. Residence—824–114. Brother named Hans, a doctor. Lives in Munich. . . .

There followed a brief summary of Kessler's academic career, the degrees obtained, the honors conferred. They were overwhelming. The professor was a learned man, and learned men often were skeptics. How would Kessler react to the call from an unknown American who traveled to Berlin without prior communication to see him about a matter he would not discuss over the telephone?

It was nearly six-thirty, time to find out the answer. And to change clothes. He got up, went to his suitcase, and took out the mackinaw and the visored cap. "Let's go," Noel said.

The prostitute stood by the phone booth while Holcroft dialed. He wanted her nearby in case someone other than Kessler answered, someone who did not speak English.

The line was busy. All around he could hear the sounds of the German language—emphatic conversations as couples and roving packs of pleasure seekers passed the telephone booth.

He wondered. If his mother had been anyone but Althene, would he be one of those outside the glass booth right now? Not where he was right *now*, but somewhere in Berlin, or Bremerhaven, or Munich? Noel Clausen. German.

What *would* his life have been like? It was an eerie feeling. Fascinating, repulsive . . . and obsessive. As if he had gone back in time, through the layers of his personal mist, and found a fork in a fog-bound road he might have taken but did not. That fork was reexamined now; where would it have led?

Helden? Would he have known her in that other life? He knew her now. And he knew that he wanted to get back to her as soon as he could; he wanted to see her again, and hold her again, and tell her that . . . *things* . . . were going to be all right. He wanted to see her laugh and have a life in which three changes of outer clothing and guns with silencers were not crucial to survival. Where the Rache and the ODESSA were no longer threats to sanity and existence.

A man answered the telephone, the voice deep and soft.

"Mr. Kessler? Doctor Kessler?"

"I shan't cure any diseases, sir," came the pleasant reply in English, "but the title is correct, if abused. What can I do for you?"

"My name is Holcroft. Noel Holcroft. I'm from New York. I'm an architect."

"Holcroft? I have a number of American friends and, of course, university people with whom I correspond, but I don't recognize the name."

"No reason for you to; you don't know me. However, I have come to Berlin to see you. There's a confidential matter to discuss that concerns the two of us."

"Confidential?"

"Let's say . . . a family matter."

"Hans? Did something happen to Hans?"

"No. . . ."

"I have no other family, Mr. Holcroft."

"It goes back a number of years. I'm afraid I can't say any more over the telephone. Please, trust me; it's urgent. Could you possibly meet me tonight?"

"Tonight?" Kessler paused. "Did you arrive in Berlin today?"

"Late this afternoon."

"And you want to see me tonight. . . . This matter must, indeed, be urgent. I have to return to my office for an hour or so this evening. Would nine o'clock be satisfactory?"

"Yes," said Noel, relieved. "Very satisfactory. Anyplace you say."

"I'd ask you to my house, but I'm afraid I have guests. There's a *Lokal* on the Kurfürstendamm. It's often crowded, but they have quiet booths in the back and the manager knows me."

"It sounds perfect."

Kessler gave him the name and address. "Ask for my table."

"I will. And thanks very much."

"You're quite welcome. I should warn you: I keep telling the manager that the food is grand. It isn't, really, but he's such a pleasant fellow and good to the students. See you at nine o'clock."

"I'll be there. Thanks again." Holcroft put the phone back in its cradle, swept by a sudden feeling of confidence. If the man matched the voice over the telephone. Erich Kessler was intelligent, humorous, immensely likable. What a relief!

Noel hung up and smiled at the woman. "Thanks," he said, giving her an additional ten marks.

"*Auf wiedersehen.*" The whore turned and walked off. Holcroft watched her for a moment, but his attention was suddenly drawn to a man in a black leather jacket halfway down the short block. He stood in front of a bookstore, but he was not interested in the pornography displayed in the window. Instead, he was staring directly at Noel. As their eyes met, the man turned away.

Was he one of the enemy? A fanatic from the Rache? A maniac of the ODESSA? Or perhaps someone assigned to him from the ranks of Wolfsschanze? He had to find out.

A confrontation is often the last thing surveillance wants. But if he does want it, you might as well know it. . . .

Helden's words. He would try to remember the tactics; he would use them now. He felt the bulges in the cloth of his mackinaw; weapon and silencer were there. He pulled the visor of his cap free of its snap, gripped the handle of his attaché case, and walked away from the man in the black leather jacket.

He hurried down the street, staying close to the curb, prepared to race out into the traffic. He reached the corner and turned right, walking swiftly into a crowd of spectators watching two life-size plastic manikins performing the sex act on a black bearskin rug. Holcroft was jostled; his attaché case was crushed against his leg, then pulled, as if being yanked aside by a victim of its sharp corners. . . . Yanked, pulled—*taken;* his attaché case could be taken, the papers inside read by those who should never read them. He had not been totally stupid; he had removed Heinrich Clausen's letter and the more informative sections of the Geneva document. No figures, no sources, only the bank's letterhead and the names—meaningless legal gibberish to an ordinary thief, but something else entirely to the extraordinary one.

Helden had warned him about carrying even these, but he had countered with the possibility that the unknown Erich Kessler might think him a madman, and he needed fragments, at least, to substantiate his incredible story.

But now, if he *was* being followed, he had to leave the case in a place where it would not be stolen. Where? Certainly not at the hotel. A locker in a train station or bus depot? Unacceptable, because both were accessible; such places would be child's play for the experienced thief.

Besides, he needed those papers—those fragments—for Erich Kessler. Kessler. The *"Lokal." The manager there knows me. Ask for my table.*

The pub on the Kurfürstendamm. Going there now would serve two purposes: On the way, he could see if he was actually being followed; once there, he could either stay or leave his case with the manager.

He pushed his way into the street, looking for an empty taxi, glancing behind him for signs of surveillance —for a man in a black leather jacket. There was a cab in the middle of the block. He ran toward it.

As he entered, he spun around quickly. And he saw the man in the black leather jacket. He was not walking now. Instead, he was in the saddle of a small motorbike, propelling it along the curb with his left foot. There were a number of other bikes in the street, cruising in and out between the traffic.

The man in the black leather jacket stopped pushing his machine, turned away, and pretended to be talking with someone on the sidewalk. The pretense was too obvious; there was no one responding to his conversation. Noel climbed in the cab and gave the name and address of the pub. They drove off.

So did the man in the black leather jacket. Noel watched him through the rear window. Like the man in the green Fiat in Paris, this Berliner was an expert. He stayed several car lengths behind the taxi, swerving quickly at odd moments to make sure the object of his surveillance was still there.

It was pointless to keep watching. Holcroft settled back in the seat and tried to figure out his next move.

A confrontation is often the last thing surveillance wants. . . . If he does . . . you might as well know it.

Did he want to know it? Was he prepared for confrontation? The answers were not easy. He was not someone who cared to test his courage deliberately. But in the forefront of his imagination was the sight of Richard Holcroft crushed into a building on a sidewalk in New York.

Fear provided caution; rage provided strength. The single answer was clear. He wanted the man in the black leather jacket. And he would get him.

24

He paid the driver and got out of the cab, making sure he could be seen by the man on the motorbike, who had stopped down the block.

Noel walked casually across the pavement to the pub and went inside. He stood on a platformed staircase and studied the restaurant. The ceilings were high, the dining area on a lower floor. The place was half full; layers of smoke were suspended in the air, and the pungent smell of aromatic beer drifted up the staircase. From the speaker system, Bavarian *Biermusik* could be heard. The wooden tables were placed in ranks throughout the central area. The furnishings were heavy, massive.

He saw the booths Kessler had described. They were along the rear wall and the sides: tables flanked by high-backed seats. Running across the fronts of the booths were brass rods holding red-checked curtains. Each booth could be isolated from its surroundings by drawing a curtain across the table, but with the curtains open one could sit at almost any booth and observe whoever came through the door at the top of the staircase.

Holcroft descended the stairs to a lectern at the bottom and spoke to a heavyset man behind it. "Pardon me, do you speak English?"

The man looked up from the reservation book in front of him. "Is there a restaurateur in Berlin who doesn't, sir?"

Noel smiled. "Good. I'm looking for the manager."

"You've found him. What can I do for you? Do you wish a table?"

"I think one's been reserved. The name is Kessler."

The manager's eyes showed immediate recognition. "Oh, yes. He called not fifteen minutes ago. But the reservation was for nine o'clock. It is only—"

"I know," interrupted Holcroft. "I'm early. You see,

I've got a favor to ask." He held up the attaché case. "I brought this for Professor Kessler. Some historical papers lent him by the university in America where I teach. I have to meet some people for an hour or so, and wondered if I could leave it here."

"Of course," said the manager. He held out his hand for the case.

"You understand, these are valuable. Not in terms of money, just academically."

"I'll lock them in my office."

"Thank you very much."

"*Bitte schön.* Your name, sir?"

"Holcroft."

"Thank you, Herr Holcroft. Your table will be ready at nine o'clock." The manager nodded, turned, and carried the attaché case toward a closed door under the staircase.

Noel stood for a moment considering what to do next. No one had entered since he had arrived. That meant the man in the leather jacket was outside, waiting for him. It was time to bait the trap, time to corner that man.

He started up the staircase, suddenly struck by a thought that made him sick. He had just done the most stupid thing he could think of! He had led the man in the black leather jacket directly to the spot where he was making contact with Erich Kessler. And to compound that enormous mistake, he had given his own name to the manager.

Kessler and *Holcroft. Holcroft* and *Kessler.* They were tied together. He had revealed an unknown third of Geneva! Revealed it as clearly as if he had taken out a newspaper ad.

It was no longer a question of whether he was capable of setting the trap. He *had* to do it. He had to immobilize the man in the black leather jacket.

He pushed open the door and walked on to the sidewalk. The Kurfürstendamm was lit up. The air was cold, and in the sky above, the moon was circled by a rim of mist. He started walking to his right, his hands in his pockets to ward off the chill. He passed the motorbike at the curb and continued to the corner. Ahead, perhaps three blocks away, on the left side of the Kurfürstendamm, he could see the outlines of the enormous Kaiser Wilhelm Church, floodlights illuminating the never-to-be-repaired, bombed-out tower, Berlin's reminder to itself of Hitler's Reich. He would use the church as his landmark.

He continued walking along the tree-lined pavement, slower than most of the strollers around him, stopping frequently in front of store windows. He checked his watch at regular intervals, hoping to give the impression that the minutes were important, that perhaps he was pacing himself to reach a rendezvous at a specific time.

Directly opposite the Kaiser Wilhelm Church, he stood for a while at the curb, under the glare of a streetlight. He glanced to his left. Thirty yards away the man in the black leather jacket turned around, his back to Holcroft, watching the flow of traffic.

He was there; that was all that mattered.

Noel started up again, his step faster now. He came to another corner and looked up at the street sign: SCHÖNBERGSTRASSE. It angled off the Kurfürstendamm and was lined with shops on both sides. The sidewalks seemed more crowded, the strollers less hurried than those on the Kurfürstendamm.

He waited for a break in the traffic and crossed the street. He turned right on the sidewalk, staying close to the curb, excusing himself through the strollers. He reached the end of the block, crossed over into the next, and slowed his walk. He stopped, as he had stopped on the Kurfürstendamm, to gaze into the storefront windows, and he checked his watch with growing concentration.

He saw the man in the leather jacket twice.

Noel proceeded into the third block. No more than fifty feet from the corner there was a narrow alley, a thoroughfare between the Schönbergstrasse and a parallel street about a hundred yards away. The alley was dark and dotted along its sides with shadowed doorways. The darkness and the length were uninviting, obvious deterrents for pedestrians during the evening hours.

But this alley, at this time, was the trapping ground, an unlit stretch of concrete and brick into which he'd lead the man who followed him.

He continued walking down the block, past the alley, toward the corner, his pace quickening with every stride, Helden's words resounding in his ears.

The amateur does the unexpected, not because he's

clever or experienced but because he doesn't know any better. . . . Do the unexpected rapidly, obviously, as if confused. . . .

He reached the end of the block and stopped abruptly under a streetlight. As if startled, he looked around, pivoting on the sidewalk, a man undecided but one who knew a decision must be made. He stared back toward the alleyway and suddenly broke into a run, colliding with pedestrians, entering the alley—a man in panic.

He ran until the darkness was nearly full, until he was at midpoint in the alley, shadows upon shadows, the lights at either end distant. There was a delivery entrance of some sort—a wide metal door. He lunged toward it, spinning into the corner, his back pressed against steel and brick. He put his hand into his jacket pocket and gripped the handle of the automatic. The silencer was not attached; it was not necessary. He had no intention whatsoever of firing the weapon. It was to be but a visible threat and, at first, not even that.

The wait was not long. He could hear racing footsteps and thought as he heard them that the enemy, too, knew about rubber-soled shoes.

The man ran by; then, as if sensing a trick, he slowed down, looking about in the shadows. Noel stepped out of his hidden corner, his hand in his jacket pocket.

"I've been waiting for you. Stay right where you are." He spoke intensely, frightened at his own words. "I've got a gun in my hand. I don't *want* to use it, but I will if you try to run."

"You did not hesitate two days ago in France," said the man in a thick accent, his calm unnerving. "Why should I expect you to stop now? You're a pig. You can kill me, but we will stop you."

"Who are you?"

"Does it matter? Just know that we will stop you."

"You're with the Rache, aren't you?"

In spite of the darkness, Noel could see an expression of contempt on the man's face. "The Rache?" he said. "Terrorists without a cause, revolutionaries no one wants in his camp. Butchers. I'm no part of the Rache!"

"The Odessa, then."

"You'd like that, wouldn't you."

"What do you mean?"

"You'll use the Odessa when the time comes. It can

be blamed for so much. You can kill so easily in its name. I suppose the irony is that we'd kill the Odessa as quickly as you would. But you're the ones we want; we know the difference between clowns and monsters. Believe me, we'll stop you."

"You're not making sense! You're not part of Wolfsschanze; you couldn't be!"

The man lowered his voice. "But we are all part of Wolfsschanze, aren't we? In one way or another," he said, a challenge in his eyes. "I say it again. You can kill me, but another will take my place. Kill him, another his. We *will* stop you. So shoot, Herr Clausen. Or should I say, son of Reichsführer Heinrich Clausen."

"What the hell are you talking about? I don't want to kill you. I don't want to kill anybody!"

"You killed in France."

"If I killed a man, it was because he tried to kill me."

"*Aber natürlich,* Herr Clausen."

"Stop calling me that."

"Why? It's your name, isn't it?"

"No! My name is Holcroft."

"Of course," said the man. "That was part of the plan. The respected American with no discernible ties to his past. And if anyone traced them, it would be too late."

"Too late for what? Who *are* you? Who sent you?"

"There is no way you can force that from me. We are not part of your plan."

Holcroft took the gun from his pocket and stepped closer. "What plan?" he asked, hoping to learn something, *anything.*

"Geneva."

"What about Geneva? It's a city in Switzerland."

"We know everything, and it's finished. You won't stop the eagles. Not this time. We will stop *you!*"

"*Eagles? What* eagles! Who's 'we'?"

"Never. Pull the trigger. I won't tell you. You won't trace us."

Noel was perspiring, though the winter night was cold. Nothing this enemy said made sense. It was possible that an enormous error had been made. The man in front of him was prepared to die, but he was not a fanatic; there was too much intelligence behind the eyes. "Not with the Rache, not with the Odessa. For God's sake, why do you want to stop Geneva? Wolfsschanze doesn't want to stop it; you must know that!"

"Not *your* Wolfsschanze. But we can put that fortune to great use."

"No! If you interfere, there won't be anything. You'll never get the money."

"We both know that doesn't have to be."

"You're wrong! It'll go back into the ground for another thirty years."

The unknown enemy drew himself up in the shadows. "That's the flaw, isn't it? You put it so well: 'back into the ground.' But, if I may be permitted, there'll be no scorched earth then."

"No what?"

"No scorched earth." The man stepped backward. "We've talked enough. You had your chance; you have it still. You can kill me, but it will do you no good. We have the photograph. We're beginning to understand."

"The *photograph?* In Portsmouth? *You?*"

"A most respected commander in the Royal Navy. It was interesting that you should take it."

"For Christ's sake! Who *are* you?"

"One who fights you, son of Heinrich Clausen."

"I told you—"

"I know," said the German. "I should not say that. In point of fact, I shall say nothing further. I will turn around and walk out of this alleyway. Shoot, if you must. I am prepared. We are all prepared."

The man turned slowly and began walking. It was more than Noel could stand.

"Stop!" he yelled, pursuing the German. Then grabbing his shoulder with his left hand.

The man spun around. "We have nothing further to say."

"Yes, we do! We're going to stay here all night, if we have to! You're going to tell me who you are and where you came from and what the hell you know about Geneva and Beaumont and—"

It was as far as he got. The man's hand shot out, his fingers clasping Noel's right wrist, twisting it inward and downward as his right knee hammered up into Holcroft's groin. Noel doubled forward in agony, but he would not let go of the gun. He shoved his shoulder into the man's midsection, trying to push him away, the pain in his testicles spreading up into his stomach and chest. The man brought his fist crashing down into the base of Holcroft's skull, sending shock waves through his ribs and spine. But he would not relinquish the gun! The man could not have the gun! Noel gripped it as if it were the last steel clamp on a lifeboat. He lurched up, springing with what strength he had left in his legs, wrenching the automatic away from the man's grip.

There was an explosion; it echoed through the alley. The man's arm fell away, and he staggered backward, grabbing his shoulder. He had been wounded, but he did not collapse. Instead, he braced himself against the wall and spoke through gasps of breath.

"We'll stop you. And we'll do it our way. We'll take Geneva!"

With those words he propelled himself down the alley, clawing at the wall for support. Holcroft turned; there were figures clustered about the alley's entrance on the Schönbergstrasse. He could hear police whistles and see the coruscating beams of flashlights. The Berlin police were moving in.

He was caught.

But he could *not* be caught! There was Kessler; there was Geneva. He could not be detained now!

Helden's words came back to him. *Lie indignantly ... with confidence ... invent your own variations.*

Noel shoved the automatic in his pocket and started toward the Schönbergstrasse, toward the slowly approaching flashlights and the two uniformed men who held them.

"I'm an American!" he yelled in a frightened voice. "Does anyone speak English?"

A man from the crowd shouted, "I do! What happened?"

"I was walking through here and someone tried to rob me! He had a gun but I didn't know it! I shoved him and it went off. . . ."

The Berliner translated quickly for the police.

"Where did he go?" asked the man.

"I think he's still there. In one of the doorways. I've got to sit down. . . ."

The Berliner touched Holcroft's shoulder. "Come."

He began leading Noel out through the crowd toward the sidewalk.

The police yelled into the dark alleyway. There was no response; the unknown enemy had made his escape. The uniformed men cautiously continued forward.

"Thanks very much," said Noel. "I'd just like to get some air, calm down, you know what I mean?"

"*Ja*. A terrible experience."

"I think they've got him," added Holcroft suddenly, looking back toward the police and the crowd.

The Berliner turned; Noel stepped off the curb, into the street. He started walking, slowly at first, then found a break in the traffic and crossed to the sidewalk on the other side. There he turned and ran as fast as he could through the crowds, toward the Kurfürstendamm.

He had done it, thought Holcroft, as he sat, coatless and hatless, shivering on a deserted bench within sight of the Kaiser Wilhelm Church. He had absorbed the lessons and put them to use; he had invented his own variations and eluded the trap he had set for another, but which had sprung back, ensnaring himself. Beyond this, he had immobilized the man in the black leather jacket. That man would be detained, if only to find a doctor.

Above all, he had learned that Helden was wrong. And the dead Manfredi—who would not say the names—had been wrong. It was not members of the ODESSA, nor of the Rache, who were Geneva's most powerful enemies. It was another group, one infinitely more knowledgeable and deadlier. An enigma that counted among its adherents men who would die calmly, with intelligence in their eyes and reasonable speech on their tongues.

The race to Geneva was against three violent forces wanting to destroy the covenant, but one was far more ingenious than the other two. The man in the black leather jacket had spoken of the Rache and the ODESSA in terms so disparaging they could not have sprung from envy or fear. He had dismissed them as incompetent butchers and clowns of whom he wanted no part. For he was part of something else, something far superior.

Holcroft looked at his watch. He had been sitting in the cold for nearly an hour, the ache in his groin still there, the base of his skull stiff with pain. He had stuffed the mackinaw and the black-visored cap into a refuse bin several blocks away. They would have been too easy to spot if the Berlin police had an alarm out for him.

It was time to go now; there were no signs of the police, no signs of anyone interested in him. The cold air had done nothing for his pain, but it had helped clear his head, and until that had happened he dared not move. He could move now; he had to. It was almost nine o'clock. It was time to meet with Erich Kessler, the third key to Geneva.

25

The pub was now crowded, as he expected it would be,
the layers of smoke thicker, the Bavarian music louder.
The manager greeted him pleasantly, but his eyes betrayed his thoughts: Something had happened to this
American within the last hour. Noel was embarrassed;
he wondered if his face was scratched, or streaked with
dirt.

"I'd like to wash up. I had a nasty fall."

"Certainly. Over there, sir." The manager pointed
to the men's room. "Professor Kessler has arrived. He's
waiting for you. I gave him your briefcase."

"Thanks again," said Holcroft, turning toward the
door of the washroom.

He looked at his face in the mirror. There were no
stains, no dirt, no blood. But there was something in his
eyes, a look associated with pain and shock and exhaustion. And fear. That's what the manager had seen.

He ran the water in the basin until it was lukewarm,
doused his face and combed his hair and wished he could
take that look out of his eyes. Then he returned to the
manager, who led him to a booth at the rear of the hall,
farthest from the room's activity. The red-checked curtain
was drawn across the table.

"Herr Professor?"

The curtain was pulled aside, revealing a man in
his mid-forties with a large girth and a full face framed
by a short beard and thick brown hair combed straight
back over his head. It was a gentle face, the deep-set
eyes alive, tinged with anticipation, even humor.

"Mister Holcroft?"

"Dr. Kessler?"

"Sit down, sit down." Kessler made a brief attempt
to rise as he held out his hand; the contact between his
stomach and the table prevented it. He laughed and

265

looked at the pub's manager. "Next week! *Ja*, Rudi? Our diets."

"*Ach, natürlich, Professor.*"

"This is my new friend from America. Mr. Holcroft."

"Yes, we met earlier."

"Of course you did. You gave me his briefcase." Kessler patted Noel's attaché case, next to him on the seat. "I'm drinking scotch. Join me, Mr. Holcroft?"

"Scotch'll be fine. Just ice."

The manager nodded and left. Noel settled back in the seat. Kessler exuded a kind of weary warmth; it was an expression of tolerance from an intellect constantly exposed to lesser minds but too kind to dwell on comparisons. Holcroft had known several men like that. Among them were his finest teachers. He was comfortable with Erich Kessler; it was a good way to begin.

"Thanks so much for seeing me. I've got a lot to tell you."

"Catch your breath first," said Kessler. "Have a drink. Calm down."

"What?"

"You've had a difficult time. It's written all over your face."

"It's that obvious?"

"I'd say you were that distraught, Mr. Holcroft."

"It's Noel. Please. We should get to know each other."

"A pleasant prospect, I'm sure. My name is Erich. It's a chilly night outside. Too cold to go without an overcoat. Yet you obviously arrived without one. There's no checkroom here."

"I *was* wearing one. I had to get rid of it. I'll explain."

"You don't have to."

"I'm afraid I do. I wish I didn't, but it's part of my story."

"I see. Ah, here's your scotch."

A waiter deposited the glass in front of Holcroft, then stepped back and drew the red-checked curtain across the booth.

"As I said, it's part of the story." Noel drank.

"Take your time. There's no hurry."

"You said you had guests at your house."

"*A* guest. A friend of my brother's, from München.

He's a delightful fellow, but long-winded. A trait not unknown among doctors. You've rescued me for the evening."

"Won't your wife be upset?"

"I'm not married. I was, but I'm afraid university life was rather confining for her."

"I'm sorry."

"She's not. She married an acrobat. Can you imagine? From the academic groves to the rarefied heights of alternating trapezes. We're still good friends."

"I think it would be difficult not to be friendly with you."

"Oh, I'm a terror in the lecture rooms. A veritable lion."

"Who roars but can't bring himself to bite," said Noel.

"I beg your pardon?"

"Nothing. I was remembering a conversation I had last night. With someone else."

"Feeling better?"

"That's funny."

"What is?"

"That's what I said last night."

"With this someone else?" Kessler smiled again. "Your face seems more relaxed."

"If it was any more relaxed, it'd be draped over the table."

"Perhaps some food?"

"Not yet. I'd like to start; there's a great deal to tell you, and you're going to have a lot of questions."

"Then I shall listen carefully. Oh, I forgot. Your briefcase."

The German reached beside him and lifted the attaché case to the top of the table.

Holcroft unlocked the case, but did not open it. "There are papers in here you'll want to study. They're not complete, but they'll serve as confirmation for some of the things I'm going to tell you."

"Confirmation? Are the things you say you must tell me so difficult to accept?"

"They may be," said Noel. He felt sorry for this good-natured scholar. The peaceful world he lived in was about to collapse around him. "What I'm going to say to you may interrupt your life, as it has mine. I don't think that can be avoided. At least, I couldn't avoid it, because I couldn't walk away from it. Part of the reason was selfish; there's a great deal of money involved that will come to me personally—as it will come to you. But there are other factors that are much more important than either you or me. I know that's true, because if it weren't, I'd have run away by now. But I won't run. I'm going to do what I've been asked to do because it's *right*. And because there are people I hate who want to stop me. They killed someone I loved very much. They tried to kill another." Holcroft stopped suddenly; he had not meant to go this far. The fear and the rage were coming together. He had lost control; he was talking too much. "I'm sorry. I could be reading a lot of things into all this that don't belong. I don't mean to frighten you."

Kessler put his hand on Noel's arm. "Frightening me isn't a concern. You're overwrought and exhausted, my friend. Apparently, terrible things have happened to you."

Holcroft drank several swallows of whiskey, trying to numb the pain in his groin and his neck. "I won't lie. They have. But I didn't want to start this way. It wasn't very bright."

Kessler removed his hand from Noel's arm. "Let me say something. I've known you less than five minutes, and I don't think being bright is relevant. You're obviously a highly intelligent man—a very honest one, too—and you've been under a great strain. Why not simply start at the beginning without worrying how it affects me?"

"Okay." Holcroft put his arms on the table, his hands around the glass of whiskey. "I'll begin by asking you if you've ever heard the names Von Tiebolt and . . . Clausen."

Kessler stared at Noel for a moment. "Yes," he said. "They go back many years—to when I was a child—but of course I've heard them. Clausen and Von Tiebolt. They were friends of my father's. I was very young, around ten or eleven. They came to our house frequently, if I recall, at the end of the war. I *do* remember Clausen; at least I think I do. He was a tall man and quite magnetic."

"Tell me about him."

"There's not much I can remember."

"Anything you can. *Please.*"

"Again, I'm not sure how to put it. Clausen dominated a room without making any effort to do so. When he spoke, everyone listened, yet I don't recall his ever raising his voice. He seemed to be a kind man, concerned for others, but extremely strong willed. I thought once— and remember, these were the thoughts of a child—that he was someone who had lived with much pain."

A man in agony had cried out to him. "What kind of pain?"

"I have no idea; it was only a child's impression. You would have to have seen his eyes to understand. No matter whom he looked at, young or old, important or not, he gave that person his full concentration. I do remember that; it was not a common trait in those days. In a way, I picture Clausen more clearly than I do my own father, and certainly more than Von Tiebolt. Why are you interested in him?"

"He was my father."

Kessler's mouth opened in astonishment. "You?" he whispered. "Clausen's *son?*"

Noel nodded. "My natural father, not the father I knew."

"Then your mother was . . ." Kessler stopped.

"Althene Clausen. Did you ever hear anyone speak of her?"

"Never by name, and never in Clausen's presence. Ever. She was spoken of in whispers. The woman who left the great man, the American enemy who fled the fatherland with their— You! You were the child she took from him!"

"Took *with* her, *kept* from him, is the way she puts it."

"She's still alive?"

"Very much so."

"It's all so incredible." Kessler shook his head. "After all these years, a man I remember so vividly. He was extraordinary."

"They were all extraordinary."

"Who?"

"The three of them. Clausen, Von Tiebolt, and Kessler. Tell me, do you know how your father died?"

"He killed himself. It was not unusual then. When the Reich collapsed, a lot of people did. For most of them it was easier that way."

"For some it was the only way."

"Nürnberg?"

"No, Geneva. To protect Geneva."

"I don't understand you."

"You will." Holcroft opened his attaché case, took out the pages he had clipped together, and gave them to Kessler. "There's a bank in Geneva that has an account that can be released for specific purposes only by the consent of three people. . . ."

As he had done twice before, Noel told the story of the massive theft of over thirty years ago. But with Kessler, he told it all. He did not, as he had done with Gretchen, withhold specific facts; nor did he tell the story in stages, as he had with Helden. He left out nothing.

". . . monies were intercepted from the occupied countries, from the sales of art objects and the looting of museums. Wehrmacht payrolls were rerouted, millions stolen from the Ministry of Armaments and the—I can't remember the name, it's in the letter—but from the industrial complex. Everything was banked in Switzerland, in Geneva, with the help of a man named Manfredi."

"Manfredi? I remember the name."

"It's not surprising," said Holcroft. "Although I don't imagine he was mentioned too frequently. Where did you hear it?"

"I don't know. After the war, I think."

"From your mother?"

"I don't think so. She died in July of 'forty-five and was in the hospital for most of the time. From someone else . . . I don't know."

"Where did you live, with your father and mother dead?"

"My brother and I moved in with our uncle, my mother's brother. It was lucky for us. He was an older man and never had much use for the Nazis. He found favor with the occupation forces. But please, go on."

Noel did. He detailed the conditions of competence required by the directors of La Grande Banque de Genève, which led him into the dismissal of Gretchen Beaumont. He told Kessler of the Von Tiebolts' clouded migration to Rio, the birth of Helden, the killing of their mother, and their eventual flight from Brazil.

"They took the name of Tennyson and have been

living in England for the past five years. Johann von Tiebolt is known as John Tennyson. He's a reporter for the *Guardian*. Gretchen married a man named Beaumont and Helden moved several months ago to Paris. I haven't met the brother, but I've . . . become friends with Helden. She's a remarkable girl."

"Is she the 'someone else' you were with last night?"

"Yes," replied Holcroft. "I want to tell you about her, what she's gone through, what she's going through now. She and thousands like her are part of the story."

"I think I may know," said Kessler. "*Die Verwünschte Kinder.*"

"The what?"

"The *Verwünschte Kinder. Verwünschung* is German for a curse. Or one damned."

"The Children of the Damned," said Noel. "She used the expression."

"It's a term they gave themselves. Thousands of young people—not so young now—who fled the country because they convinced themselves they couldn't live with the guilt of Nazi Germany. They rejected everything German, sought new identities, new life-styles. They're very much like those hordes of young Americans who left the United States for Canada and Sweden in protest against the Vietnam policies. These groups form subcultures, but none can really reject their roots. They *are* German; they *are* American. They migrate in packs and cling together, taking strength from the very pasts they've rejected. The proddings of guilt are a heavy burden. Can you understand?"

"Not really," said Holcroft. "But then, I'm not built that way. I'm not going to take on a guilt that isn't mine."

Kessler looked into Noel's eyes. "I submit you may have. You say you won't run from this covenant of yours, yet terrible things have happened to you."

Holcroft considered the scholar's words. "There may be some truth in that, but the circumstances are different. I didn't *leave* anything. I guess I was selected."

"Not part of the damned," said Kessler, "but part of the chosen?"

"Privileged, anyway."

The scholar nodded. "There's a word for that, too. Perhaps you've heard of it. *Sonnenkinder.*"

"Sonnenkinder?" Noel frowned. "If I remember, it was in one of those courses I didn't exactly shine in. Anthropology, maybe."

"Or philosophy," suggested Kessler. "It's a philosophical concept developed by Thomas J. Perry, in England in the nineteen-twenties, and before him by Bachofen, in Switzerland, and by his disciples in München. The theory being that the *Sonnenkinder*—the Children of the Sun—have been with us throughout the ages. They're the shapers of history, the most brilliant among us, rulers of epochs . . . the privileged."

Holcroft nodded. "I remember now. They were ruined by that privilege of theirs. They became depraved, or something. Incestuous, I think."

"It's only a theory," said Kessler. "We're straying again; you're an easy man to talk to. You were saying about this Von Tiebolt daughter that life is difficult for her."

"For all of them. And more than difficult. It's crazy. They're running all the time. They have to live like fugitives."

"They're easy prey for fanatics," agreed Erich.

"Like the ODESSA and the Rache?"

"Yes. Such organizations can't function efficiently within Germany itself; they're not tolerated. So they operate in other countries where disaffected expatriates such as the *Verwünschkinder* have gravitated. They want only to stay alive and vital, waiting for the chance to return to Germany."

"Return?"

Kessler held up his hand. "Please God, they never will, but they can't accept that. The Rache once wanted the Bonn government to be an arm of the Comintern, but even Moscow rejected them; they've become nothing more than terrorists. The ODESSA have always wanted to revive Nazism. They're scorned in Germany."

"Still, they go after the children," said Noel. "Helden used the phrase 'damned for what they were, damned for what they weren't.' "

"An apt judgment."

"They should be stopped. Some of that money in Geneva should be used to cripple the ODESSA and the Rache."

"I wouldn't disagree with you."

"I'm glad to hear that," said Holcroft. "Let's get back to Geneva."

"By all means."

Noel had covered the objectives of the covenant and defined the conditions demanded of the inheritors. It was time to concentrate on what had happened to *him*.

He began with the murder on the plane, the terror in New York, the rearranged apartment, the letter from the men of Wolfsschanze, the telephone call from Peter Baldwin and the subsequent brutal killings it engendered. He spoke of the flight to Rio and a man with thick eyebrows: Anthony Beaumont, ODESSA agent. He told of the doctored records at Rio's Department of Immigration and the strange meeting with Maurice Graff. He emphasized MI Five's intrusion in London and the astonishing news that British Intelligence believed Johann von Tiebolt was the assassin they called the Tinamou.

"The *Tinamou?*" broke in Kessler, stunned, his face flushed. It was his first interruption of Holcroft's narrative.

"Yes. You know something about him?"

"Only what I've read."

"I gather some people think he's been responsible for dozens of assassinations."

"And the British think it's Johann von Tiebolt?"

"They're wrong," said Noel. "I'm certain they know it now. Something happened yesterday afternoon that proves it. You'll understand when I come to it."

"Go on."

He touched briefly on the evening with Gretchen, the photograph of Anthony Beaumont. He went on to Helden and Herr Oberst, then to the death of Richard Holcroft. He described the calls between himself and a detective in New York named Miles, as well as conversations with his mother.

He told of the green Fiat that had followed them to Barbizon, and the man with the pockmarked face.

Then came the madness of the *fête d'hiver*. How he had tried to trap the man in the Fiat and had himself nearly been killed.

"I told you a few minutes ago the British were wrong about Tennyson," Noel said.

"Tennyson? Oh, the name Von Tiebolt assumed."

"That's right. MI Five was convinced that everything

that happened in Montereau, including the man with the pockmarked face who was following us, was the work of the Tinamou. But that man was killed; he *worked* for Von Tiebolt; they *knew* that. Helden even confirmed it."

"And," interrupted Kessler, "the Tinamou would not kill his own man."

"Exactly."

"Then the agent will tell his superiors. . . ."

"He can't," broke in Noel. "He was shot saving Helden's life. But identifications will be made; the British will piece it together."

"Will the British find the agent who died?"

"Word will get back to them. It has to. The police were everywhere; they'll find his body."

"Can he be traced to you?"

"It's possible. We fought in the square; people will remember. But as Helden put it: We were followed; we didn't do the following. There's no reason why we should *know* anything."

"You sound unsure."

"Before the agent died, I decided to mention Baldwin's name to him, to see if I could learn anything. He reacted as if I'd fired a gun in front of his face. He pleaded with Helden and me to get in touch with a man named Payton-Jones. We were supposed to tell him everything that happened; tell him to find out who attacked us, who killed Von Tiebolt's man, and most important, to tell MI Five he believed it was all related to Peter Baldwin."

"To Baldwin? He'd been with MI Six, you said?"

"Yes. He'd gone to them some time ago with information about the survivors of Wolfsschanze."

"Wolfsschanze?" Kessler repeated the name softly. "That was the letter Manfredi gave you in Geneva, the one written over thirty years ago."

"That's right. The agent said we were to tell Payton-Jones to go back to Baldwin's file. To 'code Wolfsschanze.' That was the phrase he used."

"In his phone call to you in New York, did Baldwin mention Wolfsschanze?" asked Kessler.

"No. He said only that I should stay away from Geneva; that he knew things no one else knew. Then he went to answer the door and he never came back."

Kessler's eyes were colder now. "So Baldwin had learned about Geneva and this Wolfsschanze's commitment to it."

"How much he learned we don't know. It could be very little, just rumors."

"But these rumors are enough to stop you from going to MI Five. Even the advantage of warning them that Beaumont is ODESSA could be too great a price. The British would question you and the girl at length; there are a thousand ways, and they're experts. Baldwin's name might surface and they would go back to his file. You can't take that chance."

"I came to the same conclusion," said Holcroft, impressed.

"Perhaps there's another way to get Beaumont away from you."

"How?"

"The ODESSA is loathed here in Germany. Word to the proper people could result in his removal. You'd never have to reach the British yourself, never have to risk Baldwin's name coming to light."

"Could that be arranged?"

"Unquestionably. If Beaumont's really an ODESSA agent, a brief message from the Bonn government to the Foreign Office would be enough. I know any number of men who could send it."

Relief swept over Holcroft. One more obstacle was being removed. "I'm glad we met . . . that you're you and not somebody else."

"Don't be too quick to make that judgment. You want my answer. Will I join you? Frankly, I—"

"I don't want your answer yet," interrupted Noel. "You were fair with me, and I have to be fair with you. I'm not finished. There was tonight."

"Tonight?" Kessler was disturbed, impatient.

"Yes. The last couple of hours, in fact."

"What happened . . . tonight?"

Noel leaned forward. "We know about the Rache and the ODESSA. We're not sure how much *they* know about Geneva, but we're damned sure what they'd do if they knew enough. We know about the men of Wolfsschanze. Whoever they are, they're crazy—no better than the others—but in their own strange way they're on our side; they want Geneva to succeed. But there's someone else. Someone—*something*—much more powerful than the others. I found that out tonight."

"What are you saying?" The tone of Kessler's voice did not change.

"A man followed me from my hotel. He was on a motorbike and stayed with my taxi across Berlin."

"A man on a motorbike?"

"Yes. Like a damned fool I led him here. I realized how stupid that was, and knew I had to stop him. I managed to do it, but I never meant it to happen the way it did. He was no part of the Rache, no part of the ODESSA. He hated them both, called them butchers and clowns. . . ."

"He called them . . ." Kessler was silent for a moment. Then he continued, regaining part of the composure he had lost. "Tell me everything that happened, everything that was said."

"Do you have any ideas?"

"No. . . . Not at all. I'm merely interested. Tell me."

Holcroft had no difficulty remembering it all. The chase, the trap, the exchange of words, the gunshot. When he had finished, Kessler asked him to go back to the words he and the man in the black leather jacket had said to each other. Then he asked Noel to repeat them again. And again.

"Who was he?" Holcroft knew that Kessler's mind was racing ahead of his. "Who *are* they?"

"There are several possibilities," said the German, "but obviously they're Nazis. Neo-Nazis, to be precise. Descendants of the party, a splinter faction that has no use for the ODESSA. It happens."

"But how would they know about Geneva?"

"Millions stolen from the occupied countries, from Wehrmacht payrolls, from the Finanzministerium. All banked in Switzerland. Such massive manipulations could not be kept completely secret."

Something bothered Noel, something Kessler had just said, but he could not put his finger on it. "But what good would it do them? They can't get the money. They could only tie it up in the courts for years. Where do they benefit?"

"You don't understand the hard-core Nazi. None of you ever did. It's not merely how he can benefit. It's of equal importance to him that others do *not* benefit. That was his essential destructiveness."

There was a sudden, loud commotion outside the booth. A single crash, then several; followed by a woman's scream that triggered other screams.

The curtain across the booth was yanked aside. The figure of a man loomed suddenly in the open space and plunged forward, falling over the table, his eyes wide and staring, blood streaming from his mouth and his neck. His face was contorted, his body wracked with convulsions; his hands lurched over the surface of the table, gripping the sides between Holcroft and Kessler. He whispered, gasping for air, *"Wolfsschanze! Soldaten von Wolfsschanze!"*

He raised his head in the start of a scream. His breath was forced out of him, and his head crashed down on the table. The man in the black leather jacket was dead.

26

The next moments were as bewildering to Noel as they were chaotic. The screaming and the shouting grew louder; waves of panic spread throughout the pub. The blood-soaked man had slipped off the table and was now sprawled on the floor.

"Rudi! *Rudi!*"

"Herr Kessler! Come with me!"

"Quickly!" yelled Erich.

"What?"

"This way, my friend. You can't be seen here."

"But he's the one!"

"Say *nothing*, Noel. Please, take my arm."

"What? Where? . . ."

"Your briefcase! The papers!"

Holcroft grabbed the papers and shoved them into the case. He felt himself being pulled into a circle of onlookers. He was not sure where he was being taken, but that it was away from the dead man in the black leather jacket was enough. He followed blindly.

Kessler pulled him through the crowd. In front of Kessler was the manager, parting the bodies in their path, the path that led to a closed door beneath and to the left of the staircase. The manager took a key from his pocket, opened the door, and rushed the three of them inside. He slammed the door shut and turned to Kessler.

"I don't know what to say, gentlemen! It's terrible. A drunken brawl."

"No doubt, Rudi. And we thank you," replied Kessler.

"*Natürlich*. A man of your stature can't be involved."

"You're most kind. Is there a way outside?"

"Yes. My private entrance. Over here."

The entrance led into an alleyway. "This way," Kessler said. "My car's on the street."

They hurried out of the alley into the Kurfürstendamm, turning left on the sidewalk. To the right, an excited crowd had gathered in front of the pub's entrance. Farther on, Noel could see a policeman running up the street.

"Quickly," said Kessler.

The car was a vintage Mercedes; they climbed in. Kessler started the engine, but did not idle it. Instead, he put the car in gear and sped west.

"That man . . . in the jacket . . . he was the one who followed me," Holcroft whispered.

"I gathered as much," answered Kessler. "He found his way back, after all."

"My *God*," cried Noel. "What did I *do*?"

"You didn't kill him, if that's what you mean."

Holcroft stared at Kessler. "What?"

"You didn't kill that man."

"The gun went off! He was shot."

"I don't doubt it. But the bullet didn't kill him."

"What *did* then?"

"Obviously you didn't see his throat. He had been garroted."

"Baldwin in New York!"

"Wolfsschanze in Berlin," answered Kessler. "His death was timed to the split second. Someone in that restaurant, outside the booth, brought him to within feet of our table and used the noise and the crowd to cover the execution."

"Oh, Jesus! Then whoever it was . . ." Noel could not finish the statement; fear was making him ill. He wanted to vomit.

"Whoever it was," completed Kessler, "knows now that I am part of Geneva. So, you have your answer; for I have no choice. I'm with you."

"I'm sorry," said Holcroft. "I wanted you to have a choice."

"I know you did, and I thank you for it. However, I must insist on one condition."

"What's that?"

"My brother, Hans, in Munich, must be made part of the covenant."

Noel recalled Manfredi's words; there were no restrictions in this respect. The only stipulation was that each family had one vote. "There's nothing to prevent him, if he wants to."

"He'll want to. We are very close. You'll like him. He's a fine doctor."

"I'd say you were both fine doctors."

"He heals. I merely expound. . . . I'm also driving aimlessly. I'd ask you out to my house, but under the circumstances I'd better not."

"I've done enough damage. But you should get back as soon as you can."

"Why?"

"If we're lucky, nobody'll give your name to the police, and it won't matter. But if someone does—a waiter or anybody who knows you—you can say you were on your way out when it happened."

Kessler shook his head. "I'm a passive man. Such thoughts would not have occurred to me."

"Three weeks ago they wouldn't have occurred to me, either. Let me off near a taxi stand. I'll go to my hotel and get my suitcase."

"Nonsense. I'll drive you."

"We shouldn't be seen together anymore. That's asking for complications."

"I must learn to listen to you. When will we see each other, then?"

"I'll call you from Paris. I'm meeting with Von Tiebolt in a day or so. Then the three of us have to get to Geneva. There's very little time left."

"That man in New York? Miles?"

"Among other things. I'll explain when I see you again. There's a taxi on the corner."

"What will you do now? I doubt there are planes at this hour."

"Then I'll wait at the airport. I don't want to be isolated in a hotel room." Kessler stopped the car; Holcroft reached for the door. "Thank you, Erich. And I'm sorry."

"Don't be, my friend Noel. Call me."

The blond-haired man sat rigidly behind the desk in Kessler's library. His eyes were furious, his voice strained and intense as he spoke.

"Tell me again. Every *word*. Leave out nothing."

"What's the *point?*" replied Kessler from across the room. "We've gone over it ten times. I've remembered everything."

"Then we shall go over it ten more times!" shouted

Johann von Tiebolt. "*Thirty* times, *forty* times! Who *was* he? Where did he come from? Who were the two men in Montereau? They're linked; where did all three come from?"

"We don't *know*," said the scholar. "There's no way to tell."

"But there is! Don't you see? The answer's in what that man said to Holcroft in the alley. I'm certain of it. I've heard the words before. It's there!"

"For God's sake, you *had* the man." Kessler spoke firmly. "If you couldn't learn anything from *him*, what makes you think we can from anything Holcroft said? You should have broken him."

"He wouldn't break; he was too far gone for drugs."

"So you put a wire to his throat and threw him to the American. Madness!"

"Not madness," said Tennyson. "Consistency. Holcroft must be convinced that Wolfsschanze is everywhere. Prodding, threatening, protecting. . . . Let's go back to what was said. According to Holcroft, the man wasn't afraid to die. What was it? '. . . I am prepared. We are all prepared. We will stop you. We will stop Geneva. Kill me and another will take my place; kill him, another his.' The words of a fanatic. But he wasn't a fanatic; I saw that for myself. He was no ODESSA agent, no Rache revolutionary. He was something else. Holcroft was right about that. Something *else*."

"We're at a dead end."

"Not entirely. I have a man in Paris checking on the identities of the bodies found in Montereau."

"La Sûreté?"

"Yes. He's the best." Tennyson sighed. "It's all so incredible. After thirty years, the first overt moves are made, and within two weeks men come out of nowhere. As if they'd been waiting along with us for three decades. Yet they do not come out in the open. Why not? That is the sticking point. Why *not?*"

"The man said it to Holcroft in the alley. 'We can put that fortune to use.' They can't get it if they expose Geneva's sources."

"Too simple; the amount's too great. If it was money alone, nothing would prevent them from coming to us—to the bank's directors, for that matter—and negotiating from a position of strength. Nearly eight hundred million; from their point of view, they could demand two thirds. They'd be dead after the fact, but they don't know that. No, Erich, it's not the money alone. We must look for something else."

"We must look at the other crisis!" Kessler shouted. "Whoever that man was, tonight, whoever the two men were in Montereau, they're secondary to our most immediate concern! Face it, Johann! The British know you're the Tinamou! Don't sidetrack that any longer. They know you're the Tinamou!"

"Correction. They *suspect* I'm he; they don't know it. And as Holcroft so correctly put it, they'll soon be convinced they're wrong, if they're not convinced already. Actually, it's a very advantageous position."

"You're mad!" screamed Kessler. "You will jeopardize *everything!*"

"On the contrary," said Tennyson calmly. "I will solidify everything. What better ally could we have than MI Five? To be certain, we have men in British Intelligence, but none so high as Payton-Jones."

"What in the name of God are you *talking* about?" The scholar was perspiring; the veins in his neck were pronounced.

"Sit down, Erich."

"No!"

"Sit down!"

Kessler sat. "I won't tolerate this, Johann."

"Don't tolerate anything; just listen." Tennyson leaned forward. "For a few moments, let's reverse roles; I'll be the professor."

"Don't push me. We can handle intruders who won't show themselves; they have something to hide. We can't handle this. If you're taken, what's left?"

"That's flattering, but you mustn't think that way. If anything should happen to me, there are the lists, names of our people everywhere. A man can be found among them; the Fourth Reich will have a leader, in any event. But nothing *will* happen to me. The Tinamou is my shield, my protection. With his capture, I'm not only free of suspicion, I'm held in great respect."

"You've lost your senses! You *are* the Tinamou!"

Tennyson sat back, smiling. "Let's examine our assassin, shall we? Ten years ago you agreed he was my finest creation. I believe you said the Tinamou might well turn out to be our most vital weapon."

"In *theory*. Only in theory. It was an academic judgment; I also said that!"

"True, you often take refuge high up in your cloistered tower, and that's how it should be. But you were right, you know. In the last analysis, the millions in Switzerland cannot serve us unless they can be put to use. There are laws everywhere; they must be circumvented. It's not as simple as it once was to pay for a Reichstag, or a block of seats in Parliament; or to buy an election in America. But for us it is nowhere near as difficult as it would be for others; that was your point ten years ago, and it is more valid today. We are in the position to make extraordinary demands on the most influential men in every major government. They've *paid* the Tinamou to assassinate their adversaries. From Washington to Paris to Cairo; from Athens to Beirut to Madrid; from London to Warsaw and even to Moscow itself. The Tinamou is irresistible. He is our own nuclear bomb."

"And he can claim *us* in the fallout!"

"He could," agreed Tennyson, "but he won't. Years ago, Erich, we vowed to keep no secrets from each other, and I've kept that vow in all matters except one. I won't apologize; it was, as they say, a decision of rank, and I felt it was necessary."

"What did you do?" asked Kessler.

"Gave us that most vital weapon you spoke of ten years ago."

"How?"

"A few moments ago you were quite specific. You raised your voice and said *I* was the Tinamou."

"You are!"

"I'm not."

"What?"

"I'm only half of the Tinamou. To be sure, the better half, but still only half. For years I trained another; he is my alternate in the field. His expertness has been taught, his brilliance acquired; next to the real Tinamou, he's the best on earth."

The scholar stared at the blond man in astonishment . . . and with awe. "He's one of us? *Ein Sonnenkind?*"

"Of course not! He's a paid killer; he knows nothing but an extraordinary life-style in which every need and appetite is gratified by the extraordinary sums he earns. He's also aware that one day he may have to pay the price for his way of living, and he accepts that. He's a professional."

Kessler sank back in the chair and loosened his collar. "I must say, you never cease to amaze me."

"I'm not finished," replied Tennyson. "An event is taking place in London shortly, a gathering of heads of state. It's the perfect opportunity. The Tinamou will be caught."

"He'll be what?"

"You heard correctly." Tennyson smiled. "The Tinamou will be captured, a weapon in his hands, the odd caliber and the bore markings traceable to three previous assassinations. He will be caught and killed by the man who has been tracking him for nearly six years. A man who, for his own protection, wants no credit, wants no mention of his name. Who calls in the intelligence authorities of his adopted country. John Tennyson, European correspodent of the *Guardian*."

"My *God*," whispered Kessler. "How will you do it?"

"Even you can't know that. But there'll be a dividend as powerful as Geneva itself. The word will go out, in print, that the Tinamou kept private records. They haven't been found, and thus can be presumed to have been stolen by someone. That someone will be ourselves. So, in death, the Tinamou serves us still."

Kessler shook his head in wonder. "You think exotically; that's your essential gift."

"Among others," said the blond man matter-of-factly. "And our newfound alliance with MI Five may be helpful. Other intelligence services may be more sophisticated, but none are better." Tennyson slapped the arm of his chair. "Now. Let's get back to our unknown enemy. His identity is in the words spoken in that alley. I've heard them! I know it."

"We've exhausted that approach."

"We've only begun." The blond man reached for a pencil and paper. "Now, from the beginning. We'll write down everything he said, everything you can remember."

The scholar sighed. "From the beginning," he repeated. "Very well. According to Holcroft, the man's first words referred to the killing in France, the fact that Holcroft had not hesitated to fire his pistol then. . . ."

Kessler spoke. Tennyson listened and interrupted and asked for repetitions of words and phrases. He wrote furiously. Forty minutes passed.

"I can't go on any longer," said Kessler. "There's no more I can tell you."

"Again, the *eagles*," countered the blond man harshly. "Say the words exactly as Holcroft said them."

"Eagles? . . . 'You won't stop the eagles. Not this time.' Could he have meant the Luftwaffe? The Wehrmacht?"

"Not likely." Tennyson looked down at the pages in front of him. He tapped his finger at something he had written down. "Here. 'Your Wolfsschanze.' *Your* Wolfsschanze. . . . Meaning ours, not theirs."

"What are you talking about?" said Kessler. "We *are* Wolfsschanze; the men of Wolfsschanze are *Sonnenkinder!*"

Tennyson ignored the interruption. "Von Stauffenberg, Olbricht, Von Falkenhausen, and Höpner. Rommel called them 'the true eagles of Germany.' They were the insurrectionists, the Führer's would-be assassins. All were shot; Rommel, ordered to take his own life. *Those* are the eagles he referred to. *Their* Wolfsschanze, not ours."

"Where does it lead us? For God's *sake*, Johann, I'm exhausted. I can't go on!"

Tennyson had covered a dozen pages of paper; now he shuffled them, underlining words, circling phrases. "You may have said enough," he replied. "It's here . . . in this section. He used the words 'butchers and clowns,' and then, 'you won't stop the eagles.'. . . Only seconds later, Holcroft told him that the account would be tied up for years, that there were conditions . . .'the money frozen, sent back into the ground.' The man repeated the phrase 'back into the ground,' saying it was the flaw. But then he added that there would be 'no scorched earth.' 'Scorched earth.' 'There will be no . . . *scorched earth.*' "

The blond man's upper body tensed. He leaned back in the chair, his sculptured face twisted in concentration, his cold eyes staring rigidly at the words on the paper. "It couldn't be . . . after all these years. Operation Barbarossa! The 'scorched earth' of Barbarossa! Oh, my God, the Nachrichtendienst. It's the Nachrichtendienst!"

"What are you talking about?" Kessler said. " 'Barbarossa' was Hitler's first invasion north, a magnificent victory."

"He called it a victory. The Prussians called it a disaster. A hollow victory, written in blood. Whole divisions unprepared, decimated. . . . 'We took the land,' the generals said. 'We took the worthless, scorched earth of Barbarossa.' Out of it came the Nachrichtendienst."

"What was it?"

"An intelligence unit. Rarefied, exclusively Junker, a corps of aristocrats. Later, there were those who thought it was a Gehlen operation, designed to sow distrust between the Russians and the West. But it wasn't; it was solely its own. It loathed Hitler; it scorned the Schutzstaffel—'SS garbage' was the term it used; it hated the commanders of the Luftwaffe. All were called 'butchers and clowns.' It was above the war, above the party. It was only for Germany. *Their* Germany."

"Say what you mean, Johann!" shouted Kessler.

"The Nachrichtendienst survives. It's the intruder. It wants to destroy Geneva. It will stop at nothing to abort the Fourth Reich before it's born."

27

Noel waited on the bridge, watching the lights of Paris flicker like clusters of tiny candles. He had reached Helden at Gallimard; she had agreed to meet him after work on the Pont Neuf. He had tried to persuade her to drive to the hotel in Argenteuil, but she had declined his offer.

"You promised me days, weeks, if I wished," he said.

"I promised us both, my darling, and we'll have them. But not Argenteuil. I'll explain when I see you."

It was barely five-fifteen; the winter night descended on Paris quickly, and the chill of the river wind penetrated him. He pulled up the collar of his secondhand overcoat to ward off the cold. He looked at his watch again; its hands had not moved. How could they have? No more than ten seconds had elapsed.

He felt like a young man waiting for a girl he had met at a country club in the summer moonlight, and he smiled to himself, feeling awkward and embarrassed, not wanting to acknowledge his anxiety. He was not in the moonlight on some warm summer's night. He was on a bridge in Paris, and the air was cold, and he was dressed in a secondhand overcoat, and in his pocket was a gun.

He saw her walking onto the bridge. She was wearing the black raincoat, her blond hair encased by a dark-red scarf that framed her face. Her pace was steady, neither rapid nor casual; she was a lone woman going home from her place of work. Except for her striking features—only hinted at in the distance—she was like thousands of other women in Paris, heading home in the early evening.

She saw him. He started walking toward her, but she held up her hand, a signal for him to remain where he was. He paid no attention, wanting to reach her quickly, his arms held out. She walked into them and they embraced, and he felt warm in the comfort of being with her again. She pulled her head back and looked at him, then pretended to be firm, but her eyes smiled.

"You must never run on a bridge," she said. "A man running across a bridge stands out. One strolls over the water; one doesn't race."

"I missed you. I don't give a damn."

"You must learn to. How was Berlin?"

He put his arm around her shoulder and they started toward the quai Saint-Bernard, and the Left Bank. "I've got a lot to tell you, some good, some not so good. But if learning something is progress, I think we've taken a couple of giant steps. Have you heard from your brother?"

"Yes. This afternoon. He called an hour after you did. His plans have changed; he can be in Paris tomorrow."

"That's the best news you could give me. At least, I think it is. I'll let you know tomorrow." They walked off the bridge and turned left along the riverbank. "Did you miss me?"

"Noel, you're mad. You left yesterday afternoon. I barely had time to get home, bathe, have a very-much-needed night's sleep, and get to work."

"You went home? To your apartment?"

"No, I—" She stopped and looked up at him, smiling. "Very good, Noel Holcroft, new recruit. Interrogate casually."

"I don't feel casual."

"You promised not to ask that question."

"Not specifically. I asked you if you were married, or living with someone—to which I got a negative to the first and a very oblique answer to the second—but I never actually promised not to try and find out where you live."

"You implied it, my darling. One day I'll tell you, and you'll see how foolish you are."

"Tell me now. I'm in love. I want to know where my woman lives."

The smile disappeared from her lips. Then it returned, and she glanced up at him again. "You're like a little boy practicing a new word. You don't know me well enough to love me; I told you that."

"I forgot. You like women."

"They're among my best friends."

"But you wouldn't want to marry one."

"I don't want to marry anyone."

"Good. It's less complicated. Just move in with me for the next ten years, exercisable options on both sides."

"You say such nice things."

They stopped at an intersection. He turned Helden to him, both his hands on her arms. "I say them because I mean them."

"I believe you," she said, looking at him curiously, her eyes part questioning, part fearful.

He saw the fear; it bothered him, and so he smiled. "Love me a little?"

She could not bring the smile to her lips. "I think I love you more than a little. You're a problem I didn't want. I'm not sure I can handle it."

"That's even better." He laughed and took her hand to cross the street. "It's nice to know you don't have all the answers."

"Did you believe I did?"

"I thought you thought so."

"I don't."

"I know."

The restaurant was half filled with diners. Helden asked for a table in the rear, out of sight of the entrance. The proprietor nodded. It was apparent that he could not quite fathom why this *belle femme* would come into his establishment with such a poorly dressed companion. In his eyes was the comment: things were not going well for the girls of Paris these days. Nights.

"He doesn't approve of me," said Holcroft.

"There's hope for you, though. You grew in his estimation when you specified expensive whiskey. He grinned; didn't you see?"

"He was looking at my jacket. It came from a somewhat better rack than the overcoat."

Helden laughed. "That overcoat's purpose was not high fashion. Did you use it in Berlin?"

"I used it. I wore it when I picked up a whore. Are you jealous?"

"Not of anyone accepting an offer from you dressed like that."

"She was a vision of loveliness."

"You're lucky. She was probably an ODESSA agent

and you've come down with a social disease, as planned. See a doctor before you see me again."

Noel took her hand. There was no humor in his voice when he spoke. "The ODESSA's no concern of ours. Neither is the Rache. That's one—or two—of the things I learned in Berlin. It's doubtful either of them knows anything about Geneva."

Helden was stunned. "But what about Beaumont? You said he was ODESSA, that he followed you to Rio."

"I think he is ODESSA, and he did follow me, but not because of Geneva. He's tied in with Graff. Somehow he found out I was looking for Johann von Tiebolt; *that* was why he followed me. Not Geneva. I'll know more when I speak to your brother tomorrow. Anyway, Beaumont'll be out of the picture in a few days. Kessler's taking care of it. He said he'd make a call to someone in the Bonn government."

"It's that simple?"

"It's not that difficult. Any hint of ODESSA, especially in the military, is enough to start a battery of inquiries. Beaumont'll be pulled in."

"If it's not the ODESSA, or the Rache, who is it?"

"That's part of what I've got to tell you. I had to get rid of the mackinaw and the cap."

"Oh?" Helden was confused by the non sequitur.

He told her why, playing down the violence in the dark alleyway. Then he described the conversation with Kessler, realizing as he came to the end that he could not omit the murder of the unknown man in the leather jacket. He would tell her brother about it tomorrow; to withhold it from Helden now would serve no purpose. When he had finished, she shuddered, pressing her fingers into the palm of her hand.

"How *horrible*. Did Kessler have any idea who he was, where he came from?"

"Not really. We went over everything he said a half-dozen times, trying to figure it out, but there wasn't that much. In Kessler's opinion he was part of a neo-Nazi group—descendants of the party, Kessler called them. A splinter faction that has no use for the ODESSA."

"How would they know about the account in Geneva?"

"I asked Kessler that. He said that the sort of manipulations required to get that money out of Germany couldn't have been kept as quiet as we think; that someone somewhere could have learned about it."

"But Geneva is *based* on secrecy. Without it, it would collapse."

"Then it's a question of degree. When is a secret a secret? What separates confidential information from highly classified data? A handful of people found out about Geneva and want to stop us from getting the money and using it the way it's supposed to be used. They want it for themselves, so they're not going to expose it."

"But if they've learned that much, they know they can't get it."

"Not necessarily."

"Then they should be told!"

"I said as much to the man in the alley. I didn't convince him. Even if I had, it wouldn't make any difference now."

"But don't you see? Someone has to reach these people—whoever they are—and convince them they gain nothing by stopping you and my brother and Erich Kessler."

Holcroft drank. "I'm not sure we should do that. Kessler said something that bothered me when I heard it, and it bothers me now. He said that we—the 'we,' I guess, meaning all of us who haven't studied the subject that closely—never understood the hard-core Nazi. From the Nazi's point of view, it wasn't simply a question of how *he* could benefit; it was just as important to him that others *do not* benefit. Kessler called it the 'essential destructiveness.' "

Helden's frown returned. "So if they're told, they'll go after you. They'll kill the three of you, because without you, there's no Geneva."

"Not for another generation. That's motive enough. The money goes back into the vaults for another thirty years."

Helden brought her hand to her mouth. "Wait a minute; there's something terribly wrong. They've tried to kill you. *You*. From the beginning . . . *you*."

Holcroft shook his head. "We can't be certain—"

"Not *certain?*" broke in Helden. "My God, what more do you want? You showed me your jacket. There was the strychnine on that plane, the shots in Rio. What more do you want?"

"I want to know who was really behind those things. That's why I have to talk to your brother."

"What can Johann tell you?"

"Whom he killed in Rio." Helden started to object; he took her hand again. "Let me explain. I think we're in the middle—*I'm* in the middle—of two fights, neither having anything to do with the other. Whatever happened to your brother in Rio has nothing to do with Geneva. That's where I made my mistake. I tied everything into Geneva. It's not; it's separate."

"I tried to tell you that," said Helden.

"I was slow. But then, no one's ever fired a gun at me, or tried to poison me, or shoved a knife in my stomach. Those kinds of things play hell with your thinking process. At least they do mine."

"Johann is a man of many interests, Noel," she said. "He can be very charming, very personable, but he can also be reticent. It's part of him. He's lived a strange life. Sometimes I think of him as a gadfly. He darts quickly from one place to another, one interest to another, always brilliantly, always leaving his mark, but not always wishing that mark to be recognized."

" 'He's here, he's there, he's everywhere,' " interrupted Holcroft. "You're describing some sort of Scarlet Pimpernel."

"Exactly. Johann may not tell you what happened in Rio."

"He has to. I have to know."

"Since it has nothing to do with Geneva, he may disagree."

"Then I'll try to convince him. We *have* to find out how vulnerable he is."

"Let's say he is vulnerable. What happens then?"

"He'd be disqualified from taking part in Geneva. We know he killed someone. You heard a man—a wealthy, influential man, you thought—say he wanted to see your brother hanged for murder. *I* know he tangled with Graff, and that means the ODESSA. He ran for his life. He took you and your sister with him, but he ran for *his* life. He's mixed up in a lot of complications; people are after him, and it's not unreasonable to think he could be blackmailed. That could shake Geneva; it could corrupt it."

"Do the bankers have to be told?" asked Helden.

Noel touched her cheek, forcing her to look at him. "I'd have to tell them. We're talking about seven hundred and eighty million dollars; about three men who did something remarkable. It was their gesture to history; I really believe that. If your brother puts it in jeopardy, or causes it to be misused, then maybe it's better that those millions get locked up for the next generation. But it doesn't have to be that way. According to the rules, you're the one who'd be the Von Tiebolt executrix."

Helden gazed at him. "I can't accept that, Noel. It must be Johann. Not only is he more qualified to be a part of Geneva; he deserves it. I can't take that from him."

"And I can't give it to him. Not if he can hurt the covenant. Let's talk about it after I see him."

She studied his face; he felt awkward. She took his hand from her cheek and held it. "You're a moral man, aren't you?"

"Not necessarily. Just angry. I'm sick of corruption in the rarefied circles of finance. There's been an awful lot of it in my country."

" 'Rarefied circles of finance'?"

"It's a phrase my father used in his letter to me."

"That's odd," said Helden.

"What is?"

"You've always called him Clausen, or Heinrich Clausen. Formal, rather distant."

Holcroft nodded, acknowledging the truth of her remark. "It's funny, because I really don't know any more about him now than I did before. But he's been described to me. The way he looked, the way he talked, how people listened to him and were affected by him."

"Then you do know more about him."

"Not actually. Only impressions. A child's impressions, at that. But in a small way I think I've found him."

"When did your parents tell you about him?"

"Not my parents, not my . . . stepfather. Just Althene. It was a couple of weeks after my twenty-fifth birthday. I was working then, a certified professional."

"Professional?"

"I'm an architect, remember? I've almost forgotten."

"Your mother waited until you were twenty-five before she told you?"

"She was right. I don't think I could have handled it when I was younger. Good Lord. Noel Holcroft, American boy. Hot dogs and french fries, Shea Stadium and the Mets, the Garden and the Knicks; and college and friends whose fathers were soldiers in the big war, each one winning it in his own way. That fellow's told his real father was one of those heel-clicking sadists in the war movies, Christ, that kid would flip out."

"Why did she tell you at all, then?"

"On the remote chance that I'd find out for myself one day, and she didn't want that. She didn't think it would happen. She and Dick had covered the traces right down to a birth certificate which said I was their son. But there was another birth certificate. In Berlin. 'Clausen, male child. Mother—Althene. Father—Heinrich.' And there were people who knew she'd left him, left Germany. She wanted me to be prepared if it ever surfaced, if anyone for any reason ever remembered and tried to use the information. Prepared, incidentally, to deny it. To say there'd been another child—never mentioned in the house—who had died in infancy in England."

"Which means there was another certificate. A death certificate."

"Yes. Properly recorded somewhere in London."

Helden leaned back against the booth. "You and we are not so different after all. Our lives are full of false papers. What a luxury it must be not to live that way."

"Papers don't mean much to me. I've never hired anyone because of them, and I've never fired anyone because someone else brought them to me." Noel finished his drink. "I ask the questions myself. And I'm going to ask your brother some very tough ones. I hope to God he has the answers I want to hear."

"So do I."

He leaned toward her, their shoulders touching. "Love me a little?"

"More than a little."

"Stay with me tonight."

"I intend to. Your hotel?"

"Not the one in rue Chevalle. That Mr. Fresca we invented the other night has moved to better lodgings. You see, I've got a few friends in Paris, too. One's an assistant manager at the George Cinq."

"How extravagant."

"It's allowed. You're a very special woman, and we don't know what's going to happen, starting tomorrow.

By the way, why couldn't we go to Argenteuil? You said you'd tell me."

"We were seen there."

"What? By whom?"

"A man saw us—saw you, really. We don't know his name, but we know he was from Interpol, We have a source there. A bulletin was circulated from the Paris headquarters with your description. A trace was put out for you from New York. From a police officer named Miles."

28

John Tennyson walked out into Heathrow Airport's crowded arrivals area. He walked to a black Jaguar sedan waiting at the curb. The driver was smoking a cigarette and reading a book. At the sight of the approaching blond man, the driver got out of the car.

"Good afternoon, Mr. Tennyson," said the man, in a throaty Welsh accent.

"Have you been waiting long?" asked Tennyson, without much interest.

"Not very," answered the driver, taking Tennyson's briefcase and overnight bag. "I presume you wish to drive."

"Yes, I'll drop you off along the way. Someplace where you can find a taxi."

"I can get one here."

"No, I want to talk for a few minutes." Tennyson climbed in behind the wheel; the Welshman opened the rear door and put the luggage inside. Within minutes they had passed the airport gates and were on the highway to London.

"Did you have a good trip?" asked the Welshman.

"A busy one."

"I read your article about Bahrain. Most amusing."

"Bahrain's amusing. The Indian shopkeepers are the only economists on the archipelago."

"But you were kind to the sheikhs."

"They were kind to me. What's the news from the Mediterranean? Have you stayed in touch with your brother on board Beaumont's ship?"

"Constantly. We use a radiophone off Cap Camarat. Everything's going according to schedule. The rumor circulated on the pier that the commander was seen going out in a small boat with a woman from Saint-Tropez. Neither the boat nor the couple have been heard from in over forty-eight hours, and there were offshore squalls. My brother will report the incident tomorrow. He will assume command, of course."

"Of course. Then it all goes well. Beaumont's death will be clear-cut. An accident in bad weather. No one will question the story."

"You don't care to tell me what actually happened?"

"Not specifically; it would be a burden to you. But basically, Beaumont overreached himself. He was seen in the wrong places by the wrong people. It was speculated that our upstanding officer was actually connected to the ODESSA."

The Welshman's expression conveyed his anger. "That's dangerous. The damn fool."

"There's something I must tell you," said Tennyson. "It's almost time."

The Welshman replied in awe. "It's happened, then?"

"Within two weeks, I'd guess."

"I can't believe it!"

"Why?" asked Tennyson. "Everything's on schedule. The cables must begin to go out. Everywhere."

"Everywhere . . ." repeated the man.

"The code is 'Wolfsschanze.' "

"Wolfsschanze? . . . Oh God, it's come!"

"It's here. Update a final master list of district leaders, one copy only, of course. Take all the microdot files —country by country, city by city, each political connection—and seal them in a steel case. Bring the case personally to me, along with the master list, one week from today. Wednesday. We'll meet on the street outside my flat in Kensington. Eight o'clock at night."

"A week from today. Wednesday. Eight o'clock. With the case."

"And the master list. The leaders."

"Of course." The Welshman brought the knuckle of his index finger to his teeth. "It's really come," he whispered.

"There's a minor obstacle, but we'll surmount it."

"Can I help? I'll do anything."

"I know you will, Ian. You're one of the best. I'll tell you next week."

"*Anything.*"

"Of course." Tennyson slowed the Jaguar at the approach of an exit. "I'd drive you into London, but I'm heading toward Margate. It's imperative that I get there quickly."

"Don't worry about me. God, man, you must have so much on your mind!" Ian kept his eyes on Tennyson's face, on the strong, chiseled features that held such promise, such power. "To be here now; to have the privilege to be present at the beginning. At the rebirth. There's no sacrifice I wouldn't make."

The blond man smiled. "Thank you," he said.

"Leave me anywhere. I'll find a taxi. . . . I didn't know we had people in Margate."

"We have people everywhere," said Tennyson, stopping the car.

Tennyson sped down the familiar highway toward Portsea. He would reach Gretchen's house before eight o'clock, and that was as it should be; she expected him at nine. He'd be able to make sure she had no visitors, no friendly male neighbors who might have dropped in for a drink.

The blond man smiled to himself. Even in her mid-forties, his sister drew men as the proverbial flame drew moths: they, scorched into satiety by the heat, saved from themselves by their inability to reach the flame itself. For Gretchen did not fulfill the promise of her sexuality unless told to do so. It was a weapon to be used, as all potentially lethal weapons were to be used—with discretion.

Tennyson did not relish what he had to do, but he knew he had no choice. All threads that led to Geneva had to be cut, and his sister was one of them. As Anthony Beaumont had been one. Gretchen simply knew too much; Wolfsschanze's enemies could break her—and they would.

There were three items of information the Nachrichtendienst did not have: the timetable, the methods of dispersing the millions, and the lists. Gretchen knew the timetable; she was familiar with the methods of dispersal; and, as the methods were tied to the names of recipients all over the world, she was all too aware of the lists.

His sister had to die.

As the Welshman had to make the sacrifice he spoke of so nobly. Once the airtight carton and the master list were delivered, the Welshman's contributions were finished. He remained only a liability; for, except for the sons of Erich Kessler and Wilhelm von Tiebolt, no one else alive would ever see those lists. Thousands of names, in every country, who were the true inheritors of Wolfsschanze, the perfect race, the *Sonnenkinder*.

PORTSEA—15 M

The blond man pressed the accelerator; the Jaguar shot forward.

"So, at last it's here," said Gretchen Beaumont, sitting next to Tennyson on the soft leather couch, her hand caressing his face, her fingers darting in and out between his lips, arousing him as she was always able to do since they were children. "And you're so beautiful. There's no other man like you; there never will be."

She leaned forward, her unbuttoned blouse exposing her breasts, inviting his caress. She opened her mouth and covered his, groaning in that throaty way that drove him wild.

But he could not succumb. When he did, it would be the last act of a secret ritual that had kept him pure and unentangled . . . since he was a child. He held her shoulders and gently pushed her back on the couch.

"It's here," he said. "I must learn everything that's happened while my mind's clear. We have lots of time. I'll leave about six in the morning for Heathrow, for the first plane to Paris. But now, is there anything you forgot to tell me about the American? Are you sure he never made the connection between you and New York?"

"Never. The dead woman across from his apartment was known to be a heavy smoker. I don't smoke, and made a point of it when he was here. I also made it clear that I hadn't been anywhere in weeks. If he questioned that, I could have proved it, of course. And, obviously, I was very much alive."

"So when he left, he had no idea that the highly erotic, straying wife he went to bed with was the woman in New York."

"Of course not. And he didn't leave," said Gretchen, laughing. "He fled. Bewildered and panicked, convinced I was unbalanced—as we had planned—thus making you next in line for Geneva." She stopped laughing. "He also fled with Tony's photograph, which we had not planned. You're getting it back, I assume."

Tennyson nodded. "Yes."

"What will you tell Holcroft?"

"He believes Beaumont was an ODESSA agent; that I was somehow embroiled with Graff and had to escape from Brazil or be shot. That's what he told Kessler. The truth is, he's not at all sure what happened in Rio except that I killed someone; he's worried about it." Tennyson smiled. "I'll play on his assumptions. I'll think of something startling, something that will stun him, convince him I'm holier than John the Baptist. And, of course, I'll be grateful that our partner has caused the removal of the terrible Beaumont from our concerns."

Gretchen took his hand, pressing it between her legs, rubbing her stockings up and down against his flesh. "You are not only beautiful; you're brilliant."

"Then I'll turn the tables, make him feel he must convince me *he's* worthy of Geneva. He will be the one who must justify his part of the covenant. It's psychologically vital that he be put in that position; his dependency on me must grow."

Gretchen locked her legs against his hand and held his wrist; the grip was abrupt and sexual. "You can excite me with words, but you know that, don't you?"

"In a while, my love . . . my only love. We've got to talk." Tennyson dug his fingers into his sister's leg; she moaned. "Of course, I'll know more what to say after I've spoken to Helden."

"You'll see her before you meet with Holcroft, then?"

"Yes. I'll call her and tell her I've got to see her right away. For the first time in her life, she'll observe me in the throes of self-doubt, desperately needing to be convinced my actions are right."

"Brilliant again." She took his hand from between her legs and placed it under her breast. "And does our little sister still run with the flotsam and jetsam? The self-imposed *Verwünschkinder*, with their beards and bad teeth?"

"Of course. She has to feel needed; it was always her weakness."

"She wasn't born in the Reich."

Tennyson laughed derisively. "To compound her striving for adequacy, she's become a nursemaid. She lives in Herr Oberst's house and cares for the crippled bastard. Two changes of cars each evening, so as not to lead the assassins of the Rache and the ODESSA to him."

"One or the other may kill her one day," mused Gretchen. "That's something to think about. Soon after the bank frees the account, she'll have to go. She's not stupid, Johann. One more murder laid at the foot of the Rache. Or the ODESSA."

"It's crossed my mind. . . . Speaking of murder, tell me: While Holcroft was here, did he mention Peter Baldwin?"

"Not a word. I never thought he would, not if I was playing my part right. I was an unbalanced, resentful wife. He didn't want to frighten me; nor did he wish to give me information dangerous to Geneva."

Tennyson nodded; they had projected accurately. "What was his reaction when you talked about me?"

"I gave him very little time to react," said Gretchen. "I simply told him you spoke for the Von Tiebolts. Why did Baldwin try to intercept him in New York? Do you know?"

"I've pieced it together. Baldwin operated out of Prague, an MI-Sixer whose allegiance, many said, was to the highest bidder. He sold information to anyone, until his own people began to suspect him. They fired him, but didn't prosecute, because they couldn't be sure; he'd operated as a double agent in the past and claimed it as his cover. He swore he was developing a two-way network. He also knew the name of every British contact in Central Europe, and obviously let his superiors know that those names would surface if anything happened to him. He maintained his innocence, said he was being punished for doing his job too well."

"What's that got to do with Holcroft?"

"To understand, you have to see Baldwin for what he was. He was good; his sources, the best. In addition to which he was a courier specialist; he could track anything. While in Prague, he heard rumors of a great fortune being held in Geneva. Nazi spoils. The rumor wasn't unusual; such stories have been around since Berlin fell. The difference with this rumor was that Clausen's name was mentioned. Again, not completely startling; Clausen was the financial genius of the Reich. But Baldwin checked out everything to the finest point; it was the way he worked."

"He went back to the courier archives," interrupted Gretchen.

"Yes. Concentrating on the Finanzministerium. Hundreds of runs were made, Manfredi the recipient in dozens. Once he had Manfredi's name, the rest was patient observation—and money spread cautiously within the bank. His break came when he heard that Manfredi was setting up contact with a heretofore-unheard-of American named Holcroft. *Why?* He studied Holcroft and found the mother."

"She was Manfredi's strategy," Gretchen broke in again.

"From the beginning," agreed Tennyson, nodding. "He convinced Clausen she had to leave Germany. She had money of her own and moved in monied circles; she could be of great use to us in America. With Clausen's help, she came to accept that, but she was essentially Manfredi's creation."

"Underneath that gnome's benign appearance," said Gretchen, "was a Machiavelli."

"Without that kindly innocence of his, I doubt he'd ever have got away with it. But Machiavelli isn't the parallel. Manfredi's interest was solely the money; it was the only power he wanted. He was a sworn companion of the gold quota. It was his intention to control the agency in Zurich; it's why we killed him."

"How much did Baldwin learn?"

"We'll never know, exactly; but whatever it was, it was to be his vindication with British Intelligence. You see, he wasn't a double agent; he was exactly what he claimed to be: MI Six's very effective man in Prague."

"He reached Manfredi?"

"Oh, yes. He implied that much by his knowledge of the Geneva meeting. He was just a little late, that's all." The blond man smiled. "I can picture the confrontation: two specialists circling each other, both wanting something desperately; one to pry out information, the other to retain it at all costs, knowing he was dealing with a potentially catastrophic situation. Certain agreements must have been made; and, true to form, Manfredi broke his word, moved up the meeting with Holcroft, and then alerted us about Baldwin. He covered everything. If your husband were to be caught killing Peter Baldwin, there would be no connection with Ernst Manfredi. He was a man to be respected. He might have won."

"But not against Johann von Tiebolt," said Gretchen, squeezing his hand beneath her breast, moving it up. "Incidentally, I received another code from Graff, from Rio. He's upset again. He says he's not being kept informed."

"His senility is showing. He, too, has served his purpose. Age makes him careless; it's no time for him to be sending messages to England. I'm afraid the moment has arrived for *unser Freund* in Brazil."

"You'll send the order out?"

"In the morning. One more arm of the hated ODESSA severed. He trained me too well." Tennyson leaned forward, his hand cupping his sister's breast. "I think we are finished talking. As always, talking with you clears my mind. I can't think of anything more to say, anything more to ask you."

"Then make demands instead. It's been so long for you; you must be bursting inside. I'll take care of you, as I always have."

"Since we were children," said Tennyson, his mouth covering hers, her hand groping for his trousers. Both of them were trembling.

Gretchen lay naked beside him, her breathing steady, her body drained and satisfied. The blond man raised his hand and looked at the radium dial of his watch. It was two-thirty in the morning. Time to do the terrible thing demanded of him by the covenant of Wolfsschanze. All traces to Geneva had to be removed.

He reached over the side of the bed for his shoes. He lifted one up, feeling the heel with his fingers in the darkness. There was a small metal disk in the center. He pressed it, turning it to the left until a spring was released. He placed the disk on the bedside table, then tilted the shoe back and removed a steel needle ten inches long, concealed in a tiny bore drilled from heel to sole. The needle was flexible but unbreakable. Inserted properly between the fourth and fifth ribs, it punctured the heart, leaving a mark more often missed than found, even during an autopsy.

He held it delicately between the thumb and index finger of his right hand, reaching for his sister with his left. He touched her right breast and then her naked shoulder. She opened her eyes.

"You are insatiable," she whispered, smiling.

"Only with you." He drew her up to him until their flesh touched. "You are my only love," he said, his right arm sliding behind her, extended a foot beyond her spine. He turned his wrist inward; the needle was positioned. He thrust it forward.

The back-country roads were confusing, but Tennyson had memorized the route. He knew the way to the hidden cottage that housed the enigmatic Herr Oberst, that betrayer of the Reich. Even the title, "Oberst," was an ironic commentary. The traitor had been no colonel; he had been general in the Wehrmacht, General Klaus Falkenheim, at one time fourth-in-command of all Germany. Praise had been lavished on him by his military peers, and even by the Führer himself. And all the while a jackal had lived in that shiny, hollow shell.

God, how Johann von Tiebolt loathed the misfit liar that was Herr Oberst! But John Tennyson would not show that loathing. On the contrary, Tennyson would fawn on the old man, proclaiming awe and respect. For if there was one certain way to get his younger sister's total cooperation, it was by showing such deference.

He had called Helden at Gallimard, telling her that he had to see where she lived. Yes, he knew she lived in Herr Oberst's small house; and again, yes, he knew where it was.

"I'm a newspaperman now. I wouldn't be a very good one if I didn't have sources."

She had been stunned. He insisted on seeing her in the late morning, before meeting Holcroft in the afternoon. He would *not* meet with the American unless and until he saw her. Perhaps Herr Oberst could help clarify the situation. Perhaps the old gentleman might allay sudden fears that had arisen.

He reached the dirt road that led through the overgrown grass into the untamed glen that protected Herr Oberst's house from prying eyes. Three minutes later he stopped in front of the path that led to the cottage. The door opened; Helden came out to greet him. How lovely she looked, so like Gretchen.

They exchanged a brother-and-sister embrace, both anxious to begin the meeting with Herr Oberst. Helden's eyes conveyed her bewilderment. She led him inside the small, spartan house. Herr Oberst stood by the fireplace. Helden introduced the two men.

"This is a moment I shall treasure throughout my life," said Tennyson. "You've earned the gratitude of Germans everywhere. If I can ever be of service to you, tell Helden, and I'll do whatever you ask."

"You're too kind, Herr von Tiebolt," replied the old man. "But according to your sister, it's you who seek something from me, and I can't imagine what it is. How can I help you?"

"My problem is the American. This Holcroft."

"What about him?" asked Helden.

"Thirty years ago a magnificent thing was done, an incredible feat engineered by three extraordinary men who wished to make restitution for the anguish inflicted by butchers and maniacs. Through circumstances that seemed right at the time, Holcroft was projected to be a key factor in the distribution of millions throughout the world. I'm now asked to meet with him, cooperate with him. . . ." Tennyson stopped, as if the words eluded him.

"And?" Herr Oberst moved forward.

"I don't trust him," said the blond man. "He's met with Nazis. Men who would kill us, Helden. Men like Maurice Graff, in Brazil."

"What are you saying?"

"The bloodlines reemerge. Holcroft is a Nazi."

Helden's face was stretched in shock, her eyes a mixture of anger and disbelief. "That's absurd! Johann, that's insane!"

"Is it? I don't think so."

Noel waited until Helden left for work before placing the phone call to Miles, in New York. Their night had been filled with love and comfort. He knew he had to convince her they would go on; there was no predetermined ending to their being together. He would not accept that now.

The telephone rang. "Yes, operator, this is the Mr. Fresca calling Lieutenant Miles."

"I thought it had to be you," said the man whose voice had no matching face for Noel. "Interpol reach you?"

"*Reach* me? There are men following me, if that's what you mean. I think it's called a 'trace.' Put out by *you*?"

"That's right."

"You gave me two weeks! What the hell are you doing?"

"Trying to find you. Trying to get you information I think you should have. It concerns your mother."

Noel felt a sharp pain in his chest. "What about my mother?"

"She ran." Miles paused. "I'll give her credit; she's damned good. It was a very professional skip. She went the Mexican route, and before you could say 'Althene Holcroft,' she was a little old lady on her way to Lisbon with a new name and a new passport courtesy of dealers in Tulancingo. Unfortunately, those tactics are outdated. We know them all."

"Maybe she thought you were harassing her," said Noel, with little conviction. "Maybe she just wanted to get away from you."

"There's no harassment. And whatever her reasons, she'd better realize that someone else is aware of them. Someone very serious."

"What are you telling me?"

"She was being followed by a man we couldn't place in any file anywhere. His papers were as counterfeit as hers. We had him picked up at the airport in Mexico City. Before anyone could question him, he slipped a cyanide capsule in his mouth."

29

A meeting ground was chosen. There was a vacant flat in Montmartre, on the top floor of an old building, its owner an artist now in Italy. Helden telephoned, gave Noel the address and the time. She would be there to introduce her brother, but would not stay.

Noel climbed the last step and knocked on the door. He heard hurrying footsteps; the door opened; Helden was in the narrow foyer. "Hello, my darling," she said.

"Hello," he answered awkwardly as he met her lips, his eyes glancing behind her.

"Johann's on the terrace," she said, laughing. "A kiss is permitted, in any event. I told him . . . how fond I am of you."

"Was that necessary?"

"Strangely enough, it was. I'm glad I did. It made me feel good." She closed the door, holding his arm. "I can't explain this," she said. "I haven't seen my brother in over a year. But he's changed. The situation in Geneva has affected him; he's profoundly committed to its success. I've never seen him so . . . oh, I don't know . . . so thoughtful."

"I still have questions, Helden."

"So does he. About you."

"Really?"

"At one point this morning, he didn't want to meet with you. He didn't trust you. He believed you'd been reached, paid to betray Geneva."

"*Me?*"

"Think about it. He learned from people in Rio that you'd met with Maurice Graff. From Graff you went straight to London, to Anthony Beaumont. You were right about him: He's ODESSA." Helden stopped briefly. "He said you . . . spent the night with Gretchen, went to bed with her."

307

"Wait a minute," interrupted Noel.

"No, darling, it's not important. I told you, I know my sister. But there's a pattern, don't you see? To the ODESSA, women are only conveniences. You were a friend of ODESSA; you'd had a long, exhausting trip. It was perfectly natural that your needs should be fulfilled."

"That's barbaric!"

"It's the way Johann saw it."

"He's wrong."

"He knows that now. At least, I think he does. I told him about the things that had happened to you—to us—and how you'd nearly been killed. He was amazed. He may still have questions to ask you, but I think he's convinced."

Holcroft shook his head in bewilderment. *Nothing is as it was for you . . . nothing can ever be the same.* Not only was nothing the same, it wasn't even what it appeared *not* to be. There was no straight line from point A to point B.

"Let's get this over with," he said. "Can we meet later?"

"Of course."

"Are you going back to work?"

"I haven't been to work."

"I forgot. You were with your brother. You said you were going to work, but you were with him."

"It was a necessary lie."

"They're all necessary, aren't they?"

"Please, Noel. Shall I come back for you? Say, in two hours?"

Holcroft considered. Part of his mind was still on the startling news Miles had given him. He had tried to reach Sam Buonoventura in Curaçao, but Sam had been in the field. "You could do me a favor instead," he said to Helden. "I've told you about Buonoventura, in the Caribbean. I put in a call to him from the hotel; he hasn't returned it. If you're free, would you wait in the room in case he does call? I wouldn't ask you, but it's urgent. Something happened; I'll tell you about it later. Will you?"

"Certainly. What shall I say to him?"

"Tell him to stay put for a few hours. Or to give you a number where I can call him later. Six to eight, Paris time. Tell him it's important." Noel reached in his pocket. "Here's the key. Remember, my name's Fresca."

Helden took the key and then his arm, leading him into the studio. "And you remember, my brother's name is Tennyson. John Tennyson."

Holcroft saw Tennyson through thick panes of leaded glass windows that looked out on the terrace. He wore a dark pinstriped suit, no overcoat or hat; his hands were on the railing as he peered out at the Paris skyline. He was tall and slender, the body tapered almost too perfectly; it was the body of an athlete, a series of coiled springs, taut and contained. He turned slightly to his right, revealing his face. It was a face like no other Noel had seen. It was an artist's rendering, the features too idealized for actual flesh and blood. And because it did not accept blemish, the face was cold. It was a face cast in marble, topped by glistening light-blond hair, perfectly groomed, matching the stone.

Then Von Tiebolt—Tennyson saw him through the window; their eyes met, and the image of marble collapsed. The blond man's eyes were alive and penetrating. He pushed himself away from the railing and walked toward the terrace door.

Stepping inside, he extended his hand. "I am the son of Wilhelm von Tiebolt."

"I'm . . . Noel Holcroft. My . . . father was Heinrich Clausen."

"I know. Helden has told me a great deal about you. You've been through a lot."

"We both have," agreed Holcroft. "I mean, your sister and I. I gather you've had your share, too."

"Our legacy, unfortunately." Tennyson smiled. "It's awkward meeting like this, isn't it?"

"I've been more comfortable."

"And I've not said a word," interjected Helden. "You were both quite capable of introducing yourselves. I'll leave now."

"You certainly don't have to," said Tennyson. "What we have to say to each other concerns you, I think."

"I'm not sure it does. Not for the moment. Besides, I have something to do," replied Helden. She started toward the foyer. "I think it's terribly important—for a great many people—that you trust each other. I hope you can." She opened the door and left.

Neither man spoke for several moments; each looked toward the spot where Helden had stood.

"She's remarkable," said Tennyson. "I love her very much."

Noel turned his head. "So do I."

Tennyson acknowledged the look as well as the statement. "I hope it's not a complication for you."

"It isn't, although it may be for her."

"I see." Tennyson walked to the window and gazed outside. "I'm not in a position to give you my blessing —Helden and I live very separate lives—and even if I could, I'm not sure I would."

"Thanks for your frankness."

The blond man turned. "Yes, I'm frank. I don't know you. I know only what Helden has told me about you, and what I've learned for myself. What she tells me is basically what you've told her, colored by her feelings, of course. What I've learned is not so clear-cut. Nor does the composite fit my sister's rather enthusiastic picture."

"We both have questions. Do you want to go first?"

"It doesn't really matter, does it? Mine are very few and very direct." Tennyson's voice was suddenly harsh. "What was your business with Maurice Graff?"

"I thought Helden told you."

"Again it was what you told *her*. Now, tell *me*. I'm somewhat more experienced than my sister. I don't accept things simply because you say them. Over the years, I've learned not to do that. Why did you go to see Graff?"

"I was looking for you."

"For *me*?"

"Not you, specifically. For the Von Tiebolts. For information about any of you."

"Why Graff?"

"His name was given to me."

"By whom?"

"I don't remember. . . ."

"You don't *remember*? Of thousands and thousands of men in Rio de Janeiro, the name of Maurice Graff just *happens* to be the one casually given to you."

"It's the truth."

"It's ludicrous."

"Wait a minute." Noel tried to reconstruct the sequence of events that led him to Graff. "It started in New York. . . ."

"*What* started? Graff was in New York?"

"No, the consulate. I went to the Brazilian consulate

and spoke to an attaché. I wanted to find out how I'd go about locating a family that had immigrated to Brazil in the forties. The attaché put the facts together and figured out I was looking for Germans. He gave me a lecture about . . . well, there's a Spanish phrase for it. *La otra cara de los alemanes.* It means the other side of the German; what's beneath his thinking."

"I'm aware of that. Go on."

"He told me there was a strong, close-knit German community in Rio run by a few powerful men. He warned me about looking for a German family that had disappeared; he said it could be dangerous. Maybe he exaggerated because I wouldn't give him your name."

"Thank God you didn't."

"When I got to Rio, I couldn't find out anything. Even the immigration records were doctored."

"At great cost to a great many people," said Tennyson bitterly. "It was our only protection."

"I was stuck. Then I remembered what the attaché had said about the German community being run by a few powerful men. I went to a German bookstore and asked a clerk about the houses. Large ones, mansions with a lot of acreage. I called them 'Bavarian,' but he knew what I meant. I'm an architect and I figured—"

"I understand." Tennyson nodded. "Large German estates, the most influential leaders in the German community."

"That's right. The clerk gave me a couple of names. One was Jewish, the other was Graff. He said Graff's estate was among the most impressive in Brazil."

"It is."

"And that's it. That's how I came to go to Graff."

Tennyson stood motionless, his expression noncommittal. "It's not unreasonable."

"I'm glad you think so," said Noel.

"I said it was reasonable; I didn't say I believed you."

"I've no reason to lie."

"Even if you do, I'm not sure you have the talent. I'm very good at seeing through liars."

Noel was struck by the statement. "That's practically what Helden said the night I met her."

"I've trained her well. Lying is a craft; it must be developed. You're out of your depth."

"What the hell are you trying to say?"

"I'm saying you're a very convincing amateur. You built your story well, but it is not sufficiently professional. Your keystone is missing. As an architect, I'm sure you understand."

"I'll be goddamned if I do. Tell me."

"With pleasure. You left Brazil knowing the name Von Tiebolt. You arrive in England and within twelve hours you're in a suburb of Portsmouth with my sister, *sleeping* with my sister. You didn't even have the name of Tennyson. How could you possibly have known about Beaumont?"

"But I *did* have the name of Tennyson."

"*How?* How did you get it?"

"I told Helden. This couple, a brother and sister named Cararra, came to see me at the hotel."

"Oh, yes. Cararra. A very common name in Brazil. Did it mean anything to you?"

"Of course not."

"So these Cararras come to see you, out of nowhere, claiming to be dear friends of ours. But as Helden told *you,* we've never heard of them. Come, Mr. Holcroft, you'll have to do better than that." Tennyson raised his voice. "Graff gave you Beaumont's name, didn't he? ODESSA to ODESSA."

"No! Graff didn't know. He thinks you're still hiding somewhere in Brazil."

"He said that?"

"He implied it. The Cararras confirmed it. They mentioned some colonies in the south—'Catarinas,' or something. A mountain region settled by Germans."

"You've done your homework well. The Santa Catarinas are German settlements. But again, we're back to the elusive Cararras."

Noel remembered clearly the fear in the faces of the young brother and sister in Rio. "Maybe they're elusive to you, but not to me. You've either got a lousy memory or you're a lousy friend. They said they barely knew Helden, but knew you very well. They risked a hell of a lot to come and see me. Portuguese Jews who—"

"*Portuguese . . .*" interrupted Tennyson, suddenly alarmed. "Oh, my God! And they used the name Cararra. . . . Describe them!"

Holcroft did. When he had finished, Tennyson said,

in a whisper, "Out of the past. . . . Out of the past, Mr. Holcroft. It all fits. The use of the name Cararra. Portuguese Jews. Santa Catarina. . . . They came back to Rio."

"Who came back?"

"The Montealegres—that's their real name. Ten, twelve years ago. . . . What they told you was a cover, so you'd never be able to reveal their identities, even unconsciously."

"What happened twelve years ago?"

"The details aren't important, but we had to get them out of Rio, so we sent them to the Catarinas. Their parents helped the Israelis; they were killed for it. The two children were hunted; they would have been shot, too. They had to be taken south."

"Then there are people in the Catarinas who know about you?"

"Yes, a few. Our base of operations was in Santa Catarina. Rio was too dangerous."

"What operations? Who's 'we'?"

"Those of us in Brazil who fought the ODESSA." Tennyson shook his head. "I have an apology to make. Helden was right: I did you an injustice. You've told the truth."

Noel had the sensation of having been vindicated when vindication had not been sought. He felt awkward questioning a man who had fought the ODESSA; who had rescued children from death as surely as if he'd taken them out of Auschwitz, or Belsen; who had trained the woman he loved to survive. But he *had* questions; it was no time to forget them.

"It's my turn now," said Noel. "You're very quick, and you know about things I've never heard of, but I'm not sure you've said a hell of a lot."

"If one of your questions concerns the Tinamou," said Tennyson, "I'm sorry, but I won't answer you. I won't even discuss it."

Holcroft was stunned. "You won't *what?*"

"You heard me. The Tinamou is a subject I won't discuss. It's not your business."

"I think it is! For starters, let's put it this way: If you won't discuss the Tinamou, we haven't *anything* to discuss."

Tennyson paused, startled. "You mean that, don't you?"

"Absolutely."

"Then try to understand me. Nothing can be left to chance now, to the offhand possibility—no matter how remote—that the wrong word might be dropped to the wrong person. If I'm right, and I think I am, you'll have your answer in a matter of days."

"That's not good enough!"

"Then I'll go one step further. The Tinamou was trained in Brazil. By the ODESSA. I've studied him as thoroughly as any man on earth. I've been tracking him for six years."

It took several seconds for Noel to find his voice. "You've been . . . for six years?"

"Yes. It's time for the Tinamou to strike; there'll be another assassination. It's why the British contacted you; they know it, too."

"Why don't you work with them? For God's sake, do you know what they think!"

"I know what someone's tried to *make* them think. It's why I can't work with them. The Tinamou has sources everywhere; they don't know him, but he uses them."

"You said a matter of days."

"If I'm wrong, I'll tell you everything. I'll even go to the British with you."

"A matter of days. . . . Okay. We'll pass on the Tinamou—for a matter of days."

"Whatever else I can tell you, I will. I've nothing to hide."

"You knew Beaumont in Rio, knew he was part of the ODESSA. You even accused me of having gotten his name from Graff. Yet in spite of all this, he married your sister. ODESSA to ODESSA? Are you one of them?"

Tennyson did not waver. "A question of priorities. Put simply, it was planned. My sister Gretchen is not the woman she once was, but she's never lost her hatred of the Nazis. She's made a sacrifice greater than any of us. We know every move that Beaumont makes."

"But he knows you're Von Tiebolt! Why doesn't he tell Graff?"

"Ask him, if you like. He may tell you."

"*You* tell me."

"He's afraid to," replied Tennyson. "Beaumont is a pig. Even his commitments lack cleanliness. He works less and less for the ODESSA, and only then when they threaten him."

"I don't understand."

"Gretchen has her own . . . shall we say, persuasive powers; I think you're aware of them. Beyond these, a large sum of untraceable money found its way into Beaumont's account. In addition to these circumstances, he fears exposure from Graff on one side . . . and from me on the other. He's useful to us both, more so to me than to Graff, of course. He's checkmated."

"If you knew every move he made, you had to know he was on that plane to Rio. You had to know he was following me."

"How could I? I didn't know *you*."

"He was there. Someone sent him!"

"When Helden told me, I tried to find out who. What I learned was very little, but enough to alarm me. In my judgment, our checkmated pig was reached by a third party. Someone who had unearthed his ODESSA connection and was using him—as Graff used him. As I used him."

"Who?"

"I wish to heaven I knew! He was granted an emergency leave from his ship in the Mediterranean. He went to Geneva."

"Geneva?" Noel's memory raced back. To a fragment of time obscured by swift movement, and rushing crowds, and screams . . . on a station platform. On a *concrete station platform.* A fight had broken out; a man had arched backward with blood on his shirt, another had gone after a third. . . . A man in panic had raced by, his eyes wide in fright, beneath . . . thick eyebrows of black and white hair. "That was it," said Holcroft, astonished. "Beaumont was in Geneva."

"I just told you that."

"That's where I saw him! I couldn't remember where before. He followed me from Geneva."

"I'm afraid I don't know what you're talking about."

"Where's Beaumont now?" asked Noel.

"Back on board ship. Gretchen left several days ago to join him. In Saint-Tropez, I think."

Tomorrow I go to the Mediterranean. To a man I loathe. . . . Everything made so much more sense now. Perhaps Tennyson was not the only man in that room who had been unfair in his judgments.

"We've got to find out who sent Beaumont after me,"

said Noel, picturing the man in a black leather jacket. Tennyson was right; their conclusions were the same. There *was* someone else.

"I agree," said the blond man. "Shall we go together?"

Holcroft was tempted. But he had not finished. There could be no unanswered questions later. Not once the commitment had been made between them.

"Maybe," he replied. "There are two other things I want to ask you about. And I warn you, I want the answers now, not in a 'matter of days.'"

"All right."

"You killed someone in Rio."

Tennyson's eyes narrowed. "Helden told you."

"I had to know; she understood that. There are conditions in Geneva that won't allow surprises. If you can be blackmailed, I can't let you go on."

Tennyson nodded. "I see."

"Who was it? Whom did you kill?"

"You mistake my reticence," replied the blond man. "I've no compunction whatsoever about telling you who it was. I'm trying to think how you can check up on what I say. There's no blackmail involved. There couldn't be; but how can you be sure?"

"Let's start with a name."

"Manuel Cararra."

"Cararra? . . ."

"Yes. It's why those two young people used it. They knew I'd see the political connection. Cararra was a leader in the Chamber of Deputies, one of the most powerful men in the country. But his allegiance was not to Brazil; it was to Graff. To the ODESSA. I killed him seven years ago, and I'd kill him tomorrow."

Noel studied Tennyson's face. "Who knew?"

"A few old men. Only one's still alive. I'll give you his name, if you like. He'd never say anything about the killing."

"Why not?"

"The shoe, as they say, was on the other foot. Before I left Rio de Janeiro, I met with them. My threat was clear. If ever they pursued me, I would make public what I knew about Cararra. The long-revered image of a conservative martyr would be shattered. The conservative cause in Brazil can't tolerate that."

"I want the name."

"I'll write it out for you." Tennyson did. "I'm sure you can reach him by transatlantic telephone. It won't take much; my name coupled with Cararra's should be enough."

"I may do that."

"By all means," said Tennyson. "He'll confirm what I've told you."

The two men faced each other, only feet apart. "There was a subway accident in London," Noel went on. "A number of people were killed, including a man who worked for the *Guardian*. He was the man whose signature was on your employment records. The man who interviewed you, the only one who could shed any light on how or why you were hired."

Tennyson's eyes were suddenly cold again. "It was a shock. I'll never get over it. What is your question?"

"There was another accident. In New York. Only days ago. A number of innocent people were killed then, too, but one of them was the target. Someone I loved very much."

"I repeat! What's your *point*, Holcroft?"

"There's a certain similarity, wouldn't you say? MI Five doesn't know anything about the accident in New York, but it has very specific ideas about the one in London. I've put them together and come up with a disturbing connection. What do you know about that accident five years ago in London?"

Tennyson's body was rigid. "Watch out," he said. "The British go too far. What do you want of me? How far will you go to discredit me?"

"Cut the bullshit!" said Noel. "What happened in that subway?"

"I was *there!*" The blond man thrust his hand up to his collar beneath the pinstriped suit. He yanked furiously, ripping his shirt half off his chest, exposing a scar that extended from the base of his throat to his breast. "I don't know anything about New York, but the experience in Charing Cross five years ago is one I'll live with for the rest of my life! Here it is; there's not a day when I'm not reminded of it. Forty-seven stitches, neck to thorax. I thought for a few moments—five years ago in London— that my head had been half cut off from the rest of me. And that man you speak of so enigmatically was my dearest friend in England! He helped get us out of Brazil.

If someone killed him, they tried to kill me, too! I was with him."

"I didn't know. . . . The British didn't say anything. They didn't know you were there."

"Then I suggest someone look. There's a hospital record around somewhere. It shouldn't be hard to find." Tennyson shook his head in disgust. "I'm sorry, I shouldn't be angry at you. It's the British; they'll use anything."

"It's possible they really didn't know."

"I suppose so. Hundreds of people were taken off that train. A dozen clinics in London were filled that night; no one paid much attention to names. But you'd think they would have found mine. I was in the hospital for several days." Tennyson stopped abruptly. "You said someone you loved was killed in New York only a few days ago? What happened?"

Noel told him how Richard Holcroft had been run down in the streets, and of the theory conceived by David Miles. It was pointless to withhold anything from this man he had come close to misjudging so completely.

In the telling was the conclusion both men had arrived at.

In my judgment, our checkmated pig was reached by a third party.

Who?

I wish to heaven I knew. . . .

Someone else.

A man in a black leather jacket. Defiant in a dark alley in Berlin. Willing to die . . . asking to be shot. Refusing to say who he was or where he came from. Someone or something more powerful, more knowledgeable, than the Rache or the ODESSA.

Someone else.

Noel told Tennyson everything, relieved that he could say it all. The relief was heightened by the way the blond man listened. His speckled gray eyes never wavered from Holcroft's face; they were riveted, totally absorbed. When he had finished, Noel felt exhausted. "That's all I know."

Tennyson nodded. "We've finally met, haven't we? We both had to say what was on our minds. We both thought the other was the enemy, and we were both wrong. Now, we have work to do."

"How long have you known about Geneva?" asked

Holcroft. "Gretchen told me that you said a man would come one day and speak of a strange arrangement."

"Since I was a child. My mother told me there was an extraordinary sum of money that was to be used for great works, to make amends for the terrible things done in Germany's name, but not by true Germans. But only that fact, no specifics."

"You don't know Erich Kessler, then."

"I remember the name, but only vaguely. I was very young."

"You'll like him."

"As you describe him, I'm sure I will. You say he's bringing his brother to Geneva? Is that allowed?"

"Yes. I said I'd telephone him in Berlin and give him dates."

"Why not wait until tomorrow or the day after? Call him from Saint-Tropez?"

"Beaumont?"

"Beaumont," said Tennyson, his mouth set. "I think we should meet with our checkmated pig. He has something to tell us. Specifically, who was his latest employer? Who sent him to that train station in Geneva? Who paid him for—or blackmailed him into—following you to New York and then to Rio de Janeiro? When we find this out, we'll know where your man in the black leather jacket came from."

Someone else.

Noel looked at his watch. It was nearly six o'clock; he and Tennyson had talked for more than two hours, yet there was still a great deal more to say. "Do you want to have dinner with your sister and me?" he asked.

Tennyson smiled. "No, my friend. We'll talk on our way south. I've calls to make and copy to file. I mustn't forget I'm a newspaperman. Where are you staying?"

"At the George Cinq. Under the name of Fresca."

"I'll phone you later this evening." Tennyson extended his hand. "Until tomorrow."

"Tomorrow."

"Incidentally, if my fraternal blessings mean anything, you have them."

Johann von Tiebolt stood at the railing of the terrace in the cold air of the early evening. Below, on the street, he could see Holcroft emerge from the building and walk east on the sidewalk.

It had all been so easy. The orchestration of lies had been studiously thought out and arranged, the rendering underpinned with outraged conviction and sudden revelation that led to acceptance. An old man would be alerted in Rio; he knew what to say. A medical record would be placed in a London hospital, the dates and information corresponding to a tragic accident on the Charing Cross underground five years ago. And if all went according to schedule, a news item would be carried in the evening papers reporting another tragedy. A naval officer and his wife had disappeared in a small pleasure boat off the Mediterranean coast.

Von Tiebolt smiled. Everything was going as it had been projected thirty years ago. Even the Nachrichtendienst could not stop them now. In a matter of days the Nachrichtendienst would be castrated.

It was time for the Tinamou.

30

Noel hurried through the lobby of the George V, eager to get to his room, to Helden. Geneva was closer now; it would be closer still when they met Anthony Beaumont in Saint-Tropez and forced the truth from him.

Too, he was anxious to learn whether Buonoventura had returned his call. His mother had said she would let Sam know her plans. All Miles knew in New York was that Althene had left Mexico City for Lisbon. Why Lisbon? And who had followed her?

The image of the man in the black leather jacket came back to Holcroft. The steady look in his eyes, the acceptance of death . . . *kill me and another will take my place. Kill him, another his.*

The elevator was empty, the ascent swift. The door opened; Noel caught his breath at the sight of the man standing in the corridor facing him. It was the *Verwünschte Kind* from Sacré-Coeur, the fashion plate who had searched him in front of the candles.

"Good evening, monsieur."

"What are you doing here? Is Helden all right?"

"She can answer your questions."

"So can you." Holcroft grabbed the man's arm and turned him forcefully toward the door of the room.

"Take your hands off me!"

"When she tells me to let you go, I'll let you go. Come on." Noel propelled the man down the corridor to the door, and knocked.

In seconds the door opened. Helden stood there, startled at the sight of the two of them. In her hand was a folded newspaper; in her eyes was something beyond her astonishment: sadness.

"What's the matter?" she asked.

"That's what I wanted to know, but he wouldn't tell me." Holcroft pushed the man through the door.

"Noel, *please*. He's one of us."

"I want to know why he's here."

"I called him; he had to know where I was. He told me he had to see me. I'm afraid he's brought us dreadful news."

"What?"

"Read the papers," said the man. "There are both French and English."

Holcroft picked up a copy of the *Herald Tribune* from the coffee table.

"Page two," said the man. "Top 'left."

Noel turned the page, snapping it flat. He read the words, a sense of anger . . . and fear . . . sweeping over him.

NAVAL OFFICER AND WIFE LOST IN MEDITERRANEAN

St.-Tropez—Commander Anthony Beaumont, captain of the patrol ship *Argo* and a highly decorated officer of Her Majesty's Royal Navy, along with his wife, who had joined him in this resort town for the weekend, were feared drowned when their small boat foundered in an angry squall several miles south along this rock-bound coast. A capsized craft fitting the description of the small boat was sighted by low-flying coastal search planes. The commander and his wife had not been heard from in over forty-eight hours, prompting second-in-command of the *Argo,* Lt. Morgan Llewellen, to issue search directives. The Admiralty has concluded that Commander and Mrs. Beaumont lost their lives in the tragic accident. The couple had no children.

"Oh, *God,*" whispered Holcroft. "Did your brother tell you?"

"About Gretchen?" Helden asked. "Yes. She suffered so much, gave so much. It's why she wouldn't see me or talk to me. She never wanted me to know what she did, why she married him. She was afraid I might sense the truth."

"If what you *say* is true," said the well-dressed man, "that Beaumont was ODESSA, we don't believe that newspaper story for a minute."

"He means your friend in Berlin," interrupted Helden. "I told him that you had a friend in Berlin who said he would transmit your suspicions to London."

Noel understood. She was telling him she had said nothing about Geneva. Noel turned to the man. "What do you think happened?"

"If the British discovered an ODESSA agent in the upper ranks of the navy, especially one commanding a coastal-patrol vessel—a euphemism for an espionage ship —it would mean they had been duped again. There's just so much they can take; there'd be no inquiries. A swift execution is preferable."

"That's a pretty rough indictment," said Holcroft.

"It's an embarrassing situation."

"They'd kill an innocent woman?"

"Without thinking twice—on the possibility that she might not be innocent. The message would be clear, at any rate. The ODESSA network would have its warning."

Noel turned away in disgust and put his arms around Helden. "I'm sorry," he said. "I know how you must feel, and I wish there was something I could do. Outside of reaching your brother, I'm not sure there is."

Helden turned and looked at him, her eyes searching. "You trust each other?"

"Very much. We're working together now."

"Then there's no time for mourning, is there? I'm going to stay here tonight," she told the well-dressed man. "Is it all right? Can I be covered?"

"Of course," said the man. "I'll arrange it."

"Thank you. You're a good friend."

He smiled. "I don't think Mr. Holcroft believes that. But then, he's got a great deal to learn." The man nodded and went to the door; he stopped, his hand on the knob, and turned to Noel. "I apologize if that appears cryptic to you, but be tolerant, monsieur. What's between you and Helden also seems cryptic to me, but I don't inquire. I trust. But, if that trust is found to be misplaced, we'll kill you. I just thought you ought to know."

The *Verwünschte Kind* left quickly. Noel took an angry step after him, but Helden touched his arm. "Please, darling. He, too, has a lot to learn, and we can't tell him. He *is* a friend."

"He's an insufferable little bastard." Holcroft paused.

"I'm sorry. You've got enough on your mind; you don't need foolishness from me."

"A man threatened your life."

"Someone took your sister's. Under the circumstances, I was foolish."

"We've no time for such thoughts. Your friend Buonoventura returned your call. I wrote down the number where you can reach him. It's by the telephone."

Noel walked to the bedside table and picked up the paper. "Your brother and I were going to Saint-Tropez tomorrow. To make Beaumont tell us what he knew. The news'll be shattering to him. On both counts."

"You said you were going to call him. I think it's best that I do. He and Gretchen were very close. When they were younger, they were inseparable. Where is he?"

"Actually, I don't know: he didn't say. He just told me he'd reach me later this evening. That's what I meant." Holcroft lifted the phone and gave Buonoventura's number to the operator.

"I'll speak to Johann when he calls," said Helden, going to the window.

The transatlantic lines were light; the link to Curaçao was made in less than a minute.

"You're a pistol, Noley! I'm glad I don't have to pay your phone bills. You're seeing the goddamn world; I'll say that for you."

"I'm seeing a lot more than that, Sam. Did my mother call you?"

"She did. She said to tell you she'll see you in Geneva in about a week. You're to stay at the Hôtel d'Accord, but you're not to say anything to anyone."

"Geneva? She's going to Geneva? Why the hell did she even leave the country?"

"She said it was an emergency. You were to keep your mouth shut. and not do anything until you see her. She was one upset lady."

"I've got to get hold of her. Did she give you a telephone number—an address—where I could reach her?"

"Not a thing, pal. She didn't have much time to talk, and the connection was rotten. It was out of Mexico. Anybody mind telling me what's going on?"

Holcroft shook his head as if Buonoventura were in

the room facing him. "Sorry, Sam. Perhaps someday. I owe you."

"I think maybe you do. We'll cut a deck for it. Take care of yourself. You got a real nice mother. Be good to her."

Holcroft hung up. Buonoventura was a good friend to have. As good a friend as the well-dressed man was to Helden, he thought. He wondered what she meant when she asked the *Verwünschte Kind* if she were covered. Covered for what? By whom?

"My mother's on her way to Geneva," he said.

Helden turned. "I heard you. You sounded upset."

"I am. A man followed her to Mexico. Miles had him picked up at the airport; he took a cyanide capsule before they could find out who he was or where he came from."

" 'Kill me, another will take my place. Kill him, another his.' Weren't those the words?"

"Yes. I was thinking about them on the way up."

"Does Johann know?"

"I told him everything."

"What does he think?"

"He doesn't know what to think. The key was Beaumont. I don't know where we go now, except to Geneva, with the hope that no one stops us."

Helden came toward him. "Tell me something. What can they—whoever they are—really do? Once the three of you present yourselves to the bank in Geneva, each of you in agreement, all reasonable men, it's over. So what can they actually do?"

"You said it last night."

"What?"

"They can kill us."

The telephone rang. Holcroft reached for it. "Yes?"

"It's John Tennyson." The voice was strained.

"Your sister wants to talk to you," said Holcroft.

"In a moment," replied Tennyson. "We must speak first. Does she know?"

"Yes. Obviously you do, too."

"My paper called me with the news. The night editor knew how close Gretchen and I were. It's horrible."

"I wish there was something I could say."

"I couldn't help you when you told me about your

stepfather. We have to live with these things by our-selves. There's nothing anyone can do or say when they happen. Helden understands."

"Then you don't believe the story that was given out? About the boat and the storm?"

"That they went out in a boat and never came back? Yes, I believe it. That he was responsible? Of course not. It's not even plausible. Whatever else he was, Beaumont was a superb sailor. He could smell a storm twenty miles away. If he was in a small craft, he'd have it in shore before any weather struck."

"Who then?"

"Come, my friend, we both know the answer. That someone else who hired him also killed him. They made him follow you to Rio. You spotted him; his usefulness had come to an end." Tennyson paused. "It was as if they'd known we were to leave for Saint-Tropez. The un-pardonable act was to kill Gretchen as well. For ap-pearances."

"I'm sorry. *God,* I feel responsible."

"It was totally out of your control."

"Could it have been the British?" asked Holcroft. "I told Kessler about Beaumont. He said he was going to work through channels. Bonn to London. Maybe an ODESSA agent commanding one of those reconnaissance ships was too much of an embarrassment."

"The temptation might be there, but no one in au-thority would grant permission. The English would put him into isolation and break him on a rack if they had to get information, but they wouldn't kill him. They *had* him. He and Gretchen were killed by someone who could be damaged by what he knew, not by anyone who could benefit."

Tennyson's reasoning was persuasive. "You're right. The British wouldn't gain anything. They'd keep him un-der wraps."

"Exactly. And there's another factor, a moral one. I think MI Six is riddled with self-seekers, but I don't be-lieve they kill to avoid embarrassment. It's not in their nature. But they'll go to extraordinary lengths to main-tain a reputation. Or revive it. And I pray to God I'm right about that."

"What do you mean?"

"I'm flying to London tonight. In the morning I'll

contact Payton-Jones at MI Five. I've an exchange to offer him, one I think he'll find difficult to resist. I may be able to give him a ground-dwelling bird that moves rapidly from one place to another, its feathers blending in with the environment."

Holcroft was as surprised as he was bewildered. "I thought you said you couldn't work with them."

"*Him.* Only Payton-Jones, no one else. He must give me his assurance of that, or we go no farther."

"Do you think he will?"

"He really has no choice. That ground-dwelling bird has become an MI obsession."

"Suppose you do? What do you get in return?"

"Access to classified material. The British have thousands of secret files. They concern the last years of the war and are embarrassing to a lot of people. But somewhere in those files is our answer. A man, a group of men, a band of fanatics—I don't know who or what, but it's there. Someone who had a connection with the Finanzministerium thirty years ago, or with our fathers; someone they trusted and to whom they gave responsibility. It could even be a Loch Torridon infiltration."

"A what?"

"Loch Torridon. It was an espionage and sabotage operation mounted by the British from 'forty-one to 'forty-four. Hundreds of former nationals were sent back to Germany and Italy to work in factories and railroads and government offices everywhere. It's common knowledge there were Loch Torridon personnel in the Finanzministerium. . . . The answer is in the archives."

"From those thousands of files, you expect to find one identity? Even if it's there, it could take months."

"Not really. I know precisely what to look for: people who may have been associated with our fathers."

Tennyson spoke so rapidly, with such assurance, that Noel found it difficult to keep up with him. "Why are you so convinced the information is there to begin with?"

"Because it has to be. You made that clear to me this afternoon. The man who called you in New York, the one who was killed—"

"Peter Baldwin?"

"Yes. MI Six. He knew about Geneva. We start with him; he's our key now."

"Then go to the file called 'Wolfsschanze,'" said Holcroft. " 'Code Wolfsschanze.' That may be it!"

Tennyson did not reply at first. He was either thinking or startled; Noel could not tell which. "Where did you hear that?" he asked. "You never mentioned it. Neither did Helden."

"Then we both forgot," Holcroft told him.

"We should be careful," said Tennyson, when Noel had finished. "If the name 'Wolfsschanze' is tied to Geneva, we must be *extremely* careful. The British can't learn about Geneva. It would be disastrous."

"I agree. But what reason will you give Payton-Jones for wanting access to the archives?"

"Part of the truth," answered Tennyson. "I want Gretchen's killer."

"And for that you're willing to give up the . . . ground-dwelling bird you've been tracking for six years?"

"For that and for Geneva. With all my heart."

Noel was touched. "Do you want me to talk to Payton-Jones?"

"*No!*" Tennyson shouted; then he lowered his voice. "I mean, it would be far too dangerous. Trust me. Do as I ask you, please. You and Helden must stay out of sight. Completely. Until I contact you, Helden must not return to work. She must stay with you, and you both must remain invisible."

Holcroft looked at Helden. "I don't know if she'll agree to that."

"I'll convince her. Let me speak with her. You and I have finished our talk."

"You'll call me?"

"In a few days. If you change hotels, leave word where Mr. Fresca can be reached. Helden has my message-service number. Let me talk with her now. In spite of our differences, we need each other now, perhaps as we've never needed each other before. And . . . Noel?"

"Yes?"

"Be kind to her. Love her. She needs you, too."

Holcroft stood up and handed the phone to Helden.

"Mein Bruder. . . ."

31

Code Wolfsschanze!

Von Tiebolt–Tennyson slammed his fist on the desk in the small out-of-the-way office he used in Paris.

Code Wolfsschanze. That sacrosanct phrase had been given to Peter Baldwin by Ernst Manfredi! The banker had played a dangerous but ingenious game. He knew that Baldwin's mere use of the phrase was enough to guarantee his death. But Manfredi would never have given the Englishman more than that; it would not have been in the banker's interests. Still, Baldwin had possessed one of the best minds in Europe. Had he pieced together more than Manfredi had considered possible? How much had he really learned? What was contained in Baldwin's file at MI Five?

Or did it matter? The British had rejected whatever it was Baldwin had to offer. One file folder among thousands upon thousands. Buried in the archives, lost because it was one more entry of rejected information.

Code Wolfsschanze. It meant nothing to those who knew nothing, and the few hundred who did—those district leaders in every country—knew only that it was a signal. They were to make themselves ready; enormous funds would soon be sent to them, to be used for the cause.

Die Sonnenkinder. All over the world, prepared to rise and assert their birthright.

Baldwin's file could not contain that information; it was not possible. But those who held that file would be used. Above all else, the British wanted the Tinamou. His capture by MI Five would reassert English supremacy in intelligence operations—a supremacy lost through years of blunders and defections.

MI Five would be handed the Tinamou, and with that gift would come an obligation to the giver. That was the splendid irony: The hated British Intelligence, that quiet, serpentine monster that had wreaked such havoc on the Third Reich, would help create the Fourth.

For MI Five would be told that the Nachrichtendienst was involved in an extraordinary conspiracy. The British would believe the man who told them; that man was giving them the Tinamou.

Tennyson walked through the London offices of the *Guardian*, receiving the compliments of his colleagues and their subordinates. As always, he accepted the compliments modestly.

He studied the women casually. The secretaries and the receptionists invited this most beautiful of men to acknowledge them, invited him, actually, to take whatever he wished. It struck him that he might have to select one of these women. His beloved Gretchen was gone, but his appetites were not. Yes, thought Tennyson as he walked toward the door of the senior editor's office, he would select a woman. The excitement was mounting, the intensity of Wolfsschanze growing with every passing hour. He would need sexual release. It was always this way; Gretchen had understood.

"John, it's good to see you," said the senior editor, getting up from behind the desk and extending his hand. "We're running the Bonn article tomorrow. Fine job."

Tennyson sat down in a chair in front of the desk. "Something has come up," he said. "If my sources are accurate, and I'm sure they are, a killing—killings—will be attempted that could provoke a world crisis."

"Good heavens. Have you written it up?"

"No. We can't write about it. I don't think any responsible newspaper should."

The editor leaned forward. "What is it, John?"

"There's an economic summit conference called for next Tuesday. . . ."

"Of course. Right here in London. Leaders from the East and West."

"That's the point. East and West. They're flying in from Moscow and Washington, from Peking and Paris. The most powerful men on earth." Tennyson paused.

"And?"

"Two are to be assassinated."

"*What?*"

"Two are to be killed; which two is irrelevant as long as they are from opposing sides; the president of the United States and the chairman of the People's Republic; or the prime minister and the premier of the Soviet Union."

"Impossible! Security measures will be airtight."

"Not really. There'll be crowds, processions, banquets, motorcades. Where's the absolute guarantee found?"

"It has to be!"

"Not against the Tinamou."

"The *Tinamou?*"

"He's accepted the highest fee in history."

"Good God, from *whom?*"

"An organization known as the Nachrichtendienst."

Harold Payton-Jones stared across the table at Tennyson in the dimly lit room that had no other furniture but the table and two chairs. The location had been selected by MI Five; it was a deserted boardinghouse in east London.

"I repeat," said the gray-haired agent curtly. "You expect me to accept the things you say merely because you're willing to go on record? Preposterous!"

"It's my only proof," replied Tennyson. "Everything I've told you is true. We haven't time to fight each other any longer. Every hour is vital."

"Nor have I the inclination to be hoodwinked by an opportunistic journalist who may be much more than a correspondent! You're very clever. And quite possibly an outrageous liar."

"For God's sake, if that's true, why am I *here?* Listen to me! I'll say it for the last time: The Tinamou was trained by the ODESSA. In the hills of Rio de Janeiro! I've fought the ODESSA all my life; that's on my record, if anyone cares to examine it. The ODESSA forced us out of Brazil, cut us off from everything we'd built there. I want the Tinamou!"

Payton-Jones studied the blond man. The argument had been vicious, lasting nearly a half hour. The agent had been relentless, pounding Tennyson with a barrage of questions, lashing out at him with insults. It was a studied technique of MI Five's, designed to separate truth from falsehood. It was apparent that the Englishman was now satisfied. He lowered his voice.

"All right, Mr. Tennyson. We can stop fighting each other. I gather we owe you an apology."

"The apologies are not one-sided. It's just that I knew I could work better alone. I had to pretend to be so many things. If ever anyone had seen me with a member of your service, my effectiveness would have been destroyed."

"Then I'm sorry for the times we called you in."

"They were dangerous moments for me. I could feel the Tinamou slipping away."

"We haven't caught him yet."

"We're close. It's only a matter of days now. We'll succeed if we're painstaking in every decision we make, every street the delegations travel—the locations of every meeting, every ceremony, every banquet. There's an advantage that's never existed before: We know he's there."

"You're absolutely convinced of your source?"

"Never more so in my life. That man in the Berlin pub was the courier. Every courier used to reach the Tinamou has been killed. His last words were 'London . . . next week . . . the summit . . . one from each side . . . a man with a tattoo of a rose on the back of his hand . . . Nachrichtendienst.' "

Payton-Jones nodded. "We'll put out inquiries to Berlin as to the man's identity."

"I doubt you'll find anything. From what little I know about the Nachrichtendienst, it was extremely thorough."

"But it was neutral," Payton-Jones said. "And its information was always accurate. It spared no one. The prosecutors of Nuremberg were continuously fed data by the Nachrichtendienst."

"I suggest," said Tennyson, "that the prosecutors were given only what the Nachrichtendienst wanted to give them. You can't know what was withheld."

The Britisher nodded again. "It's possible. That's something we'll never know. The question is, why? What's the motive?"

"If I may," replied the blond man. ". . . A few old men about to die, taking their final vengeance. The Third Reich had two specific philosophical enemies who allied themselves in spite of their antagonisms: the communists and the democracies. Now each vies for supremacy. What better revenge than for each to accuse the other of assassination? For each to destroy the other?"

"If we could establish that," interrupted Payton-Jones, "it could be the motive behind a number of assassinations during the past years."

"How does one establish it beyond doubt?" asked Tennyson. "Did British Intelligence ever have a direct connection with the Nachrichtendienst?"

"Oh, yes. We insisted on identities—to be kept locked in the vaults, of course. We couldn't act on such information blindly."

"Are any alive today?"

"It's possible. It's been years since anyone has mentioned the Nachrichtendienst. I'll check, of course."

"Will you give me their names?"

The MI-Five man leaned back in the chair. "Is this one of the conditions you spoke of, Mr. Tennyson?"

"Spoke of, but made clear that under the circumstances I could never insist upon."

"No civilized man would. If we catch the Tinamou, you'll have the gratitude of world governments; the names are minor. If we have them, so will you. Do you have other requests? Should I have brought a notebook?"

"They're limited," answered Tennyson, overlooking the insult, "and may surprise you. Out of gratitude to my employers, I should like a five-hour advance exclusive for the *Guardian*."

"It's yours," said Payton-Jones. "What else?"

"Insofar as MI Five has approached various people, implying that I was the subject of inquiries, I should like a letter from British Intelligence making it clear not only that my personal dossier is without blemish but that I've made an active contribution to your efforts to maintain— shall we say—'international stability.' "

"Quite unnecessary," said the Englishman. "Should the Tinamou be caught through the information you bring us, governments everywhere no doubt will decorate you with highest honors. A letter from us would be gratuitous. You won't need it."

"But, you see, I will," said Tennyson. "For my next-to-last request is that my name never be mentioned."

"Never be—" Payton-Jones was stunned. "That's hardly in character, is it?"

"Please don't confuse my professional endeavors with my private way of life. I seek no credit. The Von Tiebolts owe a debt; call this part payment."

The MI-Five operative was silent for a moment. "I *have* misjudged you. I apologize again. Of course you'll have your letter."

"Frankly, there's another reason for wanting anonymity. I realize that the Royal Navy and the French authorities are satisfied that my sister and her husband died accidentally while on holiday, and they're probably right. But I think you'll agree the timing was unfortunate. I have one sister left; she and I are the last of the Von Tiebolts. If anything happened to her, I'd never forgive myself."

"I understand."

"I'd like to offer you whatever assistance I can. I believe I know as much about the Tinamou as anyone alive. I've studied him for years. Every killing, every projected move he made before and after the acts. I think I can help. I'd like to be a part of your team."

"I'd be a damn fool to turn you down. What's your last request?"

"We'll get to it." Tennyson stood up. "The thing to realize about the Tinamou is that his technique is instant variation, practiced improvisation. He doesn't have a single strategy, but ten or twelve—each methodically conceived and rehearsed so that it can be adapted to the moment."

"I'm not sure I know what you mean."

"Let me explain. That killing in Madrid seven months ago, during the riots—do you remember?"

"Of course. The rifle was fired from a fourth-floor window, above the crowds."

"Exactly. A government building in a government square where the demonstrations were scheduled to take place. A *government* building. That bothered me. Suppose the guards were more alert, security measures more effective, people checked thoroughly for weapons? Suppose he could *not* have gotten to that window? It was an ideal spot, incidentally, for getting the target in his gun sight; but suppose there'd been people in that room?"

"He would have moved to another location."

"Naturally. But no matter how well concealed the

weapon—whether part of a crutch, or strapped to his leg, or sewn in sections into his clothing—it would have been awkward. He had to move quickly; timing was important; the demonstration wasn't going to last that long. The Tinamou had to have more than one location, more than one option. And he did."

"How do you know?" asked the MI-Five man, fascinated.

"I spent two days in Madrid, going over every building, every window, every rooftop in that square. I found four weapons intact, and three other locations where floorboards had been ripped out, window sashes removed, and moldings torn apart. Additional weapons had been concealed in those places. I even found two pounds of plastic explosives in a garbage can on the sidewalk. Fifty feet from the center of the demonstration. *Eight* positions from which to kill. Alternate selections for him to choose, each designed to fit a projected moment during a specific time span."

Payton-Jones sat forward, his hands on the table. "That complicates things. Standard protective measures concentrate on a single location. Which of half a hundred possibilities is the most likely? The assumption is that the killer will have stationed himself in one location. The strategy you describe adds another dimension: instant mobility. Not a single preset hiding place, but several, selected at any given moment."

"Within a given time span," finished the blond-haired man. "But as I mentioned, we have an advantage. We know he's there. There's also a second advantage, and it's one we should use immediately." Tennyson stopped.

"What is it?"

"I'll qualify that statement. We should use it only if we agree that the capture of the Tinamou is almost as vital as the ultimate safety of his targets."

The Englishman frowned. "That's a rather dangerous thing to say. There can be no risks—calculated or otherwise—where those men are concerned. Not on British soil."

"Hear me out, please. He's killed political leaders before, spreading suspicion, arousing hostilities between governments. And always steadier heads have prevailed; they've cooled things off. But the Tinamou must be stopped, on the outside chance that one day the steadier heads will not be swift enough. I think we can stop him now, if all consent."

"Consent to what?"

"To adhering to published schedules. Bring the leaders of the delegations together; tell them what you know. Tell them that extraordinary precautions will be mounted, but by keeping to schedules, there's a good chance that the Tinamou will at last be caught." Tennyson paused and leaned over the chair, his hands on the rim. "I think if you're honest, no one will disagree. After all, it's not much more than what political leaders face every day."

The frown on the MI-Five man's face disappeared. "And no one will want to be called a coward. Now, what's this second advantage?"

"The Tinamou's technique requires him to preset concealed weapons in a number of locations. To do that, he must begin days, perhaps weeks, before the designated assassination. He's no doubt begun already here in London. I suggest we start a very quiet but thorough search, staking out those areas that conform to the published reports of the summit's schedule."

Payton-Jones brought his hands together in a gesture of agreement. "Of course. We need only find one and we have not only the general location but the time span."

"Exactly. We'll know that within a given number of minutes, during a specific event at a precise area, the assassination will be attempted." Again the blond man paused. "I'd like to help in that search. I know what to look for, and, perhaps more important, where not to look. We haven't much time."

"Your offer's appreciated, sir," said the Englishman. "MI Five is grateful. Shall we begin tonight?"

"Let's give him one more day to set his guns. It'll increase our chances of finding something. Also, I'll need an innocuous sort of uniform and a permit that identifies me as 'building inspector,' or some such title."

"Very good," said Payton-Jones. "I'm embarrassed to say we have a photograph of you on file; we'll use it for the permit. I'd guess you are a size forty-four, trousers long, waist thirty-three or -four."

"Close enough. A civil-service uniform should hardly be tailored."

"Quite so. We'll take care of both items in the

morning." Payton-Jones got up. "You said you had one more request."

"I do. Since I left Brazil, I've not owned a weapon. I'm not even sure it's permitted, but I should like to have one now. Only for the duration of the summit, of course."

"I'll have one issued to you."

"That would need my signature, wouldn't it?"

"Yes."

"Forgive me, but I meant what I said before. As I want no credit for what I've brought you, I feel equally strongly about having my name listed anywhere as an associate of MI Five. I wouldn't want anyone to know the nature of my contributions. My name on a weapon's file card could lead a curious person to the truth. Someone, perhaps, connected to the Nachrichtendienst."

"I see." The Englishman unbuttoned the jacket of his suit coat and reached inside. "This is highly irregular, but so are the circumstances." He withdrew a small, short-barreled revolver and handed it to Tennyson. "Since we both know the source, take mine. I'll list it out for overhaul and have it replaced."

"Thank you," said the blond man, holding the weapon as if it were an unfamiliar object.

Tennyson entered a crowded pub off Soho Square. He scanned the room through the heavy layers of smoke and saw what he was looking for: a hand raised by a man at a table in the far corner. The man, as always, wore a brown raincoat made specifically for him. It looked like any other raincoat; the difference was found in the additional pockets and straps that often contained various handguns, silencers, and explosives. He had been trained by the Tinamou, trained so well that he often performed services contracted by the assassin when the Tinamou was unavailable.

His last assignment had been at Kennedy Airport during a rainswept night when a cordon of police surrounded the glistening fuselage of a British Airways 747. He had found his quarry in a fuel truck. He had done his job.

John Tennyson carried his pint to the table and joined the man in the brown raincoat. The table was round and small; the chairs were so close together that their heads were only inches apart, allowing both men to keep their voices low.

"Is everything placed?" asked the blond man.

"Yes," replied his companion. "The motorcade goes west on the Strand, around Trafalgar Square, through the gates of Admiralty Arch, and into the Mall toward the palace. There are seven locations."

"Give me the sequence."

"From east to west, in order of progression, we start at the Strand Palace Hotel, opposite Savoy Court. Third floor, room three-zero-six. Automatic repeating rifle and scope are sewn into the mattress of the bed nearest the window. A block west, east side, fourth floor, the men's room of an accounting firm. The weapon is in the ceiling, above the tile to the left of the fluorescent light. Directly across the street, again on the fourth floor —there's a penny arcade on the first—the offices of a typing service. Rifle and scope are strapped to the under-carriage of a photocopier. Moving on toward Trafal-gar . . ."

The man in the brown raincoat went through the locations of the remaining caches of weapons. They were within a stretch of approximately half a mile, from Savoy Court to Admiralty Arch.

"Excellent choices," said Tennyson, pushing the un-touched pint of beer away. "You understand your moves fully?"

"I know what they are; I can't say I understand them."

"That's not really necessary, is it?" asked the blond man.

"Of course not; but I'm thinking of you. If you're hemmed in, or blocked, I could do the job. From any of the locations. Why not give me one?"

"Even you're not qualified for this. There can be no room whatsoever for the slightest error. A single mis-placed bullet would be disastrous."

"May I remind you, I was trained by the best there is."

Tennyson smiled. "You're right. Very well. Make the moves I gave you and position yourself in an eighth loca-tion. Choose a room in the Government Building, beyond Admiralty Arch, and let me know which. Can you do that?"

"Ducks in a gallery," replied the man, lifting his pint

of beer to his lips. Tennyson could see the tattoo of a red rose on the back of his right hand.

"May I make a suggestion?" asked John Tennyson.

"Of course, what is it?"

"Wear gloves," said the Tinamou.

32

The blond man opened the door and reached for the light switch on the wall: two table lamps went on in the hotel room marked 306. He motioned for his middle-aged companion to follow him inside.

"It's all right," said Tennyson. "Even if the room is being watched, the curtains are drawn, and the hour corresponds to the time the maids turn down the beds. Over here."

Payton-Jones kept pace as Tennyson took a miniature metal-detector from his overcoat pocket. He touched the button, holding the device over the bed. The tiny hum grew louder: the needle on the dial jumped to the right.

Carefully, he folded back the covers and undid the sheets. "It's there. You can feel the outlines," he said, pressing his fingers into the mattress.

"Remarkable," said Payton-Jones. "And the room has been leased for ten days?"

"By telegraph and postal money order, originating in Paris. The name is Le Fèvre, a meaningless pseudonym. No one's been here."

"It's there all right." Payton-Jones removed his hands from the bed.

"I can make out the rifle," said Tennyson, "but what's the other object?"

"A telescopic sight," replied the Englishman. "We'll leave everything intact and post men in the corridor."

"The next location is down the street, in the lavatory of an accounting firm on the fourth floor. The gun's in the ceiling, wired to a suspension rod above a fluorescent light."

"Let's go," said Payton-Jones.

An hour and forty-five minutes later, the two men were on the roof of a building overlooking Trafalgar Square. Both knelt by the short wall that bordered the edge. Below was the route the summit motorcade would take on its way through Admiralty Arch and into the Mall.

"The fact that the Tinamou would put a weapon here," said Tennyson, his hand on the tar paper that bulged slightly next to the wall, "makes me think he'll be wearing a police uniform."

"I see what you mean," said Payton-Jones. "A policeman walking onto a roof where we've stationed a man wouldn't cause any great alarm."

"Exactly. He could kill your man and take up his position."

"But then he isolates himself. He has no way out."

"I'm not sure the Tinamou needs one, in the conventional sense. A taut rope into a back alley, hysterical crowds below, stairwells jammed, general pandemonium. He's escaped under less dramatic conditions. Remember, he has more identities than a telephone directory. In Madrid I'm convinced he was one of the interrogators on the scene."

"We'll have two men up here, one out of sight. And four sharpshooters on adjacent rooftops." Payton-Jones crawled away from the wall; the blond man followed. "You've done extraordinary work, Tennyson," said the MI-Five agent. "You've unearthed five locations in something over thirty-six hours. Are you satisfied these are all?"

"Not yet. However, I'm satisfied that we've established the parameters. From the Savoy Court to the end of Trafalgar—somewhere in those half-dozen blocks he'll make his move. Once the motorcade's through the arch and into the Mall, we can breathe again. Until that moment, I'm not sure I will. Have the delegations been told?"

"Yes. Each head of state will be outfitted with chest, groin, and leg plate, as well as crowns of bulletproof plastic in their hats. The president of the United States, naturally, objected to any hat at all, and the Russian wants the plastic fitted into his fur, but otherwise we're in good shape. The risk is minimal."

Tennyson looked at Payton-Jones. "Do you really believe that?"

"Yes. Why?"

"I think you're wrong. The Tinamou is no mere

marksman. He's capable of rapid-fire accuracy that would spin a shilling into figure eights at five hundred yards. An expanse of flesh beneath a hat brim is no challenge for him. He'd go for the eyes, and he wouldn't miss."

The Englishman glanced briefly at Tennyson. "I said the risk was minimal, not nonexistent. At the first sign of disturbance, each head of state will be covered by human shields. You've found five locations, so far; say there's another five. If you find no others, we've still reduced his efficiency by fifty percent, and it's a good chance—at least fifty percent—that he'll show up at one of those uncovered. The odds are decidedly against the Tinamou. We'll catch him. We've *got* to."

"His capture means a great deal to you, doesn't it?"

"As much as it does to you, Mr. Tennyson. More than any single objective in more than thirty years of service."

The blond man nodded. "I understand. I owe this country a great deal, and I'll do whatever I can to help. But I'll also be profoundly relieved when that motorcade reaches Admiralty Arch."

By three in the morning on Tuesday, Tennyson had "uncovered" two additional weapons. There were now seven in all, forming a straight line down the Strand from the Savoy Court to the rooftop at the corner of Whitehall and Trafalgar. Every location was covered by a minimum of five agents, hidden in corridors and on rooftops, rifles and handguns poised, prepared to fire at anyone who even approached the hidden weapons.

Still, Tennyson was not satisfied. "There's something *wrong,*" he kept repeating to Payton-Jones. "I don't know what it is, but something doesn't fit."

"You're overworked," said the agent in the room at the Savoy that was their base of operations. "And overwrought. You've done a splendid job."

"Not splendid enough. There's *something,* and I can't put my finger on it!"

"Calm down. Look at what you *have* put your finger on: seven weapons. In all likelihood, that's all there are. He's bound to get near one of those guns, bound to betray the fact that he knows it's there. He's ours. Relax. We've got scores of men out there."

"But something's *wrong.*"

* * *

The crowds lined the Strand, the sidewalks jammed from curb to storefronts. Stanchions were placed on both sides of the street, linked by thick steel cables. The London police stood in opposing rows in front of the cables, their eyes darting continuously in every direction, their clubs unsheathed at their sides.

Beyond the police and intermingling with the crowds were over a hundred operatives of British Intelligence, many flown back from posts overseas. They were the experts Payton-Jones had insisted upon, his insurance against the master assassin who could spin a shilling into figure eights at five hundred yards. They were linked by miniature radios on an ultrahigh frequency that could neither be interfered with nor intercepted.

The operations room at the Savoy was tense, each man there an expert. Computer screens showed every yard of the gauntlet, graphs and grid marks signifying blocks and sidewalks. The screens were connected to radios outside; they showed as tiny moving dots that lit up when activated. The time was near. The motorcade was in progress.

"I'm going back down on the street," said Tennyson, pulling out the small radio from his pocket. "I set the green arrow on the receiving position, is that correct?"

"Yes, but don't send any messages unless you feel they're vital," said Payton-Jones. "Once the motorcade reaches Waterloo Bridge, everything is on five-second report intervals each fifty yards—except for emergencies, of course. Keep the channels clear."

An agent sitting by a computer panel spoke in a loud voice. "Within five hundred feet of Waterloo, sir. Spread holding at eight MPH."

The blond man hurried from the room. It was time to put into motion the swift moves that would destroy the Nachrichtendienst once and for all and cement the Wolfsschanze covenant.

He walked out into the Strand and looked at his watch. Within thirty seconds the man in the brown raincoat would appear in a window on the second floor of the Strand Palace Hotel. The room was 206, directly beneath the room with the weapon concealed in the mattress. It was the first move.

Tennyson glanced around for one of Payton-Jones's specialists. They were not difficult to spot; they carried small radios identical to his. He approached an agent trying to keep his position by a storefront against the jostling crowds, a man he had purposely spoken with; he had spoken to a number of them.

"Hello, there. How are things going?"

"I beg your pardon? Oh, it's you, sir." The agent was watching the people within the borders of his station. He had no time for idle conversation.

An eruption of noise came from the Strand, near Waterloo Bridge. The motorcade was approaching. The crowds pushed nearer the curb, waving miniature flags. The two lines of police in the street beyond the stanchions seemed to close ranks, as if anticipating a stampede.

"Over there!" yelled Tennyson, grabbing the agent's arm. "Up *there!*"

"What? *Where?*"

"That window! It was closed a few seconds ago!"

They could not see the man in the brown raincoat clearly, but it was obvious that a figure stood in the shadows of the room.

The agent raised his radio. "Suspect possibility. Sector One, Strand Palace Hotel, second floor, third window from south corner."

Static preceded the reply. "That's beneath three-zero-six. Security check immediately."

The man in the window disappeared.

"He's gone," said the agent quickly.

Five seconds later another voice came over the radio. "There's no one here. Room's empty."

"Sorry," said the blond man.

"Better safe than that, sir," said the agent.

Tennyson moved away, walking south through the crowds. He checked his watch again: twenty seconds to go. He approached another man holding a radio in his hand; he produced his own to establish the relationship.

"I'm one of you," he said, half-shouting to be heard. "Things all right?"

The agent faced him. "What?" He saw the radio in Tennyson's hand. "Oh, yes, you were at the morning's briefing. Things are fine, sir."

"That *doorway!*" Tennyson put his hand on the agent's shoulder. "Across the street. The open doorway. You can see the staircase above the heads of the crowd. That *doorway.*"

"What about it? The man on the steps? The one running?"

"Yes! It's the same man."

"Who? What are you talking about?"

"In the hotel room. A few moments ago. It's the same man; I *know* it! He was carrying a briefcase."

The agent spoke into his radio. "Security check requested. Sector Four, west flank. Doorway adjacent to jewelry shop. Man with briefcase. Up the stairs."

"In progress," came the reply.

Across the Strand, Tennyson could see two men racing through the open door and up the dark steps. He looked to the left; the man in the brown raincoat was walking out of the jewelry shop into the crowd. There was a door on the first landing, normally locked—as it was locked now—that connected the two buildings.

A voice came over the radio. "No one with a briefcase on second to fifth floors. Will check roof."

"Don't bother," ordered another voice. "We're up here, and there's no sign of anyone."

Tennyson shrugged apologetically and moved away. He had three more alarms to raise as the motorcade made its stately way down the Strand. The last of these would cause the lead vehicle to stop, clearance required before it continued toward Trafalgar. This final alarm would be raised by him. It would precede the chaos.

The first two happened rapidly, within three minutes of each other. The man in the brown raincoat was adhering to his tight schedule with precision and subtle execution. Not once as he maneuvered his way swiftly into Trafalgar Square was he stopped by a member of British Intelligence. Across his chest were strapped two cameras and a light meter, all dangling precariously as this "tourist" tried to find the best vantage points from which to record his moment in history.

Alarm One. An arm was grabbed; an arm whose hand held a radio.

"That scaffold! Up there!"

"Where?"

The entire side of a building opposite Charing Cross Station was in the middle of reconstruction. People had scaled the pipes; they were cheering and whistling as the international motorcade came into view.

"Up on the right. He went behind the plywood!"

"Who, sir?"

"The man in the hotel, on those steps in the doorway! The briefcase!"

"Security check. Sector Seven. Man on construction scaffold. With a briefcase."

Static. An eruption of voices.

"We're all *over* the scaffolds, mate."

"No one here with a briefcase!"

"Dozens of cameras. No briefcases, or luggage of any sort."

"The plywood on the second level!"

"Man was changing film, mate. He's climbing down. No bird."

"I'm sorry."

"You gave us a start, sir."

"My apologies."

Alarm Two. Tennyson showed a policeman his temporary MI-Five identification and rushed across the intersection into a packed Trafalgar Square.

"The lions! My *God*, the lions!"

The agent—one of those Tennyson had spoken to during the morning's briefing—stared at the base of the Lord Nelson monument. Scores of onlookers were perched on the lions surrounding the towering symbol of Nelson's victory at Trafalgar.

"What, sir?"

"He's there again! The man on the scaffold!"

"I heard that report just moments ago," said the agent. "Where is he?"

"He went behind the lion on the right. It's not a briefcase. It's a leather bag, but it's too large for a camera! Can't you *see?* It's too large for a camera!"

The agent did not hesitate; the radio was at his lips. "Security check. Sector Nine. North cat. Man with large leather bag."

The static crackled; two voices rode over each other.

"Man with two cameras, larger one at his feet. . . ."

"Man checking light meter, corresponds. . . . See no danger; no bird here."

"Man descending, setting camera focus. No bird."

The MI-Five agent glanced at Tennyson, then looked away, his eyes scanning the crowds.

The moment had come. The start of the final alarm, the beginning of the end of the Nachrichtendienst.

"You're *wrong!*" shouted Tennyson furiously. "You're *all* wrong! Every one of you!"

"What?"

The blond man ran as best he could, threading his way through the packed square toward the curbside, the radio next to his ear. He could hear excited voices commenting upon his outburst.

"*He's mad as hell!*"

"*He says we're wrong.*"

"*About what?*"

"*Have no idea.*"

"*He ran.*"

"*Where?*"

"*I don't know. I can't see him.*"

Tennyson reached the iron fence that bordered the monument. He could see his colleague—the Tinamou's apprentice—dashing across the street, toward the arch. The man in the raincoat held a small black plastic case in his hand. The identification card inside was an exact replica of the one in Tennyson's pocket, except that the photograph was different.

Now!

The blond man pressed the button and shouted into the radio.

"It's him! I know it!"

"*Who's that?*"

"*Respond.*"

"*It's from Sector Ten.*"

"I understand now! I see what it was that didn't fit."

"*Is that you, Tennyson?*" Payton-Jones's voice.

"Yes!"

"*Where are you?*"

"That's it! Now I see it."

"*See what? Tennyson, is that you? What's the matter! Respond.*"

"It's so clear now! That's where we made our mistake! It's not going to happen when we thought it would —*where* we thought it would."

"*What are you talking about? Where are you?*"

"We were wrong; don't you see? The weapons. The

seven locations. They were *meant* to be found! That's
what didn't fit!"

"*What? . . . Push the red button, Tennyson. Clear all
channels. . . . What didn't fit?*"

"The hiding of the weapons. It wasn't good enough.
We found them too easily."

"*For God's sake, what are you trying to say?*"

"I'm not sure yet," replied Tennyson, walking toward an opening in the gate. "I just know those weapons
were meant to be found. It's in the progression!"

"*What progression? Push the red button. Where are
you?*"

"*Somewhere between Sector Ten and back toward
Nine,*" intruded another voice. "*West flank. In Trafalgar.*"

"The progression from one weapon to another!"
shouted Tennyson. "Going from east to west! As each
position is passed, we eliminate it. We shouldn't! They're
open limousines!"

"*What do you mean?*"

"Stop the motorcade! In the name of all that's holy,
stop it!"

"*Stop the motorcade! . . . The command's been relayed. Now, where are you?*"

The blond man crouched; two MI-Five men passed
within feet of him. "I think I've spotted him! The man
on the scaffold! In the doorway. In the hotel window. It's
him! He's doubling back; he's running now!"

"*Describe him. For God's sake, describe the man.*"

"He's wearing a jacket. A brown checked jacket."

"*All operatives alert. Pick up man in brown checked
jacket. Running north past Sector Nine, Eight, and Seven.
West flank.*"

"It has to be another weapon! A weapon we never
found. He's going to fire from behind! Distance is nothing to him. He'll hit the back of a neck from a thousand yards! Start the motorcade up again! Quickly!"

"*Vehicle One, proceed. Operatives mount trunks of
all cars. Protect targets from rear fire.*"

"He's stopped!"

"*Tennyson, where are you? Give us your location.*"

"*Still between Sectors Nine and Ten, sir,*" a voice
intruded.

"He's not wearing the jacket now, but it's the same
man! He's running across the Strand!"

"Where?"

"There's no one crossing in Sector Eight."

"Sector Nine?"

"No one, sir."

"Back farther! Behind the motorcade!"

"Sector Five reporting. Police have relaxed the lines. . . ."

"Tighten them. Get everyone out of the street. Tennyson, what's he wearing? Describe him."

The blond man was silent; he walked through the square for a distance of twenty yards, then brought the radio to his lips again. "He's in a brown raincoat. He's heading back toward Trafalgar Square."

"Sector Eight, sir. Transmission in Sector Eight."

Tennyson switched off the radio, shoved it into his pocket, and ran back to the iron fence. The motorcade had reached Charing Cross, perhaps four hundred yards away. The timing was perfect. The Tinamou's timing was always perfect.

The man in the brown raincoat positioned himself in a deserted office of the Government Building beyond Admiralty Park, a room commandeered by the bogus MI-Five identification card. The card was a license; no one argued with it, not today. The line of fire from that room to the motorcade was difficult, but it was no problem for one trained by the Tinamou.

Tennyson leaped over the iron fence and raced diagonally across Trafalgar Square toward Admiralty Arch. Two police officers stopped him, their clubs raised in unison; the motorcade was three hundred yards away.

"This is an emergency!" shouted the blond man, showing his identification. "Check your radios! MI-Five frequency, Savoy operations. I've got to get to the Government Building!"

The police were confused. "Sorry, sir. We don't have radios."

"Then get them!" yelled Tennyson, rushing past.

At the Arch, he activated his radio. "It's the Mall! Once the motorcade's through the Arch, stop all vehicles. He's in the trees!"

"Tennyson, where are you?"

"Sector Twelve, sir. He's in Sector Twelve. East flank."

"Relay his instructions. Quickly, for God's sake."

Tennyson switched off the radio, put it in his pocket, and continued through the crowds. He entered the Mall and turned left, racing across the path to the first doorway of the Government Building. Two uniformed guards blocked him; he produced the MI-Five card.

"Oh yes, sir," said the guard on the left. "Your team's on the second floor. I'm not sure which office."

"I am," said the blond man as he ran toward the staircase. The cheers in Trafalgar Square mounted; the motorcade approached Admiralty Arch.

He took the steps three at a time, crashing the corridor door open on the second floor, pausing in the hallway to shift his gun from his pocket to his belt. He walked swiftly to the second door on the left. There was no point in trying to open it; it was locked. Yet to break it down without warning was to ask for a bullet in his head.

"Es ist Von Tiebolt!" he shouted. *"Bleib beim Fenster!"*

"Herein!" was the reply.

Tennyson angled his shoulder, rushed forward, and slammed his body against the fragile door; the door flew open, revealing the man in the raincoat, crouched in front of the window, a long-barreled rifle in his hands. His hands were encased in sheer, flesh-colored gloves.

"Johann?"

"They found *everything,*" said the blond man. "Every weapon, every location!"

"Impossible!" yelled the man in the raincoat. "One or two, perhaps. Not all!"

"Every one," said Tennyson, kneeling behind the man in front of the window. The advance-security car had passed through Admiralty Arch; they would see the first limousine in seconds. The cheers from the crowds lining the Mall swelled like a mammoth chorus. "Give me the rifle!" Tennyson said. "Is the sight calibrated?"

"Of course," said the man, handing over the weapon.

Tennyson thrust his left hand through the strap, lashing it taut, then raised the rifle to his shoulder, the telescopic sight to his eye. The first limousine moved into the light-green circle, the prime minister of Great Britain in the cross hairs. Tennyson moved the rifle slightly; the smiling face of the president of the United States was now in the gunsight, the cross hairs bisecting the American's left temple. Tennyson shifted the weapon back and forth. It was important for him to know that with two squeezes of the trigger he could eliminate them both.

A third limousine came slowly into the green circle. The chairman of the People's Republic of China was in the gunsight, the cross hairs centered below the visor of his peasant's cap. A slight pressure against the trigger would blow the man's head apart.

"What are you *waiting* for?" asked the Tinamou's apprentice.

"I'm making my decision," replied Tennyson. "Time is relative. Half seconds become half hours." The fourth limousine was there now, the premier of the Soviet Union in the lethal green circle.

The exercise was over. In his mind he had done it. The transition between desire and the reality was minor. It would have been so simple to pull the trigger.

But this was not the way to destroy the Nachrichtendienst. The killing would come later; it would commence in a matter of weeks and continue for a matter of weeks. It was part of the Wolfsschanze covenant, an intrinsic part. So many of the leaders would die. But not now, not this afternoon.

The motorcade stopped; Payton-Jones had relayed Tennyson's instructions. No limousine entered the Mall. Dozens of agents began fanning out over the grass, guns drawn but held unobtrusively as they raced through the foliage, their eyes on the trees.

Tennyson held the rifle in the grip of his left hand, the strap taut from barrel to shoulder. He removed his finger from the trigger housing and lowered his right hand to his wrist, pulling the revolver from his belt.

"*Now,* Johann! They've stopped," whispered the apprentice. "Now, or they'll start up again. You'll lose them!"

"Yes, now," said Tennyson softly, turning to the man crouched beside him. "And I lose nothing."

He fired the gun, the explosion echoing through the

deserted office. The man spun wildly off his feet, blood erupting from his forehead. He fell to the floor, his eyes wide and staring.

It was doubtful that the gunshot was heard for any distance over the noise of the outside crowds, but it didn't really matter. In seconds there'd be gunfire no one would miss. Tennyson sprang to his feet, removed the rifle from his arm, and took a folded slip of paper from his pocket. He knelt beside the dead man and shoved the paper into the bloodied, lifeless mouth, pushing it as far as he could down the throat.

Strapping the weapon back on its owner's arm, he dragged the body over to the window. Pulling out a handkerchief, he wiped the rifle clean and forced the dead fingers into the trigger housing, tearing the fabric of the right-hand glove so he could see the tattoo.

Now.

He took out the radio and leaned out the window.

"I think I've spotted him! It's the same as Madrid. That's it! Madrid!"

"Madrid? Tennyson, where—"

"Sector Thirteen, sir. East flank."

"Thirteen? Specify. Madrid? . . ."

Tennyson pushed himself off the sill and back into the deserted office. It would be only seconds now. Seconds until the connection was made by Payton-Jones.

Tennyson placed the radio on the floor and knelt by the dead man. He edged the dead arm and weapon up into the open window. He listened to the excited voices over the radio.

"Sector Thirteen. East flank. Beyond the Arch to the left, heading south."

"All agents concentrate on Sector Thirteen. East flank. Converge."

"All personnel converging, sir. Sector—"

"Madrid! . . . The Government Building. It's the Government Building."

Now.

The blond man yanked at the dead finger four times, firing indiscriminately into the crowds near the motorcade. He could hear the screams, see the bodies fall.

"Get out. All vehicles move out. Alert One. Move out."

The engines of the limousines roared; the cars

lurched forward. The sounds of sirens filled Saint James's Park.

Tennyson let the dead man fall back to the floor and sprang toward the doorway, the pistol in his hand. He pulled the trigger repeatedly until there were no more shells left in the chamber. The body of the dead man jerked as each new bullet hit.

The voices on the radio were now indistinguishable. He could hear the sounds of racing footsteps in the corridor.

Johann von Tiebolt walked to the wall and sank to the floor, his face drawn in exhaustion. It was the end of his performance. The Tinamou had been caught.

By the Tinamou.

33

Their final meeting took place twenty-seven and a half hours after the death of the unknown man presumed to be the Tinamou.

Since the first account of the momentous event—initially reported by the *Guardian* and subsequently confirmed by Downing Street—the news had electrified the world. And British Intelligence, which refused all comment on the operation other than to express gratitude to sources it would not reveal, regained the supremacy it has lost through years of defections and ineptitude.

Payton-Jones took two envelopes from his pocket and handed them to Tennyson. "These seem such inadequate compensation. The British government owes you a debt it can never repay."

"I never sought payment," said Tennyson, accepting the envelopes. "It's enough that the Tinamou is gone. I assume one of these is the letter from MI Five, and the other the names pulled from the Nachrichtendienst file?"

"They are."

"And my name has been removed from the operation?"

"It was never there. In the reports you are referred to as 'Source Able.' The letter, a copy of which remains in the files, states that your dossier is unblemished."

"What about those who heard my name used over the radios?"

"Indictable under the Official Secrets Act should they reveal it. Not that it makes much difference; they heard only the name 'Tennyson.' There must be a dozen Tennysons under deep cover in British Intelligence, any one of which can be mocked up in the event it's necessary."

"Then I'd say our business is concluded."

"I imagine so," agreed Payton-Jones. "What will you do now?"

"Do? My job, of course. I'm a newspaperman. I might request a short leave of absence, however. My older sister's effects, sadly, must be taken care of, and then I'd like a brief holiday. Switzerland, perhaps. I like to ski."

"It's the season for it."

"Yes." Tennyson paused. "I hope it won't be necessary to have me followed any longer."

"Of course not. Only if you request it."

"Request it?"

"For protection." Payton-Jones gave Tennyson a photocopy of a note. "The Tinamou was professional to the end; he tried to get rid of this, tried to swallow it. And you were right. It's the Nachrichtendienst."

Tennyson picked up the copy. The words were blurred but legible.

NACHRICHT. 1360.78K. AU 23°.22°.

"What does it mean?" he asked.

"Actually, it's rather simple," replied the agent. "The Nachricht is obviously the Nachrichtendienst. The figure '1360.78K' is the metric equivalent of three thousand pounds, or one and a half tons. 'Au' is the chemical symbol for gold. The '23°.22°' we believe are the map coordinates of Johannesburg. The Tinamou was being paid out of Johannesburg in gold for his work yesterday. Something in the neighborhood of three million, six hundred thousand pounds sterling, or more than seven million American dollars."

"It's frightening to think the Nachrichtendienst has that kind of money."

"More frightening when one considers how it was being used."

"You're not going to release the information? Or the note?"

"We'd rather not. However, we realize we have no right to prevent you—especially you—from revealing it. In your *Guardian* story, you alluded to an unknown group of men who might have been responsible for the assassination attempt."

"I speculated on the possibility," corrected Tennyson, "insofar as it was the Tinamou's pattern. He was a hired assassin, not an avenger. Did you learn anything about the man himself?"

"Virtually nothing. The only identification on him, unfortunately, was an excellent forgery of an MI-Five authorization card. His fingerprints aren't in any files anywhere—from Washington to Moscow. His suit was off a rack; we doubt it's English. There were no laundry marks on his underclothing, and even his raincoat, which we traced to a shop in Old Bond Street, was paid for in cash."

"But he traveled continuously. He must have had papers."

"We don't know where to look. We don't even know his nationality. The laboratories have worked around the clock for something to go on: dental work, evidence of surgery, physical marks that a computer might pick up somewhere. *Anything.* So far, nothing."

"Then maybe he wasn't the Tinamou. The only evidence is the tattoo on the back of his hand and a similar caliber of weapons. Will it be enough?"

"It is now; you can add it to your story tomorrow. The ballistics tests are irrefutable. Two of the concealed rifles that were removed, plus the one on his person, match three guns used in previous assassinations."

Tennyson nodded. "There's a certain comfort in that, isn't there?"

"There certainly is." Payton-Jones gestured at the copy of the note. "What's your answer?"

"About what? The note?"

"The Nachrichtendienst. You brought it to us, and now it's confirmed. It's an extraordinary story. You unearthed it; you have every right to print it."

"But you don't want me to."

"We can't stop you."

"On the other hand," said the blond man, "there's nothing to prevent you from including my name in your reports, and that's one thing *I* don't want."

The MI-Five man cleared his throat. "Well, actually, there is something. I gave you my word, Mr. Tennyson. I'd like to think it's good."

"I'm sure it is, but I'm equally sure your giving it could be reappraised should the situation warrant it. If not by you, then by someone else."

"I see no likelihood of that. You've dealt only with me; that was our understanding."

"So 'Source Able' is anonymous. He has no identity."

"Right. Nor is it unusual at the levels in which I negotiate. I've spent my life in the service. My word's not questioned when it's given."

"I see." Tennyson stood. "Why don't you want the Nachrichtendienst identified?"

"I want time. A month or two. Time to get closer without alarming it."

"Do you think you'll be able to?" Tennyson pointed to one of the envelopes on the table. "Will those names help?"

"I'm not sure. I've just begun. There are only eight men listed; we're not even certain they're all alive. There's been no time to check them out."

"*Someone's* alive. Someone very wealthy and powerful."

"Obviously."

"So the compulsion to catch the Tinamou is replaced by an obsession with the Nachrichtendienst."

"A logical transfer, I'd say," agreed Payton-Jones. "And I should add, there's another reason—quite professional, but also part personal. I'm convinced the Nachrichtendienst killed a young man I trained."

"Who was he?"

"My assistant. As committed as any man I've ever met in service. His body was found in a small village called Montereau some sixty miles south of Paris. He went to France initially to track Holcroft, but found that Holcroft was a dead end."

"What do you think happened?"

"I *know* what happened. Remember, he was after the Tinamou. When Holcroft proved to be only what he said he was—a man looking for you because of a minor inheritance—"

"Very minor," interrupted Tennyson.

". . . our young man went underground. He was a first-rate professional; he made progress. More than that, he made a connection. He *had* to have made a connection. The Tinamou, the Nachrichtendienst . . . Paris. Everything fits."

"Why does it fit?"

"There's a name on that list. A man living near Paris—we don't know where—who was a general in the German High Command. Klaus Falkenheim. But he was more than that. We believe he was a prime mover of the Nachrichtendienst, one of the original members. He's known as Herr Oberst."

John Tennyson stood rigidly by the chair. "You have my word," he said. "I'll print nothing."

Holcroft sat forward on the couch, the newspaper in his hand. The headline reached from border to border. It said it all.

ASSASSIN TRAPPED, KILLED IN LONDON

Nearly every article on the page was related to the dramatic capture and subsequent death of the Tinamou. There were stories reaching back fifteen years, linking the Tinamou to both Kennedys and to Martin Luther King, as well as to Oswald and Ruby; more recent speculations touched on killings in Madrid and Beirut, Paris and Lisbon, Prague and even Moscow itself.

The unknown man with the rose tattoo on his hand was an instant legend. Tattoo parlors from cities everywhere reported a surge in business.

"My God, he did it," said Noel.

"Yet his name isn't mentioned anywhere," Helden said. "It's unlike Johann to give up credit in something as extraordinary as this."

"You said he'd changed, that Geneva had affected him. I believe that. The man I talked to wasn't concerned with himself. I told him that the bank in Geneva didn't want complications. The directors would be looking for anything that might disqualify one of us, that would put the money in potentially compromising circumstances. A man who's placed himself in a dangerous situation, who's had to deal with the kind of people your brother's had to deal with in tracking the Tinamou, could scare the hell out of the bankers."

"But you and my brother say there's someone more powerful than the Rache or the ODESSA—or Wolfsschanze—who's trying to stop you. How do you think the men in Geneva will accept all that?"

"They'll be told only what they have to be told,"

said Holcroft. "Which may be nothing, if your brother and I find out who it is."

"Can you?"

"Maybe. Johann thinks so, and God knows he's had more experience in these matters than I've had. It's been a crazy process of elimination. First we're convinced it's one thing—one group—then another; then it turns out to be neither."

"You mean the ODESSA and the Rache?"

"Yes. They're eliminated. Now we're looking for someone else. All we need is a name, an identity."

"What will you do when you find it?"

"I don't know," Holcroft said. "I hope your brother will tell me. I just know that whatever we do, we've got to do it quickly. Miles will get to me in a few days. He's going to connect me publicly to homicides ranging from Kennedy Airport to the Plaza Hotel. He'll ask for extradition, and he'll get it. If that happens, Geneva's finished, and for all intents and purposes, so am I."

"If they can find you," said Helden. "We have ways . . ."

Noel stared at her. "No," he replied. "I'm not going to live with three changes of clothing and rubber-soled shoes and guns with silencers. I want you to be a part of my life, but I won't be a part of yours."

"You may not have a choice."

The telephone rang, startling them both. Holcroft picked it up.

"Good afternoon, Mr. Fresca."

It was Tennyson.

"Can you talk?" asked Noel.

"Yes. This telephone is fine, and I doubt the George Cinq switchboard is interested in a routine call from London. Still, we should be careful."

"I understand. Congratulations. You did what you said you would."

"I had a great deal of help."

"You worked with the British?"

"Yes. You were right. I should have done so a long time ago. They were splendid."

"I'm glad to hear it. It's nice to know we have friends."

"More than that. We have the identity of Geneva's enemy."

"*What?*"

"We have the names. We can move against them now. We *must* move against them; the killing must stop."

"How? . . ."

"I'll explain when I see you. Your friend Kessler was close to the truth."

"A splinter faction of ODESSA?"

"Be careful," interrupted Tennyson. "Let's say a group of tired old men with too much money and a vendetta that goes back to the end of the war."

"What do we do?"

"Perhaps very little. The British may do it for us."

"They know about Geneva?"

"No. They simply understand a debt."

"It's more than we could ask for."

"No more than we deserve," said Tennyson. "If I may say so."

"You may. These . . . old men. They were responsible for *everything?* Including New York?"

"Yes."

"Then I'm clear."

"You will be shortly."

"Thank Christ!" Noel looked at Helden across the room and smiled. "What do you want me to do?"

"It's Wednesday. Be in Geneva Friday night. I'll see you then. I'll take the late flight from Heathrow and get there by eleven-thirty or midnight. Call Kessler in Berlin; tell him to join us."

"Why not today, or tomorrow?"

"I've got things to do. They'll be helpful to us. Make it Friday. Do you have a hotel?"

"Yes. The d'Accord. My mother's flying to Geneva. She got word to me to stay there."

There was a silence on the line from London. Finally, Tennyson spoke, his voice a whisper. "What did you say?"

"My mother's flying to Geneva."

"We'll talk later," said Helden's brother, barely audibly. "I've got to go."

Tennyson replaced the phone on the small table in his Kensington flat. As always, he detested the instrument when it was the carrier of unexpected news. News in this case that could be as dangerous as the emergence of the Nachrichtendienst.

What insanity had made Althene Clausen decide to fly to Geneva? It was never part of the plan—as she understood the plan. Did the old woman think she could travel to Switzerland without arousing suspicions, especially *now?* Or perhaps the years had made her careless. In that event she would not live long enough to regret her indiscretion. Perhaps, again, she had divided loyalties—as she understood those loyalties. If so, she would be reminded of her priorities before she took leave of a life in which she had abused so many.

So be it. He had his own priorities; she would take her place among them. The covenant of Wolfsschanze was about to be fulfilled. Everything was timing now.

First the lists. There were two, and they were the key to Wolfsschanze. One was eleven pages in length, with the names of nearly sixteen hundred men and women—powerful men and women in every country in the world. These were the elite of the *Sonnenkinder,* the leaders waiting for the signal from Geneva, waiting to receive the millions that would purchase influence, buy elections, shape policies. This was the primary list, and with it would emerge the outlines of the Fourth Reich.

But outlines required substance, depth. Leaders needed followers. These would come with the second list, this one in the form of a hundred spools of film. The master list. Microdot records of their people in every part of the globe. By now, thousands upon thousands, begat and recruited by the children sent out of the Reich by ship and plane and submarine.

Operation *Sonnenkinder.*

The lists, the names. One copy only, never to be duplicated, guarded as closely as any holy grail. For years they had been kept and updated by Maurice Graff in Brazil, then presented to Johann von Tiebolt on his twenty-fifth birthday. The ceremony signified the transfer of power; the chosen new absolute leader had exceeded all expectations.

John Tennyson had brought the lists to England, knowing it was imperative to find a repository safer than any bank, more removed from potential scrutiny than any vault in London. He had found his secret place in an obscure mining town in Wales, with a *Sonnenkind* who would gladly give his life to protect the precious documents.

Ian Llewellen: brother of Morgan, second-in-command of Beaumont's *Argo*.

And it was nearly time for the Welshman to arrive. After he had delivered his cargo, the loyal *Sonnenkind* would make the sacrifice he had pleaded to make only days ago when they drove down the highway from Heathrow. His death was mandatory; no one could be aware of those lists, those names. When that sacrifice was made, only two men on earth would have the key to Wolfsschanze. One a quiet professor of history in Berlin, the other a man revered by British Intelligence—above suspicion.

Nachrichtendienst. The next priority.

Tennyson stared at the sheet of paper next to the telephone; it had been there for several hours. It was another list—light-years away from the *Sonnenkinder*—given him by Payton-Jones. It was the Nachrichtendienst.

Eight names, eight men. And what the British had not learned in two days he had learned in less than two hours. Five of those men were dead. Three remained, one of them now close to death in a sanatorium outside of Stuttgart. That left two: the traitor, Klaus Falkenheim, known as Herr Oberst, and a former diplomat of eighty-three named Werner Gerhardt, who lived quietly in a Swiss village on Lake Neuchâtel.

But old men did not travel in transatlantic aircraft and put strychnine in glasses of whiskey. They did not beat a man unconscious for a photograph. They did not fire guns at that same man in a French village or assault that man in a back alley in Berlin.

The Nachrichtendienst had indoctrinated younger, very capable disciples. Indoctrinated them to the point of absolute commitment . . . as the disciples of Wolfsschanze were committed.

Nachrichtendienst! Falkenheim, Gerhardt. How long had they known about Wolfsschanze?

Tomorrow he would find out. In the morning he would take a plane to Paris, and call on Falkenheim, on the hated Herr Oberst. Consummate actor, consummate garbage. Betrayer of the Reich.

Tomorrow he would call on Falkenheim and break him. Then kill him.

A car horn sounded from outside. Tennyson looked at his watch as he walked to the window. Eight o'clock precisely. Down in the street was the Welshman's automobile, and inside, sealed in a steel carton, were the lists.

Tennyson took a gun from a drawer and shoved it into the holster strapped to his shoulder.

He wished the events of the night were over and he was on the plane to Paris. He could hardly wait to confront Klaus Falkenheim.

Holcroft sat silently on the couch in the semidarkness, the glow of an unseen moon filling the windows. It was four in the morning. He smoked a cigarette. He had opened his eyes fifteen minutes ago and had not been able to go back to sleep, his thoughts on the girl beside him.

Helden. She was the woman he wanted to be with for the rest of his life, yet she would not tell him where she lived or whom she lived with. It was past flippancy now; he was not interested in games any longer.

"Noel?" Helden's voice floated across the shadows.

"Yes?"

"What's the matter, darling?"

"Nothing. Just thinking."

"I've been thinking, too."

"I thought you were asleep."

"I felt you get out of bed. What are you thinking about?"

"A lot of things," he said. "Mostly Geneva. It'll be over soon. You're going to be able to stop running; so am I."

"That's what I've been thinking about." She smiled at him. "I want to tell you my secret."

"Secret?"

"It's not much of one, but I want to see your face when I tell you. Come here."

She held out both her hands and he took them, sitting naked in front of her. "What's your secret?"

"It's your competition. The man I live with. Are you ready?"

"I'm ready."

"It's Herr Oberst. I love him."

"The old man?" Noel breathed again.

"Yes. Are you furious?"

"Beside myself. I'll have to challenge him to a duel." Holcroft took her in his arms.

Helden laughed and kissed him. "I've got to see him today."

"I'll go with you. I've got your brother's blessing. I'll see if I can get his."

"No. I must go alone. I'll only be an hour or so."

"Two hours. That's the limit."

"Two hours. I'll stand in front of his wheelchair and say, 'Herr Oberst. I'm leaving you for another man.' Do you think he'll be crushed?"

"It'll kill him," whispered Noel. He pulled her gently down on the bed.

34

Tennyson walked into the parking lot at Orly Airport and saw the gray Renault. The driver of the car was the second-highest-ranking official of the Sûreté. He had been born in Düsseldorf, but grew up a Frenchman, sent out of Germany on a plane from a remote airfield north of Essen. He was six years old at the time—March 10, 1945 —and he had no memories of the Fatherland. But he did have a commitment: He was a *Sonnenkind*.

Tennyson reached the door, opened it, and climbed inside.

"Bonjour, monsieur," he said.

"Bonjour," replied the Frenchman. "You look tired."

"It's been a long night. Did you bring everything I asked for? I have very little time."

"Everything." The Sûreté official reached for a file folder on the ledge under the dashboard and handed it to the blond man. "I think you'll find this complete."

"Give me a summary; I'll read it later. I want to know quickly where we stand."

"Very well." The Frenchman put the folder on his lap. "First things first. The man named Werner Gerhardt in Neuchâtel cannot possibly be a functioning member of the Nachrichtendienst."

"Why not? Von Pappen had his enemies in the diplomatic corps. Why couldn't this Gerhardt have been one of them?"

"He may very well have been. But I use the present tense; he is no longer. He's not only senile; he's feebleminded. He's been this way for years; he's a joke in the village where he lives. The old man who mumbles to himself and sings songs and feeds pigeons in the square."

"Senility can be faked," said Tennyson. "And 'feeble' is hardly a pathological term."

365

"There's proof. He's an outpatient at the local clinic, with a bona fide medical record. He has the mentality of a child and is barely able to care for himself."

Tennyson nodded, smiling. "So much for Werner Gerhardt. Speaking of patients, what's the status of the traitor in Stuttgart?"

"Cerebral cancer, final stages. He won't last a week."

"So the Nachrichtendienst has but one functioning leader left," said Tennyson. "Klaus Falkenheim."

"It would appear so. However, he may have delegated authority to a younger man. He has soldiers available to him."

"Merely available? From the children he protects? The *Verwünschte Kinder?*"

"Hardly. They're sprinkled with a few idealists, but there's no essential strength in their ranks. Falkenheim has sympathy for them, but he keeps those interests separate from the Nachrichtendienst."

"Then where do the Nachrichtendienst soldiers come from?"

"They're Jews."

"Jews!"

The Frenchman nodded. "As near as we can determine, they're recruited as they're needed, one assignment at a time. There's no organization, no structured group. Beyond being Jews, they have only one thing in common: where they come from."

"Which is?

"The kibbutz Har Sha'alav. In the Negev."

"Har Sha'alav? . . . My God, how perfect," said Tennyson with cold, professional respect. "Har Sha'alav. The kibbutz in Israel with but one requirement for residency: The applicant has to be the sole survivor of a family destroyed in the camps."

"Right," said the Frenchman. "The kibbutz has more than two hundred men—men, now—who can be recruited."

Tennyson looked out the window. " 'Kill me, another will take my place. Kill him, another his.' The implication was an unseen army willing to accept a collective death sentence. The commitment is understandable, but this is no army. It is a series of patrols, selected at random." Tennyson turned back to the driver. "Are you sure of your information?"

"Yes. The breakthrough came with the two unknown men killed in Montereau. Our laboratories traced a number of things: clothing, sediment in shoes and in skin pores, the alloys used in dental work, and especially surgical history. Both men had been wounded; one had shell fragments in his shoulder. The Yom Kippur war. We narrowed the evidence to the southwest Negev and found the kibbutz. The rest was simple."

"You sent a man to Har Sha'alav?"

The Frenchman nodded again. "One of us. His report is in here. No one talks freely at Har Sha'alav, but what's going on is clear. Someone sends a cablegram; a few men are chosen and given orders."

"Potential suicide squads committed to the destruction of anything related to the swastika."

"Exactly. And to confirm our findings, we've established the fact that Falkenheim traveled to Israel three months ago. The computers picked up his name."

"Three months ago. . . . At the time Manfredi first reached Holcroft to set up the meeting in Geneva. So Falkenheim not only knew about Wolfsschanze, he projected the schedule. He recruited and prepared his army three months in advance. It's time he and I met each other in our proper roles: two sons of the Reich. One true, one false."

"To what should I attribute his death?"

"To the ODESSA, of course. And call a strike on Har Sha'alav. I want every leader killed; prepare it carefully. Blame it on Rache terrorists. Let's go."

For the next minutes, the blond man walking down the winding dirt road would not be John Tennyson. Instead, he would be called by his rightful name, Johann von Tiebolt, son of Wilhelm, leader of the new Reich.

The cottage was in sight; the death of a traitor approached. Von Tiebolt turned and looked back up the hill. The man from the Sûreté waved. He would remain there, blocking the road until the job was done. Von Tiebolt continued walking until he was within ten yards of the stone path that led to the small house. He stopped, concealed by the foliage, and shifted his gun from the shoulder holster to his overcoat pocket. Crouching, he stepped through the overgrown grass, toward the door and beyond it, then stood up, his face at the edge of the single front window.

Though the morning was bright with sunlight, a table lamp was turned on in the dark interior of the room. Beyond the lamp Klaus Falkenheim sat in his wheelchair, his back to the window.

Von Tiebolt walked silently back to the door and considered for a moment whether or not to break it down, as a killer from the ODESSA undoubtedly would do. He decided against it. Herr Oberst was old and decrepit, but he was no fool. Somewhere on his person, or in that wheelchair, was a weapon. At the first sound of a crash it would be leveled at the intruder.

Johann smiled at himself. There was no harm in a little game. One consummate actor onstage with another. Who would be applauded most enthusiastically? The answer was obvious: he who was there for the curtain call. It would not be Klaus Falkenheim.

He rapped on the door. "Mein Herr. Forgive me, it's Johann von Tiebolt. I'm afraid my car couldn't negotiate the hill."

At first there was only silence. If it continued beyond five seconds, Von Tiebolt realized he would have to take sterner measures; there could be no sudden telephone calls. Then he heard the old man's words.

"Von Tiebolt?"

"Yes. Helden's brother. I've come to speak with her. She's not at work, so I assume she's here."

"She's not." The old man was silent again.

"Then I shan't disturb you, Mein Herr, but if I may, is it possible to use your telephone and call for a taxi?"

"The telephone?"

The blond man smiled. Falkenheim's confusion carried through the barrier between them. "I'll only be a moment. I really must find Helden by noon. I leave for Switzerland at two o'clock."

Again silence, but it was short-lived. He heard a bolt slide back, and the door opened. Herr Oberst was there in the chair, wheeling backward, a blanket on his lap. There had been no blanket moments ago.

"*Danke, mein Herr,*" said Von Tiebolt, holding out his hand. "It's good to see you again."

Bewildered, the old man raised his hand in greeting. Johann wrapped his fingers swiftly around the bony hand, twisting it to the left. With his free hand, he reached down and yanked the blanket from Falkenheim's lap. He saw what he expected: a Luger across the emaciated legs. He removed it, kicking the door shut as he did.

"Heil Hitler! General Falkenheim," he said. "Wo ist der Nachrichtendienst?"

The old man remained motionless, staring up at his captor, no fear in his eyes. "I wondered when you would find out. I didn't think it would be so quickly. I commend you, Sohn Wilhelm von Tiebolts."

"Yes, son of Wilhelm, and something else as well."

"Oh, yes. The new Führer. That's your objective, but it won't happen. We'll stop you. If you've come to kill me, do so. I'm prepared."

"Why should I? Such a valuable hostage."

"I doubt you'd get much ransom."

Von Tiebolt spun the old man's chair toward the center of the room. "I imagine that's true," he replied, abruptly stopping the chair. "I assume you have certain funds available, perhaps solicited by the wandering children you think so much of. However, Pfennigs and francs are immaterial to me."

"I was sure of that. So fire the gun."

"And," said Von Tiebolt, "it's doubtful that a man dying of cerebral cancer in a Stuttgart sanatorium could offer much. Wouldn't you say that, too, is true?"

Falkenheim controlled his surprise. "He was a very brave man," he said.

"I'm sure. You're all brave men. Successful traitors must be imbued with a certain warped courage. Werner Gerhardt, for instance."

"Gerhardt? . . ." This time the old man could not conceal his shock. "Where did you hear that name?"

"You wonder how I could know? How I even found out about you, perhaps?"

"Not about me. The risk I took was quite apparent. I arranged for a Von Tiebolt to be near me. I considered that risk necessary."

"Yes, the beautiful Helden. But then, I'm told we're all beautiful. It has its advantages."

"She's no part of you; she never was."

"She's part of your wandering garbage, die Ver-

wünschte Kinder. A weak whore. She whores now with the American."

"Your judgments don't interest me. How did you find out about Gerhardt?"

"Why should I tell you?"

"I'm going to die. What difference does it make?"

"I'll strike a bargain. Where did you learn of Wolfs-schanze?"

"Agreed. Gerhardt first."

"Why not. He's of no value. A senile, feebleminded old man."

"Don't harm him!" shouted Falkenheim suddenly. "He's been through so much . . . so much *pain.*"

"Your concern is touching."

"They broke him. Four months of torture; his mind snapped. Leave him in peace."

"Who broke him? The Allies? The British?"

"ODESSA."

"For once they served a useful purpose."

"Where did you hear his name? How did you find him?"

Von Tiebolt smiled. "The British. They have a file on the Nachrichtendienst. You see, they're very interested in the Nachrichtendienst right now. Their objective is to find you and destroy you."

"Destroy? There's no *reason.* . . ."

"Oh, but there is. They have proof you hired the Tinamou."

"The Tinamou? Absurd!"

"Not at all. It was your final vengeance, the revenge of tired old men against their enemies. Take my word for it: The proof is irrefutable. I gave it to them."

The old man looked at Johann, his expression filled with revulsion. "You're obscene."

"About Wolfsschanze!" Von Tiebolt raised his voice. "Where? How? I'll know if you lie."

Falkenheim sank back in the wheelchair. "It doesn't matter now. For either of us. I'll die, and you'll be stopped."

"Now it is I who am not interested in *your* judgments. Wolfsschanze!"

Falkenheim glanced up listlessly. "Althene Clausen," he said quietly. "Heinrich Clausen's nearly perfect strategy."

Von Tiebolt's face was frozen in astonishment. "Clausen's wife? . . ." He trailed off the words. "You found out about her?"

The old man turned back to Johann. "It wasn't difficult; we had informers everywhere. In New York as well as Berlin. We knew who Mrs. Richard Holcroft was, and because we knew, we sent out orders to protect her. That was the irony: to *protect* her. Then word came: At the height of the war, while her American husband is at sea, she flies in a private plane to Mexico. From Mexico she goes secretly on to Buenos Aires, where the German embassy takes over and she's flown under diplomatic cover to Lisbon. To *Lisbon*. Why?"

"Berlin gave you the answer?" asked Von Tiebolt.

"Yes. Our people in the Finanzministerium. We'd learned that extraordinary sums of money were being siphoned out of Germany; it was in our interest not to interfere. Whatever helped cripple the Nazi machine, we sanctioned; peace and sanity would return sooner. But five days after Mrs. Holcroft left New York for Lisbon, by way of Mexico and Buenos Aires, Heinrich Clausen, the genius of the Finanzministerium, flew covertly out of Berlin. He stopped first in Geneva to meet with a banker named Manfredi, then he too went on to Lisbon. We knew he was no defector; above all men, he was a true believer in German—Aryan—supremacy. So much so that he couldn't stomach the flaws in Hitler's ranks of gangsters." Herr Oberst paused. "We made the simple addition. Clausen and his supposedly treasonous former wife in Lisbon together; millions upon millions banked in Switzerland . . . and the defeat of Germany now assured. We looked for the deeper meaning and found it in Geneva."

"You read the documents?"

"We read everything from La Grande Banque de Genève. The price was five hundred thousand Swiss francs."

"To Manfredi?"

"Naturally. He knew who we were; he thought we'd believe—and honor—the objectives espoused in those papers. We let him think so. Wolfsschanze! *Whose* Wolfsschanze? 'Amends must be made.'" Falkenheim spoke the words scathingly. "The thought furthest from any of their minds. That money was to be used to revive the Reich."

"What did you do then?"

The old soldier looked directly at Von Tiebolt. "Returned to Berlin and executed your father, Kessler, and Heinrich Clausen. They never intended to take their own lives; they expected to find sanctuary in South America, oversee their plan, watch it come to fruition. We gave them their pact with death that Clausen wrote so movingly about to his son."

Von Tiebolt fingered the Luger in his hand. "So you learned the secret of Althene Clausen?"

"You spoke of whores. She's the whore of the world."

"I'm surprised you let her live."

"A second irony: We had no choice. With Clausen gone we realized she was the key to Wolfsschanze. *Your* Wolfsschanze. We knew that she and Clausen had refined every move that was to be made during the coming years. We had to learn; she'd never tell us, so we had to watch. When were the millions to be taken from Geneva? How specifically were they to be used? And by whom?"

"The *Sonnenkinder*," said Von Tiebolt.

The old man's eyes were blank. "What did you say?"

"Never mind. So it was a question of waiting for Althene Clausen to make her move, whatever it might be?"

"Yes, but we learned nothing from her. Ever. As the years went by, we realized she had absorbed her husband's genius. In thirty years she never once betrayed the cause by word or action. One had to admire the sheer discipline. Our first signal came when Manfredi made contact with the son." Falkenheim winced. "The despicable thing is that she consented to the rape of her own child. Holcroft knows nothing."

The blond man laughed. "You're so out of touch. The renowned Nachrichtendienst is a collection of fools."

"You think so?"

"I *know* so. You watched the *wrong* horse in the *wrong* stable!"

"What?"

"For thirty years your eyes were focused on the one person who knew absolutely *nothing*. The whore of the world, as you call her, is secure in the knowledge that she and her son are truly part of a great apology. She's never thought otherwise!" Von Tiebolt's laughter echoed off the walls of the room. "That trip to Lisbon," he continued, "was Heinrich Clausen's most brilliant manipulation. The contrite sinner turned holy man with a holy cause. It must have been the performance of his life. Even down to his final instructions that she was not to give her instant approval. The son was to see for himself the justness of his martyred father's cause, and, being convinced, become committed beyond anything in his life." Von Tiebolt leaned against the table, his arms folded, the Luger in his hand. "Don't you see? None of *us* could do it. The document in Geneva was utterly correct about that. The fortunes stolen by the Third Reich are legendary. There could not be a single connection between that account in Geneva and a true son of Germany."

Falkenheim stared at Johann. "She never *knew? . . .*"

"Never! She was the ideal puppet. Even psychologically. The fact that Heinrich Clausen was revealed to be that holy man reaffirmed her confidence in her own judgments. She had married *that* man, not the Nazi."

"Incredible," whispered Herr Oberst.

"At least that," agreed Von Tiebolt. "She followed his instructions to the letter. Every contingency was considered, including a death certificate for an infant male in a London hospital. All traces to Clausen were obliterated." The blond man laughed again, the sound unnerving. "So you see, you're no match for Wolfsschanze."

"Your Wolfsschanze, not mine." Falkenheim glanced away. "You are to be commended."

Suddenly Von Tiebolt stopped laughing. Something was wrong. It was in the old man's eyes—flashed briefly, clouded, deep within that emaciated skull. "Look at me!" he shouted. "*Look* at me!"

Falkenheim turned. "What is it?"

"I said something just now . . . something you *knew* about. You *knew*."

"What are you talking about?"

Von Tiebolt grabbed the old man by the throat. "I spoke of contingencies, of a death certificate! In a London hospital! You've heard it before!"

"I don't know what you mean." Falkenheim's trembling fingers were wrapped around the blond man's wrists, his voice rasping under the pressure of Johann's grip.

"I think you do. Everything I've just told you shocked you. Or did it? You pretended shock, but you're *not* shocked. The hospital. The death certificate. You didn't react at all! You've heard it before!"

"I've heard nothing," gasped Falkenheim.

"Don't lie to me!" Von Tiebolt whipped the Luger across Herr Oberst's face, lacerating the cheek. "You're not that good anymore. You're too *old*. You have lapses! Your brain is atrophied. You pause at the wrong instant, *Herr General*."

"You're a maniac. . . ."

"You're a *liar!* A poor liar at that. *Traitor*." Again he struck Herr Oberst in the face with the barrel of the weapon. Blood poured from the open wounds. "You *lied* about her! . . . My God, you *knew!*"

"Nothing . . . *nothing*."

"Yes! *Everything!* That's why she's flying to Geneva. I asked myself why." Von Tiebolt struck furiously again; the old man's lip was torn half off his face. "You! In your last desperate attempt to stop us, you reached her! You threatened her . . . and in those threats you told her what she never *knew!*"

"You're wrong. *Wrong*."

"No," said Von Tiebolt, suddenly lowering his voice. "There's no other reason for her to fly to Geneva. . . . So that's how you think you'll stop us. The mother reaches the child and tells him to turn back. Her covenant is a lie."

Falkenheim shook his bloodied head. "No. . . . Nothing you say is true."

"It's all true, and it answers a last question. If you so dearly wanted to destroy Geneva, all you had to do was let the word go out. Nazi treasure. Claims would be made against it from the Black Sea to the northern Elbe, from Moscow to Paris. But you don't do that. Again, *why?*" Von Tiebolt bent over farther, inches from the battered face beneath him. "You think you can control Geneva, use the millions as *you* want them used. 'Amends must be made.' Holcroft learns the truth and becomes *your* soldier, his anger complete, his commitment tripled."

"He *will* find out," whispered Falkenheim. "He's better than you; we've both learned that, haven't we? You should find satisfaction in that. After all, in his own way, he's a *Sonnenkind*."

"*Sonnen—*" Von Tiebolt swung the barrel of his pistol again across Herr Oberst's face. "You're filled with lies. I said the name; you showed nothing."

"Why should I lie now? *Operation Sonnenkinder*," said Falkenheim. "By ship, and plane, and submarine. Everywhere the children. We never got the lists, but we don't need them. They'll be stopped when you're stopped. When Geneva's stopped."

"For that to happen, Althene Clausen must reach her son. She won't expose Geneva for what it is until she's tried everything else. To do so would destroy her son, let the world know who he is. She'll do anything before she lets that happen. She'll try to reach him quietly. We'll stop her."

"*You'll* be stopped!" said Falkenheim, choking on the blood that flowed over his lips. "There'll be no vast sums dispensed to your *Sonnenkinder*. We, too, have an army, one you'll never know about. Each man will gladly give his life to stop you, expose you."

"Of course, *Herr General*." The blond man nodded. "The Jews of Har Sha'alav."

The words were spoken softly, but they had the effect of a lash on the old man's wounds. "*No! . . .*"

"Yes," said Von Tiebolt. " 'Kill me, another will take my place. Kill him, another his.' The Jews of Har Sha'alav. Indoctrinated by the Nachrichtendienst so thoroughly they became the Nachrichtendienst. The living remains of Auschwitz."

"You're an *animal. . . .*" Falkenheim's body trembled in a spasm of pain.

"I am Wolfsschanze, the true Wolfsschanze," said the blond man, raising the Luger. "Until you knew the truth, the Jews tried to kill the American, and now the Jews will die. Within the week Har Sha'alav will be destroyed, and with it the Nachrichtendienst. Wolfsschanze will triumph."

Von Tiebolt held the gun in front of the old man's head. He fired.

35

Tears streaked down Helden's cheeks. She cradled the body of Klaus Falkenheim, but could not bring herself to look at the head. Finally, she let go of the corpse and crawled away; filled with horror . . . and guilt. She lay curled on the floor, her sobbing uncontrollable. In pain, she pushed herself to the wall, her forehead pressed against the molding, and let the tears pour out. Gradually it became clear to her that her screams and sobs had not been heard. She had come upon the horrible scene alone, and had found signs of the hated ODESSA everywhere: swastikas scratched into wood, scrawled with soap on the window, painted with Falkenheim's blood on the floor. Beyond the despicable symbols, the room had been torn apart. Books ripped, shelves broken, furniture slashed; the house had been searched by maniacs. There was nothing left but ruins.

Yet there was something . . . not in the house. Outside. In the forest. Helden pressed her hands on the floor and raised herself against the wall, trying desperately to remember the words spoken by Herr Oberst only five mornings ago: *If anything should happen to me, you must not panic. . . . Go alone into the woods where you took me for my brief walk the other day. Do you remember? I asked you to pick up a cluster of wildflowers, as I remained by a tree. I pointed out to you that there was a perfect V formed by the limbs. Go to that tree. Wedged into the branches is a small canister. Inside, there is a message to be read only by you. . . .*

Helden pried the small tubular receptacle from its recess and tore open the rubber top. Inside there was a rolled-up piece of paper; attached to it were several bills, each worth ten thousand francs. She removed the money and read the message.

376

My dearest HELDEN—

Time and danger to your person will not permit me to write here what you must know. Three months ago I arranged for you to come to me because I believed you were an arm of an enemy I have waited thirty years to confront. I have come to know you—to love you—and with great relief to understand that you are not part of the horror that might once again be visited upon the world.

Should I be killed, it will mean I have been found out. Further, it will signify that the time is near for the catastrophes to begin. Orders must be relayed to those courageous men who will stand at the final barricade.

You must go alone—I repeat, alone—to Lake Neuchâtel, in Switzerland. Don't let anyone follow you. I know you can do this. You have been taught. In the village of Près-du-Lac there is a man named Werner Gerhardt. Find him. Give him the following message: "The coin of Wolfsschanze has two sides." He will know what to do.

You must go quickly. There is very little time. Again, say nothing to anyone. Raise no alarms. Tell your employers and your friends that you have personal matters in England, a logical statement considering the fact that you lived there for more than five years.

Quickly now, my dearest Helden. To Neuchâtel. To Près-du-Lac. To Werner Gerhardt. Memorize the name and burn this paper.

Godspeed,
HERR OBERST

Helden leaned against the tree and looked up at the sky. Wisps of thin clouds moved swiftly in an easterly course; the winds were strong. She wished she could be carried by them, and that she did not have to run from point to point, every move a risk, every person she looked at a potential enemy.

Noel had said it would be over soon and she would be able to stop running.

He was wrong.

*   *   *

Holcroft pleaded over the telephone, trying to convince her not to go—at least for another day—but Helden would not be dissuaded. Word had reached her through Gallimard that her sister's personal effects were awaiting her inspection; decisions had to be considered, arrangements made.

"I'll call you in Geneva, my darling. You'll be staying at the d'Accord?"

"Yes." What was wrong with her? She'd been so happy, so elated, barely two hours ago. She sounded tense now; her words were clear, but her voice was strained.

"I'll phone you in a day or so. Under the name of Fresca."

"Do you want me to go with you? I don't have to be in Geneva until late tomorrow night. The Kesslers won't get there till ten, your brother even later."

"No, darling. It's a sad trip. I'd rather make it alone. Johann's in London now. . . . I'll try to reach him."

"You've got some clothes here."

"A dress, a pair of slacks, shoes. It's quicker for me to stop at . . . Herr Oberst's . . . and pick up others more appropriate for Portsmouth."

"Quicker?"

"On the way to the airport. I have to go there, at any rate. My passport, money. . . ."

"I have money," interrupted Noel. "I thought you'd been to his place by now."

"*Please,* darling. Don't be difficult." Helden's voice cracked. "I told you, I stopped at the office."

"No, you didn't. You didn't say that. You said you got word." Holcroft was alarmed; she wasn't making sense. Herr Oberst's hidden cottage was *not* on the way to Orly. "Helden, what's the matter?"

"I love you, Noel. I'll call you tomorrow night. Hotel d'Accord, Geneva." She hung up.

Holcroft replaced the phone, the sound of her voice echoing in his ears. It was possible she was going to London, but he doubted it. Where *was* she going? Why did she lie? God damn it! What was *wrong* with her? What had happened?

There was no point in staying in Paris. Since he had to reach Geneva on his own, he might as well get started.

He could not chance the airlines or the trains. Unseen men would be watching; he had to elude them. The assistant manager of the George V could hire him a car under the name of Fresca. The route would be mapped for him. He would drive through the night to Geneva.

Althene Holcroft looked out the window of the TAP airliner at the lights of Lisbon below; they would be on the ground in minutes. She had a great deal to accomplish during the next twelve hours, and she hoped to God she was capable of doing it. A man had followed her in Mexico; she knew that. But then he had disappeared at the airport, which meant that another had taken his place.

She had failed in Mexico. She had not dropped out of sight. Once in Lisbon, she would have to vanish; she could not fail again.

Lisbon.

Oh, *God,* Lisbon!

It had been in Lisbon where it all began. The lie of a lifetime, conceived in diabolical brilliance. What an imbecile she had been; what a performance Heinrich had given.

She had at first refused to meet with Heinrich in Lisbon, so total was her loathing, but she had gone because the threat was clear: Her son would be branded by his father. Noel *Holcroft* would never be left in peace, for the name Noel *Clausen*—only son of the infamous Nazi—would trail him throughout his life.

How relieved she'd been! How grateful that the threat had been only a device to bring her to Lisbon. And how stunned and awestruck when Heinrich calmly outlined the extraordinary plan that would take years to bring to pass, but when it did, would make the world a far better place. She listened, was convinced, and did everything he asked her to do. For amends *would* be made.

She had loved him again—during those brief few days in Lisbon—and in a rush of emotion had offered herself to him.

With tears in his eyes, he had refused. He was not worthy, he said.

It was the consummate deception! The ultimate irony!

For now, at this moment, the very threat that brought her to Lisbon thirty years ago was the threat that brought her here again. Noel Holcroft would be destroyed; he would become Noel Clausen, son of Heinrich, instrument of the new Reich.

A man had come to her in the middle of the night in Bedford Hills. A man who had gained entrance by invoking the name "Manfredi" behind the closed door; she had admitted him thinking perhaps her son had sent him. He had said he was a Jew from a place called Har Sha'-alav, and that he was going to kill her. And then he would kill her son. There'd be no specter of Wolfsschanze —the *false* Wolfsschanze—spreading from Zurich out of Geneva.

Althene had been furious. Did the man know to whom he was speaking? What she had *done?* What she *stood for?*

The man knew only about Geneva and Zurich . . . and Lisbon thirty years ago. It was all he had to know, to know what she stood for, and that stance was an abomination to him and all men like him throughout the world.

Althene had seen the pain and the anger in the dark eyes that held her at bay as surely as if a weapon had been leveled at her. In desperation, she had demanded that he tell her what he thought he knew.

He had told her that extraordinary sums were to be funneled to committees and causes throughout all nations. To men and women who had been waiting for thirty years for the signal.

There would be killing and disruption and conflagrations in the streets; governments would be bewildered, their agencies crippled. The cries for stability and order would be heard across the lands. Strong men and women with massive sums at their disposal would then assert themselves. Within months control would be theirs.

They were everywhere. In all countries, awaiting only the signal from Geneva.

Who were they?

The *Sonnenkinder*. The children of fanatics, sent out of Germany more than thirty years ago by plane and ship and submarine. Sent out by men who knew their cause was lost—but believed that cause could live again.

They were everywhere. They could not be fought by ordinary men in ordinary ways through ordinary channels of authority. In too many instances the *Sonnenkinder* controlled those channels. But the Jews of Har Sha'alav were not ordinary men; nor did they fight in ordinary ways. They understood that to stop the false Wolfsschanze, they had to fight secretly, violently, never allowing the *Sonnenkinder* to know where they were—or where they would strike next. And the first order of business was to stop the massive infusion of funds.

Expose them now!

Who? Where? What are their identities? How will proof be furnished? Who can say this general or that admiral, this chief of police or that corporation president, this justice or that senator, Congressman, or governor is a Sonnenkind? Men run for office espousing clichés wrapped in code words, appealing to hatreds, and still they are not suspect. Instead, crowds cheer them and wave flags and put emblems in their lapels.

They are everywhere. The Nazi is among us and we don't see him. He is cloaked in respectability and a pressed suit of clothes.

The Jew of Har Sha'alav had spoken passionately. "Even you, old woman. You and your son, instruments of the new Reich. Even you do not know who they are."

I know nothing. I swear on my life I know nothing. I'm not what you think I am. Kill me. For God's sake, kill me. Now! Take your vengeance out on me. You deserve that and so do I if what you say is true. But I implore you, reach my son. Take him. Explain to him. Stop him! Don't kill him; don't brand him. He's not what you think he is. Give him his life. Take mine, but give him his!

The Jew of Har Sha'alav had spoken. "Richard Holcroft was killed. It was no accident."

She had nearly collapsed, but she would not allow herself to fall. She could not permit the momentary oblivion that would have been so welcome.

Oh, my God. . . .

"Wolfsschanze killed him. The false Wolfsschanze. As surely as if they had marched him into a chamber at Auschwitz."

What is Wolfsschanze? Why do you call it false?

"Learn for yourself. We'll talk again. If you've lied, we'll kill you. Your son will live—for as long as the world lets him—but he will live with a swastika across his face."

Reach him. Tell him.

The man from Har Sha'alav left. Althene sat in a chair by the window, staring out at the snow-covered grounds throughout the night. Her beloved Richard, the husband who had given her and her son their lives again. . . . What had she done?

But she knew what to do now.

The plane touched ground, the impact pushing Althene's reveries out of her mind, bringing her back to the moment at hand. To Lisbon.

She stood at the railing of the ferry, the waters of the Tagus River slapping against the hull as the old ship made its way across the bay. In her left hand was a lace handkerchief, fluttering in the wind.

She thought she saw him but, as instructed, made no move until he approached her. She had never seen him before, of course, but that was not important. He was an old man in rumpled clothes, with heavy gray sideburns that met the stubble of a white beard. His eyes searched the passengers as if he were afraid one of them might yell for the police. He was the man; he stood behind her.

"The river looks cold today," he said.

The lace handkerchief flew away in the wind. "Oh, dear, I've lost it." Althene watched it plummet into the water.

"You've found it," said the man.

"Thank you."

"Please do not look at me. Look at the skyline across the lagoon."

"Very well."

"You spread money too generously, senhora," the man said.

"I'm in a great hurry."

"You bring up names so long in the past there are no faces. Requests that have not been made in years."

"I can't believe times have changed that much."

"Oh, but they have, senhora. Men and women still travel secretly, but not with such simple devices as doctored passports. It's the age of the computer. False papers are not what they once were. We go back to the war. To the escape routes."

"I have to get to Geneva as quickly as possible. No one must know I'm there."

"You'll get to Geneva, senhora, and only those you inform will know you're there. But it will not be as quickly as you wish; it will not be a matter of a single flight on an airline."

"How long?"

"Two or three days. Otherwise there are no guarantees. You'll be picked up, either by the authorities or by those you care to avoid."

"How do I get there?"

"Across borders that are unpatrolled, or where the guards can be bribed. The northern route. Sierra de Gata, across to Zaragoza, on the eastern Pyrénées. From there to Montpellier and Avignon. At Avignon a small plane will take you to Grenoble, another to Chambéry and to Genève. It will cost."

"I can pay. When do we start?"

"Tonight."

36

The blond man signed the Hôtel d'Accord registration card and handed it to the desk clerk.

"Thank you, Mr. Tennyson. You'll be staying fourteen days?"

"Perhaps longer, certainly no less. I appreciate your making a suite available."

The clerk smiled. "We received a call from your friend, the first deputy of canton Genève. We assured him we would do everything to make your stay pleasant."

"I'll inform him of my complete satisfaction."

"You're most kind."

"Incidentally, I'm expecting to meet an old friend here during the next few days. A Mrs. Holcroft. Could you tell me when she's expected?"

The clerk took up a ledger and thumbed through the pages. "Did you say the name was Holcroft?"

"Yes. Althene Holcroft. An American. You might also have a reservation for her son, Mr. N. Holcroft."

"I'm afraid we have no reservations in that name, sir. And I know there's no one named Holcroft presently a guest."

The muscles of the blond man's jaw tensed. "Surely an error has been made. My information is accurate. She's expected at this hotel. Perhaps not this evening, but certainly tomorrow or the day after. Please check again. Is there a confidential listing?"

"No, sir."

"If there were, I'm quite certain my friend, the first deputy, would ask you to let me see it."

"If there were, that wouldn't be necessary, Mr. Tennyson. We understood fully that we are to cooperate with you in all requests."

"Perhaps she's traveling incognito. She's been known to be eccentric that way."

The clerk turned the ledger around. "Please, look for yourself, sir. It's possible you'll recognize a name."

Tennyson did not. It was infuriating. "This is the complete list?" he asked again.

"Yes, sir. We are a small and, if I may say, rather exclusive hotel. Most of our guests have been here previously. I'm familiar with nearly every one of those names."

"Which ones aren't you familiar with?" pressed the blond man.

The clerk placed his finger on two. "These are the only names I don't know," he said. "The gentlemen from Germany, two brothers named Kessler, and a Sir William Ellis, from London. The last was made only hours ago."

Tennyson looked pointedly at the desk clerk. "I'm going to my rooms, but I need to ask you for an example of that cooperation the first deputy spoke of. It's most urgent that I find out where Mrs. Holcroft is staying in Geneva. I'd appreciate your calling the various hotels, but under no circumstances should my name be mentioned." He took out a one-hundred-franc note. "Locate her for me," he said.

By midnight Noel reached Châtillon-sur-Seine, where he made the phone call to an astonished Ellis in London.

"You'll do *what?*" Ellis said.

"You heard me, Willie. I'll pay you five hundred dollars and your expenses for one, maybe two days in Geneva. All I want you to do is take my mother back to London."

"I'm a dreadful nanny. And from what you've told me about your mother, she's the last person in the world who needs a traveling companion."

"She does now. Someone was following her. I'll tell you about it when I see you in Geneva. How about it, Willie? Will you do it?"

"Of course. But stuff your five hundred. I'm sure your mother and I will have far more in common than we ever did. You may, however, pick up the tabs. I travel well, as you know."

"While we're on the subject, travel with a little cool, will you, please? I want you to call the Hôtel d'Accord in Geneva and make a reservation for late this morning. The first plane should get you there by nine-thirty."

"I'll be on my best behavior, befitting Louis Vuitton luggage. Perhaps a minor title. . . ."

"Willie!"

"I know the Swiss better than you. They adore titles; they reek of money, and money's their mistress."

"I'll phone you around ten, ten-thirty. I want to use your room until I know what's going on."

"That's extra," said Willie Ellis. "See you in Geneva."

Holcroft had decided to call on Willie because there was no one else he could think of who would not ask questions. Ellis was not the outrageous fool he pretended to be. Althene could do far worse for an escort out of Switzerland.

And she had to get out. The covenant's enemy had killed her husband; it would kill her, too. Because Geneva was where it was going to happen. In two or three days a meeting would take place, and papers would be signed, and money would be transferred to Zurich. The covenant's enemy would try everything to abort those negotiations. His mother could not stay in Geneva. There would be violence in Geneva; he could feel it.

He drove south to Dijon, arriving well after midnight. The small city was asleep, and as he passed through the dark streets, he knew he needed sleep, too; tomorrow he had to be alert. More alert than he had ever been in his life. He continued driving until he was back in the countryside and stopped the rented car on the side of a road. He smoked a cigarette, then crushed it out and put his feet on the seat, his head against the window, cushioned by his raincoat.

In a few hours he'd be at the border, crossing into Switzerland with the first wave of morning traffic. Once in Switzerland . . . He couldn't think anymore. The mist was closing in on him; his breathing was low and heavy. And then the face appeared, strong, angular, so unfamiliar yet so recognizable to him now.

It was the face of Heinrich Clausen, and he was calling to him, telling him to hurry. The agony would be over soon; amends would be made.

He slept.

Erich Kessler watched as his younger brother, Hans, showed the airline security officer his medical bag. Since the Olympics of '72, when the Palestinians were pre-

sumed to have flown into Munich with dismantled rifles
and submachine guns, the airport's security measures had
tripled.

It was a wasted effort, mused Erich. The Palestinians'
weapons had been brought to Munich by Wolfsschanze
—*their* Wolfsschanze.

Hans laughed with the airline official, sharing a joke.
But, thought Erich, there would be no such jokes in
Geneva, for there would be no inspection by the airlines or by customs or by anyone else. The first deputy of
canton Genève would see to it. One of Munich's most highly regarded doctors, a specialist in internal medicine, was
arriving as his guest.

Hans was all that and more, thought Erich, as his
brother approached him at the gate. Hans was a medium-
sized bull with enormous charm. A superb soccer player
who captained his district team and later ministered to
the opponents he had injured.

It was odd, thought Erich, but Hans was far better
equipped than he to be the elder son. Save for the accident of time, it would have been Hans who worked with
Johann von Tiebolt, and Erich, the quiet scholar, would
have been the subordinate. Once, in a moment of self-
doubt, he had said as much to Johann.

Von Tiebolt would not hear of it. A pure intellectual
was demanded. A man who lived a bloodless life—someone never swayed by reasons of the heart, by intemper-
ance. Had that not been proved by those infrequent but
vital moments when he—the quiet scholar—had stood up
to the Tinamou and stated his reservations? Reservations
that resulted in a change of strategy?

Yes, it was true, but it was not the essential truth.
That truth was something Johann did not care to face:
Hans was nearly Von Tiebolt's equal. If they clashed,
Johann might die.

That was the opinion of the quiet, bloodless intellectual.

"Everything proceeds," said Hans, as they walked
through the gate to the plane. "The American is as
good as dead, and no laboratory will trace the cause."

Helden got off the train at Neuchâtel. She stood on
the platform, adjusting her eyes to the shafts of sunlight
that shot down from the roof of the railroad station.

She knew she should mingle with the crowds that scrambled off the train, but for a moment she had to stand still and breathe the air. She had spent the past three hours in the darkness of a freight car, crouched behind crates of machinery. A door had been opened electronically for precisely sixty seconds at Besançon, and she had gone inside. At exactly five minutes to noon the door was opened again; she had reached Neuchâtel unseen. Her legs ached and her head pounded, but she made it. It had cost a great deal of money.

The air filled her lungs. She picked up her suitcase and started for the doors of the Neuchâtel station. The village of Près-du-Lac was on the west side of the lake, no more than twenty miles south. She found a taxi driver willing to make the trip.

The ride was jarring and filled with turns, but it was like a calm, floating glide for her. She looked out the window at the rolling hills and the blue waters of the lake. The rich scenery had the effect of suspending everything. It gave her the precious moments she needed to try to understand. What had Herr Oberst meant when he wrote that he had arranged for her to be near him because he had believed she was "an arm of an enemy"? An enemy he had "waited thirty years to confront." What enemy was that? And why had he chosen her?

What had she done? Or not done? Was it again the terrible dilemma? Damned for what she was and damned for what she wasn't? When in God's name would it *stop?*

Herr Oberst knew he was going to die. He had prepared her for his death as surely as if he had announced it, making sure she had the money to buy secret passage to Switzerland, to a man named Werner Gerhardt in Neuchâtel. Who was he? What was he to Klaus Falkenheim that he was to be contacted only upon the latter's death?

The coin of Wolfsschanze has two sides.

The taxi driver interrupted her thoughts. "The inn's down by the shoreline," he said. "It's not much of a hotel."

"It will do, I'm sure."

The room overlooked the waters of Lake Neuchâtel. It was so peaceful that Helden was tempted to sit at the window and do nothing but think about Noel, because when she thought about him, she felt . . . comfortable.

But there was a Werner Gerhardt to find. The telephone directory of Près-du-Lac had no such listing; God knew when it was last updated. But it was not a large village; she would begin casually with the concierge. Perhaps the name was familiar to him.

It was, but not in a way that gave her any confidence.

"Mad Gerhardt?" said the obese man, sitting in a wicker chair behind the counter. "You bring him greetings from old friends? You should bring him instead a potion to unscramble his doddering brains. He won't understand a thing you say."

"I didn't know," replied Helden, overwhelmed by a feeling of despair.

"See for yourself. It is midafternoon and the day is cool, but the sun is out. He'll no doubt be in the square, singing his little songs and feeding the pigeons. They soil his clothes and he doesn't notice."

She saw him sitting on the stone ledge of the circular fountain in the village square. He was oblivious of the passersby who intermittently glanced down at him, more often in revulsion than in tolerance. His clothes were frayed, the tattered overcoat soiled with droppings, as the concierge had predicted. He was as old and as sickly as Herr Oberst, but much shorter and puffier in face and body. His skin was pallid and drawn, marred by spider veins, and he wore thick steel-rimmed glasses that moved from side to side in rhythm with his trembling head. His hands shook as he reached into a paper bag, taking out bread crumbs and scattering them, attracting scores of pigeons that cooed in counterpoint to the high-pitched, singsong words that came from the old man's lips.

Helden felt sick. He was only a remnant of a man. He was beyond senility; no other state could produce what she saw before her on the fountain's edge.

The coin of Wolfsschanze has two sides. The time is near for the catastrophe to begin. . . . It seemed pointless to repeat the words. Still, she'd come this far, knowing only that a great man had been butchered because his warning was real.

She approached the old man and sat beside him, aware that several people in the square looked at her as if she, too, were feebleminded. She spoke quietly, in German.

"Herr Gerhardt? I've traveled a long way to see you."

"Such a pretty lady . . . a pretty, pretty lady."

"I come from Herr Falkenheim. Do you remember him?"

"A falcon's home? Falcons don't like my pigeons. They hurt my pigeons. My friends and I don't like them, do we, sweet feathers?" Gerhardt bent over and pursed his lips, kissing the air above the rapacious birds on the ground.

"You'd like this man, if you remembered him," said Helden.

"How can I like what I don't know? Would *you* like some bread? You can eat it, if you wish, but my friends might be hurt." The old man sat up with difficulty and dropped crumbs at Helden's feet.

" 'The coin of Wolfsschanze has two sides,' " whispered Helden.

And then she heard the words. There was no break in the rhythm; the quiet, high-pitched singsong was the same, but there was meaning now. "He's dead, isn't he? . . . Don't answer me; just nod your head or shake it. You're talking to a foolish old man who makes very little sense. Remember that."

Helden was too stunned to move. And by her immobility, she gave the old man his answer. He continued in his singsong cadence. "Klaus is dead. So, finally, they found him and killed him."

"It was the ODESSA," she said. "The ODESSA killed him. There were swastikas everywhere."

"Wolfsschanze wanted us to believe that." Gerhardt threw crumbs in the air; the pigeons fought among themselves. "Here, sweet feathers! It's teatime for you." He turned to Helden, his eyes distant. "The ODESSA, as always, is the scapegoat. Such an obvious one."

"You say Wolfsschanze," whispered Helden. "A letter was given to a man named Holcroft, threatening him. It was written thirty years ago, signed by men who called themselves the survivors of Wolfsschanze."

For an instant, Gerhardt's trembling stopped. "There were no survivors of Wolfsschanze, save one! Klaus Falkenheim. Others were there, and they lived, but they were not the eagles; they were filth. And now they think their time has come."

"I don't understand."

"I'll explain it to you, but not here. After dark, come to my house on the lake. South on the waterfront road, precisely three kilometers beyond the fork, is a path. . . ." He gave her the directions as though they were words written to accompany a childish tune. When he had finished, he stood up painfully, tossing the last crumbs to the birds. "I don't think you'll be followed," he said with a senile smile, "but make sure of it. We have work to do, and it must be done quickly. . . . Here, my sweet feathers! The last of your meal, my fluttering ones."

37

A small single-engine plane circled in the night sky above the flat pasture in Chambéry. Its pilot waited for the dual line of flares to be ignited: his signal to land. On the ground was another aircraft, a seaplane with wheels encased in its pontoons, prepared for departure. It would be airborne minutes after the first plane came to the end of the primitive runway, and would carry its valuable cargo north along the eastern leg of the Rhone River, crossing the Swiss border at Versoix, and landing on Lake Geneva, twelve miles north of the city. The cargo had no name, but that did not matter to the pilots. She had paid as well as the highest-priced narcotics courier.

Only once had she shown any emotion, and that was four minutes out of Avignon, toward Saint-Vallier, when the small plane had run into an unexpected and dangerous hailstorm.

"The weather may be too much for this light aircraft," the pilot said. "It would be wiser to turn back."

"Fly above it."

"We haven't the power, and we have no idea how extensive the front is."

"Then go through it. I'm paying for a schedule as well as transportation. I must get to Geneva tonight."

"If we're forced down on the river, we could be picked up by the patrols. We have no flight registration."

"If we're forced down on the river, I'll buy the patrols. They were bought at the border in Port-Bou; they can be bought again. Keep going."

"And if we crash, madame?"

"Don't."

Below them in the darkness, the Chambéry flares were ignited successively, one row at a time. The pilot dipped his wing to the left and circled downward for his final approach. Seconds later they touched ground.

"You're good," said the valuable cargo, reaching for the buckle of her seat belt. "Is my next pilot your equal?"

"As good, madame, and with an advantage I don't have. He knows the radar points within a tenth of an air mile in the darkness. One pays for such expertness."

"Gladly," replied Althene.

The seaplane lifted off against the night wind at exactly ten-fifty-seven. The flight across the border at Versoix would be made at very low altitude and would take very little time, no more than twenty minutes to a half hour. It was the specialist's leg of the journey, and the specialist in the cockpit was a stocky man with a red beard and thinning red hair. He chewed a half-smoked cigar and spoke English in the harsh accent associated with Alsace-Lorraine. He said nothing for the first few minutes of the flight, but when he spoke, Althene was stunned.

"I don't know what the merchandise is that you carry, madame, but there is an alert for your whereabouts throughout Europe."

"*What?* Who put out this alert, and how would you know? My name hasn't been mentioned; I was guaranteed that!"

"An all-Europe bulletin circulated by Interpol is most descriptive. It's rare that the international police look for a woman of—shall we say—your age and appearance. I presume your name is Holcroft."

"Presume nothing." Althene gripped her seat belt, trying to control her reaction. She did not know why it startled her—the man of Har Sha'alav had said they were everywhere—but the fact that this Wolfsschanze had sufficient influence with Interpol to use its apparatus was unnerving. She had to elude not only the Nazis of Wolfsschanze but also the network of legitimate law enforcement. It was a well-executed trap; her crimes were undeniable: traveling under a false passport, and then with none. And she could give no explanation for those crimes. To do so would link her son—the son of Heinrich Clausen—to a conspiracy so massive he'd be destroyed. That extremity had to be faced; her son might have to be sacrificed. But the irony was found in the very real possibility that Wolfsschanze itself had reached deep within the legitimate authorities. . . . *They were everywhere.*

Once taken, Wolfsschanze would kill her before she could say what she knew.

Death was acceptable; stilling her voice was not. She turned to the bearded pilot. "How do you know about this bulletin?"

The man shrugged. "How do I know about the radar vectors? You pay me; I pay others. There's no such thing as a clear profit these days."

"Does the bulletin say why this ... old woman ... is wanted?"

"It's a strange alert, madame. It states clearly that she is traveling with false papers, but she is not to be picked up. Her whereabouts are to be reported to Interpol-Paris, where they will be relayed to New York."

"New York?"

"That's where the request originated. The police in New York, a detective-lieutenant named Miles."

"Miles?" Althene frowned. "I've never heard of him."

"Perhaps this woman has," said the pilot, shifting the cigar in his mouth.

Althene closed her eyes. "How would you like to make a very clear profit?"

"I'm no communist; the word doesn't offend me. How?"

"Hide me in Geneva. Help me reach someone."

The pilot checked his panel, then banked to the right. "It will cost you."

"I'll pay," she said.

Johann von Tiebolt paced the hotel suite, a graceful, angry animal, consumed. His audience was composed of the brothers Kessler; the first deputy of canton Genève had left minutes ago. The three were alone; the tension was apparent.

"She's somewhere in Geneva," said Von Tiebolt. "She *has* to be."

"Obviously under an assumed name," added Hans Kessler, his medical bag at his feet. "We'll find her. It's merely a question of fanning men out, after giving them a description. Our deputy has assured us it's no problem."

Von Tiebolt stopped his pacing. "No problem? I trust you and he have examined this 'no problem.' According to our deputy, the Geneva police report an Interpol bulletin on her. Quite simply, that means she's traveled a minimum of four thousand miles without being found. Four thousand miles through banks of computers, on aircraft crossing borders and landing with manifests, through at least two immigration points. And there's nothing. Don't fool yourself, Hans. She's better than we thought she was."

"Tomorrow's Friday," said Erich. "Holcroft is due tomorrow, and he'll get in touch with us. When we have him, we have her."

"He said he was staying at the d'Accord, but he has changed his mind. There is no reservation, and Mr. Fresca has checked out of the George Cinq." Von Tiebolt stood by the window. "I don't like it. Something's wrong."

Hans reached for his drink. "I think you're overlooking the obvious."

"What?"

"By Holcroft's lights, a great deal is wrong. He thinks people are after him; he'll be cautious, and he'll travel cautiously. I'd be surprised if he did make a reservation in his own name."

"I assumed the name would be Fresca, or a derivation I'd recognize," said Von Tiebolt, dismissing the younger Kessler's observation. "There's nothing like it in any hotel in Geneva."

"Is there a Tennyson," asked Erich softly, "or anything like *it?*"

"Helden?" Johann turned.

"Helden." The older Kessler nodded. "She was with him in Paris. It's to be assumed she's helping him; you even suggested it."

Von Tiebolt stood motionless. "Helden and her filthy, wandering outcasts are preoccupied at the moment. They're scouring the ODESSA for the killers of Herr Oberst."

"*Falkenheim?*" Hans sat forward. "Falkenheim's *dead?*"

"Falkenheim was the leader of the Nachrichtendienst—the last functioning member, to be precise. With his death, Wolfsschanze is unopposed. His army of Jews will be headless; what little they know, buried with *their* leaders."

"Jews? With Nachrichtendienst?" Erich was exasperated. "What in God's name are you *talking* about?"

"A strike has been called on the kibbutz Har Sha'-

alav; Rache terrorists will be held responsible. I'm sure the name 'Har Sha'alav' has meaning for you. At the last, the Nachrichtendienst turned to the Jews of Har Sha'-alav. Garbage to garbage."

"I should like a more specific explanation!" said Erich.

"Later. We must concentrate on the Holcrofts. We must . . ." Von Tiebolt stopped, a thought striking him. "Priorities. Always look to priorities," he added, as if talking to himself. "And the first priority is the document at La Grande Banque de Genève, which means the son takes precedence. Find *him;* isolate *him;* keep him in absolute quarantine. For our purposes, it need only be for thirty-odd hours."

"I don't follow you," interrupted Hans. "What happens in thirty hours?"

"The three of us will have met with the bank's directors," Erich said. "Everything will have been signed, executed in the presence of the Grande Banque's attorney, all the laws of Switzerland observed. The money will be released to Zurich, and we assume control Monday morning."

"But thirty hours from Friday morning is—"

"Saturday noon," completed Von Tiebolt. "We meet with the directors Saturday morning at nine o'clock. There was never any question of our acceptance—except in Holcroft's mind. Manfredi took care of that months ago. We're not only acceptable; we're damn near holy men. My letter from MI Five is merely a final crown. By Saturday noon it will have been accomplished."

"They're so anxious to lose seven hundred and eighty million dollars they will open the bank on a Saturday?"

The blond man smiled. "I made the request in Holcroft's name, for reasons of speed and confidentiality. The directors didn't object—they look for crumbs— and neither will Holcroft when we tell him. He has his own reasons for wanting everything over with. He's stretched to the limits of his capacities." Von Tiebolt glanced at Erich, his smile broader. "He looks upon us both as friends, as pillars of strength, as two men he desperately needs. The programming has exceeded our hopes."

Kessler nodded. "By noon Saturday he'll have signed the final condition."

"What final condition?" asked Hans, alarmed. "What does that mean? What does he sign?"

"We each will have signed it," answered Von Tiebolt, pausing for emphasis. "It's a *requirement* of Swiss law for the release of such accounts. We've met, and fully understand our responsibilities; we've come to know each other and to trust each other. Therefore, in the event one of us predeceases the others, each assigns all rights and privileges to his coinheritors. Except, of course, the stipend of two million, which is to be distributed to the individual's heirs. That two million—legally assigned and prohibited from being given to the other executors—removes any motive for double-cross."

The younger Kessler whistled softly. "Utterly brilliant. So this final condition—this death clause wherein you each assign to the others your responsibility—never had to be made part of the document . . . because it's the law. If it had been included, Holcroft might have been suspicious from the beginning." The doctor shook his head in respect, his eyes bright. "But it never was because it's the *law*."

"Precisely. And every legality must be observed. A month—six weeks—from now, it'll be irrelevant, but until we've made substantive progress, there can be no alarms."

"I understand that," said Hans. "But actually, by Saturday noon, Holcroft's expendable, isn't he?"

Erich held up his hand. "Best put him under your drugs for a period of time, available for display, as it were. A functioning mental cripple . . . until a great portion of the funds is dispersed. By then it won't matter; the world will be too preoccupied to care about an accident in Zurich. Right now we must do as Johann says. We must find Holcroft before his mother does."

"And under one pretext or another," added Von Tiebolt, "keep him isolated until our meeting the day after tomorrow. She will undoubtedly try to reach him, and then we will know where she is. We have men in Geneva who can take care of the rest." He hesitated. "As always, Hans, your brother addresses himself to what is optimum. But the answer to your question is yes. By noon Saturday, Holcroft is expendable. When I think about it, I'm not sure the additional weeks are even desirable."

"You annoy me again," said the scholar. "I defer

to your exotic mind in many things, but a deviation in strategy at this juncture is hardly welcome. Holcroft *must* be available. In your words, until 'substantive progress' is made, there can be no alarms."

"I don't think there will be," replied Von Tiebolt. "The change I'm implementing would be approved by our fathers. I've moved up the timetable."

"You've *what?*"

"When I used the word 'alarms,' I referred to legalities, not Holcroft. Legalities are constant; life spans, never."

"What timetable? Why?"

"Second question first, and you may answer it." Johann stood in front of the older Kessler's chair. "What was the single most effective weapon of war the Fatherland employed? What strategy would have brought England to her knees had there been no hesitation? What were the lightning bolts that shook the world?"

"Blitzkrieg," said the doctor, answering for his brother.

"Yes. Swift, sharp onslaughts, out of nowhere. Men and weapons and machinery, sweeping across borders with extraordinary speed, leaving in their wake confusion and devastation. Whole peoples divided, unable to reform ranks, incapable of making decisions. The *Blitzkrieg,* Erich. We must adapt it now; we can't hesitate."

"Abstractions, Johann! Give me specifics!"

"Very well. Specific one: John Tennyson has written an article that will be picked up by the wire services and flashed everywhere tomorrow. The Tinamou kept records, and there is talk that they've been found. Names of those powerful men who've hired him, dates, sources of payments. It will have the effect of massive electric shocks throughout the world's power centers. Specific two: Saturday, the Geneva document is executed, the funds transferred to Zurich. Sunday, we move to our headquarters there; they've been prepared; all communications are functioning. If Holcroft is with us, Hans has him narcotized; if not, he's dead. Specific three: Monday, the assets are deemed liquid and in our control. Using the Greenwich time zones, we begin cabling funds to our people, concentrating on the primary targets. We start right here in Geneva. Then to Berlin, Paris, Madrid, Lisbon, London, Washington, New York, Chicago, Houston, Los Angeles, and San Francisco. By five, Zurich time, we move into the Pacific. Honolulu, the Marshalls, and the Gilberts. By eight we go into New Zealand, Auckland, and Wellington. By ten, it's Australia—Brisbane, Sydney, Adelaide—then to Perth and across to Singapore, into the Far East. The first phase stops in New Delhi; on paper we're financed over three quarters of the globe. Specific four: At the end of another twenty-four hours—Tuesday—we receive confirmations that the funds have been received and converted into cash, ready for use. Specific five: I will make twenty-three telephone calls from Zurich. They will be made to twenty-three men in various capitals who have employed the services of the Tinamou. They will be told that certain demands will be made of them during the next few weeks; they are expected to comply. Specific six: On Wednesday, it begins. The first killing will be symbolic. The Chancellor in Berlin, the leader of the Bundestag. We sweep westward in a *Blitzkrieg*." Von Tiebolt paused for a moment. "On Wednesday, Code Wolfsschanze is activated."

The telephone rang; at first no one seemed to hear it. Then Von Tiebolt answered it.

"Yes?"

He stared at the wall as he listened in silence. Finally he spoke. "Use the words I gave you," he said softly. "Kill them." He hung up.

"What is it?" asked the doctor.

Von Tiebolt, his hand still on the telephone, replied in a monotone. "It was only a guess—a possibility—but I sent a man to Neuchâtel. To observe someone. And that someone met with another. It's no matter; they will soon be dead. My beautiful sister and a traitor named Werner Gerhardt."

It did not make sense, thought Holcroft, as he listened to Willie Ellis's words over the phone. He had reached Willie at the d'Accord from a booth in Geneva's crowded Place Neuve, fully expecting the designer to have made contact with Althene by now. He hadn't; she wasn't there. But his mother had said the Hôtel d'Accord. She would meet him at the *Hôtel d'Accord*.

"Did you describe her? An American, around seventy, tall for a woman?"

"Naturally. Everything you mentioned a half hour

ago. There's no one here by the name of Holcroft, or any woman fitting the description. There are no Americans at all."

"It's crazy." Noel tried to think. Tennyson and the Kesslers weren't due until evening; he had no one to turn to. Was his mother doing the same thing he was doing? Trying to reach *him* from outside the hotel, expecting *he'd* be there? "Willie, call up the front desk and say you just heard from me. Use my name. Tell them I asked you if there were any messages for me."

"I don't think you understand the rules in Geneva," Willie said. "Messages between two people aren't given to unknown third parties, and the d'Accord is no exception. Frankly, when I asked about your mother, I was given some very odd looks. Despite my Louis Vuitton, the little bastard couldn't wait for me to stop talking."

"Try it anyway."

"There's a better way. I think if I—" Willie stopped; from somewhere in the distance there was a tapping. "Just a minute; there's someone at the door. I'll get rid of whoever it is and be right back."

Noel could hear the sound of a door opening. There were voices, indistinct, questioning; a brief exchange took place, and then there were footsteps. Holcroft waited for Willie to get back on the line.

There was the sound of a cough, but more than a cough. What was it? The start of a cry? Was it the start of a *cry?*

"Willie?"

Silence. Then footsteps again.

"Willie?" Suddenly, Noel felt cold. And pain came back to his stomach as he remembered the words. *The same words!*

. . . *There's someone at the door. I'll get rid of whoever it is and be right back. . . .*

Another Englishman. Four thousand miles away in New York. And a match flaring up in the window across the courtyard.

Peter Baldwin.

"Willie! Willie, where *are* you?! *Willie!"*

There was a click. The line went dead.

Oh, Christ! What had he *done?* Willie!

Beads of sweat broke out on his forehead; his hands trembled.

He had to get to the d'Accord! He had to get there as fast as he could and find Willie, help Willie. Oh, Christ! He wished the hammering pain would get out of his eyes!

He ran out of the phone booth and down the street to his car. He started the engine, unsure for a moment where he was or where he was going. The d'Accord. Hôtel d'Accord! It was on the rue des Granges, near the Puits-Saint-Pierre; a street lined with enormous old houses—mansions. The d'Accord was the largest. On the hill . . . *what* hill? He had no idea how to get there!

He sped down to the corner; the traffic was stopped. He yelled through his window at a startled woman driving the car next to his.

"Please! The rue des Granges—which way?"

The woman refused to acknowledge his shouts; she pulled her eyes away and looked straight ahead.

"Please, someone's been hurt! I think hurt badly. Please, lady! I can't speak French very well. Or German, or . . . *please!*"

The woman turned back to him, studying him for a moment. Then she leaned over and rolled down the window.

"Rue des Granges?"

"Yes, please!"

She gave him rapid instructions. Five streets down, turn right toward the bottom of the hill, then left. . . .

The traffic started up. Perspiring, Noel tried to memorize every word, every number, every turn. He shouted his thanks and pressed the accelerator.

He would never know how he found the old street, but it was suddenly there. He drove up the steep incline toward the top and saw the flat gold lettering: HÔTEL D'ACCORD.

His hands shaking, he parked the car and got out. He had to lock it; twice he tried to insert the key but could not hold his hand steady enough. So he held his breath and pressed his fingers against the metal until they stopped trembling. He had to control himself now; he had to *think*. Above all, he had to be careful. He had seen the enemy before, and he had fought that enemy. He could do so again.

He looked up at the d'Accord's ornate entrance. Beyond the glass doors, he could see the doorman talking with someone in the lobby. He could not go through that entrance and into that lobby; if the enemy had trapped Willie Ellis, that enemy was waiting for him.

There was a narrow alley that sloped downward at the side of the building. On the stone wall was a sign: LIVRAISONS.

Somewhere in that alley was a delivery entrance. He pulled the collar of his raincoat up around his neck and walked across the pavement, putting his hands in his pockets, feeling the steel of the revolver in his right, the perforated cylinder of the silencer in his left. He thought briefly of the giver, of Helden. Where was she? What had happened?

Nothing is as it was for you. . . .

Nothing at all.

He reached the door as a tradesman in a white smock coat was leaving. He held up his hand and smiled at the man.

"Excuse me. Do you speak English?"

"But of course, monsieur. This is Geneva."

It was a harmless joke—that's all—but the foolish American with the broad smile would pay fifty francs for the cheap coat, twice its value new. The exchange was made swiftly; this was Geneva. Holcroft removed his raincoat and folded it over his left arm. He put on the smock and went inside.

Willie had reserved a suite on the third floor; its entrance was the last door in the corridor toward the street. Noel walked through a dark hallway that led to a darker staircase. At the landing, there was a cart against the wall, three small, unopened cases of hotel soap beneath one that was half empty. He removed the top carton, picked up the remaining three, and proceeded up the marble steps, hoping he looked even vaguely like someone who might belong there.

"*Jacques? C'est vous?*" The caller spoke from below, his voice pleasant.

Holcroft turned and shrugged.

"*Pardon. Je croyais que c'était Jacques qui travaille chez la fleuriste.*"

"*Non,*" said Noel quickly, continuing up the stairs.

He reached the third floor, put the cartons of soap on the staircase, and removed the smock. He put on his raincoat, felt the revolver, and opened the door slowly; there was no one in the corridor.

He walked to the last door on the right, listening for sounds; there were none. He remembered listening at another door in another hallway light-years away from this ivoried, ornamental corridor in which he now stood. In a place called Montereau. . . . There had been gunfire then. And death.

Oh, God, had anything happened to Willie? Willie, who had not refused him, who had been a friend when others could not be found. Holcroft took out the gun and reached for the knob. He stepped back as far as he could.

In one motion he twisted the knob and threw his full weight against the door, his shoulder a battering ram. The door sprang open unimpeded, crashing into the wall behind it; it had not been locked.

Noel crouched, the weapon leveled in front of him. There was no one in the room, but a window was open, the cold winter air billowing the curtains. He walked to it bewildered; why would a window be open in this weather?

Then he saw them: circles of blood on the sill. Someone had bled profusely. Outside the window was a fire escape. He could see streaks of red on the steps. Whoever had run down them had been severely wounded.

Willie?

"Willie? Willie, are you here?"

Silence.

Holcroft ran into the bedroom.

No one.

"Willie?"

He was about to turn around when he saw strange markings on the paneling of a closed door. The paneling was profuse with gold fluting and ornate fleurs-de-lis, pink and white and light blue. But what he saw was not part of the rococo design.

They were blurred handprints outlined in blood.

He raced to the door, kicking it in with such force that the paneling cracked and splintered.

What he saw was the horror of a lifetime. Arched over the rim of the empty bathtub was the mutilated body of Willie Ellis, soaked in blood. There were huge punctures in his chest and stomach, intestines protruding over his red-drenched shirt, his throat slashed so deeply that his head was barely attached to his neck, his eyes wide open, glaring upward in agony.

Noel collapsed, trying to swallow the air that would not fill his lungs.

And then he saw the word, scrawled in blood on the tiles above the mutilated corpse.

NACHRICHTENDIENST

38

Helden found the path three kilometers beyond the fork in the road leading out of Près-du-Lac. She had borrowed a flashlight from the concierge, and now she had angled the beam of light in front of her as she began to trek through the woods to Werner Gerhardt's house.

It was not so much a house, thought Helden as she reached the strange-looking structure, as a miniature stone fortress. It was very small—smaller than Herr Oberst's cottage—but from where she stood the walls appeared to be extremely thick. The beam of the flashlight caught bulging rocks that had been cemented together along the two sides she could see; and the roof, too, was heavy. The few windows were high off the ground and narrow. She had never seen a house like it before. It seemed to belong in a children's fairy tale, subject to magic incantations.

It answered a question provoked by the concierge's remarks when she had returned from the village square several hours ago.

"Did you find Mad Gerhardt? They say he was once a great diplomat before the marbles rattled in his head. It's rumored old friends still care for him, although none come to see him anymore. They cared once, though. They built him a strong cottage on the lake. No Christmas wind will ever knock it down."

No wind, no storm, no winter snows, could have any effect on this house. Someone had cared deeply.

She heard the sound of a door opening. It startled Helden, because there was no door at the side or rear walls. Then the beam of light caught the short figure of Werner Gerhardt; he stood on the edge of the lakeside porch and raised his hand.

How could the old man possibly have heard her?

"You've come, I see," said Gerhardt, no madness in

405

his voice. "Quickly now, these woods are cold. Get inside, in front of the fire. We'll have tea."

The room seemed larger than the outside structure would indicate. The heavy furniture was old but comfortable, a profusion of leather and wood. Helden sat on an ottoman, warmed by the fire and the tea. She had not realized how cold she'd been.

They had talked for a few minutes, Gerhardt answering the first question before she'd had a chance to ask it.

"I came here from Berlin five years ago, by way of München, where my cover was established. I was a 'victim' of ODESSA, a broken man living out his years in senility and solitude. I am a figure of ridicule; a doctor at the clinic keeps my records. His name is Litvak, should you ever need him. He's the only one who knows I'm perfectly sane."

"But why was your cover necessary?"

"You'll understand as we talk. Incidentally, you were surprised that I knew you were outside." Gerhardt smiled. "This primitive lakeside cottage is very sophisticated. No one approaches without my knowing it. A hum is heard." The old man's smile vanished. "Now, what happened to Klaus?"

She told him. Gerhardt was silent for a while, pain in his eyes.

"*Animals,*" he said. "They can't even execute a man with any semblance of decency; they must mutilate. May God *damn* them!"

"Who?"

"The false Wolfsschanze. The animals. Not the eagles."

"Eagles? I don't understand."

"The plot to kill Hitler in July of 'forty-four was a conspiracy of the generals. Military men—by and large, decent men—who came to see the horrors committed by the Führer and his madmen. It was not the Germany they cared to fight for. Their objective was to assassinate Hitler, sue for a just peace, and expose the killers and sadists who'd functioned in the name of the Reich. Rommel called these men 'the true eagles of Germany.' "

"The eagles. . . ." Helden repeated. " 'You won't stop the eagles . . .' "

"I beg your pardon?" asked the old man.

"Nothing. Go on, please."

"Of course, the generals failed, and a bloodbath followed. Two hundred and twelve officers, many only vaguely suspect, were tortured and put to death. Then, suddenly, Wolfsschanze became the excuse to still all dissent within the Reich. Thousands who had voiced even the most minor political or military criticisms were arrested on fabricated evidence and executed. The vast majority had never heard of a staff headquarters called Wolfsschanze, much less any attempt on Hitler's life. Rommel was ordered to kill himself, the penalty for refusal to carry out an additional five thousand *indiscriminate* executions. The worst fears of the generals were borne out: the maniacs were in total control of Germany. It was what they had hoped to stop at Wolfsschanze. *Their* Wolfsschanze: the true Wolfsschanze."

"*Their* . . . Wolfsschanze?" asked Helden. " 'The coin of Wolfsschanze has two sides.' "

"Yes," said Gerhardt. "There was another Wolfsschanze, another group of men who also wanted Hitler killed. But for an entirely different reason. These men thought he had failed. They saw his weaknesses, his diminished capacities. They wanted to supplant the madness that *was* with another madness, far more efficient. There were no appeals for peace in their plans, only the fullest prosecution of the war. Their strategies included tactics unheard of since the Mongol armies swept through Asia centuries ago. Whole peoples held as hostages, mass executions for the slightest infractions, a reign of abuse so terrible the world would seek a truce, if only in the name of humanity." Gerhardt paused; when he continued, his voice was filled with loathing. "This was the false Wolfsschanze, the Wolfsschanze that was never meant to be. They—the men of *that* Wolfsschanze—are committed still."

"Yet these same men were part of the conspiracy to kill Hitler," Helden said. "How did they escape?"

"By becoming the fiercest of Hitler's loyalists. They regrouped quickly, feigned revulsion at the treachery, and turned on the others. As always, zealousness and ferocity impressed the Führer; he was essentially a physical coward, you see. He put some of them in charge of the executions and delighted in their devotion."

Helden moved to the edge of the seat. "You say these men—this other Wolfsschanze—are still committed. Surely most of them are dead by now."

The old man sighed. "You really don't know, do you? Klaus said you didn't."

"You know who I am?" asked Helden.

"Of course. You yourself mailed the letters."

"I mailed a lot of letters for Herr Oberst. But none to Neuchâtel."

"Those that were meant for me, I received."

"He wrote you about me?"

"Often. He loved you very much." Gerhardt's smile was warm. It faded as he spoke. "You asked me how the men of the false Wolfsschanze could still be committed after so many years. You're right, of course. Most of them are dead. So it's not they; it's the children."

"The *children?*"

"Yes. They're everywhere—in every city, province, and country. In every profession, every political group. Their function is to apply pressure constantly, convincing people that their lives could be so much better if strong men protested weakness. Angry voices are being substituted for genuine remedies; rancor supplants reason. It's happening everywhere, and only a few of us know what it is: a massive preparation. The children have grown up."

"Where did they come from?"

"Now we come to the heart of the matter. It will answer other questions for you." The old man leaned forward. "It was called 'Operation Sonnenkinder,' and it took place in 1945. Thousands of children between the ages of six months and sixteen years were sent out of Germany. To all parts of the world. . . ."

As Gerhardt told the story, Helden felt ill, physically ill.

"A plan was devised," continued Gerhardt, "whereby millions upon millions of dollars would be available to the *Sonnenkinder* after a given period of time. The time was calculated by projections of the normal economic cycles; it was thirty years."

Helden's sharp intake of breath interrupted him, but only briefly.

"It was a plan conceived by three men. . . ."

A cry emerged from Helden's throat.

". . . These three men had access to funds beyond

calculation, and one of them was perhaps the most brilliant financial manipulator of our time. It was he and he alone who brought the international economic forces together that insured the rise of Adolf Hitler. And when his Reich failed him, he set about creating another."

"Heinrich Clausen. . . ." whispered Helden. "Oh, *God*, no! . . . Noel! Oh, God, Noel!"

"He was never more than a device, a conduit for money. He knows nothing."

"Then . . ." Helden's eyes grew wide; the pain in her temples sharpened.

"Yes," said Gerhardt, reaching for her hand. "A young boy was chosen, another of the sons. An extraordinary child, a fanatically devoted member of the Hitler Youth. Brilliant, beautiful. He was watched, developed, trained for his mission in life."

"Johann. . . . Oh, God in heaven, it's *Johann*."

"Yes. Johann von Tiebolt. It is he who expects to lead the *Sonnenkinder* into power all over the world."

The sound of an echoing drum inside her temples grew louder, the percussive beats jarring and thunderous. Images went out of focus; the room spun and darkness descended. Helden fell into a void.

She opened her eyes, not knowing how long she had been unconscious. Gerhardt had managed to prop her up against the ottoman and was holding a glass of brandy beneath her nostrils. She gripped the glass and swallowed, the alcohol spreading quickly, bringing her back to the terrible moment.

"Johann," she whispered, the name itself a cry of pain. "That's why Herr Oberst—"

"Yes," said the old man, anticipating her. "It's why Klaus had you brought to him. The rebellious Von Tiebolt daughter, born in Rio, estranged from her brother and sister. Was that estrangement real, or were you being used to infiltrate the ranks of wandering, disaffected German youth? We had to know."

"Used, then killed," added Helden, shuddering. "They tried to kill me in Montereau. Oh, God, my *brother*."

The old man stood up with difficulty. "I'm afraid you're wrong," he said. "It was a tragic afternoon, filled with errors. The two men who came after you were from us. Their instructions were clear: Learn everything there was to learn about Holcroft. He was still an unknown factor then. Was he part of Wolfsschanze—their Wolfsschanze? If an unknowing conduit, he was to live, and we would convince him to come with us. If part of Wolfsschanze, he was to be killed. If that was the case, you were to be taken away before you were harmed, before you were implicated. For reasons we don't know, our men decided to kill him."

Helden lowered her eyes. "Johann sent a man to follow us that afternoon. To find out who was so interested in Noel."

Gerhardt sat down. "So our people saw that man and thought it was a rendezvous with Von Tiebolt, with an emissary of the *Sonnenkinder.* For them it meant Holcroft *was* part of Wolfsschanze. They needed nothing else."

"It was my fault," said Helden. "When that man took my arm in the crowd, I was frightened. He told me I had to go with him. He spoke German. I thought he was ODESSA."

"He was the furthest thing from it. He was a Jew from a place called Har Sha'alav."

"A Jew?"

Gerhardt told her briefly of the strange kibbutz in the Negev desert. "They are our small army. A cable is sent; men are dispatched. It's as simple as that."

Orders must be relayed . . . to the courageous men who will stand at the final barricade. Helden understood Herr Oberst's words. "You'll send that cable now?"

"*You* will send it. A while ago, I mentioned a Dr. Litvak at the clinic. He keeps my medical records for any who may be curious. He's one of us; he has long-range-radio equipment and checks with me every day. It's too dangerous to have a telephone here. Go to him tonight. He knows the codes and will reach Har Sha'alav. A team must be sent to Geneva; you must tell them what to do. Johann, Kessler, even Noel Holcroft, if he's beyond pulling out, must be killed. Those funds must not be dispersed."

"I'll convince Noel."

"For your sake, I hope you can. It may not be as simple as you think. He's been manipulated brilliantly. He believes deeply, even to the point of vindicating a father he never knew."

"How did you learn?"

"From his mother. For years we believed she was part of Clausen's plan, and for years we waited. Then we confronted her and learned she was never part of it. She was the bridge to—as well as the source of—the perfect conduit. Who else but a Noel Clausen–Holcroft, whose origins had been obliterated from every record but his own mind, would accept the conditions of secrecy demanded by the Geneva document? A normal man would have asked for legal and financial advice. But Holcroft, believing in his covenant, kept everything to himself."

"But he had to be *convinced*," said Helden. "He's a strong man, a very moral man. How could they do it?"

"How is anyone convinced his cause is just?" asked the old man rhetorically. "By seeing that there are those who desperately wish to stop him. We've read the reports out of Rio. Holcroft's experience with Maurice Graff, the charges he registered with the embassy. It was all a charade; no one tried to kill him in Rio, but Graff wanted him to think so."

"He's ODESSA."

"Never. He's one of the leaders of the false Wolfs-schanze . . . the only Wolfsschanze now. I should say he was; he's dead."

"What?"

"Shot yesterday by a man who left a note claiming vengeance from Portuguese Jews. Your brother's work, of course. Graff was too old, too cantankerous. He'd served his purpose."

Helden placed the glass of brandy on the floor. The question had to be asked. "Herr Gerhardt, why haven't you ever exposed Geneva for what it was?"

The old man returned her inquisitive stare. "Because exposing Geneva would be only half the story. As soon as we did, we'd be killed; but that's inconsequential. It's the rest."

"The rest?"

"The second half. Who are the *Sonnenkinder*? What are their names? Where are they? A master list was made thirty years ago; your brother must have it. It's huge—hundreds of pages—and has to be hidden somewhere. Von Tiebolt would die in fire before revealing its whereabouts. But there *has* to be another list! A short one —a few pages, perhaps. It's either on his person or near him. The identities of all those receiving funds. These will be the trusted manipulators of Wolfsschanze. This is the list that can and must be found. You must tell the soldiers of Har Sha'alav to find it. Stop the money and find the list. It's our only hope."

"I'll tell them," said Helden. "They'll find it." She looked away, lost in another thought. "Wolfsschanze. Even the letter written to Noel Holcroft more than thirty years ago—pleading with him, threatening him—was part of it."

"They appealed and threatened in the name of eagles, but their commitment was to animals."

"He couldn't know that."

"No, he couldn't. The name 'Wolfsschanze' is awesome, a symbol of bravery. That was the only Wolfsschanze Holcroft could relate to. He had no knowledge of the other Wolfsschanze, the filth. No one did. Save one."

"Herr Oberst?"

"Falkenheim, yes."

"How did he escape?"

"By the most basic of coincidences. A confusion of identities." Gerhardt walked to the fireplace and prodded the logs with a poker. "Among the giants of Wolfsschanze was the commander of the Belgian sector, Alexander von Falkenhausen. Falken*hausen*, Falken*heim*. Klaus Falkenheim had left East Prussia for a meeting in Berlin. When the assassination attempt failed, Falkenhausen somehow managed to reach Falkenheim by radio to tell him of the disaster. He begged Klaus to stay away. He would be the 'falcon' who was caught. The other 'falcon' was loyal to Hitler; he would make that clear. Klaus objected, but understood. He had work to do. Someone had to survive."

"Where is Noel's mother?" Helden asked. "What has she learned?"

"She knows everything now. Let's hope she hasn't panicked. We lost her in Mexico; we think she's trying to reach her son in Geneva. She'll fail. The instant she's spotted, she's a dead woman."

"We've got to find her."

"Not at the expense of the other priorities," said the old man. "Remember, there is only one Wolfsschanze now. Crippling it is all that matters." Gerhardt put the poker down. "You'll see Dr. Litvak tonight. His house is near the clinic, above it, on a hill two kilometers north. The hill is quite steep; the radio functions well there. I'll give you—"

A sharp humming sound filled the room. It echoed off the walls so loudly that Helden felt the vibrations going through her and jumped to her feet. Gerhardt turned from the fireplace and stared up at a narrow window high in the left wall. He seemed to be studying the panes of glass that were too far above him to see through.

"There's a night mirror that picks up images in the black light," he said, watching intently. "It's a man. I recognize him, but I don't know him." He walked to the desk, took out a small pistol, and handed it to Helden.

"What should I do?" she asked.

"Hide it under your skirt."

"You don't know who it is?" Helden lifted her skirt and sat down in a chair facing the door, the weapon hidden.

"No. He arrived yesterday; I saw him in the square. He may be one of us; he may not. I don't know."

Helden could hear footsteps outside the door. They stopped; there was a moment of silence, then rapid knocking.

"Herr Gerhardt?"

The old man answered, his voice now high pitched and in the singsong cadence he had used in the square. "Good heavens, who is it? It's very late; I'm in the middle of my prayers."

"I bring you news from Har Sha'alav."

The old man exhaled in relief, and nodded to Helden. "He's one of us," he said, unlatching the bolt. "No one but us knows about Har Sha'alav."

The door opened. For the briefest instant Helden froze, then spun out of the chair and lunged for the floor. The figure in the doorway held a large-barreled gun in his hand; its explosion was thunderous. Gerhardt arched backward, blown off his feet, his body a contorted bloody mass, suspended in the air before it fell into the desk.

Helden lurched behind the leather armchair, reaching for the pistol under her skirt.

There was another gunshot as thunderous as the first. The leather back of the chair exploded out of its shell. *Another*, and she felt an icelike pain in her leg. Blood spread over her stocking.

She raised the pistol and squeezed the trigger repeatedly, aiming—and not aiming—at the huge figure in shadows by the door.

She heard the man scream. In panic, she crashed into the wall, a cornered insect, trapped, about to lose its insignificant life. Tears streamed down her face as she aimed again and pulled the trigger until the firing stopped, replaced by the sickening clicks of the empty gun. She screamed in terror; there were no bullets left. She hoped to God her death would come quickly.

She heard her screams—she *heard* them—as if she were floating in the sky, looking below at chaos and smoke.

There *was* smoke. Everywhere. It filled the room, the acrid fumes stinging her eyes, blinding her. She did not understand; nothing happened.

Then she heard faint, whispered words.

"My child. . . ."

It was Gerhardt! Sobbing, she pressed her hand against the wall and pushed herself away. Dragging her bloodied leg, she crawled toward the source of the whisper.

The smoke was beginning to clear. She could see the figure of the killer. He was lying on his back, small red circles in his throat and forehead. He was dead.

Gerhardt was dying. She crept to him and put her face on his face, her tears falling on his flesh.

"My child . . . get to Litvak. Cable Har Sha'alav. Stay away from Geneva."

"Stay *away?* . . ."

"You, child. They know you came to me. Wolfs-schanze has seen you. . . . You're all that's left. Nachricht—"

"What?"

"You are . . . Nachrichtendienst."

Gerhardt's head slipped away from her face. He was gone.

39

The red-bearded pilot walked rapidly down the rue des Granges toward the parked car. Inside, Althene saw him approaching. She was alarmed. Why hadn't the pilot brought her son with him? And why was he hurrying so?

The pilot climbed in behind the wheel, pausing for a moment to catch his breath.

"There's great confusion at the d'Accord, madame. A killing."

Althene gasped. *"Noel?* Is it my *son?"*

"No. An Englishman."

"Who was it?"

"A man named Ellis. A William Ellis."

"Dear God!" Althene gripped her purse. "Noel had a friend in London named Ellis. He talked about him frequently. I've got to reach my son!"

"Not in there, madame. Not if there's a connection between your son and the Englishman. The police are everywhere, and there's an alert out for you."

"Get to a telephone."

"I'll make the call. It may be the last thing I do for you, madame. I have no wish to be associated with killing; that's not part of any agreement between us."

They drove for nearly fifteen minutes before the pilot was satisfied no one had followed them.

"Why should anyone follow us?" Althene asked. "Nobody saw me; you didn't mention my name. Or Noel's."

"Not you, madame. Me. I don't make it a point to fraternize with the Geneva police. I have run into a few now and then, off and on. We don't get along very well."

They entered the lakefront district, the pilot scanning the streets for an out-of-the-way telephone. He found one, swerved the car to the curb, and dashed outside to the booth. Althene watched him make the call.

Then he returned, got behind the wheel more slowly than he had left it, and sat for a moment, scowling.

"For heaven's sake, what happened?"

"I don't like it," he said. "They expected a call from you."

"Of course. My son arranged it."

"But it was not you on the phone. It was me."

"What difference does it make? I had someone call for me. What did they say?"

"Not they. He. And what he said was far too specific. In this city, one is not that free with information. Specifics are exchanged when ears recognize voices, or when certain words are used that mean the caller has a right to know."

"What *was* the information," asked Althene, irritated.

"A rendezvous. As soon as possible. Ten kilometers north, on the road to Vésenaz. It's on the east side of the lake. He said your son would be there."

"Then we'll go."

" 'We,' madame?"

"I'd like to negotiate further with you."

She offered him five hundred American dollars. "You're crazy," he said.

"We have an agreement, then?"

"On the condition that until you and your son are together, you do exactly as I say," he replied. "I don't accept such money for failure. However, if he's not there, that's no concern of mine. I get paid."

"You'll be paid. Let's go."

"Very well." The pilot started the car.

"Why are you suspicious? It all seems quite logical to me," said Althene.

"I told you. This city has its own code of behavior. In Geneva, the telephone is the courier. A second number should have been given, so that you yourself could talk with your son. When I suggested it, I was told there wasn't time."

"All quite possible."

"Perhaps, but I don't like it. The switchboard said they were connecting me to the front desk, but the man I talked with was no clerk."

"How do you know that?"

"Desk clerks can be arrogant and often are, but

they aren't demanding. The man I spoke with was. And he wasn't from Geneva. He had an accent I couldn't place. You'll do exactly as I say, madame."

Von Tiebolt replaced the phone and smiled in satisfaction. "We have her," he said simply, walking to the couch where Hans Kessler lay holding an ice pack to his right cheek, his face bruised where it had not been stitched by the first deputy's personal physician.

"I'll go with you," said Hans, his voice strained in anger and pain.

"I don't think so," interjected his brother from a nearby armchair.

"You can't be seen," added Von Tiebolt. "We'll tell Holcroft you were delayed."

"No!" roared the doctor, slamming his fist on the coffee table. "Tell Holcroft anything you like, but I'm going with you tonight. That bitch is responsible for this!"

"I'd say *you* were," said Von Tiebolt. "There was a job to do and you wanted to do it. You were most anxious. You always are in such matters; you're a very physical man."

"He wouldn't die! That faggot wouldn't *die!*" Hans yelled. "He had the strength of five lions. Look at my stomach!" He ripped the shirt below his face, revealing a curving pattern of crisscrossed black threads. "He tore it with his hands! With his *hands!*"

Erich Kessler turned his eyes from his brother's wound. "You were lucky to get away without being seen. And now we must get you out of this hotel. The police are questioning everyone."

"They won't come here," countered Hans angrily. "Our deputy's taken care of that."

"Nevertheless, one curious policeman walking through the door could lead to complications," Von Tiebolt said, looking at Erich. "Hans must go. Dark glasses, a muffler, his hat. The deputy's in the lobby." The blond man shifted his gaze to the wounded brother. "If you can move, you'll have your chance at the Holcroft woman. That may make you feel better."

"I can move," said Hans, his face contorted in pain.

Johann turned back to the older Kessler. "You'll stay here, Erich. Holcroft will start calling soon, but he won't identify himself until he recognizes your voice. Be solicitous; be concerned. Say I reached you in Berlin and asked you to get here early, that I tried to call *him* in Paris, but he'd gone. Then tell him that we're both shocked at what happened here this afternoon. The man who was killed had been asking about him; we're both concerned for his safety. He must *not* be seen at the d'Accord."

"I could say that someone fitting his description was seen leaving by the service entrance," added the scholar. "He was in a state of shock; he'll accept that. It will add to his panic."

"Excellent. Meet him and take him to the Excelsior. Register under the name of"—the blond man thought for a moment—"under the name of Fresca. If he has any lingering doubts, that will convince him. He never used the name with you; he'll know we've met and talked."

"Fine," said Erich. "And at the Excelsior, I'll explain that because of everything that's happened, you reached the bank's directors and set up the conference for tomorrow morning. The quicker it's over, the quicker we can get to Zurich and set up proper security measures."

"Excellent again, Herr Professor. Come, Hans," Von Tiebolt said, "I'll help you."

"It's not necessary," said the bull of Munich's district soccer, his expression belying his words. "Just get my bag."

"Of course." Von Tiebolt picked up the physician's leather case. "I'm fascinated. You must tell me what you intend to inject. Remember, we want a death, but not a killing."

"Don't worry," Hans said. "Everything's clearly coded. There'll be no mistakes."

"After our meeting with the Holcroft woman," said Von Tiebolt, draping an overcoat over Hans's shoulders, "we'll decide where Hans should stay tonight. Perhaps at the deputy's house."

"Good idea," agreed the scholar. "The doctor would be available."

"I don't *need* him," argued Hans, his breath escaping between clenched teeth, his walk hesitant and painful. "I could have sewn myself up; he's not very good. *Auf wiedersehen*, Erich."

"*Auf wiedersehen*."

Von Tiebolt opened the door, looked back at Erich,

and escorted the wounded Hans out into the corridor.
"You say each vial is coded?"

"Yes. For the woman, the serum will accelerate her
heart to the point . . ."

The door closed. The older Kessler shifted his bulk in
the chair. It was the way of Wolfsschanze; there was no
other decision. The physician who had tended Hans made
it clear that there was internal bleeding; the organs had
been severely damaged, as if torn by claws possessing
extraordinary strength. Unless Hans were taken to the
hospital, he could easily die. But his brother could not be
admitted to a hospital; questions would be asked. A man
had been killed that afternoon at the d'Accord; the
wounded patient had been at the d'Accord. Too many
questions. Besides, Hans's contributions were in the black
leather case Johann carried. The Tinamou would learn
everything they had to know. Hans Kessler, *Sonnenkind*,
was no longer needed; he was a liability.

The telephone rang. Kessler picked it up.

"Erich?"

It was Holcroft.

"Yes?"

"I'm in Geneva. You got here early; I thought I'd
try."

"Yes, Von Tiebolt called me this morning in Berlin;
he tried to reach you in Paris. He suggested——"

"Has he arrived?" interrupted the American.

"Yes. He's out making the final arrangements for tomorrow. We've got a great deal to tell you."

"And I've got a great deal to tell *you*," said Holcroft.
"Do you know what's happened?"

"Yes, it's horrible." Where was the panic? Where
was the anxiety of a man stretched to the limit of his
capacities? The voice on the phone was not that of someone drowning, grasping for a lifeline. "He was a friend of
yours. They say he asked for you."

There was a pause. "He asked for my mother."

"I didn't understand. We know only that he used the
name Holcroft."

"What does *Nach* . . . *Nach-rich* . . . I can't pro-
nounce it."

" 'Nachrichtendienst'?"

"Yes. What does it mean?"

Kessler was startled. The American was in control of himself; it was not to be expected. "What can I tell you? It's Geneva's enemy."

"That's what Von Tiebolt found out in London?"

"Yes. Where are you, Noel? I must see you, but you can't come here."

"I know that. Listen to me. Do you have money?"

"Some."

"A thousand Swiss francs?"

"A thousand? . . . Yes, I imagine so."

"Go downstairs to the front desk and talk to the desk clerk privately. Get his name and give him the money. Tell him it's for me and that I'll be calling him in a few minutes."

"But how—"

"Let me finish. After you pay and get his name, go to the pay telephones near the elevators. Stand by the one on the left toward the entrance. When it rings, pick it up. It'll be me."

"How do you know the number?"

"I paid someone to go inside and get it."

This was not a man in panic. It was a rational man with a deadly purpose. . . . It was what Erich Kessler had feared. But for the arrangement of genes—and a head-strong woman—the man on the phone might be one of them. A *Sonnenkind*.

"What will you say to the clerk?"

"I'll tell you later; there's no time now. How long will it take you?"

"I don't know. Not long."

"Ten minutes?"

"Yes, I think so. But Noel, perhaps we should wait until Johann returns."

"When's that?"

"No more than an hour or two."

"Can't do it. I'll call you in the lobby in ten minutes. My watch says eight-forty-five. How about yours?"

"The same." Kessler did not bother to look at his watch: his mind was racing. Holcroft's spine was too dangerously firm. "I really think we should wait."

"I can't. They killed him. God! *How* they killed him! They want her, but they won't find her."

"Her? Your mother? . . . Von Tiebolt told me."

"They won't find her," repeated Holcroft. "They'll

find *me;* I'm who they really want. And I want *them.* I'm going to trap them, Erich."

"Control yourself. You don't know what you're doing."

"I know exactly."

"The Geneva police are in the hotel. If you speak to the desk clerk, he may say something. They'll be looking for you."

"They can have me in a few hours. In fact, I'll be looking for them."

"*What?* Noel, I *must* see you!"

"Ten minutes, Erich. It's eight-forty-six." Holcroft went off the line.

Kessler replaced the phone, knowing that he had no choice but to follow instructions. To do anything else would be suspect. But what did Holcroft expect to accomplish? What would he say to the desk clerk? It probably did not matter. With the mother gone, it was necessary only to keep Holcroft functioning until tomorrow morning. By noon, he would be expendable.

Noel waited on the dark street corner at the base of the rue des Granges. He was not proud of what he was about to do, but the rage inside him had numbed any feelings of morality. The sight of Willie Ellis had caused something to snap in his head. That sight gave rise to other images: Richard Holcroft, crushed into a stone building by a car gone wild by design. Strychnine poisoning in an airplane, and death in a French village, and murder in Berlin. And a man who had followed his mother. . . . He would not let them near her! It was *over;* he would bring it to a close himself.

It was a question now of using every available resource, every bit of strength he had, every fact he could recall, that would work for him. And it was the murder in Berlin that provided him with the single fact that could work for him now. In Berlin he had led killers to Erich Kessler. Stupidly, carelessly—to a pub on the Kurfürstendamm. Kessler and Holcroft; Holcroft and Kessler. If those killers were looking for Holcroft, they would keep Kessler in their sights. And if Kessler left the hotel, they would follow him.

Holcroft looked at his watch. It was time to call; he started across the pavement toward the booth.

He hoped Erich would answer.

And later understand.

Kessler stood in the hotel lobby, in front of the pay phone, a slip of paper in his hand. On it the astonished desk clerk had written his name; the man's hand had shaken when he had taken the money. Professor Kessler would appreciate knowing the gist of Mr. Holcroft's message to the clerk. For Mr. Holcroft's benefit. And for the clerk's, insofar as an additional five hundred francs would be his.

The telephone rang; Erich had it off the hook before the ring was finished. "Noel?"

"What's the desk clerk's name?"

Kessler gave it.

"Fine."

"Now, I insist we meet," said Erich. "There's a great deal you should know. Tomorrow's a very important day."

"Only if we get through tonight. If I find her tonight."

"Where are you? We *must* meet."

"We will. Listen carefully. Wait by that phone for five minutes. I may have to call you again. If I don't—after five minutes—go outside and begin walking down the hill. Just keep walking. When you get to the bottom, turn left and keep going. I'll join you in the street."

"Good! Five minutes, then." Kessler smiled. Whatever games the amateur indulged in were worthless. He would doubtless ask the desk clerk to relay a message or a telephone number to his mother if and when she called him—the unregistered guest; so much for that. Perhaps Johann was right: Perhaps Holcroft had reached the limits of his capacity. Perhaps the American was not a potential *Sonnenkind* after all.

Police were still in the d'Accord's lobby, as well as several journalists who sensed a story behind the clouded report of robbery the police had given out. This was Geneva. And there were the curious—guests milling about, talking with one another; reassuring one another, some afraid, some seeking sensation.

Erich stayed off to the side, avoiding the crowd, remaining as inconspicuous as possible. He did not like being in the lobby at all; he preferred the anonymity of the hotel room upstairs.

He looked at his watch; four minutes had passed since Holcroft's call. If the American did not call again during the next minute, he would find the desk clerk and . . .

The desk clerk approached, walking on his own hot fragments of glass. "Professor?"

"Yes, my friend." Kessler put his hand in his pocket.

The message Holcroft left was not what Erich had expected. Noel's mother was to remain hidden and to leave a telephone number where her son could reach *her*. The clerk had sworn not to reveal that number, of course; but then, prior commitments always took precedence. When and if the lady called, the number would be left on a piece of paper in Herr Kessler's box.

"Paging Mr. Kessler? Professor Erich Kessler."

A bellboy was walking through the lobby, shouting his name. *Shouting* it! It was *impossible*. No one knew he was here!

"Yes? Yes, I'm Professor Kessler," said Erich. "What *is* it?" He tried to keep his voice low, to remain inconspicuous. People were looking at him.

"The message is to be delivered orally, sir," said the bellboy. "The caller said there was no time for a note. It's from Mr. H. He says you're to start out now, sir."

"What?"

"That's all he said, sir. I spoke to him myself. To Mr. H. You're to start out now. That's what he told me to tell you."

Kessler held his breath. It was suddenly, unexpectedly clear. Holcroft was using *him* as the bait.

From the American's point of view, whoever killed the man in the black leather jacket in Berlin knew that Noel Holcroft had been with Erich Kessler.

The strategy was simple but ingenious: Expose Erich Kessler, have Erich Kessler receive a message from Mr. H., and leave the hotel for the dark streets of Geneva.

And if no one followed, the disparity between cause and effect might be difficult to explain. So difficult that Holcroft might reexamine his bait. Questions might surface that could blow Geneva apart.

Noel Holcroft was a potential *Sonnenkind*, after all.

40

Helden crawled through Gerhardt's house, over the smashed furniture and the blood on the floor, opening drawers and panels until she found a small tin box of first-aid supplies. Trying desperately not to think of anything but becoming mobile, rejecting the pain as an unwanted state of mind, she strapped her wound as tightly as she could and struggled to her feet. Using Gerhardt's cane for support, she managed to walk up the path and north, three kilometers, to the fork.

A farmer driving a vintage automobile picked her up. Could he drive her to a Doctor Litvak on the hill near the clinic?

He could. It was not far out of his way.

Would he please *hurry?*

Walther Litvak was in his late forties, with a balding head and clear eyes and a penchant for short, precise sentences. Being slender, he moved quickly, wasting as few motions as he did words; being highly intelligent, he made observations before replies; and being a Jew hidden by Dutch Catholics as a child and brought up by sympathetic Lutherans, he had no tolerance for intolerance.

He had one bias, and it was understandable. His father and mother, two sisters, and a brother, had been gassed at Auschwitz. Save for an appeal of a Swiss doctor who spoke of a district in the hills of Neuchâtel that had no medical care, Walther Litvak would be living in Kibbutz Har Sha'alav, in the Negev desert.

He had intended to spend three years at the clinic; that was five years ago. And then, after several months in Neuchâtel, he was told who his recruiter was: one of a group of men who fought the resurgence of Nazism. They knew things other men did not know: about thousands of grown-up children—everywhere; and about untold millions that could reach those unknown people—everywhere. There was much nonmedical work to be done. His contact was a man named Werner Gerhardt, and the group was called Nachrichtendienst.

Walther Litvak stayed in Neuchâtel.

"Come inside, quickly," he said to Helden. "Let me help you, I have an office here."

He removed her coat and half carried her into a room with an examination table.

"I was shot." It was all Helden could think of to say.

Litvak placed her on the table and removed her skirt and half slip. "Don't waste your strength trying to talk." He scissored the bandage and studied the wound, then took a hypodermic needle from a sterilizer. "I'm going to let you sleep for a few minutes."

"You *can't*. There isn't time! I have to tell you. . . ."

"I said a few minutes," interrupted the doctor, inserting the needle into Helden's arm.

She opened her eyes, the shapes around her out of focus, a numb sensation in her leg. As her vision cleared, she saw the doctor across the room. She tried to sit up; Litvak heard her and turned.

"These are antibiotics," he said. He was holding a bottle of pills. "Every two hours for a day, then every four. What happened? Tell me quickly. I'll go down to the cottage and take care of things."

"The cottage? You knew?"

"While you were under, you talked; people generally do after trauma. You repeated 'Nachrichtendienst' several times. Then 'Johann.' I assume that's Von Tiebolt, and you're his sister—the one who's been with Falkenheim. It's happening, isn't it? The inheritors are closing ranks in Geneva."

"Yes."

"I thought as much this morning. The news bulletins from the Negev are horrible. They found out, God knows how."

"What bulletins?"

"Har Sha'alav." The doctor gripped the bottle; veins swelled on his forearm. "A raid. Houses bombed, people massacred, fields burnt to the ground. The death count isn't complete yet, but the estimates exceed one hundred and seventy. Men mostly, but women and children too."

Helden closed her eyes; there were no words. Litvak went on.

"To a man, the elders were killed, butchered in the gardens. They say it was the work of terrorists, of the Rache. But that's not true. It's Wolfsschanze. Rache fighters would never attack Har Sha'alv; they know what would happen. Jews from every kibbutz, every commando unit, would go after them."

"Gerhardt said you were supposed to cable Har Sha'-alv," whispered Helden.

Litvak's eyes clouded. "There's nothing to cable now. There's no one left. Now, tell me what happened down at the lake."

She did. When she had finished, the doctor helped her off the table and carried her into the large Alpine living room. He lowered her to the couch and summarized.

"Geneva's the battleground, and there's not an hour to be lost. Even if Har Sha'alav could be reached, it would be useless. But there is a man from Har Sha'alav in London; he's been ordered to stay there. He followed Holcroft to Portsmouth. He was the one who took the photograph from Holcroft's pocket."

"It was a picture of Beaumont," said Helden. "ODESSA."

"Wolfsschanze," corrected Litvak. "A *Sonnenkind*. One of thousands, but also one of the few to work with Von Tiebolt."

Helden raised herself, frowning. "The records. Beaumont's *records*. They didn't make sense."

"What records?"

She told the angry doctor about the obscure and contradictory information found in Beaumont's naval records. And of the similar dossier belonging to Beaumont's second-in-command, Ian Llewellen.

Litvak wrote down the name on a note pad. "How convenient. Two men of Wolfsschanze commanding an electronic-espionage vessel. How many more are there like them? In how many places?"

"Llewellen was quoted in the papers the other day. When Beaumont and Gretchen—" She could not finish.

"Don't dwell on it," said the doctor. "The *Sonnenkinder* have their own rules. Llewellen is a name to add to the list that must be found in Geneva. Gerhardt was right: Above all, that list must be found. It's as vital as stopping the money. In some ways, more vital."

"Why?"

"The funds are a means to the Fourth Reich, but the people *are* that Reich; they'll be there whether or not the funds are dispersed. We've got to find out who they are."

Helden leaned back. "My . . . Johann von Tiebolt can be killed. So, too, can Kessler and . . . if it's necessary . . . even Noel. The money can be stopped. But how can we be sure the list will be found?"

"The man from Har Sha'alav in London will have ideas. He has many talents." Litvak glanced briefly away. "You should know, because you'll have to work with him. He's called a killer and a terrorist. He doesn't consider himself either, but the laws he's broken and the crimes he's committed would tend to dispute that judgment." The doctor glanced at his watch. "It's three minutes of nine; he lives less than a mile from Heathrow. If I can contact him, he can be in Geneva by midnight. Do you know where Holcroft is staying?"

"Yes. At the d'Accord. You understand, he knows nothing. He believes deeply in what he's doing. He thinks it's right."

"I understand. Unfortunately, that may be irrelevant in terms of his life. The first thing, however, is to reach him."

"I said I'd call him tonight."

"Good. Let me help you to the telephone. Be careful what you say. He'll be watched; his line will be tapped." Litvak helped her to the table where the phone was.

"Hôtel d'Accord. *Bonsoir*," said the operator.

"Good evening. Mr. Noel Holcroft, please?"

"Monsieur Holcroft? . . ." The operator hesitated. "Just one minute, madame."

There was a silence, a click, and a man spoke. "Mrs. Holcroft?"

"What?"

"This is Mrs. Holcroft, is it not?"

Helden was surprised. Something was wrong; the switchboard had not even tried to ring Noel's room. "You were expecting me, then?" she asked.

"But of course, madame," replied the desk clerk

with confidentiality. "Your son was most generous. He said to tell you it's imperative you remain out of sight, but you are to leave a telephone number where he can reach you."

"I see. Just one minute, please." Helden cupped the phone and turned to Litvak. "They think I'm Mrs. Holcroft. He's paid them to take a number where he can reach her."

The doctor nodded and walked quickly to a desk. "Keep talking. Say you want to make sure this number will not be given to anyone else. Offer money. Anything to stall them." Litvak took out a worn address book.

"Before I give you a number, I'd like to be certain . . ." Helden paused; the desk clerk swore on his mother's grave he would give the number only to Holcroft. The doctor rushed back to the table, a number written on a slip of paper. Helden repeated it to the desk clerk and hung up. "Where is this?" she asked Litvak.

"It reaches an empty apartment on the rue de la Paix, but the apartment is not at the address listed with the telephone exchange. Here it is." Litvak wrote the address beneath the number. "Memorize them both."

"I will."

"Now, I'll try our man in London," said the doctor, heading for the staircase. "I have radio equipment here. It links me with a routine-mobile-telephone service." He stopped on the bottom step. "I'll get you to Geneva. You won't be able to move around much, but the wound isn't deep; your stitches will hold under the pressure of the bandage, and you'll have the chance to reach Holcroft. I hope you do, and I hope you're successful. Noel Holcroft must walk away from Von Tiebolt and Kessler. If he fights you, if he even hesitates, he must be killed."

"I know."

"Knowing it may not be enough. I'm afraid the decision will not be yours to make."

"Whose, then? Yours?"

"I can't leave Neuchâtel. It will be up to the man in London."

"The terrorist? The killer who has only to hear the word 'Nazi' and he fires a gun?"

"He'll be objective," said Litvak, continuing up the staircase. "He won't have other pressures on him. You'll meet him at the apartment."

"How will I get to Geneva? I—" Helden stopped.

"What?"

"I asked how I would get to Geneva. Are there trains?"

"There's no time for trains. You'll fly."

"Fine. It will be quicker."

"Much quicker."

And far better, thought Helden. For the one thing she had not relayed to the doctor was Werner Gerhardt's final warning. To her.

My child. Stay away from Geneva. . . . Wolfsschanze has seen you.

"Who will take me?"

"There are pilots who fly the lakes at night," said Litvak.

Althene was irritated, but she had agreed to the condition. The pilot had asked her a single question.

"Do you know by sight the people who are looking for you?"

She had replied that she did not.

"You may before the night is over."

Which was why she was standing now beside a tree in the dark woods above the road in sight of the car. It was a sloping forest of pine that rose above the lakeside highway. She had been guided to her watch post by the pilot.

"If your son is there, I'll send him to you," he had said.

"Of course he'll be there. Why wouldn't he?"

"We'll see."

For a moment his doubts had disturbed her. "If he's not, what then?"

"Then you'll know who it is who's looking for you." He had started back toward the road.

"What about you?" she had called after him. "If my son isn't there?"

"Me?" The pilot had laughed. "I've been through many such negotiations. If your son isn't there, it will mean they are desperate to find you, won't it? Without me, they can't have you."

She waited now by the tree, no more than forty yards away, the line of sight reasonably clear considering the profusion of limbs and branches. The car was off the side of the road, pointing north, its parking lights on. The pilot had told the man at the d'Accord to be there in one hour, not before, and to approach from the south, blinking his lights repeatedly within a quarter of a mile of the rendezvous.

"Can you hear me, madame?" The pilot stood by the car and spoke in a normal tone of voice.

"Yes."

"Good. They're coming. Lights are flashing on and off down the road. Stay where you are; watch and listen, but don't show yourself. If your son steps out, say nothing until I send him to you." The pilot paused. "If they force me to go with them, get to the landing on the west side of the lake, where we flew in. It's called Atterrisage Médoc. I'll reach you there. . . . I don't like this."

"Why? What is it?"

"There are two men in the car. The one next to the driver holds up a weapon; he checks it, perhaps."

"How would I get there?" asked Althene.

"There's a second set of keys in a small magnet box under the hood." The bearded man raised one hand to his mouth, speaking loudly above the roar of the approaching automobile. "On the right side. Be still!"

A long black car came to a stop ten yards in front of the pilot. A man on the passenger side got out, but it was not her son. He was stocky, wearing an overcoat with the lapels pulled up, a heavy muffler around his throat. Large-framed dark glasses covered his eyes, giving him the appearance of a huge insect. He limped as he walked into the spill of the headlights.

The driver remained behind the wheel. Althene stared at him, hoping to recognize Noel. It was not he; she could not see the man's face clearly, but the hair was blond.

"Mrs. Holcroft is in the car, I presume," said the man with the dark glasses to the pilot. The language was English but the accent unmistakably German.

"Her son is in yours, then?" replied the pilot.

"Please ask Mrs. Holcroft to step out."

"Please ask her son to do the same."

"Don't be difficult. We have a schedule to keep."

"So do we. There's only one other person in your automobile, monsieur. He doesn't fit the description of her son."

"We'll take Mrs. Holcroft to him."

"We'll take *him* to Mrs. Holcroft."

"Stop it!"

"Stop what, monsieur? I am paid, as I'm sure you are paid. We both do our jobs, do we not?"

"I've no time for you!" the German shouted, limping past the pilot, toward the car.

The pilot nodded. "May I suggest you find the time. For you won't find Mrs. Holcroft."

"Du Sauhund! Wo ist die Frau?"

"May I further suggest, monsieur, that you don't call me names. I come from Châlons-sur-Marne. Twice you won there, and I was brought up with a certain distaste for your name-calling."

"Where is the *woman?*"

"Where is the son?"

The German took his right hand from his overcoat pocket. He was holding a gun. "You're not paid so much that it's worth your life. Where is she?"

"And you, monsieur? Perhaps you're paid too much to shoot me and not find out."

The gunshot was deafening. Dirt exploded at the pilot's feet. Althene gripped the tree in shock.

"Now, Frenchman, perhaps *you* see that payment is not so important to me as the woman Where is she?"

"Les Boches!" said the pilot in disgust. "Give you a gun and you go mad. You never change. If you want the woman, you'll produce the son and I will take him to her."

"You'll tell me where she is now!" The German raised his gun, leveling it at the pilot's head. *"Now!"*

Althene could see the car door open. A gunshot exploded, then another. The pilot lunged to the dirt. The German screamed, his eyes bulging. "Johann? *Johann!"*

There was a third explosion The German collapsed on the road; the pilot scrambled to his feet.

"He was going to *kill* you," yelled the driver, his voice incredulous. "We knew he was sick, but not insane. What can I say?"

"He would have killed me? . . ." The pilot asked the question no less incredulously. "It doesn't make sense!"

"Of course it didn't," said the blond man. "Your *request* made sense. First, help me pull him into the woods and remove his identification. Then come with me."

"Who are you?"

"A friend of Holcroft's."

"I'd like to believe that."

"You will."

It was all Althene could do to hold her place. Her legs were weak, her throat was dry, and the ache in her eyes caused her to shut them repeatedly.

The blond man and the pilot dragged the body into the woods not twenty feet below her. The pilot's instructions meant a great deal to her now. He had been right.

"Shall I take my car, monsieur?"

"No. Shut off the lights and come with me. We'll pick it up in the morning."

The pilot did as he was told, then hesitated. "I don't like to leave it so near a corpse."

"We will get it before daybreak. Have you your keys?"

"Yes."

"Hurry!" said the blond man.

The pilot's relief was in his silence; he made no further protest. In seconds, they had sped away.

Althene pushed herself away from the tree. She tried to recall the pilot's exact words. *There's a second set of keys . . . a small magnet box . . . under the hood . . . get to the landing . . . where we flew in. Atterrisage Médoc.*

Atterrisage Médoc. On the west side of the lake.

Five minutes later, her hands covered with grease, she was traveling south on the lakeside highway, toward Geneva. As the moments passed, her foot became firmer on the gas pedal, her grip on the steering wheel more relaxed. She began to think again.

Atterrisage Médoc. On the west side of the lake . . . ten or twelve miles north of the city. If she thought only of that, of the small, obscure stretch of lakefront with the gas pumps on the single dock, she might slow her heartbeat and breathe again.

Atterrisage Médoc. Please, God, let me find it! Let me live to find it and reach my son! Dear God! What have I done? A lie of thirty years . . . a betrayal so horrible, a stigma so terrifying. . . . I must find him!

Helden sat directly behind the pilot in the small seaplane. She felt the bandage beneath her skirt; it was tight, but did not cut off circulation. The wound throbbed now and then, but the pills reduced the pain; she could walk adequately. Even if she could not, she would force herself to.

The pilot leaned back toward her. "A half hour after landing you'll be driven to a restaurant on the lake where you can get a taxi into the city," he said. "Should you require our services within the next two weeks, our base for this period is a private marina called Atterrisage Médoc. It's been a pleasure having you on board."

41

Erich Kessler was not a physical man, yet he approved of physical violence when that violence brought about practical objectives. He approved of it as observer and theoretician, not as participant. However, there was no alternative now, and no time to seek one. He would have to become a part of the violence.

Holcroft had left him no choice. The amateur had sorted out his own priorities and acted on them with alarming perception. The chromosomes of Heinrich Clausen were in the son. He had to be controlled again, remaneuvered again.

Erich chose the person he needed from among the clusters of people in the lobby: a newspaperman, and, from the ease of his manner and his expertness with notebook and pencil, probably a good one.

Kessler approached the man, keeping his voice low. "You're the journalist from . . . what paper is it?"

"Genève Soir," said the reporter.

"Dreadful, what happened. That poor man. A tragedy. I've been standing here for quite a while trying to decide whether to say anything. But I simply can't get involved."

"You're staying at the hotel?"

"Yes. I'm from Berlin. I come to Geneva often. My conscience tells me to go right over to the police and tell them what I know. But my attorney says it could be misconstrued. I'm here on business; it could be detrimental. Still, they should have it."

"What kind of information?"

Erich looked at the journalist sadly. "Let's say I knew the man who was killed very well."

"And?"

"Not here. My attorney says I should stay out of it."

"Are you telling me you *were* involved?"

"Oh, good heavens, *no*. Not like that, not at all. It's just that I have . . . information. Perhaps even a name or two. There are . . . reasons."

"If you're not involved, I'll protect you as a source."

"That's all I ask. Give me two or three minutes to go upstairs and get my coat. I'll come down and head outside. Follow me down the hill. I'll find a secluded spot where we can talk. Don't approach me until I call for you."

The journalist nodded. Kessler turned toward the elevators. He would get his overcoat and two revolvers, both untraceable. The minor delay would heighten Holcroft's anxieties, and that was fine.

Noel waited in the doorway across the street from the Hôtel d'Accord. Kessler should have received the message five minutes ago. What was holding him up?

There he was! The corpulent figure walking slowly down the short steps of the d'Accord's entrance could be no one else's. The bulk, the deliberate pace, the heavy overcoat. That was it; Kessler had gone back to his room for the coat.

Holcroft watched as Erich made his stately way down the hill, nodding pleasantly to the passersby. Kessler was a gentle person, thought Noel, and probably would not understand why he was being used as the lure; it wasn't in his nature to think that way. Nor had it ever been in Holcroft's to use a man this way, but *nothing* is as it was. It was natural for him now.

And it was successful. God damn it, it worked! A man in his mid-thirties, perhaps, reached the bottom step of the d'Accord and looked directly at Kessler's receding figure. He began walking slowly—too slowly for someone going somewhere—and took up his position far enough behind Erich not to be seen.

Now, if only Kessler would do as he was told. The intersecting avenue at the bottom of the rue des Granges was made up of old three-story office buildings, manicured and expensive, but, after five o'clock in the evening, essentially deserted. Noel had done his homework; on it depended his trapping a killer from the Nachrichtendienst. Just one killer was enough; he'd lead him to others. It was not out of the question to break that man's neck to get the information. Or to fire bullets across that man's eyes.

Noel felt the gun in his pocket and took up slow pursuit, staying on his side of the street.

Four minutes later Kessler reached the bottom of the hill and turned left. The man behind him did the same. Holcroft waited until the traffic passed and both men were out of sight. Then he crossed the intersection, still keeping on the opposite side, his view clear.

Suddenly he stopped. Kessler was nowhere in sight. Neither was the man who had followed him.

Noel began running.

Kessler turned left into a dimly lit street, walked about a hundred and fifty feet, and held up a small mirror. The journalist was behind him; Holcroft was not. It was the moment to move quickly.

On the left was a cul-de-sac, designed to accommodate two or three parked automobiles, a chain across the front denoting its private ownership. There were no cars, and it was dark. Very dark. Ideal. With difficulty, he stepped over the chain and walked rapidly to the wall at the rear. He put his hand into his right pocket and took out the first gun—the first gun he would use. He had to tug at it; the silencer was caught momentarily in the cloth.

"In here!" he said, loud enough to be heard by the newspaperman. "We can talk here and no one will see us."

The journalist climbed over the chain, his eyes squinting into the shadows. "Where are you?"

"Over here." Erich raised the gun as the journalist approached. When he was within several feet, Kessler fired into the dim silhouette of the man's neck. The spit had a hollow sound; the expulsion of air from the punctured throat echoed between the two buildings. The newspaperman collapsed. Erich pulled the trigger once again, shooting him in the head.

He unscrewed the silencer from the pistol, rummaged through the dead man's clothes, extracting a billfold and the notebook, throwing them into the shadows. He took out the second gun from his left pocket and pressed the weapon into the reporter's hand, the index finger around the trigger.

Still kneeling, Kessler tore the front of his shirt and ripped two buttons off his overcoat. He rubbed the flat of his hand harshly over the oil and dirt of the parking lot and soiled his face with the residue.

He was ready. He rose to his feet and lurched toward the chain. At first he could not see Holcroft, but then he did. The American was running in the street; he stopped briefly in front of a streetlight.

Now.

Kessler walked back to the dead man, leaned over, and grabbed the hand with the gun, holding it up toward the sky and pressing the dead finger against the trigger.

The small-caliber gunshot was amplified by the surrounding stone. Erich yanked at the frozen finger twice more, let it drop, and swiftly removed the gun from his own pocket.

"Noel! *Noel!*" he screamed, throwing himself against the wall, his heavy body sinking to the concrete. "Noel, where *are* you?"

"Erich?! For God's sake . . . *Erich?*" Holcroft's voice was not far off; in seconds it was closer.

Kessler aimed his unsilenced gun toward the clump of dead flesh in the shadows. It was the last shot he would have to fire . . . and he did so the instant he saw the silhouette of Noel Holcroft in the dim spill of the light.

"Erich!"

"*Here.* He tried to *kill* me! Noel, he tried to kill me!"

Holcroft felt the chain, jumped over it, and raced to Kessler. He knelt down in the darkness. "Who? Where?"

"Over there! Johann made me carry a gun. . . . I had to shoot it. I had no choice!"

"Are you all right?"

"I think so. He came *after* me. He knew about you. 'Where is he?' he kept saying. 'Where is *H?* Where's Holcroft?' He threw me to the ground. . . ."

"Oh, *Christ!*" Noel leaped up and lunged toward the body in the shadows. He pulled his lighter from his pocket and snapped it on; the flame spread light over the corpse. Noel searched the pockets of the outer clothes, then rolled the body over to check the trousers. "Goddammit, there's *nothing!*"

"Nothing? What do you mean, nothing? Noel, we have to get out of here. Think of tomorrow!"

"There's no wallet, no license, nothing!"

"Tomorrow. We must think about tomorrow!"

"Tonight!" roared Holcroft. "I wanted them tonight!"

Kessler was silent for several seconds, then spoke softly, incredulity in his voice. "You planned this. . . ."

Holcroft got up angrily, the anger lessened by Erich's words. "I'm sorry," he said. "I didn't want you to get hurt. I thought I had everything under control."

"Why did you do it?"

"Because they'll kill her if they find her. Just as they killed Willie Ellis and . . . Richard Holcroft. So many others."

"Who?"

"Geneva's enemy. This Nachrichtendienst. I wanted just one of them! Alive, *goddammit!"*

"Help me up," said Kessler.

"Can you understand?" Holcroft found Erich's hand and lifted him up.

"Yes, of course. But I don't think you should have acted alone."

"I was going to trap him, get the names of others from him if I had to blind him for them. Then turn him over to the police, ask them to help me find my mother, protect her."

"We can't do that now. He's dead; there'd be too many questions we can't answer. But Johann can help."

"Von Tiebolt?"

"Yes. He told me he had an influential friend here in Geneva. A first deputy. He said when I found you to take you to the Excelsior. Register under the name of Fresca. I don't know why that name."

"It's one we're used to," said Noel. "He'll reach us there?"

"Yes. He's making the final arrangements for tomorrow. At the bank."

"The *bank?"*

"It'll be over tomorrow; that's what I tried to tell you. Come, we must hurry. We can't stay here; someone may pass by. Johann told me to tell you that if your mother was in Geneva, *we'll* find her. She'll be protected."

Holcroft helped Kessler toward the chain. The scholar looked back into the dark recesses of the walled enclosure and shuddered.

"Don't think about it," said Noel.

"It was horrible."

"It was necessary."

Yes, it was, thought Kessler.

Helden saw the old woman sitting on a bench at the base of the dock, looking out at the water, oblivious of the few mechanics and passengers who walked to and from the seaplanes.

As Helden drew near, she noticed the woman's face in the moonlight, the angular features and the high cheek-bones that set off the wide eyes. The woman was lost in thought, strong and distant, she was so alone, so out of place, so . . .

Helden limped in front of the bench and stared at the face below. My God! She was looking down at a face that but for years and gender could belong to Noel Holcroft. It was his mother!

What was she doing *here?* Of all the places in the world, why *here?* The answer was obvious: Noel's mother was flying into Geneva secretly!

The old woman looked up, then looked away, uninterested, and Helden hurried as best she could across the path that led to a small building that was both waiting room and radio base. She went inside and approached a man standing behind a makeshift counter beyond which were telephones and radio equipment. "The woman outside. Who is she?"

The man looked up briefly from a clipboard, studying her. "No names are mentioned here," he said. "You should know that."

"But it's terribly important! If she's who I think she is, she's in great danger. I say this to you because I know you know Dr. Litvak."

At the name, the man looked up again. It was apparent that at Atterrisage Médoc, they lived with risk and danger but avoided both where possible. And Dr. Litvak was obviously a trusted customer. "She's waiting for a phone call."

"From whom?"

The man studied her again. "From one of our pilots: '*Le Chat rouge.*' Has she trouble with the police?"

"No."

"The Corsicans? Mafia?"

Helden shook her head. "Worse."

"You're a friend of Dr. Litvak?"

"Yes. He booked the flight from Neuchâtel for me. Check if you like."

"I don't have to. We don't want trouble here. Get her out."

"How? A car's supposed to drive me to a restaurant on the lake where I'm to wait for a taxi. It'll be a half hour, I'm told."

"Not now." The man looked past her. "Henri, come here." He took a set of car keys from under the counter. "Go talk to the old woman. Tell her she must leave. Henri will drive you."

"She may not listen."

"She has to. You'll have your transportation."

Helden went back outside as quickly as her wound permitted. Mrs. Holcroft was not on the bench, and for an instant Helden panicked. Then she saw her, out on the now-deserted dock, standing motionless in the moonlight. Helden started toward her.

The old woman turned at the sound of Helden's footsteps. She held her place and offered no greeting.

"You're Mrs. Holcroft," said Helden. "Noel's mother."

At the mention of her son's name, Althene Holcroft brought her hands together; she seemed to stop breathing. "Who are you?"

"A friend. Please believe that. More than you know."

"Since I know nothing, it can be neither more nor less."

"My name is Von Tiebolt."

"Then get out of my sight!" The old woman's words were lashes in the night air. "Men here have been paid. They'll not let you interfere with me. They'll kill you first. Go join your wolfpack!"

"I'm no part of Wolfsschanze, Mrs. Holcroft."

"You're a Von Tiebolt!"

"If I were part of Wolfsschanze, I wouldn't come near you. Surely you understand that."

"I understand the filth you represent. . . ."

"I've lived with that judgment in one form or another all my life, but you're wrong! You must believe me. You can't stay here; it's not safe for you. I can hide you; I can help you. . . ."

"*You?* How? Through the barrel of a gun? Under the wheels of a car?"

"*Please!* I know why you've come to Geneva. I'm
here for the same reason. We've got to reach him, tell him
before it's too late. The funds must be stopped!"

The old woman seemed stunned by Helden's words.
Then she frowned, as if the words were a trap.

"Must they? Or must *I?* Well, I won't be. I'm going
to call out, and when I do, men will come. If they kill
you, it means nothing to me. You're thirty years of a lie!
All of you! You won't reach *anyone.*"

"Mrs. Holcroft! I love your son. I love him so much
. . . and if we don't reach him, he'll be killed. By either
side! Neither can let him live! You've got to *understand.*"

"Liar!" said Althene. "You're all liars!"

"Damn you!" cried Helden. "No one will come to
help you. They want you out of here! And I'm not a cripple. This is a *bullet* in my leg! It's there because I'm trying to reach Noel! You don't know what we've been
through! You have no right to—"

There was a loud commotion from the small building
on the waterfront. The two women could hear the words
. . . as they were meant to hear them.

"You're not welcome here, monsieur! There's no such
woman as you describe! Please leave."

"Don't give me orders! She's here!"

Helden gasped. It was a voice she'd heard all her
life.

"This is a private marina. I ask you again to leave!"

"Open that door!"

"What? What door?"

"Behind you!"

Helden turned to Althene Holcroft. "I've no time to
explain. I can only tell you I'm your friend. Get into the
water! Out of sight. Now!"

"Why should I believe you?" The old woman stared
beyond Helden, to the base of the dock and the building;
she was alarmed, indecisive. "You're young and strong.
You could easily kill me."

"That man wants to kill you," whispered Helden. "He
tried to kill me."

"Who is he?"

"My brother. In the name of God, be quiet!"

Helden grabbed Althene around the waist and forced
the old woman down to the wood of the dock. As gently
as possible, she rolled both of them over the edge and

into the water. Althene trembled, her mouth full of water; she coughed and thrashed her hands. Helden kept her arm around the old woman's waist, holding her up, scissoring the water below.

"Don't cough! We can't make noise. Put the strap of your purse around your neck. I'll help you."

"Dear God, what are you *doing?*"

"Be quiet."

There was a small outboard motorboat moored thirty feet from the dock. Helden pulled Althene toward the protective shadows of its hull. They were halfway there when they heard the crash of a door and saw the beam of a powerful flashlight. It danced in ominous figures as the blond man ran toward the pier, then stopped and shot the light out at the water. Helden struggled, her leg an agony now, trying to reach the boat.

She could not do it; she had no strength in the leg, and the weight of the wet clothes was too much.

"Try to get to the boat," she whispered. "I'll head back . . . he'll see me and—"

"Be still!" said the old woman, her arms now spreading out in quick, floating motions, easing the burden on Helden. "It's the same man. Your brother. He has a gun. *Hurry.*"

"I can't."

"You will."

Together, each supporting the other, they propelled themselves toward the boat.

The blond man was on the dock, the beam of the flashlight crisscrossing the water's surface in methodical patterns. In seconds the light would hit them; it was moving out like a deadly laser beam. The instant it centered on them, a fusillade of bullets would come and it would all be over.

Johann von Tiebolt was a superb marksman, and his sister knew it.

The blinding beam came; the hull was above them. Instinctively, both women put their faces in the water and surged underneath. The beam passed; they were behind the boat, the chain tangled in their clothes. They held on to it, a lifeline, filling their exhausted lungs with air.

Silence. Footsteps, at first slow and deliberate, then suddenly gathering momentum as Johann von Tiebolt left the dock. And then the crash of a door again, and voices again.

"Where did she go?"

"You're mad!"

"You're dead!"

A gunshot echoed through the waterfront. It was followed by a scream of pain, then a second gunshot. And then silence.

Minutes passed; the two women in the water looked at each other under the wash of moonlight. Tears filled the eyes of Helden von Tiebolt. The old woman touched the girl's face and said nothing.

The roar of an engine broke the terror of the silence. Then spinning tires and the sound of erupting gravel from an unseen drive came from the shore. The two women nodded at each other, and, once more, each holding the other, started for the dock.

They crawled up a ladder and knelt in the darkness, breathing deeply.

"Isn't it odd," said Althene. "At one point I thought about my shoes. I didn't want to lose them."

"Did you?"

"No. That's even stranger, I imagine."

"Mine are gone," said Helden aimlessly. She stood up. "We must leave. He may come back." She looked toward the building. "I don't want to go in there, but I think we have to. There was a set of car keys. . . ." She reached down to help the old woman up.

Helden opened the door and instantly closed her eyes. The man was slumped over the counter, his face blown off. For a moment the image of the mutilated head of Klaus Falkenheim flashed across her mind, and she wanted to scream. Instead, she whispered.

"*Mein Bruder. . . .*"

"Come, child. Quickly now!" Unbelievably, it was the old woman who spoke, giving the order with authority. She had spotted a ring of keys. "It's better to take their car. I have one, but it's been seen."

And then Helden saw the word, printed clearly in a heavy crayon on the floor beneath the dead man.

"*No!* It's a lie!"

"What is it?" The old woman grabbed the keys and rushed over to the girl.

"There. It's a lie!"

The word on the floor was written hastily, the letters large.

NACHRICHTENDIENST

Helden limped toward it, sank to her knees, and tried to rub the letters away, her hands moving furiously, the tears streaming down her face. "A lie! A *lie!* They were great men!"

Althene touched the hysterical girl's shoulder, then took her arm and pulled her off the floor. "There's no time for this! You said it yourself. We must leave here."

Gently but firmly, the older woman led the younger out to the drive. A single light was on above the door, creating as much shadow as illumination. There were two cars—the one Althene had driven and a gray automobile with a license plate wired to the bumper. She guided Helden toward the latter.

And then stopped. Whatever control she had managed to summon was shattered.

The body of her red-haired pilot lay in the gravel. He was dead, his hands tied behind his back. All over his face—around his eyes and mouth—were slashes made by the blade of a knife.

He had been tortured and shot.

They drove in silence, each with her own agonizing thoughts. "There's an apartment," said Helden finally. "I've been given directions. We'll be safe there. A man has flown in from London to help us. He should be there by now."

"Who is he?"

"A Jew from a place called Har Sha'alav."

Althene looked at the girl through the racing shadows. "A Jew from Har Sha'alav came to see me. It's why I'm here."

"I know."

The door of the apartment was opened by a slender man with dark skin and very dark eyes. He was neither tall nor short, but he emanated raw physical power. This was conveyed by his enormous shoulders, accentuated by the stretched cloth of his white shirt, open at the neck, with the sleeves rolled up, displaying a pair of muscular arms. His black hair was trimmed, his face striking, as much for its rigid solemnity as for its features.

He studied the two women, then nodded, gesturing them inside. He watched Helden's limp without comment; observed their drenched clothing in the same manner.

"I am Yakov Ben-Gadíz," he said. "So that we understand one another, it is I who will make the decisions."

"On what basis?" asked Althene.

Ben-Gadíz looked at her. "You are the mother?"

"Yes."

"I didn't expect you."

"I didn't expect to be here. I'd be dead if it weren't for this girl."

"Then you have a further obligation, in addition to your overwhelming one."

"I asked you a question. On whose authority do you make decisions for me? No one does."

"I've been in contact with Neuchâtel. There's work to be done tonight."

"There's only one thing *I* must do. That's reach my son."

"Later," said Yakov Ben-Gadíz. "There's something else first. A list must be found. We think it is in the Hôtel d'Accord."

"It's vital," interrupted Helden, her hand on Althene's arm.

"As vital as reaching your son," continued Yakov, staring at the Holcroft woman. "And I need a decoy."

42

Von Tiebolt spoke into the telephone, Kessler's note in his free hand. On the other end of the line was the first deputy of canton Genève. "I tell you, the address is wrong! It's an old deserted building, no telephone wires going through it. I'd say the Nachrichtendienst rather successfully invaded your state telephone service. Now, find me the right one!"

The blond man listened for several moments and then exploded. "You idiot, I *can't* call the number! The clerk swore he'd give it to no one but Holcroft. No matter what I might say, she'd be alarmed. Now, find me that address! I don't care if you have to wake up the president of the Federal Council to do it. I expect you to call me back within the hour." He slammed down the phone and looked again at Kessler's note.

Erich had gone to meet Holcroft. Undoubtedly they were at the Excelsior by now, registered under the name of Fresca. He could phone to make sure, but calling might lead to complications. The American had to be pushed to the edge of sanity. His friend from London murdered, his mother nowhere to be found; it was even possible he'd heard of Helden's death in Neuchâtel. Holcroft would be close to breaking; he might demand a meeting.

Johann was not prepared to agree to one yet. It was shortly past three o'clock in the morning, and the mother had not been located. He had to find her, kill her. There were six hours to go before the conference at the bank. At any moment—from out of a crowd, from a taxi in traffic, on a staircase or in a corner—she might confront her son and scream the warning: *Betrayal! Stop! Abandon Geneva!*

That could not happen! Her voice had to be stilled, the programming of her son carried out. Quite simply,

446

she had to die tonight, all risks eliminated with her death. And then another death would follow quickly, quietly. The son of Heinrich Clausen would have fulfilled his function.

But first, his mother. Before daybreak. What was infuriating was that she was out there. At the end of a telephone line whose accurate address was buried in some bureaucrat's file!

The blond man sat down and took a long, double-edged knife from a scabbard sewn into his coat. He'd have to wash it. The red-bearded pilot had soiled it.

Noel opened his suitcase on the luggage rack and looked at the rumpled mass of clothes inside. Then his eyes scanned the white walls with the flock paper and the French doors and the small, overly ornate chandelier in the ceiling. Hotel rooms were all beginning to look alike; he remembered the seedy exception in Berlin with a certain fondness. That he even remembered it under the circumstances was a little startling. He had settled into his unsettling new world with his faculties intact. He was not sure whether that was good or bad, only that it was so.

Erich was on the phone, trying to reach Von Tiebolt at the d'Accord. Where the hell was Johann? It was three-thirty in the morning. Kessler hung up and turned to Noel. "He left a message saying we weren't to be alarmed. He's with the first deputy. They're doing everything they can to find your mother."

"No call from her, then?"

"No."

"It doesn't make sense. Is the desk clerk still there?"

"Yes. You paid him two weeks' wages. The least he could do is to stay through the night." Kessler's expression grew pensive. "You know, it's quite possible she's simply delayed. Missed connections, a fog-bound airport, difficulties with immigration somewhere."

"Anything's possible, but it still doesn't make sense. I know her; she'd get word to me."

"Perhaps she's being detained."

"I thought about that; it's the best thing that could happen. She's traveling under a false passport. Let's hope she's arrested and thrown into a cell for a couple of days. No call from Helden, either?"

"No calls at all," replied the German, his eyes suddenly riveted on Noel.

Holcroft stretched, shaving kit in hand. "It's the waiting without knowing that drives me crazy." He gestured at the bathroom door. "I'm going to wash up."

"Good idea. Then why don't you rest for a while? You must be exhausted. We have less than five hours to go, and I do believe Johann's a very capable man."

"I'm banking on it," said Noel.

He took off his shirt and ran the hot water at full force, generating steam. The vapor rose, clouding the mirror and fogging the area above the sink. He put his face into the moist heat, supporting himself on the edge of the basin, and stayed there until sweat poured down his forehead. The practice was one he had learned from Sam Buonoventura several years ago. It was no substitute for a steam bath, but it helped.

Sam? Sam! For Christ's sake, why hadn't he *thought* of him? If his mother had changed her plans, or something had happened, it was entirely possible she'd call Sam. Especially if there was no one at the d'Accord named Noel Holcroft.

He looked at his watch; it was three-thirty-five, Geneva time, ten-thirty-five, Caribbean. If Sam had something to tell him, he'd stay by the telephone.

Noel turned off the faucet. He could hear Kessler's voice from the bedroom, but there was no one else there. Whom was he talking to, and why was he keeping his voice so low?

Holcroft turned to the door and opened it less than an inch. Kessler was across the room, his back to the bathroom door, speaking into the telephone. Noel heard the words and stepped out.

"I tell you, that's our answer. She's traveling with a false passport. Check immigration records for—"

"Erich!"

Yakov Ben-Gadíz closed the first-aid kit, stood up beside the bed, and surveyed his handiwork. Helden's wound was inflamed, but there was no infection. He had replaced the soiled bandage with a clean one.

"There," he said, "that will do for a while. The swelling will go down in an hour or so, but you must stay off your feet. Keep the leg elevated."

"Don't tell me you're a doctor," said Helden.

"One doesn't have to be a doctor to treat bullet wounds. You just have to get used to them." The Israeli crossed to the door. "Stay here. I want to talk to Mrs. Holcroft."

"No!"

Ben-Gadíz stopped. "What did you say?"

"Don't send her out alone. She's beside herself with guilt and frightened for her son. She can't think clearly; she won't have a chance. Don't do it."

"And if I do, you'll stop me?"

"There's a better way. You want my brother. Use *me*."

"I want the *Sonnenkinder* list first. We've got three days to kill Von Tiebolt."

"Three days?"

"Banks are closed tomorrow and Sunday. Monday would be the earliest they could meet with the Grande Banque's directors. The list comes first. I agree with Litvak; *it* is the priority."

"If it's so important, he's surely got it *with* him."

"I doubt it. Men like your brother don't take chances like that. An accident, a robbery in the streets . . . someone like me. No, he wouldn't carry that list around. Nor would he put it in a hotel vault. It's in his room. In a better vault. I want to get in that room, get him out of there for a while."

"Then all the more reason to use me!" said Helden. "He thinks I'm *dead*. He didn't see me at the seaplane base; he was looking for her, not me. The shock will stun him; he'll be confused. He'll go anywhere I say to find me. All I have to do is say the word 'Nachrichtendienst.' I'm *sure* of it."

"And I'm counting on it," replied Yakov. "But for tomorrow. Not tonight. You're not the one he wants tonight. Holcroft's mother is."

"I'll tell him she's *with* me! It's perfect!"

"He'd never believe you. You, who went to Neuchâtel to meet Werner Gerhardt? Who escaped? You're synonymous with a trap."

"Then at least let me go with her," pleaded Helden. "Set up a meeting and I'll stay out of sight. Give her *some* protection. I have a gun."

Ben-Gadíz thought a moment before answering. "I

know what you're offering, and I admire you for it. But I can't risk the two of you. You see, I need her tonight, and I'll need you tomorrow. She'll draw him away tonight; you'll draw him out tomorrow. It has to be that way."

"You can accomplish *both* tonight!" pressed Helden. "Get your *list*. I'll *kill* him. I swear it!"

"I believe you, but you're missing a point. I give your brother more credit than you do. No matter how we plan, he'll control the meeting with Mrs. Holcroft tonight. He has the numbers, the methods. We don't."

Helden stared at the Israeli. "You're not only using her; you're sacrificing her."

"I'll use *each* of us, sacrifice each of us, to do what has to be done. If you interfere, I'll kill you." Yakov walked to the bedroom door and let himself out.

Althene was sitting at a desk at the far end of the room, its small lamp the only source of light. She wore a deep-red bathrobe that she'd found in a closet, and it fit her loosely. The drenched clothes she and Helden had worn were draped over radiators, drying out. She was writing on a sheet of stationery. At the sound of Yakov's footsteps, she turned.

"I borrowed some paper from your desk," she said.

"It's not my paper, not my desk," answered the Israeli. "Are you writing a letter?"

"Yes. To my son."

"Why? With any luck we'll reach him. You'll talk."

Althene leaned back in the chair, her gaze steady on Ben-Gadíz. "I think we both know that there's little chance I'll see him again."

"Do we?"

"Of course. There's no point in my deceiving myself . . . or in your trying to deceive me. Von Tiebolt has to meet with me. When he does, he won't let me go. Not alive. Why would he?"

"We'll take precautions as best we can."

"I'll take a gun, thank you. I've no intention of standing there, telling him to fire away."

"It would be better if you were sitting."

They smiled at each other. "We're both practical, aren't we? Survivors."

Yakov shrugged. "It's easier that way."

"Tell me. This list you want so badly. The *Sonnen-*

kinder. It must be enormous. Volumes. Names of people and families everywhere."

"That's not the list we're after; that's the master list. I doubt we'll ever see it. The list we *can* find—we've *got* to find—is the practical one. The names of the leaders who'll receive the funds, who'll distribute them in strategic areas. That list has to be where Von Tiebolt can get it readily."

"And with it, you'll have the identity of Wolfsschanze's leaders."

"Everywhere."

"Why are you so sure it's at the d'Accord?"

"It's the only place it could be. Von Tiebolt trusts no one. He lets others deal in fragments; he controls the whole. He wouldn't leave the list in a vault; nor would he carry it on him. It will be in his hotel room, the room itself filled with traps. And he would leave it only under the direst of circumstances."

"We agree I'm that circumstance."

"Yes. He fears you as he fears no one else, for no one else could convince your son to walk away from Geneva. They need him; they always have. The laws must be observed for the funds to be released. There was never any other way."

"There's irony in that. The law is used to perpetrate the greatest illegality imaginable."

"It is not a new device, Mrs. Holcroft."

"What about my son? Will you kill him?"

"I don't want to."

"I'd like something more concrete."

"There'll be no reason to, if he comes with us. If he can be convinced of the truth and not think he's being tricked, there's good reason to keep him alive. Wolfsschanze won't end with the collapse of the funds. The *Sonnenkinder* are out there. They'll be crippled, but not exposed. Or destroyed. We'll need every voice that can be raised against them. Your son will have a vital story to tell. Together we'll reach the right people."

"How will you convince him . . . if I don't come back from my meeting with Von Tiebolt?"

The Israeli saw the hint of a smile on Althene's lips and understood her pause. His assumption had been clear: She would not come back.

"As the contact in Neuchâtel and I see it, we have

today and tomorrow; the moves at La Grande Banque will no doubt begin Monday. They'll keep him isolated, out of reach. It's my job to break that isolation, get him away."

"And when you do, what will you say?"

"I'll tell him the truth, explain everything we learned at Har Sha'alav. Helden can be extremely helpful—if she's alive, frankly. And then there's the list. If I find it, I'll show it to him."

"Show him this letter," interrupted Althene, turning back to the paper on the desk.

"It, too, would be helpful," said the Israeli.

"Erich!"

Kessler whipped around, his obese body rigid. He started to lower the phone, but Holcroft stopped him.

"Hold it! Who are you talking to?" Noel grabbed the telephone; he spoke into it. "Who is this?"

Silence.

"Who is this?"

"Please," said Kessler, regaining his composure. "We're trying to *protect* you. You can't be seen on the streets; you know that. They'll kill you. You're the key to Geneva."

"You weren't talking about me!"

"We're trying to find your mother! You said she was traveling on a false passport, out of Lisbon. We didn't understand that. Johann knows people who provide such papers; we were discussing it now."

Holcroft spoke again into the phone. "Von Tiebolt? Is that you?"

"Yes, Noel," came the calm reply. "Erich's right. I have friends here who are trying to help us. Your mother could be in danger. You can't be a part of the search. You must stay out of sight."

" 'Can't'?" Holcroft said the word sharply. " 'Must'? Let's get something straight—both of you." Noel spoke into the phone, his eyes on Kessler. "I'll decide what I do and what I don't do. Is that clear?"

The scholar nodded. Von Tiebolt said nothing. Holcroft raised his voice. "I asked you if that was *clear!"*

"Yes, of course," said Johann finally. "As Erich has told you, we only want to help. This information about your mother's traveling on a passport that's not her own could be helpful. I know men who deal in such matters. I'll make calls and keep you informed."

"Please."

"If I don't see you before morning, we'll meet at the bank. I assume Erich's explained."

"Yes, he has. And, Johann . . . I'm sorry I blew; I know you're trying to help. The people we're after are called the Nachrichtendienst, aren't they? That's what you found out in London."

There was a pause on the line. Then, "How did you know?"

"They left a calling card. I want those bastards."

"So do we."

"Thanks. Call me the minute you hear anything." Noel hung up. "Don't ever do that again," he told Kessler.

"I apologize. I thought I was doing the right thing. Just as I think you believed you were doing the right thing to have me followed from the d'Accord."

"It's a lousy world these days," Noel said, reaching for the phone.

"What are you doing?"

"There's a man in Curaçao I want to talk to. He may know something."

"Oh, yes. The engineer who's been relaying your messages."

"I owe him."

Noel reached the overseas operator and gave her the number in Curaçao. "Shall I stay on the line, or will you call me back?"

"The cables are not crowded at this hour, sir."

"I'll stay on." He sat on the bed and waited. Before ninety seconds had passed, he heard the ring of Buonoventura's phone.

A male voice answered. But it was not Sam's voice.

"Yeah?"

"Sam Buonoventura, please."

"Who wants him?"

"A personal friend. I'm calling from Europe."

"He ain't gonna come runnin', mister. He ain't takin' no more phone calls."

"What are you talking about?"

"Sam bought it, mister. Some fuckin' nigger native

put a wire through his throat. We're beating the high grass and the beaches for that son of a bitch."

Holcroft lowered his head, his eyes closed, his breath suspended. His moves had been traced to Sam, and Sam's help could not be tolerated. Buonoventura was his information center; he had to be killed, no more messages relayed. The Nachrichtendienst was trying to isolate him. He had owed Sam a debt, and that debt had been paid with death. Everything he touched was touched with death; he was its carrier.

"Don't bother with the high grass," he said, barely aware he was talking. "I killed him."

43

"Did your son ever mention the name 'Tennyson'?" asked Ben-Gadíz.

"No."

"Damn it! When was the last time you talked with him?"

"After my husband's death. He was in Paris."

Yakov unfolded his arms; he had heard something he wanted to hear. "Was it the first time you'd spoken since your husband's death?"

"His murder," corrected Althene. "Although I didn't know it then."

"Answer my question. Was it the first time you'd talked since your husband died?"

"Yes."

"It was a sad conversation, then."

"Obviously. I had to tell him."

"Good. Such times cloud the mind; things are said that are rarely recalled with clarity. *That's* when he mentioned the name 'Tennyson.' He told you he was on his way to Geneva, probably with a man named Tennyson. Can you convey that to Von Tiebolt?"

"Certainly. But will he accept it?"

"He has no choice. He wants you."

"I want him."

"Make the call. And remember, you're close to hysterics; a panicked woman is unmanageable. Throw him off balance with your voice. Shout, whisper, stutter. Tell him you were to call your pilot at the seaplane base. There's been a killing; it was swarming with police, and you're frightened out of your mind. Can you do it?"

"Just listen," said Althene, reaching for the phone.

The d'Accord switchboard connected her to the room of its very important guest Mr. John Tennyson.

And Yakov listened in admiration as Althene performed.

"You must get hold of yourself, Mrs. Holcroft," said the stranger at the d'Accord.

"Then you *are* the Tennyson my son referred to?"

"Yes. I'm a friend. We met in Paris."

"For the love of God, can you help me?"

"Of course. It would be a privilege."

"Where's Noel?"

"I'm afraid I don't know. . . . He has business in Geneva with which I'm not involved."

"You're not?" A statement made in relief.

"Oh, no. We had dinner earlier—last night, actually —and he left to see his associates."

"Did he say where he was going?"

"I'm afraid he didn't. You see, I'm on my way to Milan. . . . In Paris, I told Noel I'd stop over with him in Geneva and show him the city. He's never been here, of course."

"Can you meet with me, Mr. Tennyson?"

"Certainly. Where are you?"

"We must be careful. I can't let you take risks."

"There's no risk for me, Mrs. Holcroft. I move freely in Geneva."

"I don't. That dreadful business at Médoc."

"Come now, you're overwrought. Whatever it was, I'm sure it doesn't concern you. Where are you? Where can we meet?"

"The train station. The north entrance waiting room. In forty-five minutes. God bless you."

She hung up abruptly. Yakov Ben-Gadíz smiled in approval.

"He'll be very careful," said the Israeli. "He'll mount his defenses, and that will give us more time. I'll head for the d'Accord. I'll need every minute."

Von Tiebolt replaced the receiver slowly. The possibilities of a trap were greater rather than fewer, he thought, but the evidence was not conclusive. He had purposely made the statement that Holcroft had never been to Geneva; it was a lie, and the old woman knew it. On the other hand, she sounded genuinely panicked, and a woman of her age in panic did not so much listen as wish to be listened to. It was conceivable that she had not heard the remark, or, if she had, that she considered it subordinate to her own concerns.

Holcroft's using the name "Tennyson"—if he had—was not out of character for the American. He was subject to quick emotional outbursts, often speaking without thinking. The news of Richard Holcroft's death in New York could easily have put him in such an emotional state that the name "Tennyson" slipped out without his realizing it.

On the other hand, the American had displayed strengths where strengths had not been thought to exist. Giving the name to his mother contradicted the discipline he had developed. And further, Johann knew that he was dealing with a woman who was capable of obtaining false papers, who had disappeared in Lisbon. He would take extraordinary precautions. He would not be trapped by an old woman in panic—or by one who pretended to be in panic.

The telephone rang, breaking his concentration.

"Yes?"

It was the first deputy. They were still trying to locate the accurate address of the telephone number given the d'Accord by Mrs. Holcroft. A bureaucrat was on his way to the state telephone office to open a file. Von Tiebolt replied icily.

"By the time he finds it, it will be of no use to us. I've made contact with the woman. Send a policeman driving an official car to the d'Accord immediately. Tell him I'm a visitor of state who requires a personal courtesy. Have him in the lobby in fifteen minutes." Von Tiebolt did not wait for a reply. He replaced the phone and went back to the table where there were two handguns. They had been broken down for cleaning; he would reassemble them quickly. They were two of the Tinamou's favorite weapons.

If Althene Holcroft had the audacity to bait a trap, she would learn she was no match for the leader of Wolfsschanze. Her trap would snap back, crushing her in its teeth.

The Israeli stayed out of sight in an alleyway across from the d'Accord. On the hotel steps, Von Tiebolt was talking quietly with a police officer, giving him instructions. When they had finished talking, the officer ran to his car. The blond man walked to a black limousine at the curb and climbed in behind the wheel. Von Tiebolt wanted no chauffeur for the trip he was about to make.

Both cars drove off down the rue des Granges. Yakov waited until he could see neither, then, briefcase in hand, walked across the street to the d'Accord.

He approached the front desk, the picture of weary officialdom. He sighed as he spoke to the clerk. "Police examiners. I've been rousted from my bed to take additional scrapings from the dead man's room. That Ellis fellow. The inspectors never have ideas until everyone they need is asleep. What's the number?"

"Third floor. Room thirty-one," said the clerk, grinning sympathetically. "There's an officer on duty outside."

"Thanks." Ben-Gadíz walked to the elevator, pressing the button for the fifth floor. John Tennyson was registered in room 512. There was no time to indulge in games with a policeman on guard duty. He needed every minute—every second—he could get.

The man in the uniform of the Geneva police walked through the north entrance of the railroad station, his leather heels clicking against the stone. He approached the old woman seated at the far end of the first row of benches.

"Mrs. Althene Holcroft?"

"Yes?"

"Please come with me, madame."

"May I ask why?"

"I'm to escort you to Mr. Tennyson."

"Is that necessary?"

"It is a courtesy of the city of Geneva."

The old woman got to her feet and accompanied the man in uniform. As they walked toward the double doors of the north entrance, four additional policemen emerged from the outside and took up positions in front of the doors. No one would pass by them until permission was granted.

Outside, on the platform, flanking a police car at the curb, were two more uniformed men. The one near the hood opened the door for the woman. She climbed in; her escort addressed his subordinates.

"As instructed, no private automobiles or taxis are to leave the terminal for a period of twenty minutes. Should any attempt to do so, get the identifications and have the information radioed to my car."

"Yes, sir."

"If there are no incidents, the men may go back to their posts in twenty minutes." The police officer got inside the car and started the engine.

"Where are we going?" asked Althene.

"To a guest house on the estate of the first deputy of Geneva. This Mr. Tennyson must be a very important man."

"In many ways," she replied.

Von Tiebolt waited behind the wheel of the black limousine. He was parked fifty yards from the ramp that led out of the station's north entrance, the limousine's motor idling. He watched as the police car drove out into the street and turned right, then waited until he saw the two police officers take up their positions.

He pulled out into the street. As planned, he would follow the police car at a discreet distance, keeping alert for signs of other automobiles showing interest in that vehicle. All contingencies had to be considered, including the possibility that somewhere on her person the old woman had concealed an electronic homing device that would send out signals attracting the carrion she employed.

The last obstacle to Code Wolfsschanze would be eliminated within the hour.

Yakov Ben-Gadíz stood in front of Von Tiebolt's door. The "do not disturb" sign was posted. The Israeli knelt down and opened his briefcase. He took out an odd-shaped flashlight and snapped it on; the glow was a barely perceptible light green. He pointed the light at the bottom left of the door, worked across, and up, and over the top. He was looking for strands of thread or of human hair—tiny alarms that if removed told the occupant his room had been entered. The light identified two threads stretched below, then three vertically, and one above. Yakov removed a tiny pin recessed in the handle of the flashlight. Delicately, he touched the wood beside each thread; the pin markings were infinitesimal—unseen by the naked eye but picked up by the green light. He then knelt again and took a small metal cylinder from his briefcase. It was a highly sophisticated electronic lock-picking instrument developed in the counterterrorist laboratories at Tel Aviv.

He placed the mouth of the cylinder over the lock and activated the tumbler probes. The lock sprung, and Yakov carefully slid the fingers of his left hand along the borders of the door, removing the threads. Slowly, he pushed the door open. He reached for his briefcase, stepped inside, and closed the door. There was a small table by the wall; he put the threads down carefully on it, weighting them with the cylinder, and again snapped on the flashlight.

He looked at his watch. Conservatively, he had no more than thirty minutes to deactivate whatever alarms Von Tiebolt had set and to find the *Sonnenkinder* list. The fact that threads had been planted in the door was a good sign. They were there for a reason.

He angled the beam of green light around the sitting room. There were two closets and the bedroom door, all closed. He eliminated the closets first. No threads, no bolted locks, nothing.

He approached the door to the bedroom and threw the beam along the edges. There were no threads, but there was something else. The wash of green light picked up the reflection of a tiny yellow light recessed between the door and the frame, approximately two feet above the floor. Ben-Gadíz knew immediately what he was looking at: a miniature photoelectric cell, making contact with another drilled into the wood of the door's edging.

If the door was opened, the contact would be broken and the alarm triggered. It was as foolproof as modern technology allowed; there was no way to immobilize the device. Yakov had seen them before, tiny cells with built-in timers. Once implanted, they were there for the specific durations called for, rarely less than five hours. No one, including the person who set them, could neutralize them before the timers ran down.

Which meant that Johann von Tiebolt expected to break the contact if he wanted to enter the room. Emergencies might arise that required his tripping the alarm.

What kind of alarm was it? Sound had to be ruled out; any loud noise would draw attention to the room. Radio signals were a possibility, but signals had too limited a range.

No, the alarm itself had to release a deterrent within

the immediate vicinity of the protected area. A deterrent that would immobilize an intruder but could be defused by Von Tiebolt himself.

Electric shock was not dependable. Acid was uncontrollable; Von Tiebolt might sustain permanent injury and disfigurement. Was it a gas? A vapor? . . .

Toxin. A vaporized poison. Toxic *fumes.* Powerful enough to render a trespasser unconscious. An oxygen mask would be protection against the vapor. If Von Tiebolt used one, he could enter the room at will.

Tear gas and Mace were not unknown in Yakov's line of work. He returned to his briefcase, knelt down, and pulled out a gas mask with a small canister of oxygen. He put it on, inserted the mouthpiece, and went back to the door. He pushed the door open quickly, and stepped back.

A burst of vapor filled the door frame. It was suspended for several seconds and then evaporated rapidly, leaving the space as clear as if it had never appeared. Ben-Gadíz felt a minor stinging around his eyes. It was an irritant, not blinding, but Yakov knew that if inhaled, the chemicals that produced that stinging would inflame the lungs and cause his instant collapse. It was the proof he was looking for. The *Sonnenkinder* list was somewhere in that room.

He stepped through the doorway, past a tripod with a cylinder of gas attached to the top. To remove whatever traces might remain of the fumes, he opened a window; cold winter air rushed in, billowing the curtains.

Ben-Gadíz went back into the sitting room, picked up his briefcase, and returned to the bedroom to begin the search. Assuming that the list would be protected by a fire-resistant steel container of some sort, he took out a small metal scanner with a luminous dial. He started at the bed area and began working his way around the room.

The needle of the detector leaped forward in front of the clothes closet. The green light picked up the familiar tiny yellow dots in the door frame.

He had found the vault.

He opened the door; vapor burst forth, filling the closet as it had filled the space of the bedroom door. Only now it remained longer than before, the cloud denser. If the first alarm had malfunctioned, this one contained enough toxin to kill a man. On the floor of the closet was an overnight suitcase, its dark-brown leather soft and expensive, but Yakov knew it was not an ordinary piece of luggage. There were no wrinkles on the front or back, as there were across the top and down the sides. The leather was reinforced with steel.

He checked for threads and markings with the green light; there were none. He lifted the suitcase to the bed, then pushed a second button on the flashlight. The green light was replaced with a sharp beam of yellowish white. He studied the two locks. They were different; doubtless each triggered a different alarm.

He removed a thin pick from his pocket and inserted it in the lock on the right, careful to keep his hand as far back as possible.

There was a rush of air; a long needle shot out from the left of the lock. Fluid oozed from the point, globules dripping to the carpet. Yakov took out a handkerchief, wiped the needle clean, and slowly, cautiously, pushed it back into its recess, using his pick to press it through the tiny orifice.

He turned his attention to the lock on the left. Standing to the side he repeated the manipulations with the pick; the latch snapped up; there was a second rush of air. Instead of a needle, something shot out, embedding itself in the fabric of an armchair across the room. Ben-Gadíz rushed over, shining the light on the point of entry. There was a circle of dampness where the object had entered the cloth. With the pick, he dug it out.

It was a gelatinous capsule, its tip made of steel. It would enter flesh as easily as it had broken the threads of fabric. The fluid was a powerful narcotic of some sort.

Satisfied, Ben-Gadíz put the capsule in his pocket, returned to the suitcase, and opened it. Inside was a flat metal envelope attached to the steel reinforcement. He had reached the safety box beyond the alarms, within the successive deadly vaults, and it was his.

He looked at his watch; the operation had taken eighteen minutes.

He lifted the flap of the metal envelope and took out the papers. There were eleven pages, each page containing six columns—names, cable addresses, and cities—perhaps one hundred fifty entries per page. Approximately sixteen hundred and fifty identities.

The elite of the *Sonnenkinder*. The manipulators of Wolfsschanze.

Yakov Ben-Gadíz knelt down over his open briefcase and removed a camera.

"Vous êtes très aimable. Nous vous téléphonons dans une demi-heure. Merci." Kessler hung up the telephone, shaking his head at Noel, who stood by the window of the Excelsior suite. "Nothing. Your mother didn't call the d'Accord."

"They're certain?"

"There've been no calls at all for a Mr. Holcroft. I even checked the switchboard, in case the desk clerk had stepped out for a moment or two. You heard me."

"I don't understand her. Where *is* she? She should have called hours ago. And Helden. She said she'd phone me Friday night; goddammit, it's Saturday morning!"

"Nearly four o'clock," said Erich. "You really should get some rest. Johann's doing everything he can to find your mother. He's got the best people in Geneva working for us."

"I can't rest," said Noel. "You forget: I just killed a man in Curaçao. His crime was helping me, and I killed him."

"You didn't. The Nachrichtendienst did."

"Then let's *do* something!" cried Holcroft. "Von Tiebolt has friends in high places. Tell them about it! British Intelligence owes him one hell of a debt; he gave them the Tinamou! Call in that debt! Now! Let the whole goddamn world know about those bastards! What are we waiting for?"

Kessler took several steps toward Noel, his eyes level and compassionate. "We're waiting for the most important thing of all. The meeting at the bank. The covenant. Once that's over with, there's nothing we can't do. And when we do it, the 'whole goddamn world,' as you put it, will have to listen. Look to our covenant, Noel. It's the answer to so much. For you, your mother, Helden . . . so much. I think you know that."

Holcroft nodded slowly, his voice tired, his mind exhausted. "I do. It's the not knowing, not hearing, that drives me crazy."

"I know it's been difficult for you. But it will be over soon; everything will be fine." Erich smiled. "I'm going to wash up."

Noel went to the window. Geneva was asleep—as

Paris had been asleep, and Berlin and London and Rio. Through how many windows had he looked out at the sleeping cities at night? Too many. *Nothing is as it was for you. . . .*

Nothing.

Holcroft frowned. *Nothing.* Not even his name. His *name.* He was registered as Fresca. Not Holcroft, but Fresca! That was the name Helden was to call!

Fresca.

He spun around toward the telephone. There was no point in having Erich make the call; the d'Accord operator spoke English, and he knew the number. He dialed.

"Hôtel d'Accord. *Bonsoir.*"

"Operator, this is Mr. Holcroft. Dr. Kessler spoke to you a few minutes ago about the messages I was expecting."

"I beg your pardon, monsieur. Dr. Kessler? You wish Dr. Kessler?"

"No, you don't understand. Dr. Kessler spoke to you just a few minutes ago about my messages. There's another name I want to ask you about. 'Fresca.' 'N. Fresca.' Have there been any messages for N. Fresca?"

The operator paused. "There's no Fresca at the d'Accord, monsieur. Do you wish me to ring Dr. Kessler's room?"

"No, he's *here.* He just spoke to you!" Goddammit, thought Noel, the woman could speak English, but she couldn't seem to understand it. Then he remembered the name of the desk clerk; he gave it to the operator. "May I speak with him, please?"

"I'm sorry, monsieur. He left over three hours ago. He's off duty at midnight."

Holcroft held his breath, his eyes on the bathroom door. He could hear water running; Erich could not hear him. And the operator understood English perfectly. "Wait a minute, miss. Let me get this straight. You didn't talk with Dr. Kessler a few minutes ago?"

"No, monsieur."

"Is there another operator on the switchboard?"

"No. There are very few calls during these hours."

"And the desk clerk left at midnight?"

"Yes, I just told you."

"And there've been no calls for Mr. Holcroft?"

Again the operator paused. When she spoke, she was

hesitant, as if remembering. "I think there was, monsieur. Shortly after I came on duty. A woman called. I was instructed to give the call to the head clerk."

"Thank you," said Noel softly, hanging up.

The water in the bathroom stopped running. Kessler stepped out. He saw Holcroft's hand on the telephone. The scholar's eyes were no longer gentle.

"What the hell's going on?" asked Noel. "You didn't talk to the clerk. *Or* the switchboard. My mother called hours ago. You never told me. You *lied*."

"You must not get upset, Noel."

"You lied to me!" roared Holcroft, grabbing his jacket off the chair and going to the bed where he had thrown his raincoat—the raincoat with the gun in the pocket. "She *called* me, you son of a bitch!"

Kessler ran to the foyer and placed himself in front of the door. "She wasn't where she said she would be! We are worried. We are trying to find her, *protect* her. Protect you! Von Tiebolt understands these things; he's lived with them. Let *him* make the decisions."

"*Decisions?* What goddamn decisions? He doesn't make decisions for me! Neither do you! Get out of my way!"

Kessler did not move, so Noel grabbed him by the shoulders and threw him across the room.

Holcroft raced into the hallway, toward the staircase.

44

The gates of the estate parted; the official vehicle drove through. The policeman nodded to the guard and glanced warily through the window at the Doberman, straining on its leash, prepared to attack. He turned to Mrs. Holcroft.

"The guest house is four kilometers from the gate. We take the road that veers to the right, off the main drive."

"I'll take your word for it," said Althene.

"I tell you because I've never been here before, madame. I trust I'll find my way in the dark."

"I'm sure you will."

"I'm to leave you there and return to my official duties," he said. "There's no one at the guest house, but the front entrance, I'm told, will be open."

"I see. Mr. Tennyson is waiting for me?"

The police officer seemed to hesitate. "He'll be along shortly. He'll drive you back, of course."

"Of course. Tell me, do your orders come from Mr. Tennyson?"

"My present instructions, yes. Not the orders. They come from the first deputy, through the prefect of police."

"The first deputy? The prefect? They're friends of Mr. Tennyson's?"

"I imagine so, madame. As I mentioned, Mr. Tennyson must be a very important man. Yes, I'd say they are friends."

"But you're not?"

The man laughed. "Me? Oh, no, madame. I only met the gentleman briefly. As I said to you, this is merely a municipal courtesy."

"I see. Do you think you might extend a courtesy to me?" asked Althene, pointedly opening her purse. "On a confidential basis."

"That would depend, madame. . . ."

"It's only a telephone call to a friend who may be worried about me. I forgot to call her from the railroad station."

"Gladly," said the officer. "As a friend of Mr. Tennyson, I assume you're also an important visitor to Genève."

"I'll write out the number. A young lady will answer. Tell her exactly where you've taken me."

The guest house was high ceilinged, with tapestries on the walls and French-provincial furniture. It belonged in the Loire Valley, an adjunct to a great château.

Althene sat in a large chair, the pistol belonging to Yakov Ben-Gadíz wedged between the pillow and the base of the arm. The police officer had left five minutes ago; she waited now for Johann von Tiebolt.

The almost overpowering temptation to shoot the instant Von Tiebolt walked through the door had to be controlled. If there were things she could learn, she had to learn them. If only on the possibility she could relay them to the Israeli, or to the girl. Somehow . . .

He had arrived; the low, vibrating sound of a car motor outside was proof. She had heard that powerful engine hours before as it came to a stop on a deserted stretch of highway above Lake Geneva. She had watched through the trees as the blond man killed. As he had killed ruthlessly hours later at Atterrisage Médoc. To bring about his death would be a privilege. She touched the handle of the gun, secure in her purpose.

The door opened, and the tall man with the shining blond hair and the sculptured features walked inside. He closed the door; his movements in the soft, indirect lighting were supple.

"Mrs. Holcroft, how good of you to come."

"It was I who asked for the meeting. How good of you to arrange it. Your precautions were commendable."

"You seemed to feel they were called for."

"No automobile could have followed us from the station."

"None did. We're alone."

"This is a pleasant house. My son would find it interesting. As an architect, he'd call it an example of something or other, and point out the various influences."

"I'm sure he would; his mind works that way."

"Yes," said Althene, smiling. "He'll be walking down a street and suddenly stop and stare up at a window or a cornice, seeing a detail others don't see. He's quite devoted to his work. I never knew where he got it from. I have no talents in that direction, and his late father was a banker."

The blond man stood motionless. "Then both fathers were associated with money."

"You know, then?" Althene asked.

"Of course. Heinrich Clausen's son. I think we can stop lying to each other, Mrs. Holcroft."

"I understood it was a lie on your part, Herr von Tiebolt. I wasn't sure you knew it was one on mine."

"To be frank, until this moment I didn't. If your objective was to set a trap, I'm sorry to have spoiled it for you. But then, I'm sure you knew the risk."

"Yes, I did."

"Why did you take it? You must have considered the consequences."

"I considered them. But I felt it was only fair to let you know the consequences of a previous action on my part. Knowing it, perhaps an accommodation can be reached between us."

"Really? And what would this accommodation entail?"

"Abandoning Geneva. Dismantling Wolfsschanze."

"Is that all?" The blond man smiled. "You're mad."

"Suppose I told you that I had written a very long letter detailing a lie I have lived with for over thirty years. A letter in which I identify the participants and their strategy by name and family and bank."

"And destroyed your son in so doing."

"He'd be the first to agree with what I did, if he knew."

Von Tiebolt folded his arms. "You said, 'Suppose I told you' . . . about this letter of yours. Well, you've told me. And I'm afraid I'd have to say that you wrote about something you know nothing about. All the laws have been observed, and the pitifully few facts you claim to have would be called the ramblings of a crazy old woman who's been the object of official surveillance for a very long time. But this is irrelevant. You never wrote such a letter."

"You don't know that."

"Please," said Von Tiebolt. "We have copies of every

bit of correspondence, every will, every legal document you've written . . . as well as the substance of every phone call you've made during the past five years."

"You've *what?*"

"There's a file at your Federal Bureau of Investigation with the code name 'Mother Goddamn.' It's one that will never be released under the Freedom of Information Act, because it deals with national security. No one's quite sure why, but it does, and certain latitudes are permitted. That file is also at the Central Intelligence Agency and the Defense Intelligence Agency and in the computer banks of Army G-Two." Von Tiebolt smiled again. "We are *everywhere*, Mrs. Holcroft. Can't you understand that? You should know it before you leave this world; your remaining here would change nothing. You can't stop us. No one can."

"You'll be stopped because you offer lies! You always did. And when the lies fail, you kill. It was your way then; it's your way now."

"Lies are palliatives; death is often the answer for irritating problems that interfere with progress."

"The problems being people."

"Always."

"You are the most contemptible man on earth. You're *insane!*"

The blond killer put his hand in his jacket pocket. "You make my work pleasant," he said, withdrawing a pistol. "Another woman said those words to me. She was no less headstrong than you. I put a bullet in her head— through a car window. At night. In Rio de Janeiro. She was my mother, and she called me insane, called our work contemptible. She never grasped the necessity—the beauty —of our cause. She tried to interfere." The blond man raised the gun. "A few old men—devoted lovers of the whore—suspected me of killing her and in their feeble way tried to have me charged. Can you imagine? Have me *charged*. It sounds so official. What they didn't realize was that we controlled the courts. *No one* can stop us."

"Noel will stop you!" cried Althene, her hand edging toward the concealed weapon at her side.

"Your son will be dead in a day or two. But even if we don't kill him, others will. He's left a trail of murder from which he can never extricate himself. A former member of British Intelligence was garroted in New York.

His last conversation was with your son. A man named Graff was killed in Rio; your son threatened him. A construction engineer in the Caribbean died tonight, also garroted. He relayed confidential messages to Noel Holcroft from Rio to Paris and stops in between. Tomorrow morning a New York detective named Miles will be slain in the streets. The current case file that obsesses him has been altered somewhat, but not its subject—Noel Holcroft. In fact, for Noel's own peace of mind it would probably be better if we killed him after all. He has no life now." Von Tiebolt raised his weapon higher, then stretched out his arm slowly, his target the woman's head. "So you see, Mrs. Holcroft, you can't possibly stop us. We are *everywhere.*"

Althene suddenly twisted in her chair, thrusting her hand toward the gun.

Johann von Tiebolt fired. Then he fired again. And again.

Yakov Ben-Gadíz rearranged Von Tiebolt's suite, leaving it exactly as he had found it, airing out the rooms so that there was no evidence of entry.

Were he alive, Klaus Falkenheim would be appalled at what Yakov was doing. *Get the list. The identities. Once the names are yours, expose the account for what it is. Cause the distribution of the millions to be abandoned. Cripple the Sonnenkinder.* Those had been Falkenheim's instructions.

But there was another way. It had been discussed quietly among the elders at Har Sha'alav. They'd never had time to bring it to Falkenheim's attention, but it was their intention to do so. They called it the option of Har Sha'alav.

It was dangerous, but it could be done.

Get the list and control the millions. Don't expose the account; steal it. Use the great fortune to fight the Sonnenkinder. Everywhere.

The strategy had not been perfected, because not enough was known. But Yakov knew enough now. Of the three sons who would present themselves to the bank, one was not what the others were.

In the beginning, Noel Holcroft was the key to fulfilling the Wolfsschanze covenant. At the end, he would be its undoing.

Falkenheim was dead, Yakov reflected. The elders of Har Sha'alav were dead; there was no one else. The decision was his alone.

The option of Har Sha'alav.

Could it be done?

He would know within the next twenty-four hours.

His eyes fell on every object in the room. Everything was in place, everything as it had been. Except that in his briefcase now were eleven photographs that could signify the beginning of the end of Wolfsschanze. Eleven pages of names, the identities of the most trusted, most powerful *Sonnenkinder* across the world. Men and women who had lived the Nazi lie in deep cover for thirty years.

Never again.

Yakov picked up his briefcase. He would rethread the outer door and . . .

He stopped all movement, all thought, and concentrated on the sudden intrusion from beyond the door. He could hear footsteps, racing footsteps, muffled by the carpet but distinguishable, running up the hotel corridor. They drew near, then came to an abrupt stop. Silence, followed by the sound of a key in the lock and the frantic turning of both knob and key. The inside latch held firm. A fist pounded against the door inches from Ben-Gadíz.

"Von Tiebolt! Let me in!"

It was the American. In seconds he would break down the door.

Kessler crawled to the bed, held on to the post, and pulled his large frame off the floor. His glasses had flown off his face under the force of Holcroft's attack. He would find them in a few minutes, but right now he had to think, to analyze his immediate course of action.

Holcroft would go to the d'Accord to confront Johann; there was nothing else he *could* do. But Johann was not there, and it was no time for the American to create a scene.

Nor *would* he, thought Kessler, smiling in spite of his anxiety. Holcroft had only to gain admittance to Von Tiebolt's suite. A simple hotel key was the answer. Once inside, the American would open the bedroom door. The instant he did, he would collapse, no longer an immediate problem.

An antidote and several ice packs would revive him

sufficiently for the conference at the bank; a dozen explanations would be given to him. It was only a matter of getting Johann's room key to him.

The clerks at the d'Accord would not give him one on the strength of another guest's request, but they would if the first deputy told them to. Von Tiebolt was his personal friend; accommodations were to be granted in all things.

Kessler picked up the phone.

Helden limped about the apartment, forcing her leg to get used to the pain, angry that she had been left behind, but knowing it was the sensible thing to do—the only thing. The Israeli did not think Noel would call, but it was a contingency that had to be considered. Yakov was convinced Noel was being isolated, all messages intercepted; but there was a remote chance . . .

The telephone rang; Helden thought the blood would burst from her throat. She swallowed, and limped across the room to pick it up. *Oh, God! Let it be Noel!*

It was an unfamiliar voice belonging to someone who would not identify himself.

"Mrs. Holcroft was driven to a guest house on an estate thirteen kilometers south of the city. I'll give you directions."

He did. Helden wrote them down. When he had finished, the stranger added, "There is a guard at the main gate. He has an attack dog."

Yakov could not let the pounding continue, nor Holcroft's shouted demands. The disturbance would draw attention.

The Israeli twisted the latch and pressed himself against the wall. The door crashed open, the figure of the tall American filling the frame. He lunged into the room, his arms in front of him as if prepared to repel an assault.

"Von Tiebolt! Where *are* you?"

Holcroft was obviously startled by the darkness. Ben-Gadíz stepped silently to the side, the flashlight in his hand. He spoke rapidly, completing two sentences in a single breath.

"Von Tiebolt's not here and I mean you no harm. We are not on opposite sides."

Holcroft spun around, his hands extended. "Who are you? What the hell are you doing here? Turn on the light!"

"No lights! Just listen."

The American stepped forward angrily. Yakov pressed the button on his flashlight; the wash of green spread over Holcroft, causing him to cover his eyes. "Turn that off!"

"No. Listen to me first."

Holcroft lashed his right foot out, catching Ben-Gadíz in the knee; at contact, Noel sprang forward, his eyes shut, his hands clutching for the Israeli's body.

Yakov crouched and threw his shoulder up into the American's chest; Holcroft would not be stopped. He brought his knee into Ben-Gadíz's temple; his fist smashed into Yakov's face.

There could be no lacerations! No traces of blood on the floor! Yakov dropped the light and held on to the American's arms; he was amazed at Holcroft's strength. He spoke as loudly as he dared to.

"You must *listen!* I'm not your enemy. I've got news of your mother. I have a letter. She's been with *me.*"

The American struggled; he was breaking the grip. "Who *are* you?"

"Nachrichtendienst," whispered Ben-Gadíz.

At the sound of the name, Holcroft went wild. He roared, his arms and legs battering rams that would not, could not, be repulsed.

"I'll *kill you.* . . ."

Yakov had no choice. He surged through the hammering attack, his fingers centering in on the American's neck, his thumbs grinding into the pronounced veins of the stiffened throat. By touch, he found a nerve and pressed with all his strength. Holcroft collapsed.

Noel opened his eyes in the darkness, but the darkness was not complete. Angled against the wall was a wash of green light—the same green light that had blinded him earlier—and at the sight of it his outrage returned.

He was being pressed against the floor, a knee sunk into his shoulder, the barrel of a gun against his head. His throat was in agony but still he twisted, trying to rise from the carpet, away from the weapon. His neck could not take the strain. He fell back, and heard the intense whisper of the man above him.

"Be very clear in this. If I were your enemy, I would have killed you. Can you understand that?"

"You *are* my enemy!" answered Noel, barely able to speak through the bruised muscles about his throat. "You said you were Nachrichtendienst. Geneva's enemy . . . *my* enemy!"

"The first, absolutely; but not the second. Not yours."

"You're lying!"

"Think! Why haven't I pulled this trigger? Geneva is stopped; you are stopped; no funds are transferred. If I'm your enemy, what prevents me from blowing your head off? I can't use you as a hostage; there's no point. You have to *be* there. So I gain nothing by letting you live . . . if I am your enemy."

Holcroft tried to grasp the words, tried to find the meaning behind them, but he could not. He wanted only to strike out at the man holding him captive. "What do you want? Where have you got my mother? You said you had a letter."

"We'll take all things in order. What I want first is to leave here. With *you*. Together we can do what Wolfs-schanze never believed possible."

"Wolfsschanze? . . . Do what?"

"Make the laws work for us. Make amends."

"Make— Whoever you are, you're out of your mind!"

"It's the option of Har Sha'alav. Control the millions. Fight them. *Everywhere.* I'm prepared to offer you the only proof I have." Yakov Ben-Gadíz took the pistol away from Noel's head. "Here's my gun." He offered it to Holcroft.

Noel studied the stranger's face in the odd shadows produced by the macabre green light. The eyes above him belonged to a man who was speaking the truth.

"Help me up," he said. "There's a back staircase. I know the way."

"First we have to straighten up anything that's out of place. Everything must be as it was."

Nothing is as it was. . . .

"Where are we going?"

"To an apartment in rue de la Paix. The letter's there. So is the girl."

"The girl?"

"Von Tiebolt's sister. He thinks she's dead. He ordered her killed."

"Helden?"

"Later."

45

They raced out of the alley and down the rue des Granges to the Israeli's car. They climbed in, Ben-Gadíz behind the wheel. Holcroft held his throat; he thought the veins were ruptured, so intense was the pain.

"You left me no choice," said Yakov, seeing Holcroft's agony.

"You left me one," replied Noel. "You gave me the gun. What's your name?"

"Yakov."

"What kind of name is that?"

"Hebrew. . . . Jacob, to you. Ben-Gadíz."

"Ben who?"

"Gadíz."

"Spanish?"

"Sephardic," said Yakov, speeding down the street, across the intersection, toward the lake. "My family immigrated to Krakow in the early nineteen hundreds." Yakov swung the car to the right in a small, unfamiliar square.

"I thought you were Kessler's brother," said Holcroft. "The doctor from Munich."

"I know nothing about a doctor from Munich."

"He's here somewhere. When I got to the d'Accord, the front desk gave me Von Tiebolt's key, then asked if I wanted Hans Kessler."

"What's that got to do with me?"

"The clerk knew that the Kesslers and Von Tiebolt had dinner together in Johann's suite. He thought Kessler's brother was still there."

"Wait a minute!" broke in Yakov. "The brother is a stocky man? Short? Strong?"

"I've no idea. Could be; Kessler said he was a soccer player."

"He's dead. Your mother told us. Von Tiebolt killed

476

him. I think he was injured by your friend Ellis; they couldn't carry him any longer."

Noel stared at the Israeli. "Are you saying he was the one who did that to Willie? Killed him and knifed him like that?"

"It's only a guess."

"Oh, Christ! . . . Tell me about my mother. Where is she?"

"Later."

"*Now*."

"There's a telephone. I have to call the apartment. Helden's there." Ben-Gadíz swung the car to the curb.

"I said *now!*" Holcroft leveled the gun at Yakov.

"If you decide to kill me now," said Yakov, "I deserve to die, and so do you. I'd ask you to make the call yourself, but we haven't time for emotion."

"We've all the time we need," answered Noel. "The bank can be postponed."

"The bank? La Grande Banque de Genève?"

"Nine o'clock this morning."

"My God!" Ben-Gadíz gripped Holcroft's shoulder and lowered his voice; it was the voice of a man pleading for more than his life. "Give the option of Har Sha'alav a chance. It will never come again. Trust me. I've killed too many people not to have killed you twenty minutes ago. We must know every moment where we stand. Helden may have learned something."

Again Noel studied the face. "Make the call. Tell her I'm here and I want explanations from both of you."

They sped down the country road past the gates of the estate, driver and passenger oblivious to the sounds of an angry dog suddenly disturbed from its sleep by the racing car. The road curved to the left. Gradually, Yakov coasted to a stop off the shoulder, into the underbrush.

"Dogs' ears pick up engines that stop quickly. A diminuendo is much more difficult for them."

"Are you a musician?"

"I was a violinist."

"Any good?"

"Tel Aviv Symphony."

"What made you—"

"I found more suitable work," interrupted Ben-Gadíz. "Get out quickly. Remove your overcoat; take your weapon. Press the door closed; make no sound. The guest house will be back quite a way, but we'll find it."

There was a thick brick wall bordering the grounds, a string of coiled barbed wire on the top of it. Yakov scaled a tree to study the wire and the wall. "There are no alarms," he said. "Small animals would trigger them too frequently. But it's messy; the coil's nearly two feet wide. We'll have to jump."

The Israeli came down, crouched next to the wall, and cupped his hands. "Step up," he ordered Noel.

The ring of wire barbs on the top of the wall was impossible to avoid; there was no space on the ledge untouched by it.

Straining, Holcroft managed to get his left toe on the edge, then sprang up, vaulting the ominous coil and plummeting to the ground. His jacket had been caught, his ankles badly scraped, but he had made it. He stood up, only vaguely aware that he was breathing heavily, the pain in his throat and shins merely irritations. If the stranger had given Helden the right information on the phone, he was within a few hundred yards of Althene.

On top of the wall, the silhouette of the Israeli loomed like a large bird in the night sky; he vaulted over the coiled wire and spun down to the ground. He rolled once, as a tumbler might roll to break a fall, and sprang up next to Noel, raising his wrist in front of him to look at his watch.

"It's nearly six. It'll be light soon. Hurry."

They sliced through the forest, sidestepping branches, leaping over the tangled foliage, until they found the dirt road that led toward the guest house. In the distance they could see a dim glow of lights that shone from small cathedral windows.

"Stop!" Ben-Gadíz said.

"What?" Yakov's hand gripped Noel's shoulder. The Israeli fell on him, dragging Holcroft to the ground. "What are you doing?"

"Be still! There's activity in the house. People."

Noel peered through the grass at the house no more than a hundred yards away. He could see no movement, no figures in the windows. "I don't see anyone."

"Look at the lights. They're not steady. People are moving in front of lamps."

Holcroft saw instantly what Ben-Gadíz had seen.

There *were* subtle changes of shading. The normal eye—especially the normal eye of an anxious runner—would not notice them, but they were there. "You're right," he whispered.

"Come," said Yakov. "We'll cut through the woods and approach from the side."

They went back into the forest and emerged at the edge of a small croquet course, grass and wickets cold and rigid in the winter night. Beyond the flat ground were the windows of the house.

"I'll run across and signal you to follow," Yakov whispered. "Remember, no noise."

The Israeli dashed across the lawn and crouched at the side of a window. Slowly he stood up and peered inside. Noel got to his knees, prepared to race out from the foliage.

The signal did not come. Ben-Gadíz stood motionless at the side of the window, but made no move to raise his hand. What was wrong? Why didn't the signal come?

Holcroft could wait no longer. He sprang up and ran over the stretch of grass.

The Israeli turned, his eyes glaring. "Get away!" he whispered.

"What are you talking about? She's in there!"

Ben-Gadíz grabbed Holcroft by the shoulders, pushing him backward. "I said go *back!* We must get out of here. . . ."

"The hell we will!" Noel swung both arms up violently, breaking the Israeli's grip. He leaped to the window and looked inside.

The universe went up in fire. His mind burst open. He tried to scream, but no scream would come, only pure, raw horror, beyond sound, beyond sanity.

Inside the dimly lit room he saw the body of his mother arched diagonally in death across the back of a chair. The graceful, wondrous head was streaked with blood, scores of red rivers over wrinkled flesh.

Noel raised his hands, his arms, his whole being in the process of exploding. He could feel the air. His fists plunged toward the panes of glass.

The impact never came. Instead, an arm was around his neck, a hand clasped over his mouth; both were giant tentacles pulling his head back viciously, lifting him off his feet, his spine arching, his legs crumbling beneath him as he was forced to the ground. His face was being pushed into dirt until there was no air. And then a sharp agonizing pain shot through his throat, and the fire returned.

He knew he was moving, but he did not know how or why. Branches kept slapping his face, hands hammered at his back, propelling him forward into the darkness. He could not know how long he was in the suspended state of chaos, but finally there was a stone wall. Harsh commands barked into his ear.

"Get up! Over the wire!"

Cognizance began to return. He felt the sharp metal points stabbing him, scraping his skin, ripping his clothes. Then he was being dragged across a hard surface and slammed against the door of an automobile.

The next thing he knew he was in the seat of a car, staring through the glass of a windshield. Dawn was coming up.

He sat in the chair, drained, numb, and read the letter from Althene.

Dearest NOEL—

It is unlikely that we shall see each other, but I beg you, do not mourn me. Later, perhaps, but not now. There is no time.

I do what I have to do for the simple reason that it must be done and I am the most logical person to do it. Even if there were another, I'm not at all sure I would allow him to do what has been reserved for me.

I'll not dwell on the lie I have lived for over thirty years. My new friend, Mr. Ben-Gadíz, will explain it fully to you. Suffice it to say I was never aware of the lie, nor—God in heaven—the terrible role you would be called upon to play.

I come from another era, one in which debts were called by their rightful name, and honor was not held to be an anachronism. I willingly pay my debt in hopes that a vestige of honor may be restored.

If we do not meet again, know that you have brought great joy to my life. If ever man needed proof that we are better than our sources, you are that proof.

I add a word about your friend Helden. I think she is the lovely daughter I might have had.

It's in her eyes, in her strength. I've known her but a few hours, during which time she saved my life, prepared to sacrifice her own in doing so. It is true that we often perceive a lifetime in a moment of clarity. The moment was there for me, and she has my deep affection.

God speed you, my Noel.

My love,
ALTHENE

Holcroft looked up at Yakov, who was standing by the apartment window looking out at the gray light of the early winter morning.

"What was it she wouldn't let anyone else do?" he asked.

"Meet with my brother," answered Helden from across the room.

Noel clenched his fist and closed his eyes. "Ben-Gadíz said he ordered you killed."

"Yes. He's had many people killed."

Holcroft turned to the Israeli. "My mother wrote that you would explain the lie."

"I defer to Helden. I know a great deal of the story, but she knows it all."

"This is what you went to London for?" asked Noel.

"It's why I left Paris," she replied. "But it wasn't to London; it was to a small village on Lake Neuchâtel."

She told him the story of Werner Gerhardt, of Wolfs-schanze, of the coin that had two sides. She tried to remember every detail given her by the last of the Nachrich-tendienst.

When she had finished, Holcroft got out of the chair. "So all along I've been the figurehead for the lie. For the other side of Wolfsschanze."

"You are the code numbers that open the *Sonnen-kinder* vaults," said Ben-Gadíz. "You were the one who made all the laws work for them. Such massive funds cannot spring from the earth without a structure. The chain of legalities must be met, or they are challenged. Wolfsschanze could not afford that. It was a brilliant deception."

Noel stared at the wall by the bedroom door. He stood facing it, facing the dimly lit wallpaper, the obscure figures in the pattern of a series of concentric circles engulfing themselves. The muted light—or his own unbalanced sight—made them spin with dizzying speed, black dots disappearing, only to become large circles again. *Circles. Circles of deception.* There were no straight lines of truth in those circles, only deceit. Only lies!

He heard the scream come out of his throat and felt the impact of his hands upon the wall, pounding furiously, wanting only to destroy the terrible circles.

Other hands touched him. Gentle hands.

A man in agony had cried out to him. And that man was false!

Where was he? What had he done?

He felt tears in his eyes and knew they were there because the circles became blurs, meaningless designs. And Helden was holding him, pulling his face to hers, her gentle fingers brushing away the tears.

"My darling. My only darling. . . ."

"I . . . will . . . kill!" Again, he heard the sound of his own scream, the horrible conviction of his own words.

"You *will*," a voice answered, echoing in the chambers of his mind. It was loud and resonant, and it belonged to Yakov Ben-Gadíz, who had pushed Helden aside and had spun him around, pinning his shoulders to the wall. "You *will!*"

Noel tried to focus his burning eyes, tried to control his trembling. "You tried to stop me from seeing her!"

"I knew I couldn't," said Yakov quietly. "I knew it when you lunged. I've been trained as few others on this earth, but you have something extraordinary inside you. I'm not sure I care to speculate, but I'm grateful you're not my enemy."

"I don't understand you."

"I give you the option of Har Sha'alav. It will demand the most extraordinary discipline of which you are capable. I'll be frank: I couldn't do it, but perhaps you can."

"What is it?"

"Go through with the meeting at the bank. With the killers of your mother, with the man who ordered Helden's death, Richard Holcroft's death. Face him; face them. Sign the papers."

"You're out of your mind! Out of your fucking *mind!*"

"I'm not! We've studied the laws. You'll be required to sign a release. In it, in the event of your death, you assign all rights and privileges to the coinheritors. When you do, you'll sign a death warrant. Sign it! It won't be your death warrant, but theirs!"

Noel looked into Yakov's dark, imploring eyes. There it was again: the straight line of truth. Neither spoke for a while, and slowly Holcroft began to find the control he had lost. Ben-Gadíz released his shoulders; balance returned.

"They'll be looking for me," said Noel. "They think I went to Von Tiebolt's rooms."

"You did; the door wasn't rethreaded. You saw that no one was there, so you left."

"Where did I go? They'll want to know."

"Are you familiar with the city?"

"Not really."

"Then you took taxis; you traveled along the waterfront, stopping at a dozen piers and marinas, looking for anyone who might have seen your mother. It's plausible; they think you were in panic."

"It's almost seven-thirty," Noel said. "An hour and a half left. I'll go back to the hotel. We'll meet after the conference at the bank."

"Where?" asked Yakov.

"Take a room at the Excelsior in the name of a married couple. Get there after nine-thirty, but long before noon. I'm in four-eleven."

He stood outside the hotel door; it was three minutes past eight. He could hear angry voices from inside. Von Tiebolt dominated whatever conversation was taking place, his tone incisive, on the edge of violence.

Violence. Holcroft took a deep breath and forced himself to reject the instincts that seared through him. He would face the man who killed his mother and his father and look that man in the eyes and not betray his rage.

He knocked on the door, grateful that his hand did not tremble.

The door opened, and he stared into the eyes of the blond-haired killer of loved ones.

"Noel! Where have you been? We've been looking everywhere!"

"So have I," said Holcroft, the weariness not difficult to feign, the control of outrage nearly impossible. "I've spent the night looking for her. I couldn't find her. I don't think she ever got here."

"We'll keep trying," said Von Tiebolt. "Have some coffee. We'll be off to the bank soon, and it will all be over."

"Yes, it will, won't it?" said Noel.

The three of them sat on one side of the long conference table, Holcroft in the center, Kessler on his left, Von Tiebolt on his right. Facing them were the two directors of La Grande Banque de Genève.

In front of each man was a neat pile of legal papers, all identical and arranged in sequence. Eyes followed the typed words, pages were turned, and more than an hour passed before the precious document had been read aloud in its entirety.

There were two remaining articles of record, their cover pages bordered in dark blue. The director on the left spoke.

"As I'm sure you're aware, with an account of this magnitude and the objectives contained therein, La Grande Banque de Genève cannot legally assume responsibility for disbursements once the funds are released and are no longer under our control. The document is specific as to the burden of that responsibility. It is equally divided among the three participants. Therefore, the law requires that each of you assign all rights and privileges to your coinheritors-in-trust in the event you predecease them. These rights and privileges, however, do not affect the individual bequests; they are to be distributed to your estates in the event of your death." The director put on his spectacles. "Please read the pages in front of you to see that they conform to what I've represented, and sign above your names in the presence of one another. Exchange papers so that all signatures appear on each."

The reading was rapid; the signatures followed, and the pages were exchanged. As Noel handed his signed paper to Kessler, he spoke casually.

"You know, I forgot to ask you, Erich. Where's your brother? I thought he was going to be here in Geneva."

"With all the excitement, I forgot to tell you," Kessler said, smiling. "Hans was delayed in München. I'm sure we'll see him in Zurich."

"Zurich?"

The scholar looked past Holcroft toward Von Tiebolt. "Well, yes. Zurich. I thought we planned to be there Monday morning."

Noel turned to the blond man. "You didn't mention it."

"We've had no time to talk. Is Monday inconvenient for you?"

"Not at all. Maybe I'll have heard from her by then."

"What?"

"My mother. Or even Helden. She should be calling."

"Yes, of course. I'm sure they'll both reach you."

The last article of record was the formal release of the account. A computer had been preset. Upon the signatures of everyone in the room, the codes would be punched, the funds made liquid and transferred to a bank in Zurich.

All signed. The director on the right picked up a telephone. "Enter the following numbers on computer bank eleven. Are you ready? . . . Six, one, four, four, two. Break four. Eight, one, zero, zero. Break zero. . . . Repeat, please." The director listened, then nodded. "Correct. Thank you."

"Is it complete, then?" asked his colleague.

"It is," answered the director. "Gentlemen, as of this moment, the sum of seven hundred and eighty million American dollars is in your collective names at La Banque du Livre, Zurich. May you have the wisdom of prophets, and may your decisions be guided by God."

Outside, on the street, Von Tiebolt turned to Holcroft. "What are your plans, Noel? We must still be careful, you know. The Nachrichtendienst won't take this easily."

"I know. . . . Plans? I'm going to keep trying to find my mother. She's somewhere; she's got to be."

"I've arranged through my friend, the first deputy, for the three of us to receive police protection. Your detail will pick you up at the Excelsior, ours at the d'Accord. Unless, of course, you'd prefer to move in with us."

"That's too much work," said Holcroft. "I'm half settled now. I'll stay at the Excelsior."

"Shall we go to Zurich in the morning?" asked Kessler, deferring the decision to Von Tiebolt.

"It might be a good idea for us to travel separately,"

said Holcroft. "If the police have no objections, I'd just as soon go by car."

"Very good thinking, my friend," said Von Tiebolt. "The police won't object, and traveling separately makes sense. You take the train, Erich; I'll fly; and Noel will drive. I'll make us reservations at the Columbine."

Holcroft nodded. "If I don't hear from my mother or Helden by tomorrow, I'll leave word for them to reach me there," he said. "I'll grab a cab." He walked rapidly to the corner. Another minute and the rage within him would have exploded. He would have killed Von Tiebolt with his bare hands.

Johann spoke quietly. "He knows. How much, I'm not certain. But he knows."

"How can you be sure?" Kessler asked.

"At first I merely sensed it; then I knew. He asked about Hans and accepted your answer that he was still in München. He knows that's not true. A clerk at the d'Accord offered to ring Hans's room for him last night."

"Oh, my God. . . ."

"Don't be upset. Our American colleague will die on the road to Zurich."

46

The attempt on Noel's life—if it was going to be made—would take place on the roads north of Fribourg, south of Köniz. That was the judgment of Yakov Ben-Gadíz. The distance was something more than twenty kilometers, with stretches in the hills that rarely had traffic this time of year. It was winter, and although the climate was not Alpine, light snows were frequent, the roads not the best; drivers were discouraged from them. But Holcroft had mapped out a route that avoided the highways, concentrating on rural towns with architecture he claimed he wanted to see.

That was to say, Yakov mapped it out, and Noel had delivered it to police who were under orders from the first deputy to act as his escort north. The fact that no one discouraged Holcroft from this chosen route lent substance to the Israeli's judgment.

Yakov further speculated on the method of killing. Neither Von Tiebolt nor Kessler would be near the area. Each would be very much in evidence somewhere else. And if there was to be an execution, it would be carried out by as few men as possible—paid killers in no way associated with Wolfsschanze. No chances would be taken so soon after the meeting at La Grande Banque Genève. The killer, or killers, would in turn be murdered by *Sonnenkinder;* all traces to Wolfsschanze would be obliterated.

That was the strategy as Ben-Gadíz saw it, and a counterstrategy had to be mounted. One that got Noel to Zurich; that was all that mattered. Once in Zurich, it would be *their* strategy. There were a dozen ways to kill in a large city, and Yakov was an expert in all of them.

The trip began, the counterstrategy put into play. Holcroft drove a heavy car rented from Bonfils, Geneva, the most expensive leasing firm in Switzerland, specializing in the unusual automobile for the unusual client. It

487

was a Rolls-Royce, outfitted with armor plate, bulletproof glass, and tires that could withstand successive punctures.

Helden was a mile in front of Noel, driving a nondescript but maneuverable Renault; Ben-Gadíz was behind, never more than half a mile, and his car was a Maserati, common among the wealthy of Geneva and capable of very high speeds. Between Yakov and Holcroft was the two-man police car assigned to the American as protection. The police knew nothing.

"They'll be immobilized en route," the Israeli had said while the three of them studied maps in Noel's hotel room. "They won't be sacrificed; there'd be too many questions. They're legitimate police. I got the numbers off their helmets and called Litvak. We checked. They're first-year men from the central headquarters' barracks. As such, not very experienced."

"Will they be the same men tomorrow?"

"Yes. Their orders read that they're to stay with you until the Zurich police take over. Which I think means that they'll find themselves with a malfunctioning vehicle, call their superiors, and be told to return to Geneva. The order for your protection will evaporate."

"Then they're just window dressing."

"Exactly. Actually, they'll serve a purpose. As long as you can see them, you're safe. No one will try anything."

They were in sight now, thought Noel, glancing at the rearview mirror, applying the brakes of the Rolls-Royce for the long curving descent at the side of the hill. Far below, he could see Helden's car come out of a turn. In two more minutes she would slow down and wait until they were in plain sight of each other before resuming speed; that, too, was part of the plan. She had done so three minutes ago. Every five minutes they were to be in eye contact. He wished he could *speak* with her. Just talk . . . simple talk, quiet talk . . . having nothing to do with death or the contemplation of death, or the strategies demanded to avoid it.

But that talk could only come after Zurich. There would be death in Zurich, but not like any death Holcroft had ever thought about. Because he would be the killer; no one else. *No one.* He demanded the right. He would look into the eyes of Johann von Tiebolt and tell him he was about to die.

He was going too fast; his anger had caused him to

press too hard on the accelerator. He slowed down; it was no time to do Von Tiebolt's work for him. It had started to snow, and the downhill road was slippery.

Yakov cursed the light snowfall, not because it made the driving difficult but because it reduced visibility. They relied on sight; radio communication was out of the question, the signals too easily intercepted.

The Israeli's hand touched several items on the seat beside him; similar items were in Holcroft's Rolls. They were part of the counterstrategy—the most effective part.

Explosives. Eight in all. Four charges, wrapped in plastic, timed to detonate precisely three seconds after impact; and four antitank grenades. In addition there were two weapons: a U.S. Army Colt automatic and a carbine rifle, each loaded, safeties off, prepared for firing. All had been purchased through Litvak's contacts in Geneva. Peaceful Geneva, where such arsenals were available in quantities smaller than terrorists believed but greater than the Swiss authorities thought conceivable.

Ben-Gadíz peered through the windshield. If it happened, it would happen shortly. The police car several hundred yards in front would be immobilized, the result, probably, of cleats coated with acid, timed to eat through tires; or a defective radiator filled with a coagulant that would clog the hoses. . . . There were so many ways. But the police car would suddenly not be there, and Holcroft would be isolated.

Yakov hoped Noel remembered precisely what he was to do if a strange car approached. He was to start zigzagging over the road while Yakov accelerated, braking his Maserati within feet of the unknown automobile, hurling the plastic charges at it, waiting the precious seconds for the explosions to take place as Holcroft got out of firing range. If there were problems—defective charges, no explosives—the grenades were a backup.

It would be enough. Von Tiebolt would not risk more than one execution car. The possibility of stray drivers, unwitting observers, would be considerable; the killers would be few and professional. The leader of the *Sonnenkinder* was no idiot; if Holcroft's death did not take place on the road to Köniz, it would take place in Zurich.

That was the *Sonnenkinder's* mistake, thought the

Israeli, filled with a sense of satisfaction. Von Tiebolt did not know about Yakov Ben-Gadíz. Also no idiot, also professional. The American *would* get to Zurich, and once in Zurich, Johann von Tiebolt was a dead man, as Erich Kessler was a dead man, killed by a man filled with rage.

Yakov cursed again. The snow was heavier and the flakes were larger. The latter meant the snowfall would not last long, but for the time being it was an interruption he did not like.

He could not see the police car! Where was it? The road was filled with sharp curves and offshoots. The police car was nowhere to be seen. He had lost it! How in God's name *could* he have?

And then it was there, and he breathed again, pressing his foot on the accelerator to get closer. He could not allow his mind to wander so; he was not in the Symphony Hall in Tel Aviv. The police car was the key; he could not let it out of his sight for a moment.

He was going faster than he thought; the speedometer read seventy-three kilometers, much too fast for this road. Why?

Then he knew why. He was closing the gap between himself and the Geneva police car, but the police car was accelerating. It was going faster than it had before; it was racing into the curves, speeding through the snowfall . . . closing in on Holcroft!

Was the driver *insane?*

Ben-Gadíz stared through the windshield, trying to understand. Something bothered him, and he was not sure what it was. What were they *doing?*

Then he saw it; it had not been there before.

A dent in the trunk of the police car. A dent! There'd been no dent in the trunk of the car he had followed for the past three hours!

It was a different police car!

From one of the offshoots on the maze of curves a radio command had been given ordering the original car off the road. Another had taken its place. Which meant the men in that car now were aware of the Maserati, and, infinitely more dangerous, Holcroft was not aware of *them.*

The police car swung into a long curve; Yakov could hear continuous blasts of its horn through the snow and the wind. It was *signaling* Holcroft. It was pulling alongside.

"No! Don't do it!" screamed Yakov at the glass, holding his thumbs on the horn, gripping the wheel as his tires skidded over the surface of the curve. He hurled the Maserati toward the police car, fifty yards away. "Holcroft! Don't!"

Suddenly, his windshield shattered. Tiny circles of death appeared everywhere; he could feel glass slice his cheeks, his fingers. He was hit. A submachine gun had fired at him from the smashed rear window of the police car.

There was a billow of smoke from the hood; the radiator exploded. An instant later the tires were pierced, strips of rubber blown off. The Maserati lurched to the right, crashing into an embankment.

Ben-Gadíz roared to the heavens, hammering his shoulder against a door that would not open. Behind him, the gasoline fires started.

Holcroft saw the police car in the rearview mirror. It was suddenly coming closer, its headlights flickering on and off. For some reason the police were signaling him.

There was no place to stop on the curve; there had to be a straightaway several hundred yards down the road. He slowed the Rolls as the police car came alongside, the figure of the young officer blurred by the snow.

He heard the blasts of the horn and saw the continuous rapid flashing of the lights. He rolled down the window.

"I'll pull over as soon as—"

He saw the face. And the expression on that face. It was not one of the young policemen from Geneva! It was a face he had never seen before. Then the barrel of a rifle was there.

Desperately, he tried to roll up the window. It was too late. He heard the gunfire, saw the blinding flashes of light, could feel a hundred razors slashing his skin. He saw his own blood splattered against glass and sensed his own screams echoing through a car gone wild.

Metal crunched against metal, groaning under the force of a thousand impacts. The dashboard was upside down; the pedals were where the roof should be; and he was against that roof; and then he was not; now plummeted over the back of the seat, now hurled against glass and away from glass, now impaled on the steering wheel, then lifted in space and thrown into more space.

There was peace in that space. The pain of the razors went away, and he walked through the mists of his mind into a void.

Yakov smashed the glass of the remaining windshield with his pistol. The carbine had been jarred to the floor; the plastic explosives remained strapped in their box; the grenades were nowhere to be seen.

All the weapons were useless save one, because it was available, and in his hand, and he would use it until the ammunition was gone—and until his life was gone.

There were three men in the false police car, the third, the marksman, once again crouched in back. Ben-Gadíz could see his head in the rear window! Now! He took careful aim through the blankets of steam and squeezed the trigger. The face whipped diagonally up and then fell back into the jagged glass of the window.

Yakov crashed his shoulder once more against the door; it loosened. He had to get out fast: The fires behind guaranteed the explosion of the fuel tank. Up ahead, the driver of the police car was slamming it into the Rolls; the second man was on the road, reaching into Holcroft's window, yanking at the steering wheel. They were trying to send the car over the embankment.

Ben-Gadíz hammered his whole upper body against the door; it swung open. The Israeli lunged out on the snow-covered surface of the road, his wounds producing a hundred red streaks on the white powder. He raised his pistol and fired one shot after another, his eyes blurred, his aim imperfect.

And then two terrible things happened at the same moment.

The Rolls went over the embankment, and a roar of gunfire filled the snow-laden air. A line of bullets kicked up the road and cut across Yakov's legs. He was beyond pain.

There was no feeling left, but he twisted and turned and rolled wherever he could. His hands touched the slashed rubber of the tires, then steel and more steel, and cold patches of glass and snow.

The explosion came; the fuel tank of the Maserati burst into flames. And Ben-Gadíz heard the words, shouted in the distance. "They're dead! Turn around! Get out of here!"

The attackers fled.

Helden had slowed the car well over a minute ago. Noel should have been in sight by now. Where was he? She stopped at the side of the road and waited. Another two minutes went by; she could not wait any longer.

She swung the car into a U-turn and started back up the hill. Pushing the accelerator to the floor, she passed the half-mile mark; still there was no sign of him. Her hands began to tremble.

Something had happened. She knew it; she could feel it!

She saw the Maserati! It was demolished! On fire!

Oh, *God!* Where was Noel's car? Where was Noel? Yakov?

She slammed on the brakes and ran out, screaming. She fell on the slippery road, unaware that her own wounded leg had caused the fall, and pushed herself up, and screamed again, and ran again.

"Noel! *Noel!*"

Tears streaked down her face in the cold air; her screams tore the raw nerves of her throat. She could not cope with her own hysteria.

She heard the command out of nowhere.

"*Helden!* Stop it. Here. . . ."

A voice. Yakov's voice! From where? Where was it *coming* from? She heard it again.

"Helden! Down here!"

The embankment. She raced to the embankment and her world collapsed. Below was the Rolls-Royce—overturned and smoking, crushed metal everywhere. In horror she saw the figure of Yakov Ben-Gadíz on the ground next to the Rolls. And then she saw the streaks of red on the snow that formed a path across the road and down the embankment to where Yakov lay.

Helden lunged over the embankment, rolling in the snow and over the rocks, screaming at the death she knew awaited her. She fell by Ben-Gadíz and stared through the open window at her love. He was sprawled out, immobile, his face drenched with blood.

"No! . . . *No!*"

Yakov grabbed her arm and pulled her to him. He

could barely speak, but his commands were clear. "Get back to your car. There's a small village south of Treyvaux, no more than five kilometers from here. Call Litvak. Près-du-Lac's not so far away . . . twenty, twenty-two kilometers. He can hire pilots, fast cars. Reach him; tell him."

Helden could not take her eyes off Noel. "He's dead. . . . He's *dead!*"

"He may not be. Hurry!"

"I can't. I can't *leave* him!"

Ben-Gadíz raised his pistol. "Unless you do, I'll kill him now."

Litvak walked into the room where Ben-Gadíz lay on the bed, his lower body encased in bandages. Yakov was staring out the window at the snow-covered fields and the mountains beyond; he continued to stare, taking no notice of the doctor's entrance.

"Do you want the truth?"

The Israeli turned his head slowly. "There's no point in avoiding it, is there? At any rate, I can see it in your face."

"I could bring you worse news. You'll not walk very well ever again; the damage is too extensive. But, in time, you'll get around. At first with the help of crutches; later, perhaps, with a cane."

"Not exactly the physical prognosis needed for my work, is it?"

"No, but your mind's intact and your hands will heal. It won't affect your music."

Yakov smiled sadly. "I was never that good. My mind wandered too frequently. I was not as fine a professional as I was in my other life."

"That mind can be put to other uses."

The Israeli frowned, looking again out the window. "We'll see when we know what's left out there."

"It's changing out there, Yakov. It's happening quickly," said the doctor.

"What about Holcroft?"

"I don't know what to say. He should have died. But he's still alive. Not that it makes much difference in terms of his life. He can't go back to who he was. He's wanted in half a dozen countries for murder. The death penalty's been restored everywhere, for all manner of crimes, the laws of defense a travesty. Everywhere. He'd be shot on sight."

"They've won," said Yakov, his eyes filling with tears. "The *Sonnenkinder* have won."

"We'll see," said Litvak, "when we know what's left out there."

Epilogue

Images. Shapeless, unfocused, without meaning or definition. Outlines etched in vapor. There was only awareness. Not thought, nor any memory of experience, just awareness. Then the shapeless images began to take form; the mists cleared, turning awareness into recognition. Thought would come later; it was enough to be able to see and to remember.

Noel saw her face above him, framed by the cascading blond hair that touched his face. There were tears in her eyes; they ran down her cheeks. He tried to wipe away the tears, but he could not reach the lovely, tired face above. His hand fell, and she took it in hers.

"My darling. . . ."

He heard her. He was able to hear. Sight and sound had meaning. He closed his eyes, knowing that somehow thought would come soon, too.

Litvak stood in the doorway, watching Helden sponge Noel's chest and neck. There was a newspaper under his arm. He examined Holcroft's face, the face that had taken such punishment from the fusillade of bullets. There were scars on his left cheek and across his forehead and all over his neck. But the healing process had begun. From somewhere inside the house came the sounds of a violin being played by a very professional musician.

"I'd like to recommend a raise for your nurse," said Noel weakly.

"For which duties?" Litvak laughed.

"Physician, heal thyself." Helden joined the laughter.

"I wish I could. I wish I could heal a lot of things," replied the doctor, dropping the newspaper at Holcroft's side. It was the Paris edition of the *Herald Tribune*. "I picked this up for you in Neuchâtel. I'm not sure you want to read it."

"What's the lesson for today?"

" 'The Consequences of Dissent' would be a fair title, I imagine. The editorial staff of the New York *Times* have been enjoined by your Supreme Court from any further coverage of the Pentagon. The issue, of course, is national security. Said Supreme Court also upheld the legality of the multiple executions in your state of Michigan. The Court's opinion expresses the profound thought that when minorities threaten the well-being of the general public, swift and visible examples are to be made in the cause of deterrence."

"Today John Smith is a minority," said Noel weakly, his head resting back on the pillow. "Boom, he's dead."

This is the world news, reported by BBC of London. Since the wave of assassinations that took the lives of political figures across the globe, security measures of unparalleled severity have been mounted in the nations' capitals. It is to the military and police authorities everywhere that the greatest responsibility falls, and so that international cooperation at the highest levels may be achieved, an agency has been formed in Zurich, Switzerland. This agency, to be called Anvil, will facilitate the swift, accurate, and confidential exchange of information between member military and police forces. . . .

Yakov Ben-Gadíz was halfway through the scherzo of Mendelssohn's Violin Concerto when he found his mind wandering again. Noel Holcroft was stretched out on the couch across the room, Helden sitting on the floor beside him.

The plastic surgeon who had flown from Los Angeles to operate on his unidentified patient had done a remarkable job. The face was still Holcroft's, yet not entirely. The scars that had resulted from the facial wounds were gone, in their place slight indentations that lent a chiseled look to the features. The lines on his forehead were deeper, the wrinkles about his eyes more pronounced. There was no innocence in the slightly altered, restored face; instead there was a touch of cruelty. Perhaps more than a touch.

In addition to the changes, Noel had grown older, the aging process swift and painful. It had been four months since they had taken him from the embankment on the road north of Fribourg, but, looking at him, one might judge the time elapsed to be nearer ten years.

Still, he had his life, and his body had sprung back under the care of Helden and the rigor of the never-ending exercises ordered by Litvak, supervised by a once-formidable commando from Har Sha'alav.

Yakov took pleasure in these sessions. He demanded excellence, and Holcroft met the demands; full health was required in the physical instrument before the real training could begin.

It would begin tomorrow. High in the spring hills and mountains, beyond the scrutiny of prying eyes, but under the harshest scrutiny of Yakov Ben-Gadíz. The pupil would do what the master could do no longer; the pupil would be put through the rigors of hell until he excelled the master.

Tomorrow it would begin.

Deutsche Zeitung

Berlin, July 4 — The Bundestag today gave its formal consent to the establishment of rehabilitation centers patterned after those in America in the states of Arizona and Texas. These centers will be, as their U.S. counterparts, primarily educational in nature and will be under the supervision of the military.

Those sentenced for rehabilitation terms will have been judged by the courts to be guilty of crimes against the German people. . . .

"Wire! Rope! Chain!"

"Use your fingers! They're weapons; never forget it. . . ."

"Scale that tree again, you were too slow. . . ."

"Climb the hill and get back down without my seeing you. . . ."

"I *saw* you. Your head was blown off!"

"Press the *nerve,* not the vein! There are five nerve points. Find them. With the blindfold on. *Feel* them. . . ."

"*Roll* out of a fall; don't crouch. . . ."

"Every action must have two alternate, split-second options. Train yourself to think in those terms. *Instinctively.* . . ."

"Accuracy is a question of zero-sighting, immobility,

and breathing. Fire again, seven shots; they *must* be within a two-inch diameter. . . ."

"Escape, escape, *escape! Use* your surroundings; *melt* into them! Don't be afraid to stay still. A man standing motionless is often the last person seen. . . ."

The summer months passed, and Yakov Ben-Gadíz was pleased. The pupil was now better than the master. He was ready.

As was his colleague; she was ready, too. Together they would form the team.

The *Sonnenkinder* were marked. The list was taken out and studied.

THE HERALD TRIBUNE

Paris, Oct. 10 — The international agency in Zurich known as Anvil today announced the formation of an independent Board of Chancellors selected by secret ballot from member nations. The first Anvil Congress will be held on the 25th of the month. . . .

The couple walked down the street in Zurich's Lindenhof district, on the left bank of the Limmat River. The man was fairly tall, but stooped, a pronounced limp impeding his progress through the crowds, the shabby suitcase in his hand a further hindrance. The woman held his arm, more as though guiding an irritable responsibility than with affection. Neither spoke: They were a couple grown to an indeterminable age together in mutual loathing.

They reached an office building and went inside, the man limping after the woman toward the bank of elevators. They stopped in front of the starter; the woman asked in decidedly middle-class German the office number of a small accounting firm.

She was given a number on the twelfth floor, the top floor, but as it was the lunch hour, the starter doubted anyone was there. It did not matter; the couple would wait.

They stepped out of the elevator on the twelfth floor; the hallway was deserted. The moment the elevator door closed, the couple ran to the staircase at the right end of the corridor. Gone was the limp; gone were the somber faces. They raced up the steps to the door of the roof and stopped on the landing. The man set down the suitcase, knelt, and opened it. Inside were the barrel and stock of a rifle, a telescopic sight clamped to the former, a strap to the latter.

He took the parts out and attached them. Then he removed his hat with the wig sewn into the crown and threw it into the suitcase. He stood up and helped the woman take off her coat, pulling the sleeves through, reversing the cloth. It was now a well-cut, expensive beige topcoat, purchased at one of the better shops in Paris.

The woman then helped the man reverse his overcoat. It was transformed into a fashionable gentleman's fall coat, trimmed in suede. The woman took off her kerchief, removed several pins, and let her blond hair fall down over her shoulders. She opened her purse and took out a revolver.

"I'll be here," said Helden. "Good hunting."

"Thanks," said Noel, opening the door to the roof.

He crouched against the wall by an out-of-use chimney, inserted his arm through the sling, and pulled the strap taut. He reached into his pocket and took out three shells; he pressed them into the chamber and slapped the bolt into firing position. *Every action must have two alternate, split-second options.*

He would not need them. He would not miss.

He turned and knelt by the wall. He edged the rifle over the top and put his eye to the telescopic sight.

Twelve stories below, across the street, crowds were cheering various men coming out of the huge glass doors of the Lindenhof Hôtel. They walked into the sunlight under banners hailing the first Anvil Congress.

There he was. In the gunsight, the cross hairs centered on the sculptured face beneath the shining blond hair.

Holcroft squeezed the trigger. Twelve stories below, the sculptured face erupted into a mass of blood and shattered flesh.

The Tinamou was killed at last.

By the Tinamou.

They were everywhere. It had only begun.

ABOUT THE AUTHOR

ROBERT LUDLUM's first novel, *The Scarlatti Inheritance* (1970) brought him immediate literary success. The book and its successors, including *The Osterman Weekend, The Chancellor Manuscript* and *The Holcroft Covenant,* have all been on bestseller lists here and in England as well as in the Netherlands, Argentina, Brazil, Greece, Iran, Japan and Portugal. It was in the late sixties, at the age of forty, that Mr. Ludlum changed professions and became a writer. Listed in *Who's Who in the East* as producer-actor, Mr. Ludlum appeared in many Broadway, regional, and television dramas in the fifties, receiving excellent reviews for his performances. He also appeared in over 200 network television shows including "Omnibus," "Studio One," and "Robert Montgomery." Throughout the sixties Mr. Ludlum combined performing with producing and was responsible for over 300 productions employing major stars of the English and American stage. He was the moving force in building one of the most prestigious playhouses in the country in Paramus, N.J., and was instrumental in bringing to Broadway such hits as "The Front Page" and "The Owl and the Pussycat." His work as a producer brought him artistic citations from the American National Theatre and Academy, Actor's Equity Association, and the William Whitney Foundation. Born in New York City, and a graduate of Wesleyan University (1951), Mr. Ludlum lives in Connecticut with his wife, Mary Ryde, a former stage and television actress, and his three children.

RELAX!
SIT DOWN
and Catch Up On Your Reading!

DON'T MISS
THESE CURRENT
Bantam Bestsellers

☐	13545	**SOPHIE'S CHOICE** William Styron	$3.50
☐	13101	**THE BOOK OF LISTS #2** Wallechinsky & Wallaces	$3.50
☐	20025	**THE FAR PAVILIONS** M. M. Kaye	$4.50
☐	13752	**SHADOW OF THE MOON** M. M. Kaye	$3.95
☐	13028	**OVERLOAD** Arthur Hailey	$2.95
☐	13828	**THE RIGHT STUFF** Tom Wolfe	$3.50
☐	14140	**SMILEY'S PEOPLE** John LeCarre	$3.50
☐	13743	**MADE IN AMERICA** Peter Maas	$2.50
☐	14396	**TRINITY** Leon Uris	$3.95
☐	14611	**HOW TO SPEAK SOUTHERN** Steve Mitchell	$1.95
☐	13624	**NAME YOUR BABY** Lareina Rule	$2.25
☐	01203	**WHEN LOVERS ARE FRIENDS** Merle Shain	$3.95
☐	20134	**THE PRITIKIN PROGRAM FOR DIET AND EXERCISE** Nathan Pritikin w/ Patrick McGrady, Jr.	$3.95
☐	14174	**LONELY ON THE MOUNTAIN** Louis L'Amour	$2.25
☐	20138	**PASSAGES** Gail Sheehy	$3.95
☐	14500	**THE GUINNESS BOOK OF WORLD RECORDS 19th ed.** The McWhirters	$3.50
☐	14686	**LINDA GOODMAN'S SUN SIGNS**	$3.50
☐	14852	**ZEN AND THE ART OF MOTORCYCLE MAINTENANCE** Robert Pirsig	$3.50
☐	14736	**DR. ATKINS' DIET REVOLUTION**	$3.50

Buy them at your local bookstore or use this handy coupon for ordering:

Bantam Book Catalog

Here's your up-to-the-minute listing of over 1,400 titles by your favorite authors.

This illustrated, large format catalog gives a description of each title. For your convenience, it is divided into categories in fiction and non-fiction—gothics, science fiction, westerns, mysteries, cookbooks, mysticism and occult, biographies, history, family living, health, psychology, art.

So don't delay—take advantage of this special opportunity to increase your reading pleasure.

Just send us your name and address and 50¢ (to help defray postage and handling costs).